Dance Floor L

Brian Sellars

www.briansellars.com

Published in 2014 by Create Space

Copyright © text Brian Sellars 2013

Copyright © cover image
Picture Parade, Art Gallery and Picture Framers, Sheffield
www.pictureparade.co.uk

First Edition

ISBN-10: 1496117662
ISBN-13: 978-1496117663

The author has asserted their moral right under the Copyright, Designs and Patents Act, 1988, to be identified as the author of this work.

All Rights reserved. No part of this publication may be reproduced, copied, stored in a retrieval system, or transmitted, in any form or by any means, without the prior written consent of the copyright holder, nor be otherwise circulated in any form of binding or cover other than that in which it is published and without a similar condition being imposed on the subsequent purchaser.

Dance Floor Drowning is a work of fiction.
All characters in this publication are
fictitious and any resemblance to real persons,
living or dead, is purely coincidental

A CIP catalogue record for this title is available from the British Library.

OTHER BOOKS BY BRIAN SELLARS

The Whispering Bell
Historical fiction thriller for adult readers. Set in 7th century Anglo Saxon Mercia, it's the story of a warrior's wife, robbed of her children, her home and inheritance, when her husband is lost in battle.

Time Rocks
Stonehenge based, time travelling sci-fi adventure for teenage and adult readers.

Tuppenny Hat Detective
Period murder mystery for adult and teenage readers. Set in Sheffield, England in the early nineteen-fifties, a whodunit for young or older folk who like a mystery, without a car chase.

Thank you for choosing Dance Floor Drowning.
This murder mystery is set in the South Yorkshire *"Steel City"* of Sheffield, in the early nineteen-fifties. I hope both adult and teenage readers will enjoy it.

Like its predecessor, **Tuppenny Hat Detective**, twelve year-old Billy Perks and his friends Yvonne Sparkes and Kick Morely, team up with old Etonian, M.D., Dr Hadfield and Police Constable John Needham to take on the establishment, exposing corruption and a deadly killer.

Dance Floor Drowning is nostalgic, funny and a genuine whodunit. I hope you'll agree that the detectives being schoolchildren, brings a fresh perspective to bear, providing a new slant and added drama to detective fiction.

This work is dedicated to Lily and John
and all those young lovers who danced over
the swimming pool at Glossop Road Baths.

Dance Floor Drowning

Brian Sellars

www.briansellars.com

Chapter One

Note: Glossary of Sheffield dialect words at the back of the book

Despite rain showers, rumoured bananas quickly brought queues to the pavements of Walkley's Victorian shopping street. The hairnets and headscarves of the chattering, good natured foragers steamed and bobbed until the insistent clanging of a police car's bell silenced all, drawing them to crane and gawp.

A black police Wolseley saloon roared into view. It swerved to a halt in front of twelve-year-old Billy Perks, out shopping on his bicycle. The lad struggled to steer around it, but clattered to a tumbling halt. A precious bag of sugar, five pounds of potatoes and the family's ration book spilled onto the pavement. The driver, a sour-faced sergeant, loomed up from the car, setting his helmet on his bullet head. Billy eyed him nervously as he struggled to round up skittering potatoes from between the feet of goggling shoppers.

'Here, Perks! I've been looking for you. Get in.'

Billy's spirits plunged. He stood up, quickly fixed a kink in his National Health spectacles and stuck them back on his nose. 'I've done nowt,' he said, thumbing away a bead of blood from a grazed knee. 'Look, thaz made me squash me new glasses. I've only just gorrem. My mam'll kill me.'

The policeman bent close to the boy's freckled nose. 'Shurrup and gerrin – *if you please*,' he said with sneering sarcasm. 'The Chief Superintendent wants a word with you, my lad. We'd best not keep him waiting.'

'What about me bike? I can't leave it. It'll get nicked.'

'Stop whining. You probably nicked it anyway.'

'I never ... My dad give it me. It worra prez ...'

'Forget the damn bike and gerrin. Sharpish! We can't keep Chief Superintendent Flood waiting, now can we?'

'It'll be tha fault if it gets nicked,' said Billy. 'I'll tell me dad.'

'Ooooh, look at me, I'm shaking in my boots,' cried the sergeant, pretending to quake with fear. 'Now gerrin, or I'll handcuff you for resisting arrest.'

The clock on nearby Saint Mary's church tower struck one. Billy glanced up at the soot-blackened spire. 'Look! I'm missing me dinner.'

The officer frowned and fumbled in his back pocket. Fearing he could be looking for his handcuffs, Billy decided to cooperate. He dropped his shoulders and slouched into the car. Walkley's banana hunters watched, fascinated but unsurprised at the sight of the bedraggled, ginger-headed lad climbing into a police car. It was not the first time they'd seen Billy Perks at the centre of police activity. He was something of a celebrity. A year earlier his disconsolate features had appeared on the front pages of the Sheffield Telegraph and The Star, under the headline "Tuppenny Hat Detective Caps Cops' Killer Case".

*

Harry Clegg, senior reporter for the Sheffield Telegraph and Star newspapers, stirred five teaspoonfuls of sugar into his pint pot of tea and hungrily eyed his lunch, a towering wedge of steaming meat and potato pie. Whatever Butlers Pie Shop lacked in glamour and choice, it made up for in wholesome volume. Harry dined there often, hiding behind a copy of *The Manchester Guardian* to eat, smoke and sip tea in the relaxing hubbub and smoke filled anonymity of its dining rooms. He pulled out his notebook, shoved aside his pie to cool, and began reviewing the notes he had made that morning.

His day had started early – too early. A news desk sub-editor had telephoned his home, waking him before six-thirty. Forty minutes later, still bleary eyed and grumbling, he had steered his Austin *Sixteen* out of the traffic, rattling nose to tail along a cobbled tramway, and parked near the main entrance to

Sheffield's Glossop Road Municipal Baths.

Early morning visits to swimming pools were not high on his list of favourite things. Even as he glared at the entrance he had still nursed doubts about going inside. For a while, he'd sat gloomily watching raindrops merge into wriggling rivulets on the windscreen. Two police constables, their capes and helmets dripping, had eyed him sullenly from the scant shelter of a stone portico over a pair of regally panelled doors. A handwritten notice dripped from a sodden cat's cradle, binding the door's bronze handles together. Rain had washed out most of its message.

Harry snapped out of his reverie to concentrate on his lunch. He shovelled in a mouthful of pie and smiled appreciatively. He ate slowly and with undisguised relish. In his mid-fifties, with twenty-five years' service and a solid track record, Harry Clegg ploughed his own furrow. Winter or summer, he went about the city wearing a brown trilby hat and a camel coloured overcoat, a silk paisley scarf erupting at the neck. He looked more like an on-course bookie than a journalist. His florid complexion and purplish bulbous nose suggested a close affinity with bar stools. Yet he was a familiar sight at every conflagration, royal visit, punch up, and car crash in the city - day or night. His small, glittering blue eyes flittered over traffic deaths, burglaries, murders, naughty vicars and plucky have-a-go-pensioners, with never a hint of boredom.

Occasionally swapping fork and pencil, he steadily ate his pie whilst editing his notes; his attention wandering easily between recollections of the morning's events and the smooth meaty excellence of Butler's beef gravy.

His morning had gone like this:

7:30 am. Stooping against the downpour, Harry climbed from his car, nodded at the frowning constables and hurried inside through a service door a few yards beyond their post. He found the main pool almost drained. The bright, humid space above it echoed to whirring, slurping sounds from unseen machinery. In the dry shallow end, a white sheet covered what was, unmistakably, a corpse. At the deep end, several grim-faced men, wearing wellington boots and laboratory coats, paddled around, ankle-deep. Unmoved by his arrival they continued their meticulous work. Armed with tweezers and little wooden spatulas they were grazing the Victorian pool's shiny tiles, pausing here and there to peck and scrape at bits of unpleasant looking flotsam. With unconcealed satisfaction, they bagged, labelled and set aside their sordid trophies for later examination.

Harry recognized Chief Superintendent Flood, overseeing matters at the poolside, despite the angry remonstrations of half-a-dozen elderly men bobbing and jostling around him. Two were in business suits; the others wore only white towelling bathrobes. All were extremely agitated, and clearly held Flood responsible. One, a haughty, military type, whose robe kept flapping open, revealing a good deal more than a potbelly, led the onslaught. His main concern, as far as Harry could make out, was that the Chief Superintendent had ordered the closure of the Turkish bath, a facility used almost exclusively by the city's toffs. According to the bathrobe-flasher, this was "utterly unnecessary" as the facility was outside, what he several times referred to as, "Flood's necessary field of inquiry."

Chief Superintendent Flood seized on Harry's arrival to escape the tirade. 'Ah, Clegg, so glad you could come,' he called, his trumpeting voice echoing across the empty pool. 'This way please.'

Harry, who had never known such hospitality from the police, raised an eyebrow and traipsed after him. His was usually the last face the police wanted to see at a crime scene.

Fending off the flasher and his retinue, Flood led him along a dingy corridor to the pool manager's office, which he had evidently commandeered for his inquiry. On the way, a constable handed Flood a folded sheet of paper. He quickly read it and waved the young man away.

Inside the cramped, untidy office, Flood motioned that Harry should shut the door. 'Don't get excited, Clegg,' he said. 'You're getting nothing. I just needed to escape those old farts ...'

Harry shrugged, as if unconcerned. He eyed the Chief Superintendent, noting as always, the stark contrast between his impeccable, blue-black uniform, and his cadaverous, sallow complexion. Harry had always found Flood's rapid rise in the force, and his exceptional rate of arrests and convictions, baffling. He didn't come across as particularly bright, yet his record suggested he must be. Flood invariably got his man. That meant Harry usually got a good story out of it. Hiding a smile, Harry watched him move round the desk, his deliberate reaching movements giving him the look of a stalking heron. His sharp skeletal features and long nose added to the illusion.

'Now now, Mister Flood,' Harry said, a twinkle in his eyes. 'That's the cream of Sheffield society you're talking about.'

'God help us,' Flood said, warming slightly to his visitor.

'Come on, Super – give me something. What happened here?'

Flood sat in the swimming bath manager's rickety swivel chair and gave it a test spin. He eyed Clegg thoughtfully as he came round to face him, appearing to relax somewhat. 'Oh, why not? But don't quote me, Clegg. If you do, I'll have your …' He unfolded the sheet of paper the young constable had handed him, and read from it. 'Male, late fifties or sixty, wearing nothing but one of the establishment's bathrobes, – bla – bla – bla - hip flask in pocket – empty – face down in the main pool.' He peered across the untidy desk. Clegg was scribbling into a notebook. 'Almost certainly drowned, of course,' he went on, 'but we'll need the post mortem to confirm that ...'

'Any marks on the body?'

Flood scanned the paper. 'Nothing obvious, but, as I say, we'll need a post mortem.'

'It doesn't sound much like murder, does it?' Harry said. 'He could've just slipped, couldn't he? Sounds like he was in the Turkish bath next door – hitting the old hip flask a bit – maybe had a drop too much – took a wrong turn through the connecting doors - and splash ...'

Flood shrugged. 'You may well be right.'

'So, why all the coppers then?'

Flood stared at him, pursing his lips in a supercilious frown.

'Why all that forensics' mob,' Harry persisted, 'in their special issue wellows?'

'Ah well, that's the thing,' said Flood, tapping his finger against the side of his long nose. 'He's been in there at least thirty-six hours.'

Harry Clegg stiffened. 'Since Saturday? Wasn't there a dance? The Summer Ball.'

'Precisely. He had to be in there thirty-six hours ago - before the dance floor was put over the pool.' Flood paused, watching Harry scribble fiercely into his notebook. 'He had to. It couldn't happen otherwise.'

'But how? Surely somebody must have seen him?'

Flood's head wobbled on his thin neck. He gave Harry a superior stare. 'Exactly. And you can't do that accidentally, can you? No matter how big your hip flask might be.'

Harry whistled a long, low note and scribbled some more. 'When was the floor fitted?'

'They finished it Saturday afternoon,' replied Flood absently. He was opening and closing desk drawers and nosily poking around inside them with a pencil. He looked up suddenly. 'They were taking it up again when they found him this morning. It's a night shift that do it. We got the call at five-thirty-two. I was here by seven. I told 'em to finish the job and drain the pool - to give us a better look.'

'Got a name yet?'

'I.D. card in his wallet, but of course, it mightn't be his. In any case, I can't give you the name yet – you know, family first and all that …'

'Where were his street clothes?'

'Locker, Turkish bath, next door. We'll need to confirm they fit him, but it seems likely. Nobody remembers when he came in.'

'So, unknown man drowned by unknown person who accessed the pool by unknown means.' Harry shook his head, frowning cynically. 'Huh, great story that'll make.'

'Or he may have quietly climbed in on his own when nobody was looking.' Flood grinned, tapping his teeth with his pencil.

'Suicide? D'you really think so?'

'Of course I don't.'

0o0o0

Chapter Two

To Billy's eyes, Notre Dame School for Girls was bandit country. There, behind its sooty brick walls, the dark arts of *besting* boys were studied and refined to deadly elegance. Luckily, it was the school's summer break. The only Furies haunting its hideous tranquillity that day were the black-veiled nuns of Notre Dame de Namur. Their Order had founded the school in the mid-nineteenth century, evidently to teach girls to scratch, kick, scream and deploy killer put-downs against boys. When not doing so, Billy imagined them endlessly reciting the Rosary, or colouring in pictures of soppy-faced saints kneeling before even soppier faced Madonnas.

He had climbed Notre Dame's lofty perimeter wall, hoping it would offer a useful vantage for spying into Glossop Road Swimming Baths. It did not. All he could see was the combined entrance to the Turkish baths and Slipper baths. Further along the grimy coping, a clear view of the boiler room's coke hatch proved equally unrewarding.

An hour earlier, he'd been in Chief Superintendent Flood's office, enduring a puzzling verbal battering, after being picked up like Al Capone and driven to what the troll of a driver had told him was to be life imprisonment or execution. It had left him feeling worried and queasy but above all, baffled. Flood had threatened and harangued him, and poked him in the chest. He had shown him etchings, evidently culled from ancient books, showing people hanging in chains. He had ranted over them with such venom that Billy had feared imminent torture in a dripping dungeon. Then, inexplicably, he had ordered him to stay away from the swimming baths.

Finally, as he had pushed him out of his office, the chief superintendent's parting lash was to tell him sourly that there would be no lift home in a police car. 'You'll have to walk, my lad,' he had snarled. 'I suggest you use the time to consider what I've said.'

That petty meanness would seriously backfire.

*

As the crow flies, Billy's home in Walkley lay about two and half miles from Police Headquarters at Castle Green in the city centre. It might just as well have been fifty miles, for he had no certain idea how to get there. Tram fare, he supposed, would be a penny or tuppence. Not that it mattered, he didn't have a farthing. However, he knew perfectly well that trams ran to Walkley, and reasoned that all he had to do was follow the tramlines. That would surely get him home.

Sick with worry, head down and knees wobbly from Flood's dire warnings, he started for home, chewing over all the chief had said. Flood had seemed puzzlingly resentful that Billy had solved the Star Woman's murder case a year before. Why should this be a problem? Surely, that had been helpful? They should be pleased with him. Instead, Chief Superintendent Flood had accused him of trying to make fools of the police. It was most baffling. Nevertheless, even if Flood was completely off his trolley, Billy reasoned it would be wise to heed him. So, he told himself, no more playing detective, and stay away from the swimming baths, exactly as Flood had instructed.

Following the tramlines, he plodded home passed shops, *little mester* forges, offices and the bombed out shells of buildings damaged in the blitz, many still shored up by great timber buttresses and girders. In a miserable daze, he repeatedly reviewed Flood's words, until a tramcar's discordant bell clanged into his thoughts, making his heart jump. He looked around in surprise, suddenly becoming aware of his surroundings. A cold sweat slicked his face when he realised where he was. There, in front of him, not fifty yards away, stood Glossop Road Swimming Baths. The very place he had sworn to avoid. In panic, he dodged into a shop doorway, terrified the chief superintendent might drop from on high and drag him away to be hung drawn and quartered - or even worse.

He peered out at the forbidden building, wondering what secrets it could possible hold. It looked perfectly innocent, its red brick façade generously piped with stone dentils, cornices, and pediments. Why had Flood warned him off it? What menace could it contain? It looked so inviting and friendly. What was it the Chief Superintendent was so keen to hide?

In an instant, his thoughts switched, recharging his deflated spirits. Why shouldn't he go wherever he wanted? It's a free country! Flood had no right to stop him having a swim. The city council even encouraged it with posters of apple-cheeked families splashing each other's perfect teeth with the sparkling water.

Moments later, he had climbed the encircling wall of Notre Dame Girls' School. It was the swimming bath's closest neighbour. From there he hoped he might see what secret Chief Superintendent Flood was hiding.

He quickly realised it was pointless. Opaque glass filled every window in the art nouveau façade. He could see nothing, and such activity as there was around the building suggested no more than *business as usual.* Patrons were casually wandering in and out of entrances to the Turkish baths, or the respectfully segregated plunge pools. He swept his gaze along the walls wondering, with crumbling confidence, how he might get a look inside. Pipes from the slipper baths steamed and chugged. Bathers came and went – pale faced before their swim, pink faced afterwards. The only unusual thing he spotted was a notice posted on the double doors at the entrance to the large, mixed bathing pool. On closer inspection he found rain had washed almost all the ink from it. He could just make out the words *"Closed for maintenance"*. Nothing particularly suspicious about that, he thought.

Pulling up a pretend raincoat collar, he slowly walked the cobbles of Convent Walk, the narrow lane between the swimming baths and the girls-school. Inside his head, the sound of a zither playing the Harry Lime theme chimed up. He had recently seen the movie, and adopted its theme as the perfect accompaniment for stalking around in detective mode. Slinking into a door recess, he exhaled imaginary cigarette smoke and looked out from under the brim of his imaginary trilby hat. If there was something going on in the swimming baths that Flood wanted to hide, the only way to find out about it was to dive in for a closer look.

The imagined zither music faded away. He set off home at a brisk pace, flicking his pretend cigarette over the wall of Notre Dame School. He was hungry. He had missed lunch. But it was still early afternoon, plenty of time left to get home, grab some bread and dripping, pick up his swimming trunks and get back to the swimming baths. There was just one snag. As usual, he was skint; stony broke, penniless, poorer than a church mouse's poor relation. He hadn't a penny towards the entrance fee or the tram fare. At a pinch, he could manage without the tram fare, but there was no way to get through the tines of the full length iron turnstile at the swimming bath's entrance without buying a ticket. About a bob would be enough, twelve pence. That would even leave enough for a mug of Bovril after his swim. Somehow, he would have to raise the cash.

He could start with a bottle search, his old standby. This involved checking out every dustbin, backdoor step, and forgotten corner of the neighbourhood, in the hope of finding discarded beer or pop bottles. Local beer-off shops would happily refund a deposit of tuppence on every one he returned to them. The trouble was, every other kid in Sheffield was doing the same.

His granny Smeggs would gladly give him money. Unfortunately, his mother had placed her off limits, having discovered his over exploitation of granny's soft heart. She had already warned him, in blood chilling detail, of the horrific retribution that would follow any attempt to tap her up.

That left only subterfuge and trickery. Old Pop Meason kept empty pop bottles in crates behind his sweet shop, awaiting collection by the soft drinks' company. Billy knew he could easily pinch a few and run round to the front of the shop to return them for the deposit. Local scallywags often tricked the poor old boy with this ruse. Billy recalled, with shame, that he had once done it himself. It had made him miserable for weeks. Guilt eventually drove him to hand over four pennies to the old boy, which he pretended to have found on the floor of the shop. Old Pop Meason had been so pleased that he rewarded Billy with sixpennyworth of free sweets. Billy daren't go back to the shop nowadays, because the old man would insist on giving him treats. Even worse, he would crow to his other customers about what a wonderful honest young lad Billy was. Billy shuddered, he could not go through that again.

It would be pointless asking his pals, Kick and Yvonne, for money. They wouldn't have any, and even if they did they wouldn't give it to him. There was nothing else for it; he would have to ask his mother for an advance on his Friday sixpence – plus a bit – quite a bit. The trouble was it was only Monday. He knew he'd be on a sticky wicket. Blood from stones didn't come close.

He found the door to his house thrown wide open. Steam puthered from inside where his mam was leaning over a washtub, pounding dirty clothes with a copper posher. Her hair hung in her eyes. Water slopped around her feet. Throughout the kitchen and living room, saucepans and kettles bubbled and simmered on the stove, the gas ring and the fireplace. She glanced up at him and wriggled her nose to stop her steamed up spectacles sliding off into the foaming washtub.

Billy saw instantly that she looked less likely to give him an advance than any person he could imagine. He turned away miserably and headed for his usual perch in times of extreme gloom, a river smoothed rockery stone overlooking the Perks' long, narrow garden.

The Perks' house was unusual in that at the bottom of the garden, next to the outside toilet, was a small brick built washhouse. It was equipped with a cold-water tap over a stone sink and a coal fired copper clothes boiler. It had room to store washtubs, scrubbing boards and the big cast iron mangle. It was perfect for scrubbing, boiling, and rinsing clothes. Using it saved considerable time and effort, not to mention household disruption. Why then, he wondered, was his mam doing the laundry in the house? The place was in chaos. She had moved all the furniture and rolled up the carpet. He realised she must have carried the two wash tubs, posher and rubbing board, all the way up from the washhouse. Why?

He stepped back into the chaotic living room. 'What's up, mam? Why aren't you using the washhouse?'

She looked up at him, flat-eyed, her face red and sweating. Running a hand over her forehead, she peeled back damp curls and threaded them behind her ears. 'Copper's leaking. It won't light. It just wets the kindling and puts it out.'

Billy gazed round at the shambles that was his home. She had even banished the dog to a distant corner. The little wire haired terrier cringed in the unfamiliar surroundings, shivering from fear of the disruption all about him.

Then, Billy had a brilliant idea - a super idea - an idea so brilliant and super that he almost fainted at the thought of his brilliance and superiority: the slipper baths!

Along with steam rooms and swimming pools, Glossop Road Baths offered its patrons Slipper Baths; private bathtubs brimming with hot water. For a modest few pence, people who seldom saw more hot water than could be contained in a kettle, could have their own private bathtub and cubicle. They could bathe, right up to their chins, in clean hot water.

He had been there several times with his mam, though he'd soon realised it was not just him she expected to scrub. It was her method of dealing with coal shortages. When she couldn't afford coal for the washhouse boiler, she would take Billy to the slipper baths. Dirty pants, vests, shirts and socks would be smuggled in with him, for a secret wash in the luxurious hot water.

She would lock the cubicle door and wait as the attendant filled the bathtub from outside, using a variety of spanners and valve keys. The man would shout through the door; 'Don't be long – there's a queue outside.'- or - 'Does tha want any more cold?' Billy noticed they never asked if you wanted "more hot". Asking for it was futile. He'd say something like, 'No, you can't. You're not in bloody Hollywood tha knows!'

With the bathtub brimming his mam would plop Billy in to it, and dump the smuggled dirty washing and soap powder on top of him. His job was to punch and kick it around while she rubbed at stubborn stains with a large block of carbolic.

Slipper bath attendants seemed to be a notorious breed of humanity-hating individuals. They would bang on cubicle doors, grumpily urging people to hurry up. It seemed to Billy that their two greatest pleasures in life were emptying the bathtubs before people had finished, and exposing the illicit laundering of smalls. If you were not a favoured client, or a relative, a relaxing snooze in the tub was definitely out of the question.

Customers had no control over water, either coming in or going out. When they deemed a bather's allotted time was up, attendants would ruthlessly drain the tub from outside the cubicle, using a special valve key. They would then crouch over the open sluice to inspect the water flowing out into the main drain. If it looked blue and scummy, from the use of washing soda, they would rant, rage, and threaten. This made illegal laundering a risky business.

As he watched his mother slopping sheets from the poshing tub into the rinsing tub, Billy refined his plan. He knew he held a trump card, and would now play it with silky coolness.

'Mam, I hate to see you struggling like this,' he said, his voice oozing concern. 'Why don't I take the clothes to the slipper baths and run them through for you. I know how to.'

Missis Perks gaped at her son - the apple of her eye - the saviour of the day. 'Ooooooh, Billy love! Would you?'

'Of course I will, Mam. Gi' me the money. I'll get me trunks. I might as well have a swim an' all, while I'm there.'

Missis Perks beamed and wiped her glasses on her apron. 'Find me my purse, love.'

*

There was a queue outside the slipper baths. It strung along Convent Walk under the steaming pipes snaking in and out of the building. Billy was surprised to find so many people waiting. It was Monday. Friday was the usual day for a bath, but then, he realised, Monday was washday.

As he joined the line, he noticed how podgy many of the women looked. Rather like him, they too appeared a bit thick around the waist. A few were already overheating under their extra layers of badly concealed washing. Billy sympathized, he was wearing several pairs of scruffy underpants and knickers, three of his dad's shirts and something unmentionable of his mother's. Even the rolled up towel and swimming trunks, tucked under his arm, concealed intimate items of illegal laundry.

He paid at the ticket office window and the cashier released the turnstile. He had a bit of a struggle getting through due to his lack of flexibility. He had so many socks stuffed up the sleeves of his coat, he couldn't bend his arms. The woman following him struggled too. She leaked vests, knickers and three liberty bodices. Only quick thinking and surprising agility prevented her being discovered. Billy watched her kick her smalls through the gate, whilst telling the turnstile operator that a wasp was about to attack him. As the attendant wafted and spun around in panic, she squeezed through and winked at Billy.

The slipper baths were up a flight of stairs. The attendant grunted, eyed him suspiciously and pointed to a cubicle. Once inside, Billy relaxed and stripped off his illicit layers. Soon he was floating in hot, scummy blue water and washing the family's smalls. When he was done, he put on his swimming trunks. His plan was to slip out of the tub as soon as it was safe, and take a quick look round. Frustratingly, the attendant clattered up and down the row of cubicles nonstop, turning taps, draining drains, and bullying his unseen customers with his constant recitation of council rules.

Billy waited for things to quieten. Then, wearing just his swimming trunks, he climbed over the partition wall, dropped down to the duck boarded floor and headed for the stairs. He crept down unnoticed and slipped into a line of men and boys going into the men's pool. Nobody seemed concerned. Seconds later, he was swimming. After a quick splash about, he looked around to get his bearings. He suspected that the mixed bathing pool, with its *closed for maintenance* notice, was probably the centre of the mystery. Somehow, he had to get in there. A pair of anonymous doors in a far corner suggested a possible route. He swam towards them, climbed out onto the poolside, and waited for the chance to make a dash for them.

It was not long before rowdy teenagers, bombing off the diving board, distracted the sour-faced lifeguard. Billy seized his chance and sneaked through the doors. Unexpectedly, he found himself in the Turkish bath. It was like stepping back in time. He closed the double doors gently behind him and tiptoed into a hot, steamy hall. His glasses had fogged up, blinding him. He wiped the lenses with his fingers and looked about in awe. Above him, a balcony, edged with ornate balustrade, swept around a large octagonal room. He saw men with towels wrapped around their waists ambling around it, others were sitting reading in the daylight from hidden skylights somewhere in the roof. Ceramic tiles covered the walls with geometric patterns of dove blue, lemon and white. In the middle of the floor, a large, mosaic star motif, radiated intricate patterns into shaded alcoves beneath the balcony. Behind curtains drawn haphazardly across the alcoves, elderly men, swathed in white towels and bathrobes, snoozed on narrow beds, their sonorous snoring borne aloft on the steamy gloom.

Deeply engrossed in a sporting newspaper, a silver haired old chap with a sweating red face and spectacles on the end of his nose, ambled in to view from a side door. He stiffened with outrage as he saw Billy, and casting aside his Racing Times, marched towards him, as though on a parade ground, his loosely tied bathrobe flapping like a luffing spanker. 'What the damn-dicky-doodly are you doing here, boy?'

Billy panicked and tried to retreat back through the double doors, but couldn't open them. 'Oh, er - sorry, sir. I must have taken a wrong turn.'

'Bet your boots you did, old lad.' The man made a grab for him, but Billy ducked and jinked passed him. Stairs up to the balcony suggested an escape route. He took them two at a time. At the top he faced a row of elderly pink faces, all bearing the same look of startled outrage. Beyond them, he spotted a narrow door and made a dash for it. Crashing through, he found himself in a cold, empty darkness. Luckily, it felt ripe with the promise of escape, and, as his eyes accustomed to the gloom, he saw he was in a service area with a long flight of concrete steps down into a darker space smelling of heat, oil and fire. He looked round for something to bar the door behind him. In a pile of junk, he found old bathrobes, odd shoes, a gas mask, and a rusty umbrella. He grabbed the gamp and wedged it in the door handle.

The gritty concrete steps hurt his bare feet as he picked his way down, fearful that his pursuers might appear at any moment. A door at the bottom of the steps opened into a cavernous subterranean room dominated by a great furnace. He peered around it. High in one wall was a grubby strip of window. He could see people's feet tripping by on the pavement outside, heels clicking on metal grating as they passed. At the furnace, a man, stripped to the waist, was polishing a pressure gauge. Billy watched him tap it gently with his knuckles and then lean to peer into the fire through a small observation window.

'What's up, son?' asked the man without turning from his work. 'Are tha lost?'

Billy approached him slowly. 'I – err - ... Somebody were chasing me. I don't know how I got here.'

'Chasing thee - eh? Why, what's tha done?'

'Nowt. I never did nowt.'

The man turned and faced him. He was not much taller than Billy, but his shoulders were wide and muscular. His square, grimy face gleamed like oiled metal. Two bright blue eyes shone out from beneath sooty eyebrows. His mouth was wide with lips that were oddly clean against his soot-smudged skin. Billy smelled menthol as the man exhaled.

The sounds of joyous, echoing shrieks and laughter suddenly burst into the great void of the boiler room. Evidently, a door from the swimming pool had been opened. The stoker looked at Billy with sudden concern. 'Tha'd better hide thee sen, lad.'

Billy crouched, staring about wildly. 'Where?'

'Get thee sen o'er theer, behind them chunter pipes, ' He pointed to a gently throbbing pump at the junction of four large pipes, two of which branched off into a duct in the wall.

'Chunter pipes?' Billy eyed them curiously and slid into the narrow space behind them. He waited, hardly daring to breath. His anxious gaze swept his surroundings. Several people had entered from behind a towering run of steel piping. The man from the Turkish bath led them, brandishing his rolled up racing paper like a swagger stick. At his shoulder was the glowering slipper bath attendant. A fat man in a brown overall and two admin types in suits followed.

'Did you see anybody, Daniels?' boomed the officious military type.

'No, sir. I've not got no time to see nowt,' said the stoker combatively. 'I'm too busy down here for gazing round looking at things. And what wi' Mike being off sick, it's even worse than usual.'

The two suited types shot weary glances at each other and fiddled with the knots in their neckties.

The stoker pressed on. 'They told me I was to have somebody to give me an 'and. Weer is he? I've not seen nobody. D'yer know that I've not even had my snap today.. I've bin here sin' five this mornin'. I've not even had a mash yet. I bet they've all had theirs though, them in t'office.' He pointed an accusing finger at the admin guys. 'I've to keep this fire up. That pressure gauge moant drop more than five pounds. And that pump o'er theer needs a new impeller. When am I going to get one? Tell me that, will tha?' He stuck out his chin and took a step towards the military type. 'There's always folk with time to look round, but not me.'

The group backed off, abandoning their leader to face the

truculent stoker alone.

'Well, if you see a boy, Daniels, let me know – eh?' said the military type, unmoved by the stoker's comprehensive response.

'I'll do what I can, Doctor Longden,' the stoker said. 'As I always do.'

The doctor turned away and marched off, barging disdainfully through his cowardly entourage. The boiler man waited, showing Billy a staying hand. The unseen door opened and closed, choking off the jolly sounds of the adjoining swimming pool. As Billy waited, he noticed a couple of tightly rolled up sweet papers on the floor by his foot. He recognized the wrappers, Halls Mentholyptus sweets. He liked them too, as the stoker evidently did.

'Tha can come out now, mi owd,' the boiler man said. He faced Billy and looked him over, grinning and chuckling to himself.

Billy beamed at the stoker and glanced back at his hiding place. 'Chunter pipes?'

The man laughed. 'Yeah we call 'em that. It's because you can hear the old fools chuntering in the cold room - through the duct.' He pointed to where the pipes snaked into a neatly tiled opening in the wall. 'Mike listens to 'em, but I don't. They talk rubbish, if you ask me. Mike's off sick just now. He thought he'd got himself onto a good thing the first time he heard 'em chuntering and whispering. It was that fool Longden telling his pal about some bloody horse, a red-hot tip. A dead cert that couldn't lose, he was saying. Poor old Mike backed it. Lost five quid. I knew he would. I warned him about Longden. He never wins owt. If I had a shilling for every quid that old fool's lost, I'd be a rich man.' He chuckled, looking Billy over from top to toe. 'So, what's thee name then, lad?'

'Billy, sir.'

'Well, Billy. I'm Mister Daniels, chief engineering genius in this palace of wonders, but tha can call me Stan.' He held out a massive paw to shake hands. Billy grabbed it, feeling very grown up.

'So, what's tha done to upset Doctor Nasty?'

Billy shrugged. 'Nasty? He looks crazy, more like. Who is he?'

'Doctor Longden, one of our regulars, but not a very nice bloke, Billy. You want to watch out for him. One of these days, he'll come badly unstuck, especially if I get my way.' Stan's expression had darkened. He shot a threatening glance at the door through which Longden and his cronies had departed. It made Billy feel uncomfortable. Stan looked back to him and shrugged apologetically, his mood lifting instantly.' Yeah, he's in here all the time. God knows how he gets away with it. He's the top man at the city morgue. It's a good job his patients are already deeyad, is all I can say.' He laughed at his quip and picked up a shovel. Billy watched him flick open the furnace door with it, releasing intense heat that forced him back a step. Stan seemed quite unaffected by it and bending even closer, peered inside. He began stoking the furnace with a smooth, steady rhythm. It looked effortless; though Billy was sure it could not be.

Stan was sweating when, after a minute or two stoking, he shut the fire door and leaned his shovel beside it. He wiped his face on a sweat towel, conveniently hung on an overhead pipe. 'So, what's all this fuss and mystery abaht then?'

Billy explained, including everything from the moment he had been knocked off his bike by the police car.

Stan listened intently, occasionally moving off to turn a valve, read a gauge, or throw a switch. When Billy had finished, Stan shook his head, perplexed. 'Shall we have a mash up?' he asked, not waiting for an answer. Billy followed him to a sink in a corner and watched him set about the task. He was very well organized. Enamelled mugs of steaming tea quickly appeared. Stan dusted off a couple of old dining chairs, cleared a motor cycle crash helmet and goggles out of the way, and invited Billy to join him. Billy sat down at a small table bearing a bottle of milk, a paper twist of sugar and a snap tin that had once contained Thornton's toffee. He looked around the snug little corner and realised he was being accorded full honours and hospitality. He grinned proudly and sipped the sweet, milky tea.

'So, own up then. Did tha drown him?' Stan was eyeing Billy across his tea mug with comic sternness.

'Drown who?'

'Don't tell me tha dunt know? Papers'll be full of it toneet. It'll definitely be in t'Star.'

'What will?'

'Murder! They found a dead body in the pool. The *dance floor drowning,*' he announced grandly. 'That's what they're gonna call it in t'paper. That bloke Clegg from the Telegraph and Star told me. He's been here all morning taking notes and asking questions. We've had coppers all o'er the place, poking their noses in everywhere.' He pointed to a dusty clock on the wall. 'They dint leave until dinnertime. There's still a couple of 'em here now, in white overalls. They've had us all in the office – questioning us.' He blew his nose, sniffed experimentally a few times, unwrapped a menthol sweet and popped it in his mouth. 'The copper in charge is that slimy toad, Flood. Ever heard of him?'

Billy both nodded *and* shook his head, slightly unsure as to what he should admit to at this early stage in the conversation.

'He's a right big eeyaded bugger,' Stan went on. 'Chief Superintendent slimy toad they should call him. He damn near accused me of doing it.' He laughed loudly. 'I told 'im straight. I said if ever I killed somebody, I'd shove 'em in that furnace. That gets hot enough to get rid of owt. They'd never find nowt left of him but his clog irons. I'd certainly not leave bodies floatin' about in a swimming pool.' He laughed again and wiped a tear from his eye. 'I think that put the wind up him. He couldn't get me out of the office quick enough.'

Billy shuddered and stared at the furnace door. It was easy to see that Stan was even less fond of chief superintendent Flood than he was. The idea of Stan scaring him off with veiled threats of cremation struck him as most welcome. 'So what happened then? Who got killed?'

'Well, like I said, they found a body. I had to empty t'pool – every last drop. That's why I'm having to fill it up ageeyan.' He pointed to the machine behind which Billy had hidden. 'That old pump's still chugging away, burrit waint last much longer. Trouble is, they waint spend any money. Tha knows what councils are like …'

'But the drowning …' Billy interrupted. 'What happened?'

'Oh aghh, well I don't know really? They don't tell us much down here. All I know is some bloke were drowned in t'big pool – mixed bathing. They found him when they were taking the dance floor up this morning. We have contractors who come in overnight to do it. Useless sods, they are.'

Billy's eyes could not open wider. He gaped, swallowed, gasped and gulped as Stan told him the tale. When he had finished, Billy's head was so full of questions, he could neither think nor speak.

Stan looked at the wall clock 'Ayupp! thar'd better be going home now, lad,' he said leaping up and rinsing his mug under the cold tap. 'It's nearly half past four, sithee. I knock off at five. I've been here sin' five this morning tha knows. I've to do everything while Mike's off sick. Thi promised me an assistant – weer izzi? Scotch mist. Will o' the whizz – that's all he is.' He dried his mug on his trouser front. Billy thought about correcting his wisps and whizzes, but Stan suddenly burst out with: 'Ayup! Weerz thi clothes?'

'Oh no!' cried Billy, 'And my weshing. Worramma gonna do about me dad's pants?'

Stan rocked back on his heels, his face rigid with concern. 'Reight – nah don't thee worrit thi sen. It'll be alreight. I expect thi'll all still be in t'slipper baths. I'll go and fetch 'em for thee.'

*

Billy stood at the tram stop, his mother's washing bundled inside his bath towel. Water dripped from it onto the pavement. Luckily, when a tram arrived, the conductor was collecting fares on the top deck. Billy could slip aboard without his dripping bundle drawing comment. The tram's lower deck was almost empty. He slipped quickly into a seat by a window and slid his soggy baggage under the seat in front of him. As the tram rattled on towards Walkley, a puddle slowly formed around Billy's feet. Unaware, he gazed out of the window at the passing sights.

An old man, sitting in the seat in front, was the first to notice the expanding puddle. He peered down bemused, and picked up his feet as the tram started up Barber Road, the steepest hill on the Walkley tram route. Gravity immediately took the water away from his feet, leaving him in the dry, so the old guy shrugged and put it from his mind. The conductor clattered down the steel spiral staircase just in time to see a thin ribbon of water heading towards him on the rear platform. He glared angrily along the row of seats. His fierce gaze passed over Billy and stopped at the old man, who, he thought, seemed to be directly above the source of the little stream.

Hearing him coming, Billy held up tuppence for his fare. The conductor ignored it and stomped passed. Billy looked up and seeing that the conductor was obviously on the warpath, surreptitiously dragged his illegal bundle closer to his feet, just in case he had to make a swift getaway. Blissfully unaware, the old man in front gazed out of the window as the tram crested the brow of Barber Road and began to plunge, like a switchback, down the other side of the hill towards Springvale.

The conductor was apoplectic. The trickle of water reversed, and surged back inside the tram, picking up dust and discarded tickets as it went. Towering over the old man, his face red with fury, the conductor glared down at him. 'What the chuffin eck?' he spluttered.

The old man turned, looked up innocently, and gave the conductor a bewildered smile.

'Look! What ... ?' the conductor shrieked, dismay robbing his voice of power. 'You've – you've – look what thaz done, Albert. It's only two stops afore thar gets off. Couldn't tha hold it in?'

OoOoO

Chapter Three

In sheep pastures above Man's Head Rock, Harry Clegg drove his stately Austin between dilapidated dry-stone walls. The car lurched over the rutted bumps and puddles of a narrow lane more suited to farm animals than wheeled traffic. Sheep scrutinized his arrival through gaps in the wall.

Much loved by rock-climbers, naturalists, and hikers, Man's Head Rock is a grim-faced colossus overlooking Sheffield's Rivelin Valley. Beneath its craggy stare, a peaty river tumbles into the city from high on Hallam Moor in the newly created Peak National Park. Wild and beautiful as it is, Man's Head Crag was the last place Harry wanted to be; the last story he wanted to cover. For almost a week he had revelled in reporting the "Dance Floor Drowning", and was reluctant to drop it for some grubby murder on the moors. Unfortunately, his ambitious young editor believed that coming, as it did, so soon after the so-called *Dance Floor Drowning*, the story was sure to make it to the front pages of the national dailies, and was insisting that Harry Clegg covered it.

Fifty yards ahead Harry spotted several police cars parked nose to tail. He drove up behind them and switched off the engine. Gazing about miserably, he swung his feet out of the car and began swapping his highly polished brogues for Wellington boots. Apart from a solitary bird watcher, bundled up against the stiff breeze and loaded down with camera equipment, rucksack and binoculars, there was nobody about. Harry locked his car, though it hardly seemed necessary in such a remote spot. He picked his way through the ruined wall into a field of sheep, pausing briefly to scan woodland on the far side of the valley before setting off across springy turf. The sheep parted grudgingly before him as he plodded through their afternoon snack. A barbed wire fence, strung haphazardly at the edge of the field, marked the cliff top from whose craggy walls glared Man's Head Rock.

A stiff breeze whipped tears from his eyes and tugged at his trilby hat. Grabbing a fence post for support, he leaned out to peer over the cliff edge. Fifty feet below, a dozen policemen clambered over a rock-strewn, bracken-covered slope. They were searching an area cordoned off by sad bunting, draped between wooden stakes. From his vantage, above the ear of the colossus, the cliff looked quite unlike the grimacing giant seen from the valley below. But this was not the head Harry had come to see. It was rumoured that two hikers had seen a severed human head gaping up at them from the bracken. So far, the police had found neither head nor torso.

*

Later that same day twelve-year-old "Kick" Morley burst into an old greenhouse, his eyes wide with excitement. 'There's a man's eeyad at Mans eeyad,' he cried.

'You don't say,' said Yvonne Sparkes, sniffing testily from a deckchair amid the horticultural dereliction. She was engrossed in a copy of the Girl's Crystal, and did not shift her gaze.

'Did tha 'ear worra just said? Thiv found a bloke's eeyad. He's deeyad.'

'Who sez?'

'Me mam. She heard it at Lipton's butter counter. They said it were down in t'rocks, reight under t'giant's chin.'

Kick glanced around the desiccated greenhouse as if noticing his surroundings for the first time. Its flaking woodwork and whitewashed glass panes made a bright, dry, gang den for him and his pals, Billy Perks and Yvonne Sparkes. Tucked away in half an acre of neglected garden, and screened by rampant shrubs and twelve feet high advertising hoardings, it was the perfect hideout. Seed boxes and a couple of old deckchairs provided seating. A little iron stove could be fired up for toasting pikelets. Behind the stove, in its place of honour, hung a dusty grey board about the size of a large tea tray. Smudgy chalk lines marked it out in three equal columns. This was the famous "MOM board". The three pals had used it to crack the case of the old Star Woman's murder. It had been placed in its present position by Harry Clegg, almost a year before. He had posed the trio of youngsters before it to photograph them for the front page of his newspaper. The story of their detective work had caused quite a stir. Billy Perks, the gang's default leader, with Yvonne and Kick, the only members, had enjoyed limelight and celebrity for several days.

'Weerz Billy?'

Yvonne reluctantly put aside her reading. 'I'm off,' she said, flicking her dark curly hair behind her ears. It's my granny's birthday. I've gorra take her a card and have tea wi' her.'

'I asked thee weerz Billy? Are tha deaf?'

'I heard you. I don't know where he is. I think he went looking for Doctor Hadfield.'

'Does he know about the bloke's eeyad? Are we gunna be detectives again?' He turned to the MOM board and lifted it down from its hook. 'I'd better get this ready.'

Kick's discovery that detectives often evaluate the potential guilt of suspects by listing their Motive, Opportunity, and Means, had been the inspiration behind *his* creation of the M.O.M. board. It was his main contribution to their famed exploits. He'd been dying to use it on another case ever since.

*

Doctor Hadfield, a young man of yet ill-defined ambition, lived in the single storey, octagonal gatehouse of a large Victorian villa. Barely a year to the day he had arrived in Walkley as locum for an elderly GP. His experience since medical school amounted to little more than a short stint in the Army. Initially, life in the staunchly working class suburb had been a bit of a shock for the graduate of Eton and Oxford. Things took a distinctly worse turn when, upon the death of his old employer, he found himself promoted to junior associate. This rapid elevation had thrown him into a state of bewilderment and dread.

Worse was to come. The replacement for his late boss turned

out to be a tyrannical woman who had been one of his tutors at Oxford; Clarissa Fulton-Howard. She claimed to have taken the appointment as a sort of semi-retirement post. Now in her late fifties, Miss Fulton-Howard was returning to her Sheffield roots. She had purchased an idyllic stone cottage in the Peak District, a mere fifteen minutes' drive away, and was not pleased to find her idyll sullied by the presence of young Hadfield, a former student whom she had not only thought lazy and flippant, but one she suspected of having painted her bicycle saddle with golden syrup.

Wearing his customary off duty cricket whites and carpet slippers, Hadfield peered at his young visitor across a marmalade-stained dining table. 'I'm twenty-eight, Billy. Not fifty,' he said, with a gesture suggestive of smoking a pipe, or perhaps imitating Popeye the sailor. Billy wasn't sure.

A whistling kettle came to the boil on a Baby Belling hotplate. Hadfield turned it off. He poured boiling water into a couple of enamelled mugs and dribbled a bottle-top measure of Camp Coffee essence into each, filling the room with its enigmatic aroma.

'Have I been up the Amazon? No. Have I trekked the arctic wastes? No. Have I worked in an African field hospital, or discovered the cure for malaria? No! I've done nothing, Billy!'

He cast around miserably, his shoulders slumping in despair. 'Even in the army I got little further than Aldershot.' He poured milk and plopped a couple of saccharin tablets into each mug before stirring them vigorously with a pencil. He offered one to Billy, and eyed him closely, hoping for a sympathetic response. Instead, he found him leafing through a medical book, occasionally turning it sideways to better appreciate its colourful images of human reproductive organs.

'Are you listening, Billy?'

Billy had mistakenly assumed that the young doctor was off on one of his frequent rants against society in general, or Test Match cricket in particular. He had not expected to have to vouchsafe opinions. Flummoxed, he nodded apologetically and tried to look fascinated.

Scowling, Hadfield withdrew the proffered coffee mug and confiscated the medical book. 'All I've done is what my father wanted,' he went on. 'This is my first proper job, Billy. Can you believe that? I only took it because I thought it wouldn't last long.' He scowled at the bare walls of his tiny living room and sighed. 'I want to see the world. I don't want to be a GP in ruddy Walkley for the rest of my life. The only excitement I've had here was that bit of detective work we did last year.'

He studied his visitor again, and sank back into a battered armchair. 'You do see my itch, don't you, old bean? I mean, I'm not just being selfish, am I? I want a bit of excitement; some adventure, some worthwhile experiences. I want to be useful in the world - and you know what they say about travel?'

'They don't know how that bloke drowned, tha knows. My friend Stan told me.'

Hadfield blew a sigh and sipped his coffee. 'I might as well talk to a wall.'

'Now thiv found a man's eeyad at Mans eeyad,' Billy went on.

Hadfield gaped. 'A man's head at…'

'How can tha tell 'ow somebody died if thaz only gorriz eeyad?'

'Only-got-his-head,' Hadfield enunciated. 'Speak English, for God's sake, Billy. What do you have against using the letter aitch?'

Billy frowned, 'But how can you tell?' he said, with some small concession to Received Pronunciation.

'Its detachment is a strong clue, old lad,' Hadfield quipped. 'Mind you, even then, pathologists will stir the metaphorical entrails in search of ambiguity. No pathologist worth his salt will pass on the enigmatic, Billy.'

Billy scowled. 'I don't know what tha'rt saying,' he grumbled. 'How though? How can tha tell what they died of?'

'Do you know what, Billy? You really are the worst possible company for a chap down in the doldrums,' said Hadfield. 'You don't talk to one, except to ask ludicrous questions. You certainly don't listen, and you spend your entire visit looking for the dirty bits in one's medical books. Aren't you the least bit interested in anything I say?'

Billy sat up and straightened his shoulders. 'Sorry. Err – so - how much curing have you done today?' he asked, attempting interest.

Hadfield deflated miserably. 'You make me sound like a pork butcher, or a tanner.'

Billy shrugged his shoulders. 'Ooh well, if tha 'rt going to be a narky owd mardy arse, I'm off,' he said. 'I came to see thee for nowt. I thought we were friends.'

'OK, stop right there.' Hadfield raised a staying hand. 'You never visit me for no reason. And frankly, old lad, I can always tell when you're up to something. So, what is it this time? Why are you here? Are you in detective mode again? Is that why you're asking about drowning and headless corpses?'

'I'm norra detective no-more. I told thee that before. I were asking because thiv found a man's eeyad at Mans eeyad.'

'Forgive me, old lad, but that's a downright fib. I mean to say, if you're really not a detective, why would you want to know about headless corpses?'

Billy dropped his gaze. 'I just want to know. It's all a bit fishy. Sommat's going on. There are bodies floating in swimming pools and dead eeyads popping up all o'er.'

The doctor frowned. 'I think you've flipped, old lad. What could possibly be going on?'

'I don't know, but the coppers are acting reight weird about it,' he said. 'Thiv warned me to stay away. They were gonna handcuff me. They had me down at the main cop-shop on Monday. They said they'd lock me up forever if I didn't stay out of it.'

'They can't do that. We fought the Nazis to stop that sort of thing.'

'That's all reight for thee to say, tha'rt posh. It's different for me. They don't care what they do to me. I nearly lost me bike and us ration book.' He looked about giving the air a righteous sniff before going on. 'If old Fishy Wragg hadn't taken it in for me it would've got nicked. Now it stinks of fish and I lost two pounds o' sugar. My mam went barmy. I thought she'd kill me.'

'Billy, this is serious.' Hadfield scratched his head. 'Why were you at the police station?'

'I told thee! They arrested me - took me in a police car. They wunt bring me back though. I had to walk home. It's miles. I could've got lost. I'm only a little child tha knows.' He tried to look pathetic.

'Who did you see? Who spoke to you there?'

'A big-wig. Chief Superintendent Flood, or sommat. He were ranting on abaht all sorts. He poked me in t'chest and said he'd lock me up if I didn't stay out of it.'

Hadfield stood up and paced his cramped room. 'This's not cricket, old lad,' he said, his brow furrowing with concern. 'Leave it with me, Billy. I'll get to the bottom of this. Have you told your parents?' Billy shook his head. 'Perhaps it's best not to - until we know more about it. I'll poke around a bit - see if I can get to the bottom of it. How's that?'

'But worra about my mam's sugar ration? She sez I've got to mek it up. How can I?'

'Hum, better start growing beets, old lad.'

OoOoO

Chapter Four

A week had passed since the "*Dance Floor Drowning"*. A wolfish frenzy of pressmen had milked the story from every possible angle, and, as their attention veered to the *"Man's Head Murder"* yet more salivating hacks flapped into the city from the capital like crows to a carcass.

Rivelin Valley crawled with reporters and photographers. Dog walkers and hikers with any old cock and bull story to tell, no matter how improbable, achieved overnight celebrity. Old men on their allotments were snapped and quoted in the national dailies, especially the red tops. Even when the *decapitated head* turned up, still firmly attached to a body, the press struggled to cling on grimly to the *"man's head at Man's Head"* headlines, until they had exhausted every possible spin they could put on it.

It had taken the police two days of poking and peering under bracken and rocks to unearth the head - and its body. Tangled briar and bracken had covered the head which gazed out from rocks, some as big as bags of cement. The body was covered up to the neck. It was not surprising that the hikers who had reported its discovery had thought they were seeing a severed head.

When the police finally carried away the disappointingly intact corpse, the crowds that had gathered to watch, rapidly dwindled. Fleet Street headline writers were inconsolable. Shredding blizzards of unusable alliterative iterations, they fled to Sheffield's Midland, and Victoria Stations and boarded trains for London.

Billy clamped his hand on his dog's muzzle and tried to keep him calm and quiet. Wire Haired Terriers are not good at calm, or quiet. True to the breed, Ruff, as he was called, had two operational modes, ecstasy and sleep. Even when sleeping, his dreaming was often as ecstatic as his waking life.

From the cover of birch trees on the hillside opposite the murder site, Billy viewed the search area. Apart from a solitary constable sitting on a low wall, all that remained of police activity were two poles, like broom staves, with a string of grubby bunting hanging limply between them.

Billy released Ruff and climbed down through the woods to the river. Four yards wide and a foot deep, the River Rivelin eddied and tumbled chaotically around rocks and tree roots. The pair crossed it on stepping stones made from old millstone grit grinding wheels, like giant cotton reels. Ruff crossed it several times, twice, fully immersed in the peaty waters. Once across, Billy grabbed the dog by its collar and passed by the Round Dam, an old millpond whose glassy waters had powered mill wheels since the time of Henry the VIII. The valley road ran above the now ruined mill. Beyond it, steep, rough pasture rose to a craggy edge from where the fearsome Man's Head Rock overlooked the murder site.

The solitary policeman pretended not to notice Billy's approach until he was almost within an arm's reach. 'Why are you still here?' Billy asked. 'I heard you'd found a body and its head.'

The constable eyed him gravely, gently batting the wet dog from his trouser leg. 'And who might you be - the Chief Constable?'

'No, I'm Bil ...' He stopped himself, recalling Chief Superintendent Flood's dire warnings. 'I'm – err - just a member of the public who's interested in what happened.'

'Well then, *oh great and valued member of the public*, forgive me,' said the constable. He stood up, pulled his tunic straight and saluted theatrically. 'I am Police Constable John Needham, at your service, sir. Forgive me, for a moment there, I thought you were that nosy kid called Billy Perks, the dead-eye detective of Walkley.' PC Needham smiled eyeing him craftily.

At six feet two, with a broad athletic build, Needham towered over him. Billy felt dizzy looking up at him, but much reassured by his open, friendly face and cheerful blue eyes.

'Now that thiv found it, I was just wondering why you're still here. Are they still looking for sommat else, or what? And I'm norra detective no more.' For emphasis, he adopted his best portrayal of injured innocence.

Constable Needham laughed. 'Well I hope you're a better detective than you are an actor, cos that performance were rubbish.' His expression softened and he smiled at the lad. 'Still, it's a pity you're not that Billy Perks kid, cos this'd be a really good case for him.' He paused and gave Billy a quizzical look, before going on. 'I mean to say, headless first - then not headless – makes you think don't it? It's not unusual for a corpse to lose a head, but they don't often gain one, do they? I'd have thought it'd be a real challenge for a lad like – that there Billy Perks.'

'I've been told not to get involved. I'll gerrin to trouble if I do.'

'Who said that – thee dad?'

'No, Chief Superintendent Flood.'

'Crickey! Chief Superintendent Flood. You've got some important friends haven't you?'

'Huh, he's not me friend,' said Billy. 'He said I'd go to jail for life if I stick me nose in.'

The constable's eyes narrowed. 'When did he tell you that?'

'Last Monday.'

'So here you are now, just a week later, interrogating me at the murder site.' Chuckling softly he looked around the silent, leafy valley. 'Tha dunt seem to be taking him too seriously.' Resuming his seat on the low wall, he looked down at his boots and brushed away a smear of muddy earth. Ruff helped him by licking it. 'Well you can rest assured, lad. We did find a body. It most definitely had a head on its shoulders, and it's been taken away for examination.'

'Was it a man? How was he killed?'

'Oooh that was nasty.' The constable pulled a face as if smelling rotten fish. 'His head was bashed in. Sommat big and round, like a beer mug, or a piece of pipe. I heard our blokes talking about it.'

Billy's eyes widened. 'But he weren't in pieces?'

PC Needham eyed him gravely. 'Only the one. They don't know what happened yet. I think the so-called experts are a bit baffled – seem to be talking rubbish, from what I've heard.'

'Why?'

'Well some of 'em said he must have been run over by a truck and then buried up here.'

'Run over?' Billy sneered dismissively. 'How did he get up here then - walk by his sen?'

'That's just what I said. The killer would have had to carry him all the way up from the road. It couldn't be done. It's too steep and rough. Even Tommy Ward's elephant would find it a struggle.'

'Maybe he was chucked off the crag,' suggested Billy doubtfully. They both turned to look up at the rocks. Billy snorted, regretting his suggestion. He couldn't imagine how even a strong man could have carried a fully clothed corpse all the way up from the road and thrown it back down again.

The constable was having similar doubts. 'More than likely,' he suggested, 'he wasn't dragged or thrown anywhere. I think he was here already, and was killed here.'

'The killer might've had a car,' said Billy, still struggling with his *"Thrown off the crag theory"*. 'He could'ave run over him, put him in the boot and driven up to the top lane, and chucked him off.'

'No – no - no, you can't park near enough, and you'd never carry a corpse all the way across that sheep field up there. It's too far and it's all rough and tussocky.' He looked expectantly at Billy and then added, 'And a sheep might bite thee bum.'

Billy giggled.

'And if you could carry him, you'd be seen. There's always folks up there looking around; hikers, climbers, bird watchers.'

'Unless it was night,' said Billy.

'Now thart talking rubbish. You'd never attempt it at night. Besides a dead body weighs a ton, especially when it's all floppy. Has tha ever tried to lift a drunk up?' Constable Needham shrugged his broad shoulders and held out his palms as if they contained evidence for his explanation. 'And don't forget that it were buried under t'rocks. That means the killer would have had to climb down here to bury it after he'd carried it all that way up and chucked it off the cliff top. And some of them stones on him were big ens. He'd have to be a giant to 'ave done all that.'

'Was it only his head that was bashed in?'

'Blimey! Int that enough? You're a bit bloodthirsty aren't you?'

'No I mean, if he was run over by a truck why wasn't he injured in other places?'

'What, d'you mean like Doncaster and New York?'

Billy giggled again. It took him several attempts to calm himself sufficiently to clarify his question. 'No, I mean other parts of his body. Like broken legs or arms, not just his head.'

'I didn't see the body close up. All I know is, they said his head were clubbed wi sommat round.'

Billy looked down to the gently stirring lime trees shading the valley road out to Kinder Scout and the Snake Pass. 'It's lonely round here. Aren't tha scared, all by thee sen? A monster-beast might come and bash your head in.'

'You're the only one who's doing my head in. I hate to think what you'll be like when you grow up and join the police force.'

'Who sez I will?' Billy thought for a moment. 'Folks are always saying that, burra don't want to. I used to want to be a tram driver. Now I want to be a furnace mason - like me dad.'

'Furnace mason? What's so good about working in a scorching steelworks?'

'You get *Hot Money*.'

'What?'

'They have to line the furnaces with special fire-bricks while it's still really hot, so they pay 'em extra money. It's called Hot Money. It's brilliant, int it?'

The policeman looked doubtful. 'Hum, I suppose it's all right - until it kills thee.'

Billy shot him a stricken glance.

PC Needham didn't notice. He was looking at the sky. 'You'd

better get thee sen home, lad. It looks like it'll rain soon.'

Billy looked at the lowering sky, and nodded agreement. 'Yeah but first I'm going to have a look from his head. Have you been up?'

'What, up there, you mean?' Needham pointed to the craggy features of Man's Head rock. 'Not flipping likely, and neither should you, tha'll get soaked in a minute.' PC Needham moved off to unpack his police cape from a haversack he had tucked under the wall. He swung it round his shoulders, and laughed at the irony as he watched Billy set off up the steep path at the edge of the crag. 'You'll never prove he was chucked off the top. It's a barmy idea.'

Billy waved and scrambled up the relatively easy, ramblers' climb to the top. The killer could have dragged the body down that way too, he realised. It would not have been easy, but it might explain how they did it. At the top, the muddy ground was as slippery as ice. Billy had to be careful not to go skating over the edge. Staring sheep moved away warily as they spotted little Ruff scrambling up behind him. A stiff breeze ruffled their fleeces as Billy peered out across the valley. He waved to PC Needham, then set off across the field to look for signs of a motor car, or lorry. He did not expect to find anything. The idea that a grown man had been run over, driven up there and thrown off, seemed ridiculous, but if he had, Billy thought, there should be some sign of it.

A dry stone wall, badly patched here and there with odd bits of wire netting, ran along the side of the field. Beyond it he found the narrow muddy lane, churned into a tangled mess of tyre marks. Numerous vehicles had used the track recently. Any evidence there might have been for the unlikely theory of a killer with a car or truck, had long been obliterated.

Billy climbed over the wall into the lane and waited mockingly for his little dog to manage the same feat. When he finally did, they set off home together through the first raindrops. Ruff cocked his leg and peed on the crumbling wall, as if to show the staring sheep, his mastery of their terrain. Billy noticed he had picked a spot where one of the cars that had parked there recently had evidently scraped into the tumbled stonework, leaving flakes of black paint behind.

*

Between a particularly bad case of haemorrhoids and a carbuncle, Dr Hadfield called Police HQ from his surgery. It was his third attempt to contact the chief superintendent. Promised call-backs had not materialized, and he was now feeling cross and quite ill-used. Being kept hanging on the silent line for what seemed ages, did not improve his humour either. The woman at the other end of the line eventually clicked back on and apologized for keeping him waiting. 'In what connection was it that your enquiry is in connection with?' she asked in a ridiculously snooty and ungrammatical telephone voice.

'I've explained it all before,' said Hadfield wearily. 'I need to speak to the Chief Superintendent. It's about a young patient of mine.'

'But he's been out. He's very busy you know. He may not be - oh – err – no - just a moment, sir, I believe he's coming into his office now. Please hold. I'm putting you through.'

Flood's brassy voice came on the line. 'Hello, Doctor – err - Heathfield. How can I help?'

'Hadfield, Chief Superintendent, it's Hadfield. I've been calling you for days.'

'Oh really? I'm very sorry to hear that,' Flood said. 'I've been – er - they had to find me. We're really very busy here. You probably heard about our murders. Just like tramcars, what? Don't get one for ages then two come along at once. Now how can I help – er - Doctor – err -?'

'Young Billy Perks,' said Hadfield, trying to keep calm. 'He told me you arrested him ...'

'Good Lord no - not arrested, no no no no no. We spoke to him on a police matter, but that was over a week ago. Why are you involved? He *is* alright, isn't he?'

'He's fine, but I was concerned to hear how he'd been treated ...'

'Treated. What on earth do you mean? He was cautioned on a serious police matter.'

'You cautioned him?'

'Well not exactly *A Caution* – not in the legal sense. You see, Doctor – er – the lad got involved in a murder investigation once before - last year. Sad to say, some rather misguided adults assisted him. Thoroughly irresponsible, I thought. You may recall it.'

Hadfield blushed guiltily, aware that Flood was having a dig at him, as he had been one of the adults involved.

'It was only a game to him, of course,' Flood went on. 'He was just playing at being a detective. The trouble is, it was a very dangerous situation, you see. He and his friends could have come to serious harm. I wanted to make sure he didn't get any ideas about these latest cases, especially as they're somewhat unusual. I expect you've read about the murder at Man's Head Rock? Well perhaps you don't know, Doctor – erm – er – Heathfield, but we know that Billy Perks and his friends often play near there. I just wanted to make sure he stays out of it – for his own safety. We could be dealing with a lunatic. The last thing I want is children and – err - misguided adults too, for that matter, putting themselves at risk.'

Hadfield squirmed with annoyance, but pressed on calmly. 'But you interviewed him before the Man's Head murder?'

'Yes – yes.'

'So you could hardly have warned him to stay away from it?'

'No – yes – no - err - I meant that I wanted him to stay away from the swimming baths case, but then, a few days later the other one popped up right where he and his friends play.'

Hadfield preened minimally, sensing that Flood was slightly rattled. 'The boy said you poked him in the chest? Did you? He also said you told him he'd go to jail for life?'

Flood laughed, a little too heartily to be genuine, the doctor thought. 'Look Doctor, you know young Billy Perks, he's a bit of a scamp. I needed to make an impression on him, put the wind up him a bit, nothing more than that. However, if you're concerned, I'll speak to his parents. Frankly, I'd hoped to avoid formality.'

Hadfield felt deflated. Apart from his one small slip, Flood's reasoning seemed valid, and although the rules about the interrogation of minors had been stretched a little, he could see why. 'OK, thank you, Chief Superintendent. I'll be speaking to Billy's parents myself. If you're happy to leave it with me, you needn't worry about visiting them. As you say, "avoid formality". However, I'm sure you will agree with me that the rules about minors are there for very good reason. You will no doubt understand my concern.'

'Don't worry, Doctor – err - Heathfield ...'

'Hadfield. It's Hadfield.'

'I quite understand. And, if I may say so, I'm delighted that you take such a close interest in your patient's welfare.'

The line went dead.

*

'Birch!' Flood yelled at his office wall. He slammed the telephone receiver onto its base on his desk, toppling an artillery shell case that served as a pencil holder. Its contents scattered across the floor. 'Birch! For God's sake where are you?'

The office door opened. Miss Birch, his flustered civilian secretary, rushed in, crunching pencils beneath her tripping feet. Thin and gangly, with grey hair wrapped around her head like a turban, she bobbed and bowed as if kowtowing to a Chinese emperor. Muttering apologies, she dropped to her knees and began scooping up pencil debris, in the process spilling the contents of the folder of mail she was carrying.

'Stop it! Stop it, woman!' cried Flood. 'For God's sake leave all that. Where's Lackey?'

Miss Birch's spectacles slid down her nose as she swung her terrified gaze to her boss's reddening face. 'Sergeant Lackey is in the canteen, Sir.'

'Get him!'

Five minutes later, Miss Birch announced Sergeant Lackey, waving him into Flood's presence as if fanning dying embers.

'That bloody kid's causing trouble already,' Flood said without ceremony. 'I've had his doctor on the 'phone. Hadfield, remember him? That meddling, posh bugger who teamed up with him last year. He as good as accused me of police brutality.'

Sergeant Lackey picked his way to Flood's desk, avoiding Miss Birch's fluttering fingers as she cleared a path through splintered pens and pencils. 'He's a brassy little devil that kid,' said the sergeant. 'He was cheeky to me when I picked him up the other day.'

'Did he say much in the car?' Flood was polishing the artillery shell case on his sleeve

'No, he just moaned about his bike or sommat. Oh, and a ration book.'

'Do you know the family?' Flood said, half-heartedly tidying his desk.

'The father's a steelworker, a big bloke. They're no trouble as far as I know.'

Flood looked disappointed. 'No unpaid fines, or anything?' He moved to his office window.

Lackey followed him with his eyes, his brow furrowed with concentration. 'It – err - it wouldn't be hard to get some sort of – err - hold on the lad. Keep him quiet, like,' he said craftily. 'Maybe even get him put away for a month or two.'

Flood turned sharply. 'No! I wouldn't want him put away, no courts.' He turned back to the window and looked down at the traffic in the street below. 'Who's the local copper?'

Lackey frowned. 'Oh, he's no bloody use. John Needham, ex-navy bloke. He wouldn't help us. He's too – err - too …' He shuffled his feet, leaving the sentence unfinished. 'Anyway, we don't need him. Leave it to me, Sir. I'll soon get a tight rein on the lad.'

'No details,' instructed Flood. 'Just make sure he stays out of police business, nothing more than that.'

OoOoO

Chapter Five

Kick Morley was playing keepy-uppy with a football against the gable end of Billy's house. Almost two weeks had passed since the dance floor drowning and the so-called headless corpse murder. Kick Morley, in the absence of more headless corpses, had reinstated football as his major obsession, despite it being the cricket season.

Smothering her annoyance, Missis Perks approached him from her back door. 'He's not here, Michael,' she said stiffly. 'I've told you already, he went off on his bike.'

'Yeah, burrill be back soon,' said Kick reasonably, rolling the ball off his head, around his neck, onto his shoulder and down onto a knee before catching it.

'Yes, love, he will, but can't you wait somewhere else?'

'But that'd be no good, Missis Perks. I have to wait somewhere where he's gonna be when he comes back. It's no good waiting somewhere where he's not gonna be …'

Missis Perks pursed her lips, briefly rocked by the child's implacable logic. 'Yes, but you must stop banging that – B-B-BALL! Billy's dad's on nights. He's not well. He needs his sleep.'

'Can I wait if I don't bounce the ball?'

'Oh I suppose so, but don't do anything with the ball. Just be quiet – please. And anyway he has jobs waiting for him when he gets back. He's still got lavvie paper to tear up. I told him yesterday to do that.'

At that moment, Billy returned on his bike, skidding to a dramatic stop and saving his mother further debate.

Missis Perks glared at the pair. 'Just keep it down,' she said, through gritted teeth. 'And you,' she was pointing a stabbing finger at Billy, 'can get that lavvy paper done. I don't want your father going down the yard to find none on the nail.'

Billy shrugged contritely. 'Sorry mam.'

'And remember, Billy, your dad's on nights, and he's not well. Keep the noise down.'

Billy dismounted, and cheekily drew his index finger across his lips. He began to tip toe theatrically towards the street. Kick followed in similar mode. They looked like a pair of pantomime clowns.

'Don't go disappearing, Billy,' Missis Perks told him. 'Your dinner'll be ready soon.'

The lads climbed onto the front gate and swung it gently back and forth. 'Thiv opened the big swimming bath at long last.'

'About time an' all,' said Kick. 'It's two weeks sin' they found that floater.'

Billy cocked his leg over the gate's top rail so that he could swing hands free. 'My dad says millions o' kids have been playing hell about it being shut in t'school holidays. He said, they had to open it or there would have been riots and commotions.'

'Maybe they've solved who did it,' Kick said.

'I don't think so. We still need to do some poking around. We should go for a swim.'

'Errgh!' Kick's expression signalled disgust. 'Worrif thiv not changed watta. We'd be swimming in deeyad man's body juice.'

Billy squinted up from fixing a kink in his wire-framed glasses. 'It'll mek a change from swimming in tha piddle. Tha'rt always piddlin in it.'

Kick laughed, blushing slightly. 'I never!'

Billy threaded his specs back on to his nose and around his ears. 'Thiv not even said who he were yet.' He climbed down from the gate and headed off towards his house door. 'I've gorra tear up some lav paper,' he said gloomily. 'Will tha call for us this affs?'

Kick eyed him doubtfully. 'No, I'm not going swimming in no deeyad body juice.'

'Okay then, we'll meet at t'greenhouse. We need to mek a plan, and tha needs to get thee MOM board sorted out. We aren't mekkin any progress on these murders.'

The pair parted. Billy headed for the garden shed where his dad's old newspapers were saved for a million jobs around the house and garden, not the least important of which was as toilet paper.

'Make sure they're neat and tidy,' called his mother as she spotted him going into the shed. 'I don't want 'em all ragged and different sizes. It looks common.'

Billy gave her a resentful nod. He closed the shed door behind him and stuck his tongue out, once he was sure she couldn't see him. Selecting several sheets of newsprint, he laid them out on his father's workbench and began tearing them neatly over the back of on old hacksaw blade. He divided each broadsheet into pieces roughly the size of a library book page. He was good at it, and made a nice neat job. It was a slow job, mainly because distracting stories he spotted in the old newspapers were hard to resist. That was how he learned the name of the Man's Head murder victim. There, on a couple of sheets of lavvy paper, he saw the announcement of the poor man's funeral.

Henry Darnley, professor of history and chairman of the Board of Trustee Curators of Sheffield Museum, who was brutally murdered at Man's Head crag, will be buried at Crookes Cemetery on ...

Billy blew a long whistling sigh as he studied the details. Somehow, he had missed the announcement, even though he always scanned the newspapers when his dad had finished with them. He could not imagine how he had missed it. The newspaper was three days old. The funeral was to take place tomorrow afternoon. He should go, he told himself. We all should. He wondered briefly if he could convince his pals to join him. It would be a fine opportunity to see who turned up. They would learn who the victim's friends and family were. And, though they might never know it, one of them could even be the killer.

He quickly sorted his sheets of toilet paper into a pad and punched a hole through one corner with an awl. He threaded string through the hole and tied a loop for a hanger. Admiring his handiwork, he set off to install it on the special nail at the back of the lavatory door.

*

Billy's house clung to a steep street of small, artisan dwellings, most built at the end of the nineteenth century. Though many had walls of similar grey sandstone and roofs of welsh slate, they were a curious mixture of shapes and sizes. Steps, low walls and stone terraces linked them, as if to prevent them sliding down onto Walkley's main shopping street where double-decker tramcars pounded between pavements crowded with shoppers. Few motor vehicles could make the steep climb up Billy's street without considerable drama and clouds of exhaust smoke. Once a week however, the greengrocer's horse and cart accomplished it without fuss.

'Any headless corpses today?' This from Mister Leaper perched high on the driving seat of his mobile fruit-and-veg shop. Beattie, his heavy grey mare, snorted and shook her head, seeming to share the joke as she stopped at the curb where Billy stood, waiting with his mother's shopping list.

'Very funny,' grumbled Billy, as he helpfully lifted down a wheel-chock from its hanger under the cart's tailboard and kicked it into place behind a wheel. 'Me mam says thee carrots are rubbery and thee runner beans are stringy.'

Mister Leaper lifted an eyebrow. He had a weather beaten, russet face, that would better suit a trawler man than a greengrocer. An ancient cap, worn shiny at the neb by years of handling, covered his head. A leather belt, with the badge of the Royal Artillery on its buckle, held a brown warehouse coat firmly in place over his ample frontage. Wheezing and grunting, he climbed down to the pavement and stamped his feet, as if testing his safe arrival on terra firma. He set the cart's handbrake and expertly secured it with a mystical hitch. 'Oh does she now?' he said, nodding and bobbing his head as if acknowledging applause from around the street. 'She waint be wanting nowt then!'

Billy rubbed Beattie's powerful neck and looked into her soft, brown eyes. 'Nay she does,' he said loftily. 'She wants carrots and runner beans, but not rubbery 'ens.'

'Has thy heard owt else about them murders?' Mister Leaper asked, looping a nosebag over Beattie's head.

'Only that thiv reopened t'swimming baths, but I've not heard nowt at all about t'other one at Man's Head. Has tha?'

'No, nowt. I know they're burying one of 'em at Crookes cemetery tomorrow afternoon. But I expect tha'll already know that, thee being a genius detective an' all.' Mister Leaper armed himself with a spirit level and a few well used slivers of plywood. He bent to levelling his set of large brass weighing scales. When he'd done he demonstrated their accuracy with a theatrical flourish of a cast iron test-weight.

From neighbouring houses, women were gathering at the cart. They smiled and nodded, greeting each other, as, armed with baskets and shopping bags, they formed an orderly queue on the pavement. Mister Leaper smiled at each one as they joined the line. 'Good day, girls. Lovely day for it?' he said. 'I've got some smashing Savoys today – only threppenz a-piece.'

'Threppenz!' one woman cried, seeming most alarmed. 'Who do you think I am, Lady chuffing Docker? I'm not made of money tha knows.'

Billy's mind was not on cabbages, or diamond dripping millionairesses. He quickly completed his mother's shopping and ran back into the house with it. The funeral announcement in the newspaper had been the only information to emerge about either the so-called Man's Head murder, or the drowning. The police remained tight-lipped on both. In particular, it was as if the *"dance floor drowning"* had never even happened. Billy and his pals had become increasingly concerned and had convinced themselves that if *they* didn't act, the killers might go free - perhaps to strike again.

Since reading about the funeral, Billy had repeatedly turned over his thoughts and ideas about it, but he had not changed his mind. He was convinced they should attend, and reasoned that if they could discover who were the dead man's friends and relations, a reason for his death might begin to reveal itself. It might only be a short step from there to the identification of those with reason, or the desire, to kill him.

*

At noon on the day of the funeral, Billy and Kick reconnoitred the cemetery. They were looking for a good hiding place, close enough to see the mourners' faces without being spotted. They arrived to find the sexton putting the final touches to a new grave. They watched him, unseen, from a stand of rhododendron bushes. 'If that's where they're going to bury him,' Billy whispered, 'this'll be a great hiding place.'

Kick agreed, though he seemed somewhat distracted. He was staring at the open grave, a puzzled frown on his face.

'What's up?' Billy asked him.

'Will they have a separate coffin for his eeyad?'

Billy gaped at him astonished. 'Worra tha talking abaht? He's gorriz eeyad on his shoulders, tha wazzock!'

Kick shuffled defensively. 'Well why are they all saying he were eeyadless then?'

Billy could hardly believe his ears. 'I've told thee already. At first they thought he were eeyadless, burriz not. It's the papers' fault. They kept on saying it because of Man's Head rock. It just gen 'em better headlines, – more gory like. They like it gory, wi missing eeyads and stuff .'

'Huh huh, headlines,' Kick sniggered at Billy's unintentional pun.

Billy frowned. 'That copper I met said the head was sticking out from some bracken. He said that at first glance it looked like it were chopped off.'

Kick sighed, disappointed. 'It would've been better chopped off.'

Billy shook his head disdainfully. 'I've told thee all this once. I think th'art barmy.' He started towards the cemetery gates. 'Come on. I'm going for me dinner. I'll see thee later. Don't forget, they're burying him at three. We need to be hidden before anybody comes.'

*

It was raining when Yvonne, Kick and Billy crept into hiding in the rhododendron bushes. The funeral cortege was due to arrive shortly. Billy and Kick had fastened elderberry branches to themselves for extra camouflage. Yvonne said they looked stupid. She was wearing her dark green school raincoat, and smugly pointed out how it kept her dry as well as perfectly camouflaged, without having caterpillars and spiders crawling out of it.

Billy wiped a finger across his rain-spattered glasses and peered from the rhododendrons. Apart from his earlier reconnoitre, he had only visited the cemetery once before. That had been in the late summer of the previous year. His granny Smeggs had forced him to help her gather blackberries from the abundance of brambles growing around the graves. Since then he had often wondered about the blood red juice from his granny's blackberry pies, flowing like blood from berries grown in earth containing so many rotting corpses. He shuddered and swung his gaze around the wide expanse of gravestones.

The cemetery ensured its corpses remained at rest by enclosing them within a six feet high stone wall. At its main entrance a pair of regal, cast iron gates swung between ornamental pillars. Nearby, a brass tap dribbled into a stone water trough. Beside it rose a mountainous heap of composting flowers where visitors, tidying up the graves of their loved ones, tossed dying wreaths and bouquets. Rows of gravestones, some bearing carved swags of acanthus leaves, angels and urns, lurched at each other across weed-grown paths. A few monuments had toppled over, and lay beneath veils of bramble, ivy and old man's beard; excellent habitat for wrens, grass snakes, hedgehogs and foxes. A small, gothic chapel overlooked all, its mullioned windows as dark and shiny as coal.

A metallic squeal drew Billy's attention to the gates. A Daimler hearse, followed by two black limousines, slowly entered and began their stately progress up the drive. The hearse stopped at the chapel porch. The driver and three frock coated ushers climbed out and began offloading a coffin onto a folding bier. After carefully arranging floral wreaths on it, they wheeled it into the chapel porch.

With great solemnity, two middle aged women stepped from the second of the limousines. A rather effete young man followed and joined them. The three paused, waiting self-consciously for the first car to disgorge its passengers. One of the women frowned and poked the young man into action, making him step up to open the first limousine's door. A stern faced woman of about fifty-five climbed out. She glared at the young man and edged him aside, deferring to her fellow passenger. It was an older, elegant woman wearing a veiled, black straw hat. She leaned on a silver topped, ebony cane with which she testily beat away all offers of help from her grave faced companion.

With the minimum of fuss and formality, the sad little group mustered behind the bier and followed it into the chapel's shadowy interior. Three more family groups arrived on foot; middle aged, middle class couples, each with a pair of young adults sporting either university scarves, or smart school uniforms. Billy did not recognize anyone; even the school uniforms were unknown to him.

However, he did recognize one of the last to arrive, Doctor Longden, the man who had chased him out of the Turkish baths. He and a fat, slovenly man arrived in a taxicab. The fat one exchanged angry whispers with the cabby before grudgingly paying him. As Billy watched them enter the chapel, he thought what an odd couple they made, Longden swinging a walking stick and marching to some imagined military band, his fat friend, slouching behind.

Two other men arrived. Both hung back in the rain watching from a distance. When the chapel doors closed behind the mourners, the pair moved in to the porch to shelter. Billy watched them light cigarettes and kick their heels, not speaking to each other. He guessed they were reporters. A few minutes later Harry Clegg arrived. He nodded to the smokers in the porch, removed his hat and went quietly into the chapel.

'Not many,' Billy said. 'You'd think there'd be more.'

'What about him?' Yvonne flicked a dark, wayward curl behind her ear and pointed to a small, balding man, wearing a navy blue three-piece suit. He was shaking the rain from his trilby hat. A silver badge glinted from his lapel. He replaced his hat, turned up his jacket collar and continued to watch the chapel doors from the hillside. 'D'you think he's here for t'funeral, or sommat else?'

'Why dunt he go in to t'church?' Kick asked.

'He might be nowt to do with 'em,' said Billy.

'Why's he up there then?' asked Yvonne. 'It's siling down. He's gerrin soaked. He could be in the church - keeping dry.'

He had seemed innocuous to Billy, but Yvonne's suspicions led him to study the old guy more closely. Quietly smoking as he watched events at the chapel door, he struck Billy as being more curious than grieving. 'Humm, I don't know,' he said. 'We'll keep an eye on him.'

Kick soon became restless. He stood up and stretched, shrugging off his elderberry camouflage. 'I'm fed up wi' this. How long 'ave we gorra stay 'ere?'

'Half an hour at least,' said Yvonne. 'They'll have prayers and then sing sommat.'

'Chuffing 'eck! I'm not waiting half an hour. We've seen 'em all now, and we didn't recognize nobody. We might as well tek-us-hooks.'

Billy too was disappointed, though at least he had seen Doctor Longden, and that might be a clue. But, he had hoped for more. He needed a lead, some useful clue to spark off the case. Instead, he'd learned little more than the dead man's name. Henry Darnley, the victim of the Man's Head murder, still remained a mystery. And now, soaked to the skin and prickled by his elderberry disguise, it was not difficult to agree with Kick. 'Yeah, this worra dead loss. Let's tek-us-hooks.'

'Look! He's gone,' cried Yvonne, pointing to the rise where the old man had been standing. 'He was right there - then puff – he's gone.'

'He's left sommat behind,' said Kick. 'Look - on that gravestone.'

Billy wiped his glasses with his fingers and peered through the rain. He could just make out a small, rectangular object, about the size of a cigarette packet. 'I think it's just his fags.'

'We'd better 'ave a look,' said Yvonne. 'It could be us first clue.'

Shedding elderberry branches, Billy stomped up the hill, his eyes fixed on the little object on the gravestone. He was soon disappointed when it turned out to be nothing more than a cigarette packet – an empty one. Yvonne picked up a wind-blown memorial card, shook the rain off it, and began scribbling notes on it.

Billy examined the cigarette packet, swore at it, and tossed it aside. 'Nowt! Another waste o' time.'

Yvonne frowned at him and retrieved the packet from the ground. She wiped it on her raincoat and inspected it closely. 'Everything has to be recorded,' she said. 'It's all evidence until you know that it's definitely not.' She made more notes, then, eyeing the boys crossly, pocketed her *evidence.*

OoOoO

Chapter Six

Ruff repeatedly nudged Billy with his nose, desperate to attract his attention. The little dog hated it when Billy sat reading, or crayoning, or doing anything that did not involve him. Billy elbowed him away and carried on reading. Deep in the pages of his dad's copy of The Star evening newspaper, under the headline: Dance Floor Drowning, he had found a brief report of the second murder victim's funeral. The article revealed little more than the dead man's name; James Hepburn, a solicitor.

Once again, the thought that such an unusual death should receive so little press coverage, troubled him. After a brief initial frenzy of sensational headlines, the story had vanished from the pages of the local and national newspapers. It had been the same with the Man's Head murder. At first, both deaths had attracted major press interest. Newspapers had revelled in the opportunities for gory headlines. Editors exploited every angle in the telling and retelling of the stories until all of them lost interest, seemingly at the same time. It was as if someone had thrown a switch. Even with neither murder solved, the nation's top story was the last journey of London's last tramcar.

It had to be a cover up, Billy thought. Trams were terrific, he loved them, but surely, the tabloids would prefer a juicy murder to the last run of an old tram.

If it was a cover up, why was it? And, was there a link between the two deaths? Had the victims known each other? They were of a similar age, around sixty, and were both respected professionals. The more he thought about it, the more convinced he became that the police, or some other powerful agency, was smothering the story. Only a year before, the authorities' grubby efforts to hide the old Star Woman's murder had started him and his friends on the road of crime detection. It seemed, once again, that there was cause to be concerned. He shrugged, tightened his lips across his teeth and briefly took on the persona of Humphrey Bogart in the Maltese Falcon. If this is how the cookie crumbles, they'd better watch out.

He shrugged Humphrey from his mind and switched to thinking about The Star's reporters. He thought of them struggling to write their stories with police, armed with blue pencils, breathing down their necks. He imagined faceless coppers striking out anything they did not want revealed. This brought Harry Clegg to mind. It was Harry who had given him the nickname The Tuppenny Hat Detective. They'd got on very well when he'd reported on the Star Woman's murder, although Harry had often tried to put words into his mouth. He decided to pay him a visit. He would go to his office in the city centre. Harry would know if there was a cover up. Better than anybody, Harry Clegg understood the city's political eddies and tides, especially its hidden undertow. Billy knew that if minded to, Harry would be able to suggest ways through any official smokescreen, without even admitting there was such a thing.

Sounds of his father waking and moving about upstairs interrupted his thoughts. His dad was on nights and would be getting up ready to go to work. Billy knew he'd be down any minute to wash at the kitchen sink, grab a mug of tea and a slice of bread and dripping, and dash out to catch the tram to the steelworks across town. Billy carefully refolded the newspaper, smoothed out its creases and placed it on the dining table next to the ex-army gasmask bag in which his dad carried his snap, mashings' tin, milk bottle and cigarettes.

Frank Perks shied a half-eaten cream cracker at Billy as he entered the room. 'D'you give Ruff them biscuits? There's crumbs all up the stairs. Your mam'll skin you.'

'It weren't me. He sniffs out the packet if it's not put away properly,' Billy explained.

'Blimey! Must've been me then,' his dad confessed. 'Still, no harm done. I told your mam it was you.' He grabbed Billy playfully and wrestled him to the floor. Ruff seized the opportunity to finish off the cream cracker.

After a brief tumble, laughing and coughing breathlessly, the pair leaned back against the settee. 'D'you like work, Dad?'

'No choice, Billy. Everybody has to work, even the king - ugh, I mean queen. Cripes, I'll never get used to us having a queen.'

Billy ignored his slip. 'But, is it Hot Money that's making you ill, Dad?'

Frank Perks eyed his son, smiled and dropped his arm around the lad's shoulders. 'No of course not. That's just working in a bit of heat, that's all. Yer gerra bit sweaty. That's why they only let us do a bit at a time.'

'But if it's so hot, why do you have to wear a sports coat?' Billy thought of the times his mother had begged old tweed jackets that neighbours were throwing out. Even the rag and bone man saved them for her.

'A thick jacket keeps the heat off. I can keep working a bit longer. And when they're all dried out and scorched, I just chuck 'em away and start wi' another one.' He studied his son's expression, and hugged him fiercely. 'Hey, what's brought this on?'

Billy looked back at him sheepishly. 'Somebody told me, Hot Money can kill you.'

'That's rubbish. Hot money's good for us, Billy. It means we can gerra week at Scarborough or Bridlington every year, as well as a good Christmas and a fat capon.'

'What's a capon?'

'Oh shurrup wi thee questions. I've gorra go to work. I've gorra make up for them sick days I've had off . And *no!*, before you say owt, it weren't because of *hot money*.'

*

Later, in the old greenhouse, the pink tip of Yvonne's tongue popped out as she concentrated on transcribing notes into a school exercise book. Kick stood behind her, rubbing at the MOM board with a filthy handkerchief. Occasionally he stopped to peek over her shoulder at what she had written. 'Why bother wi' that?' he asked, spotting something unexpected.

'It was carved on the gravestone where that old man was standing.'

'So what?'

'I don't know what, but it might turn out to be evidence or sommat.' Yvonne stiffened her shoulders and plied on resolutely. 'You can never tell what'll be useful.'

Kick read out the note in a derisory tone. 'Mary Scott, born 8th December 1895 - died 12th December 1940. "*Brutally murdered in the Marples Massacre.*"

Billy sat up sharply in his creaking deckchair. 'Marples Massacre!' He leaned closer to Yvonne and read the note for himself.

Kick frowned at the pair. 'What's the Marples' Massacre?'

'Gerries dropped a bomb on the Marples Hotel,' Yvonne told him. 'We did it at school. It were full o' people. They were all blown to smithereens,'

'What – how many?'

'I don't know - burrit worra lot,' she said.

'She must have been one of 'em,' Billy said sadly. 'I know a bit about it, because my uncle Fred was there. He got out though. It was just before Christmas - in the war.'

'In Sheffield?' Kick queried.

'Aye, in Fitzalan Square. It's all boarded off now, but tha can still see into t'ruins from upstairs on a tram.'

Kick was silent for a moment, deep in thought, before he said: 'I'm sorry for her, an' all that, but what's it got to do wi' the dance floor drowning or the Man's Head murder?'

Yvonne cast him a withering glance. 'Who said it did? All I said was, we should keep notes of everything we find out until we know if it's a clue or not.'

Billy perked up again, setting his deck chair creaking. 'Everything? How the 'ell can we do that?' he asked. 'We don't even know what we're looking for. We only went to that chuffin funeral to find out who the bloke was, and look what's happened? We've come away wi' more cummerbunds than we had to start with.'

'Conundrums,' Yvonne corrected despairingly. 'Cummerbunds are belts, yer wassock.'

Billy ploughed on undeterred. 'We shouldn't get us-selves bogged down with stuff that dunt matter, and you can't save everything anyway. That's a daft idea.'

With a final precise stroke of his handkerchief, Kick demonstrated his satisfaction that the MOM board was clean and ready for use. He carefully leaned it against a stack of upturned terracotta plant pots. Taking a stick of chalk, he drew two vertical lines to create three columns of equal width. Across the top he entered the headings, *Means / Opportunity / Motif.*

'Vee – Vee, it's a Vee,' cried Yvonne. 'Motive not motif.'

Kick made the correction without a hint of chagrin.

'And why don't you put an extra column in for notes and other names instead of having to squeeze 'em in at the front? You can't read 'em when they're all squashed up.' She eyed him flatly and fingered her dark curls into place behind her ears.

Kick ignored her suggestion. Yvonne snapped shut her notebook and began pacing between ghostly ranks of desiccated tomato plants. After a moment she stopped and faced the boys. 'They told us at school there's a special grave for all them killed in the blitz. It's like a memorial – same as they have for soldiers.' Looking off thoughtfully she pulled a curl to the corner of her mouth and released it. 'I don't understand it.'

Billy looked up from cleaning his spectacles. 'Why not?' he said. 'It's better to have a proper memorial than some scrappy little grave that'll fall over and be forgotten.'

'No, I mean, why isn't she buried with all the others – Mary Scott? And why does it say she was *murdered*. People never said *murdered* about the blitz. They said "*killed in the blitz*," not murdered. It's what they all said – everybody.'

Billy and Kick exchanged solemn glances. 'I think you should write that down, Wy,' said Billy. 'You might be on to sommat there.'

For a while the three sat gazing miserably at the MOM board, its empty columns seeming to mock them. 'Wiv gorra do sommat,' said Kick. 'How can we have a dead swimmer and dead bloke at Man's Head - and still have no clues.'

'And nowhere to write names,' Yvonne said, giving her suggestion another plug.

'We need to go back to the day before it all started,' said Billy.

Kick shot him a derisory glance. 'Oh aahh! How do we do that? Chuffin time travel.'

'Research,' Yvonne said, coming swiftly to Billy's aid. 'We can look at old newspapers; back numbers they call 'em. Find out what was in 'em the day before and on the day it happened.' She paused and looked at each of the lads. 'Was it raining? Did anything strange happen? We could ask the farmer if he were moving his sheep up at Man's Head? Did he see any climbers on the rocks, or hikers?'

'And who were them two hikers that found the body?' Kick suggested.

Billy looked relieved. He knew what must be done, but hadn't known how to do it until Yvonne spoke up. 'Yeah and I'll go and see Mister Clegg,' he said. 'I bet he can tell us sommat.'

'Me and Kick can make a list of all the things we want to check up on. We can split it up between us,' Yvonne said. 'We'll soon have 'em all done.'

*

It was later that same day when Harry Clegg placed two pennies on the telephone box shelf above the coin box and squinted out through the kiosk window. He consulted his notebook, put the telephone receiver to his ear and fed the coins into the slot. A tramcar rattled by as he dialled Doctor Hadfield's home number. He waited, listening to the ring tones. His thumb hovered over Button A, ready to press it when the call was picked up. There was no answer so he pressed Button B to get his tuppence back and grumpily shouldered his way out of the telephone box.

His mood lifted suddenly when he spotted Yvonne Sparkes. He had photographed her a year before, when working on the *Star Woman Murder* story. He waved and crossed the busy road to her, losing his hat in his haste. Yvonne laughed and picked it up for him.

'Thanks!' he said, dusting it down with his cuff. 'You're Yvonne aren't you? Do you remember me?'

Yvonne looked up at him through a tangle of dark curls. 'Of course I do; Mister Clegg. My friend Billy, you know, Billy Perks, he wants to talk to you.' She fingered her hair coyly and moved it into place behind her ears.

'Oh, so you're still friends are you? And what's his name - the other boy?'

'Michael Morley, Kick we call him, yes we're all still friends.'

'You three made a great detective team.' He eyed her craftily. 'And there was that chap who helped you – now, what was his name?' Harry knew very well who he meant, but played the innocent, hoping to draw Yvonne on to his side.

'Doctor Hadfield? she queried. 'Yes, he and Billy are still great friends.'

'And does he still help you with your detective work?'

'Well, we aren't really detectives any more, but if we were I'm sure he'd like to help us.'

'Not detectives? Gosh, not even with the Dance Floor Drowning?' he spoke in a jokey, sotto voce, and glanced around as if sharing a great secret. 'I made that up, you know; Dance Floor Drowning. Good int it?'

Yvonne giggled, not sure what to say.

'Surely you'll try to solve that one. And what about the Man's Head murder – that was really spooky wasn't it?'

Yvonne began to feel slightly awkward. She suspected that Harry was simply fishing for a story for his paper. She remembered how he had tried to put words in their mouths the last time they had dealt with him. 'Excuse me, but is there something you want, Mister Clegg? Is it about Billy and Doctor Hadfield?'

Clegg smiled and shrugged, turning up his palms as if caught out. 'OK. You got me,' he said. 'I can see I can't fool you. Yes, I do want something. I wanted to know if the old detective team was together again. And also, will the doctor be helping you like last time?' He laughed and gestured with his hands as if scribbling notes. 'It'll make a nice little story.'

Yvonne bit her lip for a second. 'We really aren't detectives this time.' she told him, thinking about Billy's problems with chief superintendent Flood. 'Although, like anybody else, we'd like to know what happened. We sometimes ask Doctor Hadfield about things, you know, dead bodies and stuff. He gives us his advice and he tells us if we get the wrong idea. He's a good friend. He's also my sister's young man.'

Harry Clegg chuckled quietly. 'Her young man, you say? Oh well then, I guess that puts him firmly on the detective team, whether he wants to be or not.'

OoOoO

Chapter Seven

PC John Needham tried the door to Walkley Post Office. Finding it securely locked, he strolled on to the adjoining premises, a sweet shop still open for business until late. The storekeeper smiled and waved though his window as John moved on checking the door locks of the other shops in the row; Maypole grocery, Wraggs the fishmonger, and Rumpleys chip shop, before vanishing for a smoke in a lock up behind an ironmonger's shop.

John unlocked the wooden storage shed with a key provided by the ironmonger upon his initiation into the secrets of the Walkley beat. Inside, he switched on a small lamp bulb casting a weak light over boxes, crates and shelves packed with assorted ironmongery. An old church pew pushed up against one wall provided seating and served as a worktop for a primus stove, kettle, teacups and milk bottle. He frowned at an apple core and an unwashed tea cup left by the day shift copper, and made a mental note to tell his colleague to clean up after himself in future.

Leaning back in the old pew he daydreamed wearily in the silence as he waited for the kettle to boil. Billy Perks barged in through the door, giving him a heart stopping shock.

'Eddie! Chuffing 'eck,' Needham gasped in confusion.

Billy slid in alongside him on the bench. 'Eddie? Who's that? It's me.'

Needham coughed, appearing flustered and embarrassed. 'I know. I can see yer now,' he said, quickly regaining his composure. 'Captain Trouble. What's tha want?'

Billy grinned, pushing his specs up his nose. 'I came to see thee. I've been waiting ages.'

'How did you find me?'

Billy shot him a surprised look. 'Tha always comes here for a smoke and a mash.'

'Oh aye, and who told you that?'

'Everybody knows. All t'coppers come here. That's why they leave this old bench and a kettle and everything.'

'Hum, is that so?'

Billy pointed up to a shelf above the door. 'Thiz an old wireless set up there an' all. Tha can get t'Test match on it, and t'football.'

Being fairly new to the Walkley beat, PC Needham hadn't yet discovered the radio. 'Tha seems to know more about this job than I do.'

Billy's thoughts had moved on. His face now wore a look of urgent enquiry. 'What's the latest? Have they got the killers yet?'

PC Needham groaned and rocked back on the bench. 'Look, forget about all that. You're a kid. It's not healthy to be moping around over corpses and stuff.'

'On no, I can't forget it,' said Billy. 'I have to find out. It's not just being nosey or playing a game, tha knows. This's important. I think they're trying to cover it up. Both of 'em.'

'Who is?'

'I don't know. Some bigwigs, I expect. They won't let anything be in the papers. They don't even say who the victims were. They've warned me to stay out of it. And now they've changed your beat and sent you up here instead of where you were before ...'

'Ayup, now hang on a minute, lad. You're gerrin carried away wi' thee sen. I've been pestering for this beat for months. I like Walkley. I only live round t'corner.'

'Well why isn't it in t'papers then?' Billy asked. 'You'd think a story like this would be top news until it's solved. Instead there's only little snippets, hardly anything at all.' Billy walked around the cluttered shed absently peering into sacks and boxes. 'It's all very fishy, and I'm not the only one who thinks so.'

John Needham blew out his cheeks and shook his head. 'The trouble with people like you is, you see bogey-men behind every tree. There is *no* cover up, Billy. There is *no* conspiracy.' He fixed Billy with his smiley blue eyes. 'You should be playing and having fun, not worrying about corpses and cover ups.'

Billy gritted his teeth and frowned at him. 'I'm going to see Mister Clegg. Him and Doc Hadfield are the only ones who listen to me. If tha wain't do sommat about it, they will.'

'Get proof, lad. If you can show me some proof, believe me, there's plenty of folk who'll listen to you.' He looked Billy in the eye and put a hand on his shoulder. 'What do you think the police are doing? We're not trying to hide owt. If there's a crime, believe me, nobody is going to take it more seriously than us. And if you can prove I'm wrong about that, I'll team up wi thee me sen. We'll capture the baddies together.'

*

The following morning Billy faced a starchy receptionist across her desk at Kemsley House, headquarters of Sheffield's local press. 'You can't just walk in and expect a red carpet,' she told him with chilling finality. She swivelled on her typist-chair like the gun barrel of a Churchill tank, presenting Billy with the rigidly coiffed elegance of the back of her head.

'I don't want a carpet,' he told her. 'I want to see Harry Clegg. He told me I could come and see him anytime.'

The Churchill swung back again and took aim. 'Don't be a silly little boy. *Mister* Clegg would never say such a thing – especially not to – er - a boy like you.'

'Well he did. We're - er - working on a story together. I'm his assistant. I helped him last year. I was in the paper - on the front page.'

The black telephone at the woman's elbow suddenly emitted a strangulated whirring sound, as if ringing inside a boxing glove. She sneered icily, removed her spectacles and one dangly earring, and lifted the telephone receiver to her ear. 'Good morning: Sheffield Press, how may I help?' Her rigid expression softened, evidently melted by the voice on the other end of the line.

Billy seized his chance. He knew the layout of the building very well. The year before, during his brief moment of fame,

Harry Clegg had given him a conducted tour. He dashed up the stairs and battered through the double swing doors on to the main news floor. His gaze swept the clutter and bustle of the large, open office. Faces turned enquiringly up to his, then quickly fell away again, in disappointment.

'I'm looking for Mister Clegg,' he announced.

'Aren't we all, luv,' said the nearest minion, without looking up from her clanking Underwood typewriter. 'He's gone – scarpered - vanished without a word.'

Firm hands gripped Billy's shoulders. He felt himself hauled backwards through the double doors. 'Right, mi lad. Out you go.' A uniformed commissionaire, his chest covered in medal ribbons and gold braid, frog marched him down the stairs and out onto Sheffield's busy High Street. 'Bye bye, now. And don't come back.'

Billy watched him re-enter the building between its impressive Portland stone columns. The lead glazed doors swung shut, seeming to render the place impregnable. The burly commissionaire glared out at him, powerful evidence that it probably was. He retreated a few steps and looked up to where the newspaper's gilded Star emblem floated proudly on the domed roof above the grand entrance. He thought wistfully of how, only a few months earlier, he had been the Star's hero, the face on the front page. Now he couldn't even get in the door.

With disappointment etched into his freckled face, he sloped away. What had happened to Harry Clegg? Why had he disappeared? Was this suspicious, or was he simply on his summer holidays? Either way, it was a spanner in the works. He was sure there was much that Harry Clegg could have told him.

Billy sat on the steps of the Cutlers Hall, in Church Street, at the heart of Sheffield's blitzed city centre. Facing him, the clock on the cathedral tower ticked towards eleven-thirty. Around the cathedral, most of the buildings had escaped the bombing. Behind their windows, inky fingered solicitors, accountants and clerks, pored over dusty deeds, ledgers, stock cards and forms. Should they bother to lift their heads to look out, they would see sunlight gilding every corbel, castellation, cartouche and cornice of the sooty cityscape, adding texture and vitality to both medieval and Victorian gothic. Billy looked about unseeing, his mind greatly troubled.

'You seem much taken by our lovely church, young man.' The speaker, an elderly cleric, let out a stifled gasp as he struggled to sit beside him on the Cutlers Hall steps. 'I come almost every day to take it in from here, but I've never had the good sense to sit on these steps like you, young man. What a very good idea.'

Billy cast him a sidelong glance, not sure what to say. He shuffled up to make room. 'I'm just waiting for the tram,' he said lamely.

The old man did not seem to hear him. 'I like to look at it each day, you see. It changes with the sun – often it looks quite different.' His shoulders shook gently as if he was laughing inside. 'We're going to be changing it quite a lot soon; a new extension on the west there.' He pointed, and then waved his hand as if rubbing out an image in the air. 'I'm not sure about it, personally. I'd rather not change it, but everyone seems to think it's a good idea.' He gave Billy a studying look and smiled. 'There's been a church here since at least the ninth century, you know. Did you know they found an Anglo-Saxon stone cross that probably stood right there.' He pointed vaguely. 'It's in the British Museum now. I've seen it, of course. It's quite splendid.' He laughed, shaking his head incredulously. 'You won't believe this, but it'd been hollowed out to make a quenching trough in a blacksmith's forge.' He rolled back on his buttocks and laughed softy. 'It's a miracle it survived.'

A Walkley bound tramcar shook the ground as it rattled to a halt at the tram-stop. Billy stood up. 'I've got to go. Tarraahh.'

'Don't give up, young man. Keep trying.'

Billy looked back curiously as he boarded the tram. He paid his fare, and climbed the stairs to the top deck. From the tram window, he looked down at the old cleric seated on the steps of the Cutler's hall. He was looking back at him, a knowing smile creasing his face beneath his silver hair.

'Any more fares please?' The conductor's voice sounded weary with repetition. He rang the bell. 'Hold on very tight now please!' The tram shuddered into life, throwing Billy onto a hard seat in the back-bay windowed area of the upper deck. He shuffled along the empty leather bench and looked back to the old cleric. He was still there and still watching, until the tram turned a corner and lost line of sight.

Billy glanced around the top deck. Most of the seats were empty. He counted only eight other passengers, all men, sitting alone and taking full advantage of the freedom to smoke on the upper deck. He jerked upright suddenly when he saw that one of them was the old man he had seen at the funeral. He turned and spotted Billy at the same moment and immediately came over to join him in the back-bay. 'Hello, lad.'

'I saw you at the funeral,' said Billy, slightly startled.

'I saw thee an' all.' The old guy smiled cheekily and began the ritual of rolling a cigarette. 'You were there with that young lass …'

'Yvonne.'

'Smart as paint, that one. And I know your other pal an' all; a good little footballer.'

'What's the badge for?' Billy asked eyeing the splash of silver pinned to the old man's lapel.

'Union, I'm shop steward at Cranks Forge. As a matter of fact I'm on union business right now,' he said, adding a muffled harrumphing sound to emphasize the gravity of his position. 'The bosses have sacked a comrade. I've gorra gerrim his job back, the daft bugger. Between me and thee, he dunt deserve it. He's a lazy sod, but we can't have t'bosses trampling all o'er us can we?'

Billy had no opinion. 'Why did you go to the funeral? You never went in the church.'

He fixed Billy with a hard stare. 'Some go to remember. Some go to remind.'

Billy frowned, unsure what to make of his response. He said, 'There's sommat fishy going on. I think somebody's trying to cover it all up. It's the same with him at the swimming baths. Is that what you think an' all?'

Again the steady gaze. 'Spring Heeled Jack will know the answer.'

'Who? Spring Heeled Jack? Who's he? '

'It all started in his dark realm,' said the old man, in deadly earnest. He turned and glanced out of the window and then stood up sharply, grabbing a strap handle to stop himself skittling down the aisle as the tram bucked and lurched. 'I gerrof at the next stop.' He smiled and doffed his trilby hat. 'I run a gym most evenings. It's in the coach house behind the relish factory. D'you know it? Leavygreave Road. If tha needs to talk to me, tha can find me there.' He winked and ruffled Billy's hair. 'Don't worry, I know thee dad. He knows me an' all. He were a reight good footballer thee dad. Tell him thaz seen Walter Mebbey. He'll know me. Tha can bring that pal o' thine an' all, but not the young lass. We don't have lasses. It's boxing, catch-as-catch-can, and weightlifting. It's not fit for lasses.'

'Who's Spring Heeled Jack?'

'Find out for thee sen , and pray tha never meets him on a dark neet.'

OoOoO

Chapter Eight

'Billy!' The voice was Dr. Hadfield's, his tone, angry. 'What the devil have you done?'

Billy was scroamin into the greenhouse garden by his usual route under the advertising hoardings. He was not expecting to be challenged, and especially not by Doctor Hadfield. He scrambled to his feet, dusted himself down and faced the young man. 'What's up? How did you gerrin?'

The doctor's face was red with rage. 'Never mind about that. What have you done, Billy?' he yelled. 'I can't protect you now, you idiot. You've left me no choice. I have to go to the police.' He pulled a large envelope from inside his jacket and waved it under Billy's nose. 'Where the devil did you get this? This is theft, Billy. Even worse, it's tampering with legal evidence. People go to jail for this sort of thing.'

Baffled, Billy eyed the envelope and backed away towards the greenhouse. 'I haven't the faintest idea what tha'rt going on about,' he said. 'Honest I've never seen it afore.'

The doctor followed him inside, glancing about warily. He closed the door behind them. 'Billy, please do not insult my intelligence. It is obviously you who put this through my letterbox. Who else could it be? But how the devil did you get it?'

'I-don't-know-worrit-is,' Billy said, annunciating forcibly. 'I've never seen it afore.' He flopped into a deckchair. 'Anyway, why would I be so sneaky about it? If I'd got sommat to show thee, I'd bring it round, like I usually do. We'd look at it together and talk about it.'

Hadfield looked shaken. He sat in the remaining deck chair and toyed nervously with the envelope. Billy reached out and gently took it from him. It was made of very stiff paper, and had a concertina like pleat down its sides to allow for expansion. The opening flap had a string fastener to facilitate reuse. Billy did not say so, but he had seen similar envelopes in Harry Clegg's office at the newspaper. A handwritten note on the front read, *Neither is what it seems.*

Billy blew out his cheeks and shook his head. 'It weren't me, Doc. Honest.'

Hadfield sighed and looked about him at the whitewashed panes of glass, the tinder dry seed boxes and rows of dead plants, as if counting cobwebs. 'Good place this,' he said quietly after a while. 'Whose is it?'

Billy glanced around mirroring the young doctor. 'Hum, it's old Mister Eadon's place. He dunt use it anymore. My granny says he's got bad legs, but I expect you know about that.'

'Hum, no he's not my patient.' He sighed and knuckled his eyes as if weary. 'What a mess,' he said miserably. 'D'you have any idea who it could be from?'

Billy shook his head. Harry Clegg sprang to mind, but for the time being, he decided to keep his thoughts to himself. Peering inside the envelope, he drew out a thin sheaf of papers. There were two foolscap pages of rough sketches and two of handwritten notes. Another slim bundle contained several extracts, none more than four lines long, cut from typewritten documents.. A single staple held them together. There were no printed sheets, or letterheads; nothing to indicate their origin, or ownership.

'I believe you, Billy old lad. I should know better, but who could it be?'

'I've a vague idea, but I don't want to say anything until I know for certain. It's best if I keep it to myself.'

'Thank God one of us is acting like a grown up,' Hadfield said apologetically and gently retrieved the papers. 'These are absolute dynamite. I think the typed bits are from Coroner's Office documents. As you can see, they're carbon copies. Hopefully, that means whoever pinched them left the originals safe and intact. There's not much to go on, but the language and style is pretty typical of the Coroner's court.' He cleared a space on some upturned seed trays and laid the pages out on them. 'This one says there'll be an inquest, but the deceased's remains can be released to the family for burial. That's definitely from the coroner's office.'

'Yeah, and the date's about right,' Billy said reading it from the page. 'Both victims have been buried now, one in Crookes cemetery and I read about the other in the paper.'

The doctor smoothed out the hand written pages on his thigh. 'The writing's terrible, but I think these might come from the pathologist's own notes, just the rough versions, of course. They look like hastily made copies. It's as if somebody had sight of the pathologist's notes, but had only seconds to crib from them. Some of it looks like shorthand that's been rubbed out and then written over.'

Billy knew that Harry Clegg often used shorthand, and was now sure it must be him who stole them and posted them through the doctor's door. He imagined him scribbling away as he riffled the pathologist's files, one eye on the office door, his ears cocked for the sounds of approaching footsteps.

'Whatever it is, it's obviously an illegal copy,' said Hadfield. 'I'll have to tell the police.'

'What's it say?'

'Well, in summary; death was by drowning. This must be the man in the swimming pool.' He shrugged apologetically for having stated the obvious. 'This other one seems to be the Man's Head victim. It's a list of injuries ...' He stopped, a puzzled expression on his face. 'All but one is post mortem.' He went over all the reports again. 'It's as if the *corpse* was battered about – post mortem.'

Billy's heart raced as he peered over the doctor's shoulder and read for himself. He saw that someone, in a different hand, had recorded the location of the body as Man's Head rocks, above Round Dam.

'This is weird,' said the doctor, throwing his head back and holding up a page. 'It says: *Damage to corpse – bla –bla –bla - consistent with being struck by blunt object - bla - bla - bla –*

partial burial at Man's Head Rock.'

Billy wrinkled his face in a puzzled frown. 'What's the weird part?' He extended his arms, palms upward. 'Man gets hit by something, and buried. It's simple.'

Hadfield shook his head. 'No, it's not, Billy. It's this word "*damage*",' he said. 'Saying *damage* to the corpse merely confirms that it was post mortem. Yet it's included here as if it's contributory to death. That's all wrong. And, on another tack, why on earth would anybody hit a corpse? It's already dead. And then here, right at the end, the actual cause of death is left open. It's confused and ambiguous. This's all nonsense.'

Billy stared hard at him. 'So are you saying the pathologist is hiding sommat, or lying?'

'Well no, actually I'm not. Quite possibly he's doing the very opposite. I think he may be trying to avoid lying, but may be under pressure of some sort.' He brandished the sheaf of papers briefly, then slapped them down on to the seed trays. 'These scraps and scribbles are useless. Obviously, they are not the finished pathology report. It's pointless to speculate on what that might eventually say. But I'm pretty sure that word "Damage" instead of "Injury" will not be in it as a contributory cause of death.'

The doctor scooped the papers together and slid them back into the envelope. He stood up, a sheepish grin on his face. 'Look, old lad, I'm sorry I went off at you. I hope we're still friends.'

Billy was distracted, and didn't hear him. 'What about the other bloke, Doc, the dance floor drowning? D'you think they could be connected.'

'Connected? Why do you say that? The deaths are quite dissimilar.'

'Well think about it - two men about the same age, both murdered in mysterious circumstances, both murders covered up by the big-wigs. It just all makes me think there's a connection.' Billy chewed his cheek, frowning. 'What will you do with 'em - the papers?'

'Hum, good question.' Hadfield tapped the envelope against his chin. 'I'm not sure yet. Maybe I should take them to the police, but that could put me right in the middle of this mess. I certainly don't want that. Also there may be more to come from whoever's passing this stuff to me. If it is a conspiracy, our informant may turn out to be one of the good guys.' He gently kicked a desiccated onion along the dusty aisle and started slowly towards the door.

'Why not give 'em back to the pathologist?' Billy said, 'Only the pencilled bits, of course. It'd be a good excuse to get friendly with him. He might show you his real notes.'

'Crickey! You're a dark horse, aren't you? A proper little Machiavelli.'

'You could ask him about the swimming pool floater at the same time. If there is a connection, he might've already found it.'

The doctor scratched his head. 'I really should give them to the police. They were obviously obtained under questionable circumstances. I just don't want the police trampling all over my life.'

'Who's Maxy Velly?'

' Machiavelli. Go to the library. Read The Prince.'

*

Frank Perks was having breakfast when his son, pyjama clad and bleary eyed, joined him at the table. Billy loved the early mornings when his dad came home from a night shift. He would get up and rush downstairs to him, as soon as he heard Ruff barking his welcome. Stripped to the waist, Frank Perks would wash at the kitchen sink, hands, face, armpits and hair, usually in cold water. While the kettle boiled, he'd rub liquid paraffin into his hands to soften them after handling fire bricks and mortar all night. Billy's mother would join them a few minutes later, smelling of soap and flowers. She would have washed at the washstand in her bedroom.

He'd watch his mam and dad squeezing passed each other in their tiny kitchen, as tea, porridge, and toast, or bread and dripping were made. Often they would lark about, pretending to bump into each other in the barely corridor width space. There was always laughter and horsing around on night-weeks.

Billy asked his dad about the old man he'd met on the tram.

'Yeah I know him; little bloke, weightlifter, strong as an ox, bandy as a duck. He used to run a gym before the war, back when I was footballing.'

Billy watched him fill his pint pot with tea and plop four saccharin tablets into it from a small, sugar encrusted, aspirin bottle kept in the sugar bowl.

'He still does. It's near the relish factory. He wants me to join. He said I could take Kick Morley and thee an' all.'

'Don't thee and thou, Billy,' his mother called from the kitchen. 'Talk nicely. You don't hear me thee-ing and thou-ing, do you?. Frank, tell him!'

'Don't thee and thou, Billy,' said his dad, giving him a secret wink.

'Sorry, Mam.'

'What's he want?' his dad asked. 'I haven't seen him for years.'

Billy looked away sheepishly. He decided it was not the time to bring up his detective work. 'I don't know. He just said I could join.'

Marion Perks placed bowls of steaming porridge before father and son. 'I'm not having him boxing,' she said. 'You're not going, Billy. He'll get cauliflower ears and a nose like a flat iron; anyway we can't afford boxing gloves. It's not five minutes since we bought him that Scouts uniform. We're not made o' money you know.'

Billy's dad laughed. 'Blimey, I thought we were.'

'It's alright you laughing, Frank, but it all costs money,' Billy's mam said. 'There's his piano lessons, scouts' uniform, he'll be wanting new football boots after the school holidays, and he never stops growing out of things.'

'For God sakes, Billy,' his dad cried feigning despair. 'What do you mean by growing all the time? How do you expect us to keep up if you keep growing out of things.'

Missis Perks swatted her husband with a tea towel. 'It's easy for you to laugh. You don't see the price of stuff. Half the time you can't get anything but rabbit and offal, and when I can get sommat we can't afford it.'

Frank Perks put his arm around his wife. 'Don't worry, love. I'll find out what old Walter Mebbey wants. It's years since I've seen him, but he was never one for wasting folk's time.'-

0o0o0

Chapter Nine

Rivelin Valley Road runs west from Sheffield out to the Peak District National Park. At three and a half miles long before it joins the Manchester Road, it is the second longest avenue of lime trees in Europe. Winding gently between bilberry and heather covered hills, pasture and mixed woodland, it is one of the loveliest roads in England. Despite the steep and often craggy hills overlooking it, it's seldom so steep as to bother a bulky bishop on his bicycle.

Billy pedalled his bike in the dappled sunlight beneath the limes. He had the road to himself, and thrilled to its its beauty. Sheep grazed the hills overseen by jubilant skylarks. Below, on the wooded valley floor, songbirds sang to the echo. He dismounted and hid the bike behind a stone wall. Unseen the peaty river murmured and chortled. Across the road, a lane between fields, branched uphill to the Rivelin Hotel, a remote, stone built pub. Above its slate roof, ranged against the sky, Man's Head Rock glared down.

Billy turned away and looked down into the valley. The *Round Dam*, a millpond that had once powered an old cutler's forge, quietly filled and emptied with barely a ripple on its surface. Billy's dad had told him that from medieval times until the coming of the steam power, men had worked iron and steel into knives, shears, and scythes in Rivelin's water driven mills. The very anvil at Gretna Green, across which runaway lovers take their marriage vows, was made in one of Rivelin's water mills.

The coming of steam, and then electricity, sealed the fate of the old water mills. The great wheels, tilt hammers and grindstones stopped forever. The mill owners in their broughams, phaetons and landaus, built new hearths, forges and grinding troughs in the east of the city nearer to the canal and the new railways. They swapped their horses for chauffeur driven motor cars and built large villas in the city's western suburbs. The workers had to leave their idyllic cottages and gardens, and move into the teeming courts of back-to-back houses springing up around the new factories. Woodland and wilderness gradually reclaimed the valley, breaking ancient beams and toppling walls. Along the banks of fish filled millponds, enigmatic ruins quietly crumbled under moss and fern, turning with the years into beautiful dripping grottos hiding beneath willow, alder, rosebay and bramble. A necklace of reedy waters is strung out along the bright, noisy river linking each sculptural ruin with its past and defining its future.

Billy stepped off the road and climbed the steep lane up to Man's Head Rock. By now he knew precisely where they had found Professor Henry Darnley's body, having thoroughly grilled the hapless John Needham. He had also learned that the police had no conclusive evidence as to how the corpse came to be there. Forensic experts, apparently, could not agree. Various theories had been tested and dismissed, even including hurling a kit bag full of sand, intended to represent a corpse, from the cliff top and having some poor constable climb down to it and drag it to the burial spot. They also ruled out dragging the corpse up from the road below. Everything pointed to Darnley having been killed right there, where he was found. If so, what was he doing there? Had the killer followed him, or lain in wait? How had they known he would be there? Was he lured to his death, or accompanied to it?

Billy had asked PC Needham if Henry Darnley had been hiking. The constable said he was not dressed for it. He was wearing ordinary day clothes; flannels, shirt, and tie, but oddly, no jacket. His shoes were expensive, handmade Oxfords, 'Last thing you'd wear for scroamin o'er rocks,' the copper had said.

Billy found it difficult approaching the burial site. Loose scree slid about underfoot setting off little avalanches. Firm footing was impossible, and in his view certainly ruled out anyone carrying a body to the spot. He paused, turning his back to the giant's chin to look down to where the police had cleared away the bracken and exposed the shallow grave. It was only about twenty feet away. Dressed and shod as he was, Darnley would have found the going difficult. Why would he want to do it? Even more baffling was, how could the killer have surprised him on such a difficult surface?

Darnley's head had been sticking out above ground. Before clamming up, the newspapers had reported that his dead eyes were staring up at the crags. Billy tottered over the loose stones and skidded to a halt at the gravesite. It was no more than a slight depression in the scree, and would have gone unnoticed but for the stripped out bracken. He stepped into the grave and sat down. The bottom of it was solid rock, no doubt the reason it was so shallow. Darnley's head must have been sticking out because the killer couldn't get it far enough down to cover it. He looked up at the rock face where the dead eyes had gazed.

The idea that the killer had deliberately placed the corpse that way had, at first, seemed tempting. It hinted at some mysterious coded message. The reality however, did not support such a theory. It was probably simply that the killer had no choice. Billy could not bring himself to rule it out completely, but accorded the idea little importance. The biggest mystery, he thought, was, why had Darnley gone there. What had drawn him to his death? And how had he travelled; bike, or bus, or did he drive? If so where was his car? And also, where was his jacket?

*

Doctor Hadfield could not help himself. He knew he should not be poking his nose into a police murder enquiry, but he always found mysteries irresistible. Since accidentally teaming up with Billy Perks and his friends on the old Star Woman murder case, amateur sleuthing had firmly captured his interest.

He ballooned his cheeks and shook his head thoughtfully. 'Grasp the nettle, old lad,' he told himself. 'Go and see the dratted pathologist. You know you want to.'

Circumstances seemed to have conspired to make such a visit

easy for him. He had an afternoon off, having worked the previous night *on call*. His girlfriend was not speaking to him, and he had no sensible demands on his time. So, even though common sense screamed that he should stay away, he decided to ignore it.

A first class honours graduate, he had been an exceptional student, twice winner of the Fleming-Vesalius award. Even so, not a day of general practice in Walkley, passed without some reminder of how much there remained to be learned. He wanted to do more, be more useful, but did not know how to go about it. He often felt he was teetering between ignorance and ignominy. His overbearing boss, his ex-tutor, did not help him, either. Her undisguised disapproval could bring his spirits clattering down. She particularly disliked what she called, "his childish detective games". Hardly a day passed without her raising her eyebrows and tut-tutting about it, and she had told him flatly to end his contact with Billy and his pals, or, as she had put it, "with those scruffy urchins".

At two in the afternoon, after a lunch of grilled Spam on toast, he slid into the driving seat of his Austin Ruby. His mind rattled through the names of those who would disapprove of his actions. As ever, his father topped the list, but, as he managed to disappoint him so often and in so many ways, it no longer mattered. Dr Clarissa Fulton-Howard, came next on the list, and she was an altogether more dangerous critic. He shook her carping image from his thoughts and set off.

The Pathology Department was across the city in a wing of a large, down-at-heel Victorian hospital. He parked the Ruby in a tree-lined street, opposite its tall iron gates. For two minutes, he sat staring at them, feeling sick with tension. He knew it made no sense, but he was undeniably scared of what might be about to happen. Handing over the illicit notes would either bring trouble tumbling down upon him, or, as Billy had suggested, smooth the way to a productive relationship with a helpful pathologist.

When he finally plucked up the courage to get out of his car, he realised he did not know how many pathologists worked behind the impassive walls, or to which of them he should address himself. Why hadn't he checked? What an idiot! Luckily, he spotted a police constable patrolling near the gates, and was soon directed to the nearest public telephone box, a mere fifty yards away. He looked up the telephone number and dialled it. After a few false starts, he learned that he needed to speak to a Doctor Sarah Becket.

As he walked back to the hospital, he rehearsed possible opening gambits to try on Dr Becket, but rejected them. Passing through the prison-like gates, he wondered how many laws he might already have broken and be about to break. Once inside, he stiffened his shoulders and stepped boldly, trying to look as though he had a perfect right to be there.

The corridors smelled of cabbage and disinfectant. Green tiles faced the walls to shoulder height, thickly coated cream paint above that. He explored thoroughly, all the while pretending to know exactly where he was. There were few signs to help him. Only by listening and avoiding the sounds of bustle and urgent activity did he manage to stick to the gloomy backwaters he hoped would lead to *PATHOLOGY* and *THE MORGUE*.

He found Sarah Becket, the only living occupant of a dimly lit room containing three operating tables, each bearing a corpse beneath a faded green sheet. She was standing at a writing shelf, fiddling with a large reel-to-reel tape recorder. He could see her only in silhouette, back lit by a frosted glass partition wall. Two men, probably porters, were moving about quietly beyond it, their images distorted by the glass. Neither one reacted to his presence.

Dr Becket was a slight young woman with fair, curly hair. Her regulation white overall hung open over a grey skirt and red blouse. Her pale, heart shaped face was dominated by horn-rimmed glasses, through which peered large blue eyes. She looked exhausted. Hadfield knew the look. At teaching hospital, he'd seen many an intern with the same drained appearance after a double shift. He'd been one himself, and needed no convincing that Sarah Becket was out on her feet. He approached her smiling. 'Doctor Becket?'

'I'm sorry, but whatever it is, I'm just off home.' She disconnected the tape recorder cable from the electric lamp holder it was plugged into, and refitted the displaced light bulb.

'I'm Doctor Hadfield. Reginald Hadfield...'

She eyed him critically. 'They never said you were coming. Who are you?' She stifled a yawn, and shrugged apologetically.

'I must talk to you. Please. It's a very delicate matter. I'm Clarissa Fulton-Howard's junior at Walkley ...'

'Oh, you poor dear!' She beamed at him, a cheeky sparkle coming to her tired eyes. 'And I thought my lot in life was bad ...'

'You know Clarissa?'

'I have that dubious honour,' she said wincing theatrically. 'She thinks she's still teaching at Cambridge, or wherever it was. She's lectured me on practically everything I do - even how to wash my stockings.' She looked at Hadfield with increased curiosity. 'I really am sorry, but I do have to go. Nobody said you were coming.'

Hadfield suddenly had a bright idea. 'Can I give you a lift home? We can talk in the car – if you promise not to fall asleep.'

OoOoO

Chapter Ten

After teatime, the three friends gathered at the greenhouse. Billy arrived last having stayed to listen to Dick Barton on the BBC's Light programme at a quarter to seven.

Kick held out a small padlock fastened to a bent staple. 'This were on the door.'

Billy examined the door jamb and the scars of the unwelcome padlock's removal. 'Who purrit on? Worrit Mister Eadon? He said he dint mind us coming in here.'

'It weren't him,' Yvonne said. 'I've been and asked him. He said we can play here as long as we don't break owt.'

'I bet it's coppers,' Kick said. 'They're just spoil sports. They know we come in here and they want to stop us, even though it's got nowt to do wi' 'em.'

Billy strode into the greenhouse. 'Well chuff 'em! It belongs to Mister Eadon, and he says we can come here. So that's that.' He immediately wrote something on the MOM board. The other two pressed close to read it.

Spring Heeled Jack.

Seeing that he had their full attention he added question marks – three of them.

'What's it mean?' Kick stared at the words as if they might suddenly explain themselves.

'I don't know,' said Billy. 'That's the point.' He eyed the pair solemnly, and then chalked a fourth question mark on the board. 'D'yer remember the old bloke at the cemetery?'

They nodded.

'Well, I met him on the tram. We only talked for a bit because he had to gerrof. But he said, "*Spring Heeled Jack knows*," or sommat like it.'

'Who is he? Why didn't he go inside t'church wi' the others?' Yvonne asked.

'I asked him. All he said was, "Some go to remember, some go to remind.".'

Kick made a ghostly hooting sound. 'Oooooo, spooky. Remind 'em of what?'

'I don't know. It's a mystery. But I know where to find him. He's gorra gym near the relish factory. He wants me to go there.' He gave them an eager glance. 'That shows he must 'ave got sommat else to tell us.' He turned to Kick. 'He wants me and thee to go.'

Yvonne reared up indignantly. 'What about me?'

'Lasses can't go. It's a gym club. They do boxing. It's for lads,' Billy explained.

'Way, I could flatten thee, any-road-up.' Yvonne pawed the air in front of his nose.

Billy ducked and danced back a step. 'Thaz no chance,' he said, trying to look tough. 'And it's not about who can flatten who. It's for lads only and tha 'rt not one.'

Yvonne flopped into her deckchair. 'I could've been,' she cooed, 'but I chose brains instead.'

Kick ignored her. 'We could look in t'library,' he said. 'They might have sommat about Spring Healed Jack.'

Billy was astonished to hear such a sensible suggestion from him. He'd assumed Kick's experience of the library was limited to his ejection for making farting noises during the *Story Time Reading Circle*. 'That's a very good idea,' he gasped.

*

Doctor Clarissa Fulton-Howard eyed her junior despairingly. 'Hadfield, do you possess a wristwatch?' She had summoned him to her consulting room, which she now paced with menacing deliberate strides, bouncing on the balls of her feet as if testing the floor.

Hadfield knew perfectly well that he owned a rather nice Omega, a graduation present from his father, yet he clutched at his wrist as if to confirm the fact. 'Yes ma'am.'

'Does it work?'

Puzzled, he put the watch to his ear and listened. 'Yes ma'am, it works fine.'

'Then what am I to assume, Doctor Hadfield?'

She had him with that one. He gaped, wondering what avalanche of grief and effluent was about to engulf him.

'I trust you *can* tell the time? Or is it that you don't care to interrupt your busy schedule of tomfoolery with anything so mundane as *your duties to your patients and colleagues?*'

'But I had the afternoon – err - off.' His protest punctured, leaking certainty as he uttered it.

'Really? So our conversation yesterday evening, when you agreed – *nay promised* –you would forego your afternoon off, so that I could do the measles' round, was all pure fantasy, was it? Did I dream it – make it up – imagine it?' She prowled her office, moving as if through treacle. An untimely memory of her bicycle saddle flashed through his mind.

The doctor wore her hair pulled into a tight bun at the back. It shone like a pewter helmet. Through thick framed spectacles, her gaze flitted about the room as if shooting flies. She reminded him of some sort of Wagnerian praying mantis.

He felt sick as he recalled the conversation and realised his error. The memory of it flooded back to him like a nightmare. He had indeed agreed to stand in for her. There were dozens of measles cases. Oh my God, she had every right to be annoyed. 'I – I was at the err - pathol – look, I'm so sorry. I completely messed up. You're absolutely right. I don't know how I could …'

She glared at him, seeming to swallow her bottom lip. 'Were you about to say - pathology? Why would you go there?'

'Oh, nothing, just something personal. Nothing to do with here.'

Suspicion furrowed her brow. She stomped around her desk and took her seat without releasing him from her steely glare. 'I'm not happy about this. In fact to be frank, Hadfield, I'm not happy about you at all. You're lazy, careless and you seem to think life is some sort of playtime. Huh fun! Ask the mothers I saw this afternoon if they're having fun, with their distressed and squalling infants.'

'I'm sorry, Professor – er - Doctor. I am utterly in the wrong, and again, I apologise. I don't know what … I can't say more, but if you *do* have other specific issues about my work here, then perhaps you should tell me what they are – er - so I can address them.'

She continued to stare at him, her thumbs rapidly winding the air beneath her tweed-encased bosom. 'The matter is closed, for now. We'll speak of it at the end of the month when you've had chance to show me a considerable improvement.'

She waved him away and reached for a telephone directory. 'Now, I'm very busy. I have much to catch up on.'

Hadfield backed out of her office, furious with himself for giving her the ammunition to shoot him down so comprehensively. He had only himself to blame. He had armed her and even taken aim for her. All she had had to do was pull the trigger.

Doctor Fulton-Howard watched the door close on her junior before running her finger down the columns of names and numbers in the phone book. She quickly found the listing for the Pathology Department and dialled. As the call rang out, she eased back in her chair. 'Doctor Amos Longden, please.'

After a few clicks and buzzes, a confident voice came on the line. 'Longden.'

'It's Clarissa. What was my junior doing there this afternoon?'

'Who? Here? What?'

'Hadfield. He's an idiot. There's no reason for him to have been there. If he wasn't seeing you, Amos, who the devil did he see?'

'Umm yes, gosh, I see. Leave it with me, Clarry, old girl. I may know exactly what this is about.'

*

Yvonne and Kick insisted on accompanying Billy to Walkley's library. A sneezing librarian, smothered in a pink woollen cardigan and smelling of eucalyptus took their enquiry. She led them to a battery of little oak drawers. Each had a brass pull handle incorporating a hand written label bearing cryptic abbreviations. She pulled one open and began searching for references to Spring Heeled Jack. Billy opened another, almost losing a finger as the librarian snapped it shut. 'Leave that, young man,' she said glaring at him through red-rimmed eyes.

Her fingers riffled through dozens of cards, disturbing dust to spiral slowly in shafts of sunlight spearing the room's charged silence. She found a reference, withdrew a card and read it to herself. The pals waited in rapt anticipation.

'There's a carving of him on a building called the Queens Head. It's a pub. It says here it's thought to be the oldest secular building in Sheffield.' She looked up from the card, wiped her dripping nose and nodded at them. 'I know where it is. I've seen it. It's a beautiful old beamed building near the bus station.' She stifled a sneeze. 'It says here it was built in 1475 as a hunting lodge. Spring Heeled Jack is carved on a beam end.'

'We'd best go an' have a look at it,' Billy said, and turning to Yvonne eyed her sheepishly, 'Ayup Wy, can tha gi' us a lend o' tuppence for me tram fare?'

'Pay thee own tram fare. I'm not yer mam.' Yvonne produced a purse from her pocket and ostentatiously hugged it to her chest. She smiled as Billy stormed off in a huff.

The librarian turned out a second card from her index, and began reading it aloud. 'It was called the Queens Head because of Mary Queen of Scots who was imprisoned in Sheffield.' She beamed at Kick and Yvonne. 'What a story. Isn't that wonderful, children?'

Yvonne thanked her politely and trotted outside to catch up with Billy. She found him skulking in the Pikelet shop doorway. He was watching a tram parked at the terminus.

Walkley library's main entrance overlooked the tram terminus. Trams from the city centre and beyond rolled up there to wait a while before setting out on their return journeys. Tramcars could be driven from either end. They did not need to be turned around for their return trips. The driver would wind the blind-box handle, with furious energy, to change the destination display. Next, he'd remove the drive lever, and uplift a bell striker pedal from its slot in the floor. He would carry these through the car to the other end of the tram where he'd install them for the return trip.

Meanwhile the conductor flipped the backs of all the seats to face them in the new direction of travel. He or she would then go outside, and, with a long pole with a hook on its end, reach up and snag the trolley wheel on the overhead power line. Holding it off the wires, the conductor would walk round the tram with it and connect it to the return direction power-cable. The tram was then ready to go.

Regular passengers were familiar with his ritual. Billy Perks certainly was, and being unable to pay for a ticket, he seized upon its diversions to sneak aboard and hide under a seat while the driver and conductor were distracted.

Yvonne and Kick boarded and paid their fare. After a few stops, when the tram had filled up a bit, Billy crawled out of hiding and joined them. To make it look, at a glance, as if he had bought a ticket, he picked up a discarded one and stuck it behind his ear.

A few minutes later the pals dropped off the tram in High Street in front of the blitzed, art deco shell of Burton's Tailoring store. Their route to the bus station and the Queens Head would take them through Fitzalan Square, a large Edwardian quadrangle favoured by picnicking office workers, pigeons and random sermonisers. Variously bounded by stone balustrades, cloister-like tram stops and a taxi rank, the square was constantly awash with a tide of travellers and shoppers beneath the stern gaze of a statue of King Edward VII. Out of sight, beneath the royal feet lay subterranean public conveniences, which led some wags to say "the king was on the toilet". These facilities were spotless with pristine, gleaming ceramics, brass and copper plumbing, and dark mahogany woodwork, their mosaic floors endlessly swabbed by rightfully proud attendants.

The buildings on two sides of the square lay in ruins, destroyed by Nazi bombs. The north and west sides however, boasted an architectural treasure trove, including gothic banks, the city's main post office, and an art deco cinema. Billy pointed out the bombed site of The Market Street Wine Vaults, commonly known as "Marples Hotel". A screen, made of old domestic doors, surrounded it. The three pals peered through the redundant keyholes and letterboxes to view the extent of the Marples' devastation.

Down the hill passed the princely General Post Office, the Queens Head Inn huddled in the shadow of taller buildings including iron foundries and a factory where an old lead works with a massive water wheel had once turned.

Despite its neighbours, the Queens Head Inn was a striking sight; a black and white beamed, crooked roofed building, standing incongruously amidst its sooty surroundings. Like a puppy dog seeking adoption, it seemed to beg to be carried away to sunnier pastures, far from the ground shaking forges, foundries and soot black railways. Not all the old pub's walls and beams were accessible from the gloomy street. Billy felt uneasy as he and his friends self-consciously searched the ancient facade for Spring Heeled Jack, an image they had never seen and might not even recognize if they found it.

Flicking her head sideways and arching her eyebrows, Yvonne tried, surreptitiously, to alert the boys to a middle-aged woman peering suspiciously from one of the pub's crooked windows. They backed off and tried to pretend they were not remotely interested in the pub. They did not fool the woman, who rushed out wanting to know their business.

Billy gulped and stared at her. She was wearing a low cut frilly blouse, a tight pencil skirt and black high heels. She wore her long bleached hair curled over one eye like the actress Veronica Lake. Billy gawped, thinking how beautiful she looked.

Yvonne dug him in the ribs and prompted him to answer. He stumbled over an explanation. Unexpectedly, it met with the woman's approval and she happily pointed out the carving to them. Unfortunately, they could not get near enough for a clear view, and had to take her word for much of its appearance.

Yvonne scribbled a description into her exercise book. *A*

figure with a wide, cruel mouth, arms raised ready to pounce. He's wearing a Tudor style doublet - legs hidden - no sign of sprung heels. 'What's he supposed to be?' she asked.

The woman's face took on a look of pantomime horror. She hunched her shoulders and raised her hands, splaying her fingers like claws, as if about to pounce. 'Ooooooh Spring Heeled Jack - he's a real bad 'en lovie,' she said, her eyes rolling and flicking about as if terrified. 'He lives underground in the old castle tunnels and leaps out on folk when they're just laikin about or doodling. He can jump o'er a house, or even a church steeple. He chops folk's heads off and sucks out their juices.'

'Tunnels? What tunnels?' asked Kick gazing adoringly at the woman.

The woman gave him a hard stare. 'You don't know much do you?' She pointed to the road branching off opposite where they were standing. It was a straight lane between industrial buildings, and ran away to disappear under an arch carrying a main road and tram lines. Billy could see the tops of tramcars rattling over it. 'You see that road? That leads to Castle Market and Castle Gate. Once upon a time, all round here was a great stone castle.' The three pals gaped, following the direction indicated by her red polished fingernail. 'It's all gone now, of course, or has it?' she asked suddenly, startling them. 'Right underneath us could be dungeons and cellars. Some folks say there are secret passages going all the way out to Beauchief Abbey and the Manor Castle, where they imprisoned Mary Queen of Scots. D'you know that she probably lived in Sheffield longer than she lived anywhere. This pub's named after her.'

'Only her eeyad,' argued Kick.

The woman stared at him as though watching a slug froth in salt. 'He's a cheerful soul isn't he? He's like somebody's cranky old granddad.'

'Where do you think the tunnels go?' Billy asked.

'Truth to tell, lovie, nobody knows. They keep finding bits of 'em when they're clearing bombsites and such.'

A man's voice interrupted angrily. 'Ayup, Ruby! Does tha still work in this chuffin pub or not? We've gorra bar full of thirsty blokes and tha'rt out here chatting to daft kids.'

Billy looked passed the woman to the man leaning out of the pub's front door. 'I'm sorry missis. It's my fault. Will tha get the sack?'

She laughed out loud, throwing her head back. 'He'd berra not, love. He's me hubby. If he did, I'd bloody kill 'im.'

Yvonne thanked her, and headed back to the Walkley tram stop in High Street. The boys thanked her too, grinning sheepishly as she turned on her high heels and tottered back into the pub, swinging her hips.

Billy slipped an arm on Yvonne's shoulder, 'Ayup Wy, gi' us a lend o' tuppence.'

OoOoO

Chapter Eleven

'It's no good moaning. Nowt comes of it,' Yvonne chided. The two lads looked at her and raised their eyebrows, sensing she was not yet about to stop lecturing. They had gathered in the greenhouse to review progress. The boys were saying they hadn't made any, but Yvonne disagreed. She was pacing the dusty aisle between dead tomato plants, shifting and weighing invisible points of evidence and circumstance from one hand to the other as she argued her case. 'We know a heck of lot more than we did a couple of days ago,' she insisted. 'We just don't understand it yet.'

Kick frowned at her and glanced at Billy inviting his views. 'What's she going on abaht?'

Yvonne picked up the MOM board, flipped it over impatiently, and propped it up against a rickety stack of terracotta plant pots, almost knocking them over. Kick dived from his deck chair and caught the wobbling tower before it tumbled spectacularly.

'Watch it!' he cried. 'Tha'll topple 'em o'er.' He steadied the stack and adjusted the angle of the MOM board. 'I've only just gorrem straight again. I think somebody's been mucking abaht wi 'em.'

Yvonne sighed impatiently and waited for him to stop fiddling and sit down again. When she had their attention she said, 'Let's look at what we know, and see if owt's connected.'

Billy got the idea right away. 'Yeah, I were just gonna say that.'

Yvonne's fiery glare pressed him back in his deck chair. 'We've got Mary Scott and the bombing that killed her – or did it?' She wiped the back of the MOM board with her palm, looked around to locate a stubby chalk-stick and wrote: Mary Scott /

Marples bomb / old man at cemetery …'

'Walter Mebbey,' Billy reminded her. 'That's his name.'

'And why did he leave a fag packet on that grave?' asked Kick.

'Maybe it's not about the fag packet, but the gravestone he put it on,' Billy suggested. 'He wanted us to notice that particular grave, and read worrit said.'

Yvonne nodded agreement. 'Yes, and we have Spring Heeled Jack.' She wrote as she spoke, her animation unleashing a tumble of dark curls across her face.

'I think Walter said, "Spring Heeled Jack knows that realm.", or sommat like it, any road.'

'What realm?' Kick asked.

'We don't know yet, do we? But it was searching for Spring Heeled Jack that led us to the Queen's Head pub,' said Yvonne, chalk poised. 'The pub woman said Spring Heeled Jack lived in the old tunnels.' Her face suddenly lit up with excitement. 'That's his realm – the old tunnels.' She dropped her shoulders and frowned. 'But what's next? I'm stuck.'

'I don't think Spring Heeled Jack's got owt to do with it,' Billy said. 'He chops heads off. He dunt drown 'em in swimming pools.'

Kicks face lit up. He spluttered, trying to speak through his sudden excitement. 'Mary Queen of Scots!'

Yvonne and Billy gaped at him.

'She's called Mary Scott – on the gravestone - and the pub's named after Mary Queen of Scots.'

Yvonne scowled at him. 'Are you nuts? Mary Queen of Scots was hundreds of years ago. Mary Scott is just some poor woman who was killed in the blitz.'

Billy reared up defensively. 'But, tha said we've to record everything. Tha said we can't never know what's not evidence until tha knows it definitely int.'

Billy chuckled and pulled a yah-boo face at her.

Yvonne gritted her teeth, wrote on the board and then stepped back to review it.

Mary Scott / Marples bomb / Walter Mebbey
Spring Heeled Jack / Queen's Head pub / Mary Queen of Scots

Billy took the chalk from her and stepped up to the board. 'And we also know that Henry Darnley, the Man's Head victim, was killed where he stood on that day. And another thing is…' He stopped, chalk poised, frowning with concentration, 'I think the bigwigs are trying to gag the pathologist.' He wrote: *Darnley killed at MH / Who is gagging corpse doc?*

'What's M H?' asked Kick

'Man's 'eeyad!' chorused Yvonne and Billy. Kick shrugged. All three fell silent and stared at the board. Time passed, a bee bumbled about the whitewashed glass panes trying to find its way out, repeatedly ignoring the hole through which it had entered. The stack of terracotta pots emitted faint grating sounds as it settled to its use as an easel for the MOM board. Yvonne's deck chair squeaked with her every gloomy exhalation. Billy forgot he was not alone and picked his nose.

'Oh sithee - tha mucky pup,' said Kick, pulling a face at Billy's nasal excavations. 'Gi' o'er picking, tha'll pull thee brains aht.'

It was Billy's turn to hide his face.

Kick refocused on the MOM board. 'I can't see owt connecting owt wi' nowt,' he said. 'And any road up, what's t'Marples' bomb got to do wi' it? And why Spring Heeled Jack? That's just an owd tale for scaring chabbies.'

'I don't know, but somehow they're all connected,' said Billy. 'We just can't see it yet.' He took the MOM board and hung it back on its nail behind the stove. 'We'll keep it facing out this way so we can look at it every day until sommat clicks.' He glanced at their faces. 'Sommat's bound to click sooner or later.'

Yvonne stood and faced the two lads. 'I know what we can do.'

'What? Billy asked, looking up expectantly.

'For a start tha could tek us to thee granny's,' Yvonne said. 'She knows all about history. She's always goin' on about the olden days.'

Kick brightened. 'Aah, we could ask her about Marples. She knows everything about bombs and the war.'

Billy narrowed his eyes. 'Hum, tha could be reight, Wy. Come on, let's go now.'

Granny Smeggs lived in a one-up-one-down stone cottage at the end of a terrace of three identical dwellings. Well-kept flower gardens fronted the neat row, behind a six-foot high sandstone wall. The display of pink rambler roses around granny's cottage door would have done justice to the lid of any chocolate box.

A shared picket gate opened onto the gardens. A powerful spring, recycled from some forgotten industrial purpose, held it shut against all but the most determined visitor. Billy pushed passed it, recalling how the postman often claimed that granny's gate was "*more vicious than a wild dog*".

A wild, hummocky space at the back of the cottages had been Billy's favourite playground. It had scrubby trees, long grass, brambles and the mysterious foundations of long lost buildings, whose original purpose not even granny Smeggs could explain.

The side of granny's garden adjoined the site of the old Star Woman's brutal murder, a ramshackle terrace of Tudor, oak beamed cottages. The three pals glanced in respectful silence as they passed by it, each recalling their part in tracking down the old woman's killer.

Granny opened her door. 'What, all three of you?' she hooted. 'There's not enough cake for three. You'll have to have toast. Seed cake's not 'lastic. It won't stretch.'

Billy launched himself into the only free armchair. Granny's big rocker, with its complex arrangement of loose cushions, was the only other comfortable chair, and no one would dare to take that. Kick pulled out a dining chair and sat at the table. Yvonne did the same, but not until she had asked permission.

'Yes lovie, you sit down,' Granny said smiling graciously. 'If he was a gentleman, he'd budge up and let you sit with him instead of sprottling out like a drunk's dishcloth. That's the cat's pog anyway.' She gave Billy a stern look. 'You'll have to shift if she comes in.'

Missis Smeggs removed the tea towel covering half a loaf of bread on her table, and began slicing. Billy had always admired the precision of granny's slicing. His pals took a slice each and moved to the fireplace to toast them. Granny always had a fire, even in summer; without it there would be no hot water for tea.

'How's your mam, Yvonne?' Granny Smeggs asked. 'I saw her in the co-op. She'd a lovely camel jacket on. It looked too good for a Tuesday.'

'She's very well, Missis Smeggs, thank you. She said she'd seen you.'

'We wanted to ask about the Marples' bombing, Missis Smeggs,' said Kick, not wishing to waste time on talk of camels' coats. 'Do you know owt about it?'

'I should think I do know. I'd a friend who was in it. Billy calls him his uncle Fred. He's not a real uncle though. Him and his wife are just very good family friends. Anyway, he got out somehow, but he would never speak of it. They were badly shaken, all them that got out.'

'Were many hurt?'

'Oh it was awful, lovie. They were having such a good time, you see - when the siren went. It was coming up to Christmas. The twelfth of December. The pub was packed. Then bang! More than seventy killed in one terrible blast.' She looked skyward and sighed shaking her head sadly. 'First the shop across the road, C&A Modes, took a direct hit. The blast from that injured some of 'em in the pub. It took all the windows out, you see - glass flying everywhere. Them that weren't already sheltering dashed down into the cellars after that. There was nowhere else to go, not with all the bombs dropping. They had no choice.'

'Then it happened; a direct hit. The whole roof and everything blew apart and crashed down on them. It killed them all, except only about six or seven. The papers said the survivors had been in a little cellar. Some university expert said it was stronger because it was so small.' She dabbed her eyes and bit her lip, blinking rapidly. 'The all-clear didn't go until about four in the morning. Huh, Friday the thirteenth. They were digging them out for days – bodies. A lot were so badly mangled up and blown apart that they couldn't tell what bit went with what. More than seventy died. It was awful.' She dug into her apron pocket and pulled out a large handkerchief, eschewing the delicate lace one peeping decoratively from the same place. She blew her nose and wiped her tears. The children watched in silence.

The tick of her clock seemed extra loud as she took a sip from her cup. She pulled a face on finding only cold dregs and tea leaves. Yvonne swung the kettle hob over the heat of the fire and lifted the kettle lid to check there was enough water for another cup.

'There were stories about folk never being seen again,' Granny said softly as she stared into the fire. 'One minute they would have been drinking happily with somebody. They'd see them take shelter, but then they'd vanish. They weren't even found among the dead.' She looked up suddenly, the firelight glinting on her spectacles. 'And you'll never believe this, but on that very same night, some black-hearted thieves broke into the bank opposite Marples and robbed it. Can you believe that?'

'How much did they pinch?' asked Kick.

'Nobody knows. They got in through a hole in the wall made by the bombing. The police said they couldn't get into the bank's safe where the money was kept, but they got into a room where the safety deposit boxes were. Some of the boxes were damaged by the bomb blast. They'd come open, so I expect the robbers just took whatever they wanted.'

'What's a deposit box?' asked Yvonne.

'It's what rich folks keep their jewellery in.' She gave a little chuckle. 'I didn't have mine in one that night,' she joked.

'What did they steal?' Kick asked.

'Nobody knows, love, and I don't suppose they ever will. Rich folk keep some very secret stuff in safety deposit boxes; not just jewels and treasures, but papers and dark secrets. Believe me, some secrets are worth more than a bucketful of diamonds to some folk.'

Billy thought of the thieves working in secret while barely fifty yards away scores of people were dying under tons of rubble, as even more bombs rained down. What could be so valuable that you would ignore the cries of dying people and risk your life with bombs screaming down all around you?

OoOoO

Chapter Twelve

'Do you allow just anyone to wander in here when they feel like it?' Chief Superintendent Flood paced, director of pathology, Doctor Amos Longden's shabby office, as though it was his own private space. He glared around at the glass-partitioned walls, haughtily condemning the obvious lack of security, as well as the man, shuffling awkwardly, seated behind the desk.

Though well known to each other, Longden and Flood were not friends. Their ingrained hostility went back to the war and in particular the blitz. Flood was then a police sergeant and Longden a senior pathologist. They had taken a dislike to each other for no very good reason leading them to cross swords several times since. Flood's bullying tactics, invariably prevailed, and so Longden generally avoided him.

The Coroner's office had reported a breach of security. Flood had seized upon the chance to embarrass his old adversary by personally taking charge of the resulting investigation. A cleaner had found an envelope containing illegal copies of pre-hearing notes in a public area of the Coroner's court. Flood had marched into Longden's office, unannounced, and spread the papers out across his desk. They concerned the so-called Dance Floor Drowning, and Man's Head murders. Flood flicked them about with a theatrical flourish as he railed against Longden's lack of security.

Beneath his calm exterior, Doctor Amos Longden seethed, but returned Flood's glare unflinchingly, well aware the chief superintendent was milking the situation to cause him, and his department, as much embarrassment as possible.

'We know that Hadfield was here, Longden. One of my men saw him - spoke to him. Ten minutes later he saw him leave with Doctor Becket and drive her off in his car.' He placed his palms on Longden's desk and leaned towards him. 'Did she write these to give to him? Or could he have pocketed them unknown to her?'

'Of course not. It's not her handwriting.' Longden picked up the papers and tossed them aside disdainfully. 'I don't know whose scribble it is, but I doubt Sarah Becket has ever seen them. And if she had, why would she give them to Hadfield? For that matter, why would he bother to take them? He wouldn't even know they existed.

'Hadfield is an interfering nuisance. Worse still, he's in league with that bloody Perks boy. I'm sure you remember the newspapers crowing about him last year. He made your department look like a bunch of fools.'

'My recollection, chief superintendent, is that it was the police, not my department that looked foolish. What was it the papers called the lad, The Tuppenny Hat Detective? In fact, I believe the same front page article mentioned you by name. Good photograph too.'

Flood bristled, his baton quivering against his leg. 'We can only deal with actual evidence, and whatever professional interpretation you and your department place upon it. We don't make it up, unlike some.'

Longden smiled, feeling he had struck a nerve. 'Anyway, I suspect he and Sarah are just friends. After all they're young, single and medical doctors. Why shouldn't they be friends?'

'Nonsense! She could be passing him information,'

'About what, for God's sake?'

'About the post mortems …'

'Dr Becket is a professional, a respected member of my team. She would not do such a thing. She knows perfectly well not to discuss cases with anyone but an appointed officer of the court, in other words *the coroner or me.* Also, she's fully aware that as neither of these cases is yet before the coroner, it would not only be professional misconduct, it'd be *sub judice,* a criminal matter.'

Longden rose from his desk and crossed the room to a filing cabinet. He unlocked it with a key from his waistcoat pocket and took out a green cardboard folder. It had a stiff flap closure tied with pink tape. He dropped the folder onto his desk and retook his seat. 'All the papers are in here, even her rough notes, and tape recordings. I have the only key to that cabinet. Nothing leaves here without my permission.'

'So how did important extracts find their way onto a table in the coroner's court?'

'Simple. They are not *our* notes. From the look of them, they're extracts from some sort of unofficial preliminary report. That's not the sort of thing we see here. I think you should be looking for your spy at police headquarters. You can't pin this on us.'

The Chief Superintendent passed his hand over his chin, his face reddening with fury. He tapped the glass partition wall with his baton. 'They're not from my office, but this place has more holes than a sieve. Glass walls! Huh, ridiculous. It wouldn't stop a child. And you've already admitted Harry Clegg was in here last week - on his own - with the run of the place.'

'Nonsense, I was expecting him. I found him sitting reading the office copy of Country Life. He hadn't time to steal anything. He'd only been here a few minutes.' Longden sighed with impatience and wafted his hands over the papers on his desk. 'Look, Flood, I'm very busy. You will not find your thief here, and I won't let you invent one out of thin air. As I've already said, these papers are not from this office. They are most likely discussion notes taken by your people or the coroner's office.'

'One more thing,' said Flood. 'I understand you've taken Sarah Becket off the Rivelin murder case – why is that?'

'That's an internal matter, nothing to do with you.'

*

Rivelin Street, arguably the steepest in Sheffield, offered spectacular views across the valley to a broad expanse of deer park at Stannington. The only buildings to be seen were a few old cottages and a row of spanking new prefabs, built for people bombed out of their houses in the blitz. Billy was on his way to see Francis Simmons, an old friend. Like his granny, Simmons was a mine of information about the old days. He was an old soldier with a treasure chest of stories about Africa and the Boer war, as well as his experiences of the trenches in Flanders. Nowadays he confined his digging to his allotment on the riverbank near the Holly Bush Inn.

'By eck! Kill the fatted scarf. Look what's weshed up.' The old man straightened up from hoeing a row of carrots and arched his back gratefully. 'Tha mun be reight desperate, young Billy. Tha never comes near me unless tha wants sommat.'

Billy felt mildly offended, though the image of old Frank attempting to kill a *fat scarf* made up for it. He hadn't seen him since before Easter when he'd called on him in search of a pot-rabbit for his mam. 'I came t'other day but tha were out,' he lied lamely.

Francis knew it was a fib, but went along with it. 'So, to what do I owe the pleasure,' he said, adopting a posh tone and doffing his tweed cap with a courtly flourish. 'Don't tell me, I bet I know. It's that bloke they found at Man's 'eeyad, int it? Thart a detective again. Well if tha thinks I did it, I dint. I never even heard o' the poor fella.'

'Wrong. It's not about that. It's about the Marples' bombing. I keep hearing different things, an' I don't know what's reight or wrong. Me Granny sez somebody robbed the bank while the Marples were still burning.'

'Oh aaarh, they did an' all,' Francis faced him, suddenly excited by a thought. 'Tha should ask him – tha knows - that bloke from The Star newspaper. Him who took thi - err – photo - last year. He knows better than anybody. He were theer – in it!'

'Mister Clegg? He was in the hotel?'

'Oh aargh, he were there alreight. He wrote all about it in the t'Star. Tha'll still be able to read it an' all, if tha wants to, int – err - wotsit - library. They keep all them owd newspapers for history. Thiv gorram going back years, even to the South African war.'

Fearing the onset of one of Corporal Simmons' tales of army life, Billy dived in quickly to divert him with a question. 'I thought only a few escaped from the Marples; my granny said seven?'

Francis chewed his cheek for a second, shrugging off mild disappointment. 'She's reight. More than seventy poor souls died, God rest 'em. Only six or seven came out alive. But then there were plenty more who said they got out beeyart nobody seeing 'em. Mind you, they might be just mekkin it up – tha knows, to mek the sens look important like. Tha can't prove nowt one way nor t'other. And there were some that got out and just walked away beeyart telling nobody. Shock tha sees. It makes 'em a bit puddled, because of the horror of it all.' He shook his head and started towards his garden shed. 'Are tha stopping for a mash, or are tha too busy these days for thee pals?' He paused to peer at a rose bush. 'Look at this poor thing, it's snided wi' greenfly. It wants some soapy watta on it.'

Billy trailed after him, casually eyeing the stricken rose. 'Was Mister Clegg puddled?'

'I don't know, but he were big on the story at one time, always going on abaht it in his paper. Then he dropped it, and we never heard no more.'

Inside the cosy little shed with its stove and battered old kitchenette, Billy slid into a chair at a dining table. A yellowing newspaper, stained with tea mug rings, served as a tablecloth. 'What do you know about the bank robbers?'

Francis lit a paraffin stove and set a scorched kettle on it to boil. He polished two enamelled mugs on the front of his threadbare cardigan. 'I know they never caught nobody,' he said inspecting his attempts at hygiene. 'And I know they didn't get very much.' He wafted a fly away from his head. 'They gorrin through an oyal a bomb made in a wall. They could only reach a small part of the bank. Not the money in the main safe. That's why they only robbed some safety deposit boxes. I don't know how many – burrit weren't a lot.'

'Can you still see where the hole was in the wall?'

'Oh no, it were all below ground. It was in one of them old tunnels from Sheffield Castle. The bombing had opened it up again. Somehow the thieves gorrin and followed it round to the bank. They say it were some of them who'd escaped from the Marples Hotel. That's just across from the bank. They said they weren't proper bank robbers - just ordinary people who were escaping through them old tunnels. Whoever they were, I bet they thought Christmas had come early. I bet they just grabbed as much as they could and - wotsit - scarpered. It'd pay for a good neet's boozing wunt it?' He doubled up with laughter, tears sparkling in his pale blue eyes.

Billy frowned. 'Is it true that nobody knows what was nicked?'

Francis wiped his face and calmed himself. 'Aye, as far as I know it is.' He shrugged his thin shoulders. 'Any rooad up, them who's got safety deposit boxes don't brag about what's in 'em. As a rule, they want to keep it quiet. That's why they have 'em. Burrit meks yer think, dunt it? Thi could have all sorts stashed away – and I don't mean liquorice allsorts.'

*

The walk back up Rivelin Street is hard work. As Billy slowly trudged home to Walkley, he thought of old Mister Simmons' comments about the contents of the safety deposit boxes. Surely someone knew what was in them? The bank would have records, wouldn't they?

'Ayup, mi owd. Are tha all reight?'

Billy lifted his bowed head from the steep climb to see PC John Needham grinning down at him. 'Oh it's you. Hello.'

'Are tha all reight,' asked John.

'Aye, I'm champion.'

'You don't look champion. You look knackered. A young un like you should be skipping up this hill, not crawling up it like an owd man. What's up wi thee? Are yer badly?'

Billy laughed, deliberately wobbling his legs as if they were made of rubber. 'I'm just tired. This 'ill's killin' me,' he said jokily, and sat down on the causey-edge to look up at the towering policeman. 'I've just been talking to somebody about a bank robbery.'

PC Needham squatted down beside him. 'Oh aye, well if you

did it, wait until my shift's finished. I've got enough work on already without you mekkin more for me.'

'No, it's not me robbing a bank. This one was robbed in 1940. It were the old United Counties Bank in Fitzalan Square, the one that's called Barclays now. It were robbed the same night that Marples got bombed.'

'Aaagh well, Fitzalan Square's not on my beat. And in 1940 I'd just been called up. The Lords of the Admiralty had graciously invited me to give the Royal Navy the benefit of my vast knowledge and salty experience.'

'It got robbed cos a bomb knocked an oyal in it. Tha could just walk in and rob stuff.'

'Gerraway!'

'True! But I need to know more about it. How can I find out?'

'Like what?'

'Like what did they steal? Did they catch any of 'em? Who were they? And owt else I can find out.' He gave the constable a stern look over his spectacles. 'Everything is evidence until tha knows it definitely int.'

PC Needham frowned thoughtfully. 'And you think I can find out, do you?'

'Well tha 'rt a copper. They'll tell thee. They're bound to have records and files on it, but they won't tell a kid owt, will they?'

'OK, I'll see what I can do.' He laughed and stood up, stretching to his full height. 'Shall I get you an ambulance, or can tha walk now?'

Billy got up and set off up the hill, marching briskly and swinging his arms. He stopped suddenly and faced the constable. 'Oh, I forgot to ask thee sommat else.'

'What?'

'When its football season, do they ever give thee free tickets for Hillsborough, cos you're a copper?'

The constable performed a clowning retch, as though about to vomit. 'Ugh, Hillsborough! Oh no. If they did, I'd have to shoot me sen,' he cried, frowning as if assailed by a bad smell.

Billy gaped in horror. 'Oh no!' he cried, 'Tha 'rt norra chuffin

Blade, are tha?'

'I most certainly am, lad.' He raised his arms triumphantly. 'United till I die. United through and through, Billy lad. Up the Blades!'

'Oh no, that's terrible.'

*

At the weekend, Billy joined a jabbering line of children queuing for Walkley Palladium's Saturday matinee. The film was Sugarfoot, a western starring Randolph Scott. Interest in it temporarily cooled as rumours of yet another strike by what the newspapers were calling "the biscuit barrel burglar," buzzed along the queue. The target this time had evidently been Doctor Fulton-Howard's surgery. Drugs, bandages, and a sphygmomanometer had vanished.

This was the latest in a series of burglaries. The police claimed that the city's many open windows, due to the hot summer weather, made it easy for someone, small and agile, to climb in and out of people's unguarded homes. Usually, only highly portable valuables were taken; the favourite being any cash that people had put aside in biscuit barrels for the rent, the tally man, or the man from the Pru. Stealing sphygmomanometers, or as most people called them, blood pressure thingies, did not fit the usual pattern.

Billy joined in the gabble of speculation until a cheer went up as the cinema queue finally started moving. The stirring music of the film's overture flooded out onto the street. He was not to know that the police had found a tangle of gardeners' green twine at the surgery break-in, and were connecting it, perhaps a little too quickly, to him and his pals, because they met in a greenhouse. As Randolph Scott duked it out with the bad guys, plain clothed police officers were knocking at Billy's door.

In stunned silence, Frank and Marion Perks listened to police claims of "strong evidence" connecting Billy and his pals to the robbery. They were not told that the so-called evidence comprised no more than a bit of gardeners' twine, such as any ironmonger might sell.

When Billy came out of the pictures, blinking in the late afternoon sunshine, PC Needham was waiting for him. He pulled him aside and led him to a quiet passage behind the cinema. Taking out his notebook, he looked around warily and whispered out of the corner of his mouth, 'If anybody comes, pretend I'm questioning you. And try to look worried.'

'I am worried. What's up wi' thee?'

The constable glanced around surreptitiously. 'I don't know what's going on yet, but I don't like it. I've had that creep, Sergeant Lackey breathing down my neck about you and your pals. He seems to think you've been nicking stuff. It doesn't make any sense, but sommat very strange is going on.' He leaned against the passage wall, his shoulders dropping in a sigh. 'When I left the *Andrew* I wanted to be a copper more than owt else – well, except for a footballer, maybe. But there are things going on now that I don't like, and I'm buggered if I know what to do about it.' He paced back and forth, frowning with concentration. 'Billy, I need to talk to your dad, but in secret and unofficially. Is he at home?'

Billy eyed him with concern. 'Yeah, burril be going to the Reform Club at seven. It's his old time dancing. He takes me mam if he's not working on a Saturday.'

PC Needham thought for a moment. He reached absently into his tunic pocket and pulled out his cigarettes. 'Right, you dash home and tell him that I'll be there after six when I finish my shift.' He patted Billy on the shoulder. 'I can't go while I'm on duty, see. It's gotta be unofficial.'

Billy left, as the constable lit a fag. He was puzzled, but strangely pleased at the idea of this friendly copper meeting his dad. He felt sure that when the two men met, the great mystery, whatever it was, would soon be revealed.

OoOoO

Chapter Thirteen

December 12th 1940

'These are no good, Frank love. I asked her for coloured pages,' said Granny Smeggs, disappointment marring her face. 'I told her, "only cut out coloured ones".'

Frank Perks gave his mother-in-law a bemused frown and patted the wad of torn out magazine pages he had brought to her. 'Worra they for, any road up?'

'Paper chains of course. Look.' She fished out a large cardboard box from under her table and lifted out a colourful paper chain, each link made from a strip of paper, carefully cut from a magazine page and stuck down with flour paste. 'It's for Christmas. It wouldn't be Christmas without paper chains. There's no tinsel, nor tranklements to be found anywhere cos 'o this ruddy war.'

'I think she thought you wanted it for fire twists or sommat. Shall I tek 'em back?'

Granny guarded them with a sweep of her arm. 'No, I'll keep 'em, now they're here. I can maybe use a few of 'em. The rest'll make fire twists, or – er - sommat else.'

Frank made to leave. 'I'd better get going. I don't want to be caught outside if there's a raid again tonight.'

Granny escorted him to the door of her small room and opened it on to a clear frosty night. She looked up at the sky. 'It's a bombers' moon tonight,' she said. 'There's not a cloud.'

Frank Perks glanced at the starry sky. 'Will you be all right, ma? You can come to ours if you'd rather.'

'What? And spend the night in that tin duck pond you call an air raid shelter. No thank you. I'm better off in my own cellar. It's dry and I've everything I want down there.'

'Aye, you're probably right. We don't use t'shelter anymore. It fills up wi' watta as soon as it rains - meks everything claggy.

We go down the cellar an' all now. I've built some bunk beds, and we've got t'wireless and everything. There's even that well of ours down there,' he said with a laugh. 'Thiz not many can say they've gorra well in their cellar.'

The wail of air raid sirens interrupted them. Their mournful howl instantly resetting the thoughts, fears, hopes and priorities of all who heard it. It was just after seven-o-clock. 'Crickey! I'd better dash afore they get here,' said Frank. 'Does tha need a hand to get owt down into your cellar?'

'No, you go. Get a move on, Frank. God bless you, love, and thanks.'

'Good night, ma.' he said, turning to leave. 'Don't forget to turn your gas off.'

'PUT THAT BLOODY LIGHT OUT!' This from an unseen air raid warden somewhere in the blackness of the street. Frank Perks made a swift goodbye and closed granny's door, sealing the blackout. He set off down the path in the moonlight. Not a chink of light showed from the houses he passed as he jogged the two or three hundred yards to his house where his wife waited anxiously. The cheerful sounds of the BBC's light programme escaped up into the darkness from coal cellar grates, blackened windows, and Anderson shelters in gardens. By the time he reached his house, the first rattling pulse of ack ack had started and searchlights probed the starry sky.

Like thousands of Sheffielders that night, Frank and Marion Perks snuggled together in their coal cellar. They sipped tea, listened to the wireless, and pretended the blast and crump of bombs raining down did not terrify them.

Throughout the city, the pre-Christmas festivities interrupted by the bombing, shifted from pubs, dance halls, and cafes, and continued in public air raid shelters and cellars. Strangers joined in community singing and joked about the danger. Couples who had been dancing at a ball in the Cutlers Hall tried to protect their smart clothes as they crowded into basements and dusty public shelters. Women cursed the Nazi bombers and bemoaned the clothing coupons sacrificed to buy their frocks. Incendiary bombs rained down in thousands. Fires flared up all across the city. When the Central Cinema caught light, four hundred people good-naturedly booed the projectionist for switching the film off. Hard-pressed policemen urged the audience out to the shelters, repeatedly suffering the same old jokes about ticket refunds, or what a bad film it was and how the bombers deserved credit for ending it.

In the Marples hotel in Fitzalan Square, manager Mister Burgess and his staff, shepherded patrons down into the hotel's maze of inter-connected cellars. It was not difficult; most people were making the best of it, laughing and joking as they carried their drinks and pre-yuletide festivity with them. The cellars were deep, and there was singing to the strains of an accordion. It seemed an enjoyable and perfectly safe refuge. Everybody was having fun. Perversely, the air raid made it all seem even more enjoyable.

The jollity faltered when C&A Modes, a large fashion store across the High Street from the Marples, took a direct hit. Flying glass from the exploding storefront injured some Marples' clients, making revellers head for the cellars with increased urgency.

About an hour later, the Marples hotel took a direct hit from a five hundred pounder. The seven-storey building blew apart. A thousand tons of rubble fell into the cellars. The building next door caught fire. The blaze roared hungrily through the ruins.

Walter Mebbey had been playing his accordion and leading the singing. He'd been strolling round from one cellar to the next, jollying the crowd along, when the bomb struck. The blast blew him off his feet and rammed him into a narrow, stone alcove. The lights went out. His ears felt blocked up, loud whistling sounds filled his head. He felt around in the darkness and scrambled deeper into cover as the building collapsed around him.

A second or two behind him Henry Darnley, a professor of history at Sheffield University, blundered into the same alcove and fell into Walter's unseen arms. 'Ugh, sorry. Are you OK?' he asked, untangling himself from the unintentional embrace. The pair tumbled into churning rubble and were pushed aside like litter before a broom.

Walter couldn't hear or see. He shoved the unseen body aside and tried to regain his footing. The flint on his cigarette lighter had given up and wouldn't spark. He felt the man flinch and push deeper into the alcove as more debris came crashing down. Grit and choking dust sprayed into Walter's face. He tried the cigarette lighter again, still without success. He shuffled deeper into the recess, trying to make room for the man struggling beside him. He tried talking to him. 'Hello. Hello, can tha hear me? Has tha gorra light? Mine's bust' he shouted.

No answer.

Deaf and blind, Walter dared to creep out of hiding, hoping to find a light, or anything visible to head for. Unable to see what was above or around him, he kept his head down and crawled on hands and knees over the rubble. It was loose and kept shifting and slipping taking him with it. The accordion strapped to his chest bumped and snagged on unseen obstruction, it kept hitting him under the chin, its musical honking unheard by any.

Walter felt the warm, softness of another person's body. It made him jump as he touched it. He apologized and pulled back sharply, but there was no response. He tentatively felt around again until he found it, and quickly realised it was a man's still warm corpse - the clothing wet and sticky with what was undoubtedly blood. Gritting his teeth and trying not to vomit Walter searched the dead man's pockets, hoping to find a torch, or cigarette lighter, or matches. He struck lucky and struck a match.

He found himself entombed by rubble in a space about ten feet square. The man who had sheltered with him was crawling towards him from a deep alcove set into the cellar wall. Walter saw it had a large stone table built into it, for keeping food cool, He realised that was what had protected him from the blast and the tons of falling rubble. He crawled towards the other man and clasped hands with him, relieved to see another living soul. They were both jabbering excitedly, faces animated, lips moving, but neither could hear the other.

'I can't hear thee,' Walter shouted. The man stood up groggily, poking his ears and shaking his head as if to dislodge a blockage. Walter saw him speak again, but still heard nothing. 'It's no good I can't hear thee.'

The man shrugged and stopped trying to make himself heard.

Walter yelped as the match burned his fingers. He dropped it, sucked his finger ends and struck another. Suddenly his ears popped and a rush of indistinguishable sound crashed into his brain. He shook his head, hearing what sounded like an escape of steam. Gradually other sounds bubbled through into his head; screams and shouting, and above it all the ear splitting crunch and scrape of rubble settling into the cellar's voids, as if in its own tortured agony.

The match burned out, and in the blackness, the cries of the dying seemed even more desperate. Wetness oozed from the shifting rubble. The air was thick with dust and smoke. It stank of urine and blood. Above his head, the sagging ceiling strained and creaked beneath untold weight, its tormented wailing seeming almost human.

A glimmer of light feebly picked out the chaotic shapes of rubble blocking a doorway. Walter beckoned his companion towards it.

'Hello! Are you there?' The voice coming through the wreckage sounded small and distant. 'I'm alive in here. Is there anybody there?' Sounds of scrabbling and digging followed.

'Yes we're here – two of us.' Walter answered. 'Go easy with that digging! Tha might bring the whole bloody lot down on thi sen. It's all blocked solid on this side. Tha waint get no further this way. ' He scrambled nearer to the light. 'Is there somebody else wi' thee? How many of you are there?'

'It's me and three others – maybe more – I can't really see much. I've only got a few matches left. There's a dead person and one of us is hurt.'

'If tha can clear a bit more on tha side we'll try to squeeze through to you, but be very careful, or we could kill us senz. The roof in here look's like it'll come down any minute.'

'Hello! Are you there?' It was a different voice, a more cultured, authoritative male voice. 'We can feel cold air coming in. Perhaps there's a way out on this side.'

Walter's neighbour from the alcove pressed forward beside him. 'Is that you Longden? I can't hear very well – my ears are shot. It's me. Are you hurt?'

'Darnley? Darnley, Good heavens, is that you, old boy? You're alive. Good show. We thought you'd had it. Are you hurt?'

'A bit deaf, and bruised a bit, but nothing broken. Who's there with you? Is Clarry there? Is she all right? '

'I'm with Mary. She's unhurt. We're looking for Clarry. I think there's a couple more chaps. We can hear them but we haven't seen them yet. I'm afraid they weren't in our crowd. One of 'em sounds pretty badly injured.' There was silence for a moment then Longden spoke again. 'Mary said she could feel air coming in. She squeezed through to try to find out where it's coming from. It might be a way out.'

Walter interrupted. 'Look, stop thee nattering, you two. We need to get out of here before this bloody roof comes down.'

'Who's that?' Longden called.

'It's the chap who was playing the accordion,' Darnley replied. 'We're in some sort of alcove together. Mercifully, he's not playing at the moment. There's another fellow here, but he's dead.'

'We'll all be dead if we don't get a bloody move on,' said Walter, cautiously picking at the rubble jammed between him and Longden.

'Can I help?' asked Darnley.

'Aye, but tek it steady. We don't want the whole lot coming in.'

For an hour they worked slowly and with great care until Walter grabbed Darnley's wrist. 'Stop! Hold on a minute. We're gonna have to shift this big un next,' he explained. He struck a match. A conglomeration of broken brickwork, about the size and thickness of an armchair cushion, still blocked the escape hole they were excavating.

Darnley shook his head doubtfully. 'We can't do that, the whole lot will come down.'

Walter did not agree. 'Look. See that?' He pointed to a shaped block of stone sticking out above the blockage. 'I reckon that's one end of a stone lintel or a door step. That's what's supporting this lot, not them bricks. I think we can pull them out and scroam through.'

Both men studied the rubble until the match burned Walter's fingers and darkness engulfed them again. Darnley said nothing. Walter wriggled the cushion sized block, and gradually worked it free. 'It's coming. Gi' us a hand. Come on pull. It's coming out.'

Darnley helped to drag it aside, exposing a hole big enough to scramble though. The pair waited for signs of a collapse, almost too scared to move, or even breath. After a moment, Darnley spoke and blew a sigh of relief. 'Well done, old chap. I think you've done it.'

Walter shouted into the hole. 'Does it look alreight at thar side?'

A match flared at the far end of the short tunnel. 'It seems OK,' Longden answered, 'but you'd better be dashed careful.'

Walter immediately passed his accordion through the hole, and followed it as quickly as he could, trying not to disturb the rubble. Grunting and wheezing Darnley followed. Walter turned and pulled him through a second before the lot caved in, filling the air with dust.

'Thanks old boy. That was a damn close shave, what?'

Someone struck a match. 'Darnley! Good to see you. Thank heavens you're safe,' said Longden, his moustachioed face gurning in the match light. 'And you too, old boy. Well done.' He handed Walter his dusty accordion. 'Here you'd better have this back. I enjoyed your playing,' he told Walter. 'Bloody rude of Gerry to interrupt you like that – what?'

A woman's voice broke in from the darkness, like a headmistress stilling a noisy assembly. 'I've found it! It's down here. I can feel fresh air coming in.'

Longden lurched towards the sound of the woman's voice. 'Clarry darling, thank God you're safe. I've been looking for you.'

Everyone began moving towards the the snooty voice. Walter struck another match and glanced back the way he and Darnley had come. The walls supporting the cellar's steel beamed ceiling had collapsed on three sides. It sloped crazily, bearing down on the heap of rubble through which they had crawled. He noticed Darnley was staring at it, terror on his face. 'That'll go any second. We'd better get a move on,' he told him.

They caught up to the woman who had called them. She was crouched beside the escape hole she had found. It was in a wall whose masonry was quite unlike the rest of the cellar. She beckoned them excitedly. Walter could not see her face. She had a scarf wrapped around her mouth and nose as protection against the dust. Soot and dust covered her hair and clothes.

Longden helped her to widen the hole, pulling out stones and clearing them away. He stopped suddenly. 'Listen,' he said.

Everyone stopped what they were doing and cocked an ear.

'I can't hear anything,' said Darnley. 'What did you hear, Longden?'

'The screaming's stopped.'

For a moment the little group were silent and thoughtful. A man with a silk paisley scarf wrapped around his face suddenly burst into action. He scrambled up to the hole in the wall and vanished into it. After a few seconds he reappeared. 'It's perfectly clear in here,' he said. 'It's a tunnel. I can't tell how far it goes, but it looks absolutely clear and as solid as a rock.'

'Follow it for a bit and come and tell us,' Darnley instructed without reticence.

'OK. Shan't be a mo.'

As he watched him go Walter heard a faint sound from the direction they had come. He thought it sounded like a woman's cry. 'D'you hear that?' He struck another match, and paused, listening.

Darnley glared at him crossly. 'One thing at a time, old boy,' he snapped. 'Let's be sure we can save ourselves before we start digging others out.'

'It sounds like a woman,' said Walter, poking fiercely at his still whistling ears. 'I'll go back and see if we can help her.'

'No, stop! You can't do anything,' cried Darnley. 'There are dozens trapped back there. We'll be overrun. We can't help them all.' He grabbed Walter's shoulder and pushed him towards their escape route. 'Come along, this way. Get through there. If we find a way out we can send the firemen back this way. They're the ones to give help, not you. What the hell are going to do anyway - sing to them?'

Walter angrily shrugged free of him. He faced up to the much taller man. 'Ayupp, who's tha think tha 'rt shoving, pal? I'm not thee skivvy tha knows. I can please me sen who I help, and whether tha likes it or not, I'm going back to help that lass.' He shouldered Darnley aside, picked up his accordion and set off back the way he had come. After a few steps, he turned and faced Darnley again in the flickering match light. 'And I'll tell thee sommat else, if all I can do for her is play her a song, then that's worral do.' He glared at Darnley for a second, his chin jutting pugnaciously, then headed off into the blackness.

Darnley shrugged and climbed through the hole in the wall. The others followed him.

Walter found a young woman trapped by a fallen beam. He struck a match. She had tried to work herself free, but, like an alligator's jaw, a large crack in the beam held her leg in its bite. Blood sprayed from the wound.

'Alreight, love. Hang on. Let's see what we can do.' Walter tried lifting the beam. She screamed in agony. He stopped and struck another match. Her leg was a mess of mangled flesh and splintered bone. He stripped off his necktie, wrapped it around her thigh as a tourniquet to stem the pulsing fountain of blood. It seemed to make no difference. She sobbed as he tried to tighten it. He took off his jacket, ripped off his shirt and bound her leg hoping that would staunch the flow. 'Hold on tight, love. Press on the bandage. We've got to stop thee bleeding. '

The match flame burned his finger. In the darkness, the woman found his hand. He gripped it warmly and felt her die. For a while he sat in the darkness, holding her dead hand. Unseeing he straightened her clothes as best he could and covered her face with his blood sodden shirt. He patted around to find his jacket and accordion then made his way back to join the others.

Though he shouted them and even heard the distant sounds of their reply, he never saw them again. He stumbled blindly through a maze of tunnels for what seemed an age. Eventually he happened on a narrow padlocked gate where the tunnel fed into a dimly lit room crowded with boxes and sacks. It smelled of food, like a pantry. He peered inside, and guessed it must a storeroom beneath Castle Market, a large indoor market hall built on the site of the old castle. The gate was sturdily built of timber and chain link mesh. Its hinges and lock had rusted solid. Shouldering and kicking it made no impression. It was obvious the others could not have come this way.

'Stand back!' The voice belonged to a steel helmeted firefighter. He came barging through the storeroom's bales and boxes, and took a swing at the gate with an axe. The blow ripped away chain-link mesh. Walter bent it aside and passed his accordion through the gap. The fire-fighter grabbed it cheerfully and helped him squeeze through after it. 'Ayup what's all this then? Are tha doing requests? I'll have a chorus o' Nellie Dean.' He helped Walter into the storage cellar and sat him down on a wooden crate. 'Are tha wi' thee sen? Thart lucky I saw thee. I were just going back up into t'market.'

'A woman, but she's dead,' said Walter. 'There are some others an' all, about four or five on 'em. I was with 'em, but they must've gone out another way.'

'Come on, mi owd. I'll show thee weer tha can gerra cuppa. Tharz earned it.'

0o0o0

Chapter Fourteen

Bang on six-o-clock, PC Needham rapped on the Perk's back door. Frank Perks let him in, his greeting stiff with concern.

'Would you like a cup of tea, constable?' asked Missis Perks, her head appearing in the kitchen doorway.

'Call me John. John Needham. You'll know my mother, I expect - in Industry Street?'

'May Needham? Oh yes, I've known May for years,' said Marion Perks. 'We worked together on the hotplate at the University Refec.'

'Oh aye, she loved that job. She's had to retire though, bad ankles.'

'What's this all about?' asked Frank Perks, a touch impatient. 'We've had the police round already, talking bloody nonsense about our Billy.'

Marion Perks shot her husband a critical glare. 'He's hopeless. He was shouting at 'em. I had to stop him. Another minute and they'd have arrested him, never mind our Billy.'

Frank gestured for John to take an armchair, and moved to the settee to sit facing him. Marion Perks handed the constable a cup of tea and offered him her best cut glass sugar basin. The constable stirred two teaspoonfuls of sugar into his cup, and looked around the little room. 'It's nice,' he said. 'I've never been in any of these houses.'

Frank sniffed. 'It's too small. There's only this room and that kitchen – no wider than a passage. We've just the one bedroom. Our Billy sleeps in the attic.'

Marion joined them and the three sat facing each other – a triumvirate of concern. John sipped his tea as an awkward silence enveloped them. Frank Perks spoke first: 'What're the coppers doing? They just kept saying the same rubbish. Billy had nowt to do wi' it. All this biscuit barrel burglar stuff, it's bloody nonsense. Even they seemed embarrassed to be accusing him. I'm wondering if it's owt to do with that telling off Billy got from that Flood bloke, Chief Superintendent or whatever he is. Did yer know about that?'

Needham nodded. He had not been officially informed, but had heard enough from Billy and others to fill in the blanks.

'Why try to scare a little lad like that?' Frank asked. 'He warned him not to play detectives, as though he's some sort of criminal. I was livid when I heard. I would've gone down there, but for that young doctor. He persuaded me to leave it.'

'He went off like a roman candle,' said Marion Perks. 'I couldn't have stopped him on my own. Thank goodness it was Doctor Hadfield telling us. He calmed him down. If he hadn't done they'd both be in trouble, father and son. How would that look to the neighbours?'

'Where is Billy?' John asked.

'I sent him upstairs. I was puzzled why you'd asked to talk to us. I thought it sounded – well - I don't know what I thought. Did you want *him* here an' all?'

The constable shook his head, frowning. 'You decide,' he said. 'I don't know. You see, I think somebody is trying to make life difficult for your Billy. First, he's had that telling off, and speaking off the record, I agree with you about that. It wasn't right.'

'Doctor Hadfield told us not to worry. I wasn't happy about it, but he seemed to think it made sense, though it was misguided. The way he put it, the chief superintendent was only trying to protect the kids.'

PC Needham sipped his tea. 'Maybe, but this business about the burglaries is stupid. It makes no sense at all, and it's definitely not right.' He put his cup aside and sat forward in his chair. 'You see, I've grown to like your Billy, and I think I'm getting to know him – you know, how he ticks. I had a little brother. He died when I was fifteen, appendicitis.' He looked around the room as if gathering his thoughts. 'Your Billy's a bright lad, and he's a good lad an' all. There's no way he'd be nicking stuff, nor his pals neither. They're all good kids. I know all the families.'

Frank Perks lowered his gaze. 'Well thanks, John. I appreciate that.'

'I remember your Eddie,' said Missis Perks sadly. 'He was a smashing little lad, all smiley and full of life.' She looked into her teacup for a moment. 'It's funny, but when our Billie got his first pair of glasses he reminded me of your Eddie.'

Needham laughed softly. 'Aye, I see flashes of Eddie in him all the time. They even sound the same - well – I mean they would if …' He blew a sigh and rotated his police helmet in his hands. 'They say they can cure it now, you know, appendicitis. Well peritonitis really. They give 'em lots of that Penicillin.' He stood up and edged towards the door. 'Anyway, what I wanted to say is that I think Billy is being watched, or maybe even targeted by somebody. Probably some *brown-noser* on Flood's staff.' He looked at the Perks' concerned faces. 'Try not to worry. This biscuit-barrel-burglar will be caught soon, but until then we must make sure we don't give 'em a chance to pin it on Billy, or his friends. There's a rumour they've got some evidence against him. I don't know what, but we'll need to be careful. Did they look at his room?'

'Aye, I took 'em upstairs, said Marion. 'They just looked under the bed. They didn't find anything - not even fluff. I clean up there every week …'

John frowned. 'No, but did they plant owt there?'

Marion gasped and looked to her husband. 'They'd never do that, would they?'

'I hope not,' Needham said. 'I'm probably overreacting, but we have to be careful. It only takes one person to be a rotten apple in the barrel. Flood's not liked. He's crafty and conniving. I've heard that most of our senior officers don't like him or his methods.' He blew a sigh, puffing out his cheeks. 'You see, your Billy made the police look a bit stupid last year. Some officers, including Flood were dragged over the coals after that. Maybe he's still smarting.'

Marion Perks looked worried. 'We'll have to search that attic from top to bottom, Frank.'

'It won't do any harm,' said John. 'You don't want them coming back for another look round and miraculously finding sommat incriminating.'

'I can't believe it.' Marion dabbed her eyes.

'If they do come back, ask 'em if they've got a search warrant. They most likely won't have, and I don't think they'll try to get one either. That should stop 'em in their tracks.' He got up and started towards the door.

Frank Perks rose and stood facing him. 'What do you think's going on? I mean. How can a little lad be so important?'

'Good question, I wish I knew,' he said reaching out for the doorknob.

Mister and Missis Perks followed him. 'Thanks, John. I appreciate this,' said Frank Perks. 'If owt happens, I'll let you know.'

Billy crept back upstairs to his bedroom. He had been hiding behind the door at the foot of the stairs and had heard every word. It had not cleared up anything for him. He was just as puzzled as his parents.

Billy's mam and dad searched his attic bedroom. His mother stripped the bed while his dad peered underneath it. Billy and Ruff watched as even the bit of the old carpet the dog slept on was given a thorough shake before being shoved back under the bed. Ruff reclaimed it with an indignant growl.

They found nothing.

Frank Perks scratched his head, a puzzled frown on his face. 'Well there's nowt here. Have they been in that greenhouse of yours?' he asked Billy.

'No, it's secret. Nobody knows about it.'

'Well I do, don't I? I just asked thee about it.'

'Don't thee-and-thou, Frank,' said Missis Perks sharply. 'How can you expect him to talk nicely if you keep theeing-andthouing?'

'Sorry, love.'

Billy smiled secretly at his father's faked remorse. 'I meant that I don't think they know about the greenhouse,' Billy explained. 'But even if they do there's nowt for 'em to find only old seed trays and plant pots.'

'Well your friend John Needham seems sure they'll try some dirty tricks, so you'd better be on your guard.'

*

The following morning Billy was up early, determined to be first at the greenhouse. Clutching his day clothes, he ran downstairs to the kitchen, and splashed his face and arms with cold water. He wanted to get out before his mother woke and stopped him going.

He heard her start to move about upstairs and knew that she'd be down any minute.

'Billy, is that you? Are you up already? What are doing?' she called down the stairs.

'It's OK, mam. Ruff's been sick,' he lied. His mam hated mess, dog vomit in particular. She could become quite ill at the mere thought of it. Billy knew he'd played a trump card.

Ruff looked up at him adoringly, wagging his tail in response to hearing his name. 'I'm cleaning it up,' Billy called up to her. 'There's no need to come down. I'd better take him out. He looks like he's gonna do it again.' Half dressed, he cut and spread a slice of bread with pork dripping, meaty with brown jelly, and dashed outside. Ecstatic, the little dog preceded him.

Despite the early hour, he was not the first at the greenhouse. Harry Clegg was waiting for him. He looked tired and scruffy. Instead of his customary camel overcoat, silk paisley scarf and brown trilby hat, he was almost unrecognizable in army dungarees, wellingtons and an old tweed cap. He peered out furtively as he closed the door behind Billy. 'Did anybody follow you?'

'What's up with you? You look awful.'

'Has anything happened to you – anything strange, or weird

like?'

'Yeah, I met this scruffy bloke in the greenhouse, acting all puddled. What's going on?'

'Never mind, just listen and do exactly what I say. You're in danger …'

'I know about the burglary thing, if it's that. It's all in hand. We're ready for 'em.'

Clegg looked at him blankly. 'What burglary thing? What're you babbling about?'

'They're trying to frame me for a burglary. We think they're going to plant some evidence so they can pretend to find it and blame it on me.'

Harry Clegg chewed his cheek thoughtfully. 'Police, you say? Hum, it's probably that idiot Flood. He must think you know something – something special. He's scared of you. It's worse than I thought. He's involved somehow, but I don't know how.' He slowly paced the greenhouse's dusty aisle. He was frowning, deep in thought. Suddenly he stopped and fixed Billy with a steely gaze. 'They want to shut you up, me too. Somebody's been sending my editor poison pen letters about me. They never sign 'em of course – bloody cowards. I'm taking a few weeks off until it all blows over. The wife's got me painting the bedroom.'

'Any idea who it is?'

'Could be anybody,' he said ruefully. 'Over the years I've upset a lot of people in this city. Some criminals can get very self-righteous when you expose 'em in the paper, not to mention the husbands I catch doing naughty things behind their wives' backs.' He paced about peering into every corner and looking under pots and seed boxes. 'You'd better keep a sharp look out, Billy. The nearer you get to solving this murder the nearer you are to getting your head bashed in.'

'Blimey, it can't be that bad.'

'Why not? If the killer thinks you're getting close, he'll try to stop you. He doesn't want to swing on the hangman's rope.'

Billy shuddered. 'Well he's pretty safe at the moment. We're not getting anywhere. I think I might know how it was done, but

I don't have a clue about motive or who it was.'

A tense silence followed. Harry bit his lip thoughtfully and looked around. Billy watched him prowl the aisle fiddling aimlessly with the old plant labels, pots and bits of string. 'Do you know about Spring Heeled Jack?' Billy asked.

Clegg looked bemused. 'Yes, it's a kid's rhyme. Why?'

'It talks about the old tunnels under the city.'

'So what?' he snapped. 'He's not the killer. I can promise you that.'

'Was it you who gave those notes to Doc Hadfield?' Billy asked. 'He says it's illegal. He's probably already been to the cops about it.'

Clegg smiled and nodded. 'I thought he would do, but I guessed he'd at least read them first. He did, didn't he?'

Billy nodded. Clegg looked relieved.

'The doc said they show that someone's trying to hide the truth. He's going to see the post mortem doctor.' There was no reaction from Clegg. 'Did you know that Professor Darnley's jacket is missing? The forensic people think he was killed where they found him, and yet he had no jacket, and no way of getting there.'

Clegg eyed him critically. 'Who told you that?'

'Nobody. I just said it to me sen.'

'You're not as daft as you look, Billy Perks. But watch out! Killers are ruthless. Somebody has been sitting on a massive secret for more than ten years. I don't know exactly what it is, but I think it's got something to do with a bank robbery during the war…'

'You mean when the Marples was bombed?'

Clegg stared at Billy, astonished. 'Good Lord, how do you know about that?'

'I don't. That's what I'm trying to find out about.'

'Leave it alone, Billy. Please. You don't know what you're getting into.'

'You were in that hotel,' Billy said unmoved. 'You escaped and wrote about it afterwards.'

Clegg grabbed at the greenhouse door. He cracked it open a fraction and peered outside. 'Listen. Somebody might be coming.' He shut the door and turned back to Billy. 'Yes I was there. And I'm pretty sure that what happened that night is behind all of this. One of the victims was there too. Did you know that?'

'Who?'

'I wish I knew for sure, but I haven't quite worked it all out yet. I think Flood is also involved somehow, but I don't know how. Two of them are dead already. That's the two murders, Hepburn and Darnley. There could be more to come.' He leaned his head back and looked up at the bright morning sunlight striking the whitewashed windowpanes. He seemed to be gathering his thoughts. Billy watched him and waited silently.

'It was terrible that night. We couldn't see for the dust and dark, and I was deaf for days afterwards. All I can say with any certainty is that there were six or seven of us in that cellar; two women and five men, at least I think so. One man, the pub's accordionist, went back to help somebody. We never saw him again. We'd found a tunnel. We didn't know where it led to, but cold air was coming in. We split up into two groups so that we could search in both directions. My group got lucky and came out near the fish market. We tried to go back to tell the others but the police stopped us. They sent in two coppers to find them instead. Believe it or not, one of 'em was that creep Flood. He was just a sergeant back then.'

'Did he find them?'

'No. They must have got out somewhere else and just walked off into the night.'

'And now you think one of 'em is murdering the others?'

'Yes, and there'll be more,' warned Harry.

'Spring Heeled Jack knows their realm,' said Billy, closely watching Clegg's reaction.

'Shuddup with the bloody Spring Heeled Jack nonsense; this's serious, Billy. You could get yourself hurt – even killed. It's not a game. You've got to keep out of it, Billy. Somebody is watching you, and me too.' He picked up the MOM board from where it leaned against the rickety stack of plant pots and began reading it. 'Is this all you've got?'

'So far, but we'll get more.'

'Not if they get you first.' He shoved the MOM board disdainfully back into place. The stack of plant pots reeled and rocked. Clegg tried to catch it, but too late. It toppled, crashing to the floor. Something shiny with polished wood and glittering brass work clattered into view amid the scattering shards. Clegg gaped at it. 'What the hell's that?' He bent close and picked up a sphygmomanometer. It was made of burr-elm effect Bakelite with brass fittings and dial. It glinted in the early morning sunshine.

Billy gaped at it. 'Chuffing eck! That's the thing that was nicked.'

'It's a blood pressure tester. Where the devil did you get it?' Clegg asked.

'I never!'

'Well, I warned you, Billy. You've got to be very careful. Obviously somebody's trying to set you up.' Clegg glanced at his wristwatch. 'We'd better get rid of it before they come to search and find it here.' He reached out to pick it up.

Billy grabbed it away from him. 'Don't worry. I'll take care of it.'

'Where will you put it?'

'Somewhere they'll never see it.' He ran out of the greenhouse before Clegg could object, and disappeared into the rampant lilac, privet and rhododendron shrubs surrounding the overgrown garden.

Clegg stepped back into the greenhouse and glanced around. He picked up the MOM board and hung it where he had placed it the year before to photograph the trio of pals. It had all been so positive then, he thought. Now it was deadly dangerous. He shook his head ruefully. Perhaps if he and his newspaper had not made the three children quite so famous, they would not now be in danger. He left and headed for his car, wondering what perils lay ahead for him and the three young detectives.

Meanwhile, Billy was in familiar territory, a derelict, shadowy space, like a forgotten footpath; the domain of prowling cats, urban foxes and kids *backnacking*. It ran between the old garden, and the hedges and fences of adjoining properties. Ducking low he crept to where it ended at the walled junction of two streets; Highton Street, perilously steep, and Camm Street, running on the level across the breast of the hillside.

Before the luxury of tap water, Camm Street had given access to a public well, now hidden behind a high wall. It had supplied most of upper Walkley's drinking water, and still flowed to a succession of wells down into the valley and the River Don. He scroamed over the wall and dropped into the secret well-space, where, for years folk had met daily and chatted as they filled their buckets and ewers. Worn smooth by years of use the stonework and pavers were now overgrown and skewed. Between them, the crystal waters gurgled softly as they churned to the surface in the old stone cistern.

Billy hid the sphygmomanometer under a loose paving stone and then started to climb back out to the street. First he peered cautiously over the wall to make sure it was clear. Apart from a patrolling tomcat, the street of grey stone cottages was empty. He was on the point of jumping out when a police sergeant, his old enemy, the sneering driver who had picked him up and taken him to Flood's office, turned into Camm Street from Highton Street. Two other people followed him; PC Needham and Marion Perks, his mam.

Unseen, Billy watched them pass. His mam looked worried. So did John Needham, who kept patting her gently on the shoulders to comfort her. Billy surmised that she was being led to the greenhouse. No doubt the sergeant would pretend to search it and discover the blood pressure tester, while she looked on. This was the very set up that John Needham had warned him about.

Billy felt a sudden moment of panic and wondered if Harry Clegg would still be there. Tears fogged his sight as he watched the three go by. He wanted to wave to his mam and assure her it was all right. He felt scared and confused, but even so, he wished he could be there to see the look on the sergeant's face when he searched the greenhouse and found nothing but broken plant pots.

0o0o0

Chapter Fifteen

If it had not been such a comical sight, Billy might have found it scary: Walter Mebbey wearing clodhopping boots, knee-length gym shorts and a floppy vest. He was straining beneath the weight of an enormous barbell; face bright red, cheeks puffed out, and his eyes shut tight as if to prevent them popping out of his head. Billy feared that at any moment the old guy might explode in a mess of pluck and bootlaces. At last, the barbell headed sedately for the floor. It clanged dully onto a thick coconut fibre mat.

Red and sweating, Walter's cheeks puffed out as he blew with relief. He ran a finger over each separate disc of weight on the bar, checking the total loading. He looked smugly satisfied, and approached Billy with a big smile on his sweating face. 'There's only Julian Creus, at my weight, who could lift more than that, and he gorra medal at the Olympics. He towelled his face and arm pits, bouncing on his short bowed legs and heavy work boots. 'Int thee dad wi thee?'

'He's at work.'

'Good footballer thee dad were. I don't know why he never played for t'Blades.'

Billy almost choked on the thought. 'No, the Owls!' he cried in alarm. 'Me dad's norra Blade.'

Walter chuckled, well aware that his deliberate slip would set the lad's heart thumping. 'Lets gerra cuppa tea and have a talk. I expect that's why tha'rt here?'

'Yeah, I want to know about the Marples' bomb and the bank robbery.'

Walter led him to a quiet corner where a brass tap dripped into a sink. Beside it, an upturned tea chest served as a table for a kettle steaming on a gas ring. Tin mugs, a battered teapot, milk bottle and a jar of saccharin sweeteners cluttered its stained surface.

Walter poured strong tea into two mugs and expertly spooned off the tealeaf floaters, flicking them at the sink where they stuck like sleeping ants. 'I thought thar'd get round to wondering about the Marples' bomb sooner or later,' he said, nodding his hotly pink bald head. 'That's worrit's all about, tha knows.' He stirred saccharin into his tea and sipped it. Billy sat on a gym bench pushed up against the wall and waited for him to go on. 'I guess there were about six or eight of us trapped in that cellar that night.'

'You were there?' cried Billy. 'Chuffing 'eck!'

'Aye, and him from t'paper an' all.'

'Mister Clegg? Yeah, I knew about him.'

'But I can't be sure who else. It were coal black, tha sees. Bricks and plaster and bottles and bits of furniture kept falling on us - even a bloody piano. Folks were screaming. We'd got separated from t'others. It weren't one big cellar, tha sees. It were lots of little uns. Some were snided wi' folk, packed in like sardines. Some just had a few in 'em. Afterwards, they said seventy were killed. It always seems a damn sight more to me. The place were packed out before the bomb. The bar were jumping - you could hardly get served.' He took another swig of his tea and nodded reflectively. 'When we all went down to t'cellars I were walking about playing my accordion. They were all singing and laughing. There were still folk upstairs in t'main bar. I've always thought it seemed a lot more than seventy, but you don't go round counting folk, do you?' He took another sip of tea and pressed his muscular shoulders back against the wall, as if to ease some deeply felt pain.

'The explosion was massive - not loud, but massive. It stuffed your whole body full, like a hard punch that hit you everywhere all at once, even in your feet and fingers. Then there's no air left. You try to breathe in, but there's nowt there. You can't inhale – it's weird. Then it were pitch black. You're blind and deaf and choking. You don't even know if you're the reight way up. You scroam about like a squalling bairn. You can't tell where to go or what to do.' He shook his head and nipped the beginnings of tears from his eyes, blinking furiously. 'Then comes the worst part; the part you never forget. The part that comes over and over in your nightmares. It starts when your ears pop, and at first you thank God for that, but then you hear it. It rushes in on you like a peep into Hell, and you wish you were deaf again.'

'What does?' Billy's eyes were wide with alarm.

'Screaming!' the old man sniffed and wiped a hand over his face. 'They're all screaming – everybody; men and women alike; weeping and screaming – terrible, desperate cries, but thiz nowt tha can do. Tha can't see, but tha knows that folks are dying all around thee. They beg for help, - crying out like bairns - begging for their mams, their husbands and wives. And there's nowt tha can do. You're just stuck there like soft Mick. You can't see 'em. You can't get to 'em, and if you could there's nowt you can do for 'em.' He shook his head, and then towelled his face and neck.

Billy waited, watching the old man. It was obvious that he was seeing it all happen again in his mind's eye. When he spoke again, his gestures were weaker, almost flippant and despairing. 'I scrambled around in t'dark until I found a few others. We joined forces and started searching for a way out. After a bit, the cries get quieter. You're glad for that first, until you realise why. It's because they're dead, or dying – lots of 'em. They can't scream no more.' He sniffed and looked around, taking a moment to compose himself. 'It's when the quiet comes that you realise just how many there were. You even start thinking of yourself as one of 'em – dead – but not yet. And still the silence grows. It get's thicker and thicker.'

He finished his tea and towelled his face again. 'I remember we all stopped digging and waited, listening to that deep, thick silence. It was as if we all knew that we were part of some massive "*dying moment*". The soundless din of souls departing. It's the quietest thing I've ever known.' He sniffed and fished a handkerchief from a pocket in his shorts. He didn't use it, but went on talking. 'After a bit the crying started up again, but not as much, just a few this time; a faint, sobbing few. They sounded far away. We knew we couldn't get to 'em. Then I heard a woman, she sounded closer. I went back to look for her. She had a beam on her leg. She knew she were dying. She was calm and brave – no panic, no self-pity. She just grabbed me hand and died. I think she just wanted somebody to know – not just do it with nobody to see.'

'When I crawled back to t'others, they'd all gone. It was still pitch black. I only had a few matches left so I dint strike one. Anyway, you can always tell if you're alone or not. It's a feeling you get. I realised they must've found a way out, so I scroamed around until I found it an' all. It worra big enough hole to easily get through. I struck a match and saw this passage. It were as clean and sound as a new built netty. I found out later that it was part of some old Sheffield Castle tunnels and dungeons. Seven hundred years old, they told me.'

'The woman who died,' said Billy. 'Was that her grave - Mary Scott?'

'No, I never knew who she was.' He made a strange little harrumphing noise, as if to emphasize the point. 'Mary Scott was different. I think she was with the others; one of those that went out through the hole in the wall before I got there.'

'But she died that night. It says so on the gravestone.'

'Aye, I know it does, but she survived the bomb blast. She was killed later.'

'But you just said she was with the people who found their way out.'

'I think she was, but I told thee, it were dark. I never saw nobody's face. I know Clegg was there because he wrote about it in his paper later on. And I heard the names of two of 'em; Longden and Darnley. They spoke to each other; they were friends, but I couldn't have recognized either of 'em. It were pitch dark remember. And yes, I believe Mary Scott was with them, alive and well at that stage. It was her and another woman, I think they called her Clarry, who found the tunnel, but she had her face wrapped in a scarf, because of the dust. We could hardly breathe.'

'Darnley?' Billy asked.

'Aye, I thought that might interest thee.' He smiled nodding his head. 'Darnley, him they found murdered at Rivelin.' Walter drained his tea mug, tested the weight of the teapot and decided against a second cup. 'I found out later that he was a professor at the university. He had a lot to do with Weston Park Museum, 'an all. He was an expert on ancient manuscripts. Apparently he went all over the world giving talks.'

'Why did you go to his funeral?'

'Two reasons. I know Mary Scott was not the poor woman I tried to help, but in a strange way she represented her - in my head. It might be stupid, but since December 1940 I've often thought of that poor woman.' He paused, silent for a moment, rapidly blinking his eyes.

Billy waited a heartbeat then asked, 'And the second reason?'

'Second? Huh, I was suspicious about how Mary Scott died.'

'Why?'

'Mainly because apart from Clegg, none of 'em – not one, came forward afterwards to say they'd escaped.' He paused again staring at Billy. 'Why not? Why hide it?'

Billy shrugged his shoulders, unable to think of a reason. 'So, they're not in the seven people that escaped?'

'No they're not; that was seven innocent people who the authorities knew all about. Darnley and his lot never told anybody. Nobody knew they were there - not officially anyway. And then, sure enough, about a week later, fire-fighters checking all the tunnels, found her body. It was in the paper. Clegg wrote about it. He said that she was found more than a hundred yards from the Marples Hotel. That's when I started wondering. After the war, Harry Clegg helped me to trace the fireman who'd found her body. He was a volunteer, cos of the war. He said he'd always had his suspicions, because she was found under builders' stone, not rubble from the bomb blast.'

'Builders' stone. What do you mean?'

'Well, it goes back to when they were building the Post

Office, back in 1910. The builders accidentally broke through into the tunnel. Some of their stone fell through. They just left it there and covered the tunnel over again.'

Billy's eyes widened. 'That means Mary Scott couldn't possibly have been underneath it thirty years later, unless ...'

'You've gorrit - unless it were deliberately piled on top of her.'

Billy ballooned his cheeks. 'Chuffin eck! They killed her, didn't they?'

'That fireman told me, him and the bloke he was working with that day both guessed straight away that she'd been killed. Murdered! They told the authorities so, an' all. But all they got was a blank stare. They were instructed to say nowt. The authorities wanted it hushed up because of public morale.'

'Public morale?'

'Yes, they said that because of the blitz and the Marples and everything, people were very upset. The Government wanted to keep bad news to a minimum. It made everybody feel helpless, thar sees. They thought it would be better for - you know - for public morale if they kept it quiet.'

'But it was murder, you can't sweep that away.' Billy stood up, paced around, then sat down again. 'Somebody killed her, why? What had she done?'

Walter sighed and smiled at him. 'I can't tell thee that, lad. Even after all these years, I still don't know. But think of this, Billy, somebody robbed the bank that night. Was it them? If so, was it all of 'em, or was it just one of 'em? Did Mary Scott see something criminal and refuse to be part of it? Is that why she was killed? One person alone could easily have robbed that bank. That same person could also have killed Mary Scott.' He paused letting his words sink into Billy's thoughts, then went on, 'I heard that they split up into two groups to find their way out. Maybe one group never knew anything about it. Maybe the other group did. And now, all these years later, somebody is killing 'em off. Is someone still trying to hide the same wicked secret?'

'If they all robbed the bank, that might explain why they never came forward after they escaped,' said Billy.

'Smart lad, you've gorrit in one. That's why I went to Darnley's funeral. I wanted *them* – whoever they are – to know that I've not forgotten Mary Scott. I'm still around and I still want to find out who killed her. And I want 'em brought to justice.'

'Who did you say Darnley was with that night?'

'I heard him say Longden. He was a posh sounding bloke too, like Darnley.' Walter rubbed his eyes with the heels of his hands and smoothed wisps of silvery hair back over his baldhead. 'I've never found out who he is. He's nowt to do with the museum, not like Darnley was. So they weren't colleagues.'

'But it's weird that none of them came forward to say they'd escaped,' Billy said. 'That definitely makes it look like they were all in on the robbery, or the murder, or both.'

Walter eyed Billy steadily. 'No no, you can't be totally sure about that, Billy. You have to be careful. Those people had all been enjoying a night out in a pub. Maybe some of 'em had wives or families that didn't know about it. They might simply have wanted to keep it quiet for no better reason than that. Don't assume they're all murderers. For all we know they could have just had a secret bit of fluff with 'em.' He rubbed his knees and blew a sigh of exasperation. 'But I've often thought that when Mary's body was found a week later, if you had nowt to do with it, surely that would have started you thinking. You'd have been worried sick that your little secret affair was about to be exposed. My guess is they would have deliberately decided to keep out of it. The trouble is, Billy, you can't sweep evil under the carpet. It sticks to everything. And from the moment they decided to turn a blind eye, they all took a share in the murder.'

'What about the other man, Mister Hepburn? Was he in Marples cellar?'

'I can't say for sure, Billy. I never heard him mentioned, and never saw him.'

'Do you know owt about the dance floor at the swimming baths? I mean how do they get it over the water?'

'I don't know. I suppose it slides out somehow, burra don't know. Why?'

'I was wondering how you'd drown somebody if the dance floor was already in place?'

'Oh, thaz got me wi that one, lad. I've no idea, and to be frank, one murder is plenty for me to worrit me sen abaht.'

*

Yvonne scooped the last shards of the shattered plant pots into a seed box. 'It must've been a cat, or a fox, or sommat that knocked 'em over,' she grumbled. 'The whole stack was toppled. We need a padlock on the door.'

Kick glanced around gloomily. 'Even if we had a padlock there's still a million places cats can gerrin.'

'This was no cat,' Billy said helping to clear up the last few bits. 'It was a chuffin rat.'

The three flopped gloomily into their usual places. Billy began to update them, starting with Constable Needham's unofficial visit to his home.

'Well then, we'd better step up the action,' said Yvonne when he had finished. 'If they're going to play rough with us, we'd better stop messing about and prove 'em wrong - fast.'

'Who's messing about? Not me.' Kick's frown was condemning. He dragged the MOM board out and set it up ready for use.

Billy searched round for the stick of chalk and took stance next to the board. 'We've got two murders – three if you count Mary Scott. We don't know why any of 'em was killed, but there is a something that links 'em all –'

'The Marples' bombing,' Kick suggested.

Yvonne looked doubtful. 'No we don't,' she said. 'We know Mister Darnley was there and Mary Scott, but what about Mister Hepburn? What's his connection?'

'Hepburn the floater? No we can't connect him to owt, can we?' Kick said.

Billy was staring at the MOM board. 'We should talk to Missis Hepburn,' he said. 'She could tell us.'

Kick liked this idea. 'Yeah, she could tell us all sorts,' he said eagerly.

'Yeah, liquorice allsorts,' quipped Yvonne dismissively. 'Why would a poor widow woman talk to us? Especially with her husband hardly cold in his grave yet.'

Billy looked at her critically. 'She might do,' he said lamely. 'She might be glad that we're on the same side.'

'What do you mean, "same side"?'

'Well we're looking for her husband's killer. That puts us on the same side. She'll be glad to tell us whatever she knows. The only trouble is, we don't know where she lives.'

Yvonne sniffed. 'Well, you're supposed to be a detective. You'll just have to find out. And this time, I'm coming an' all. I'm not letting you spoil a breakthrough.'

'Huh breakthrough,' Kick said sourly. 'We'll never even find her address. Sheffield's a big place, tha knows.'

Yvonne tossed her head and flounced to the door. 'You're pathetic, you two. Have yer never heard of a telephone book?'

Kick jumped up from his seat. 'Wharrif she's not on t'chuffin phone? Big eeyad!'

'Then look in the voting - wotsit - register.' She stormed out, slamming the door.

*

'Why didn't they examine Mary Scott's body. Worrit because of the war?'

Doctor Hadfield looked up from under the bonnet of his Austin Ruby, his face smeared with auto grease. Billy had tracked him down to the stately coach house behind the large Victorian villa where the doctor's surgery was located. 'Didn't they? Surely they did.'

'This old bloke I know told me about it. He said they found her body in a tunnel about a week after the Marples' bombing. It was more than a hundred yards from the bombsite, and the rubble on top of her wasn't from the bomb blast. It came from when they built the Post Office on top of the tunnel in 1910. That proves it had nowt to do wi' the Marples bombing. It also proves that somebody had to bury her there deliberately.'

'Crikey Moses! Are you sure about that, old bean?'

'Well tha can ask him thee sen if tha don't believe me.'

'No, of course I believe you. It's just a bit of a shocker to hear it like that.' He wiped his hands on a rag, carefully lowered the old car's bonnet, and secured it. 'There most certainly should have been an autopsy whether it was wartime or not. I'll ask Sarah. Maybe she can shine some light onto it for us.'

'Ooooh, Sarah,' said Billy, a soppy smirk on his face.

Hadfield flashed a scowl. 'You really are a ninny at times, Billy. Have I mentioned that?'

Billy shrugged off the reproof. 'Have you told Marlene that you've dumped her?'

'I haven't dumped her. Sarah and I are just friends, Billy. One is allowed to have friends. I don't need to tell Marlene anything, and I certainly don't have to explain myself to you.'

'Anyway, Yvonne's told her.'

Hadfield looked panic stricken. 'Crickey! She hasn't, has she?'

'Well they are sisters. What d'yer expect?'

He shrugged and wiped oily fingerprints from his car's hood. 'Well, no harm done really, I suppose. To tell the truth we haven't seen much of each other for a while. Actually, maybe I'm *the dumpee* in this scenario. It's difficult to tell with women. You'll find that out for yourself when you're older. One can tell most things about the heart with a jolly good examination and a stethoscope, but the old courtship business is all smoke and mirrors for a chap. Nothing is ever what it seems.'

'Humm, a bit like these murders.'

'Oh come on now. You seem to be making good progress, surely.' He began washing his hands in a chipped enamel washbowl.

'We haven't really,' Billy said miserably. 'We don't know why they were killed, or if they knew each other. We need to question the floater's wife.'

'Missis Hepburn? Oooh no, Billy. One needs to be careful about that sort of thing, old bean. That's a most delicate matter, talking to the bereaved. One never quite gets the hang of it.'

'She might be glad to have us on her side.'

Hadfield looked doubtful. 'No disrespect, Billy, but you're – well - you're children. Missis Hepburn will be finding this a very difficult time. She'll have lots on her mind, quite apart from feeling pretty miserable about – you know ...'

'Yes but when we tell her that we're looking for her husband's killer, she'll be glad that we are. She'll be on our side then. That'll make her one of us.'

'I shouldn't count on it, old bean.' The doctor chewed his lip and frowned. 'I really don't think you should disturb her, Billy. It's absolutely not the thing to do.' He shook his head frowning. 'Forgive me for being frank, old lad, but it'd be dashed bad form. Think of it this way, Billy, it would be extremely - er - *unkind* at this time. Perhaps in a few weeks you could drop her a polite little note - to test the water, but seeing her and asking questions is really not cricket.'

'But we can't wait. We've got to get moving. The cops are after me. I've told you about the Sviggy-mamooter.'

'Humm, sviggy-mamooter,' repeated the doctor. 'You're such an accomplished neologist, Billy. That's a far better name for it, but look here, I'm trying to give you some serious advice. You simply can't burst in on old ladies and trample all over their grief. That's my advice, Billy, and frankly, if you don't take it, it'll be a pretty poor show. Now look here, about that ruddy sphygmomanometer, you'd better sneak it to me at the house. I'll make sure it reappears in my dreaded leader's surgery. But don't let anyone see you with it.'

Doctor Clarissa Fulton-Howard appeared suddenly at the open doors of the coach house. Hadfield blushed and straightened up in panic, overturning the washbowl and spilling its contents on to his shoes. 'Will you be joining us any time today, Doctor, or have you become a motor mechanic now?'

Hadfield shuffled with embarrassment. 'It's my lunch break.'

'Luncheon breaks are for shop girls, Doctor Hadfield. The sick make no distinction between breakfast, luncheon or dinner.' She turned to Billy. 'What's this boy doing here?'

'This is Billy Perks, he's a friend of ...'

'Ah yes, of course, Billy Perks. I've heard you're a very clever boy. Perhaps you're just what we need to solve the mystery of my missing medical equipment. Has Doctor Hadfield told you that we had a burglary here? They stole a sphygmomanometer. The police say they have a lead, but I don't think they have. You'll help us, won't you?'

'I don't think so, ma'am. I mean, the police don't like me butting in on their cases.' Billy shrugged apologetically.

'Surely Billy, you could do a bit of sleuthing for Doctor Fulton-Howard?' Hadfield said, recovering composure. 'We won't tell anyone, will we profes – er - doctor?'

Dr Fulton-Howard forced a smile. 'Of course not. Mum's the word' she said peering suspiciously at the pair.

'Right then, Billy,' Hadfield said. 'Run along now, there's a good lad. Don't forget that little job we discussed. I'll expect you after six.'

OoOoO

Chapter Sixteen

Billy's mam was waiting for him. He found her perched on the arm of the settee like an eagle eyeing its prey. At first she gave him the silent treatment – the worst. Her eyes followed him around the room. He could feel them burning into his skull. What had he done wrong? Panic swelled in his chest. Desperately, he reviewed the day's events, trying to work out what he'd done that might account for her threatening demeanour. Why was he getting the silent treatment? He had seen her look more fondly at dog poop on the carpet. Oh lor, this was serious.

At last she spoke. Her voice was flat and calm – the worst. 'Where have you been?'

Before he could answer, she stood up and peered down at him, her gaze dulled with disappointment. 'Why have I had the police? Why did I have to see what you did? Why did I have to hear all about your wicked behaviour?' She walked into the kitchen and banged pots around, noisily filling the kettle and lighting the gas ring. 'Don't deny it. They showed me what you did, you wicked boy.'

This was getting really confusing. His defences bristled. What could she mean? He'd already found the police trap and sprung it, what else could it be? Suddenly, he felt sick and whoozy. The fear that the police may have hidden something else in the greenhouse, as well as the sphygmomanometer, struck him. He had thought he had been clever and foiled their set up, but no – it looked as if they had beaten him after all. They must have hidden something else to incriminate him. What else could make his mother so upset? 'What is it, mam? I haven't done nowt,' he said miserably.

'I saw them. I saw what you did. All them plant pots ... Do

you know what them things cost? Who's going to pay for 'em? That greenhouse belongs to poor old Mister Eadon. It's only his bad legs that stop him using it. Them plant pots were his property. That policeman called it criminal damage, Billy. Do you hear that? *Criminal* damage!'

Faced with such confusing and accusatory questioning, experience had taught Billy that the most obscure answer would always be the most usefully distracting. 'The new *"old doctor"* wants me to help her find the biscuit barrel burglar. I was talking to her while I helped Doctor Hadfield to repair his car.'

'Don't try to get out of it. What were you thinking - breaking all them plant pots, for God's sakes?'

'It weren't on purpose, mam. It was an accident. And it weren't me, any road, it were Mister Clegg. He did it - him from *The Star*. He did it when he found the sviggymamooter. They'd hidden it there, just like Constable Needham warned us they would. They're trying to make it look like I'm the biscuit barrel burglar. They can't now, can they? Especially now that the new *"old doctor"* wants me to help her to find it.' Feeling immensely pleased with himself, he began setting the table for tea. Ruff followed him around, sniffing his every step, trying to work out where he'd been all day without him.

'You needn't think I'm feeding you, Billy Perks. You'll get no more food in this house. If you can't be bothered to come home for your dinner, or even tell me where you're going, you'll never eat a meal here again. This is not a hotel, you know. You walked out of here at half past seven this morning. Look at that clock. Look at it!' she pointed to the mantel clock, her finger wagging with fury. 'What time is it?'

'I'm sorry, mam. I didn't ...'

'What time does it say?'

'Ten past six, mam.'

'Yes, ten past flipping six and this is the first I've seen of you all day. I've had errands that wanted doing. That dog's been an absolute pain because you left him behind. Your father's on lates. And what are you? What are you, young man?'

On such occasions, Billy was never sure quite what he was. Whenever he did manage to bowl her a googly, and force her onto the back foot, she would become incredibly cryptic. There was nothing to do then but hang his head remorsefully and wait. Eventually she would tell him precisely "what he was" and what she thought about it.

'You are scotch mist, young man. Scotch-flipping-mist.'

There it was, a Caledonian meteorological phenomenon, as Doctor Hadfield had once referred to it. 'I'm sorry, mam.' He had no firm yardstick for assessing the likely punishment for being Scotch mist, but saw clearly that it agitated his mother. So, whatever it was to be, it would not be good.

*

The following day, after washing the cellar steps, filling the coalscuttle, chopping kindling, and carrying two bags of groceries for her, Billy mounted his bike and set out to find PC Needham. He pedalled round the usual places that the local beat coppers used when they wanted to disappear for a while. He started with the Bole Hills with its breezy sports fields, playgrounds, and rugged terraces, beloved of dog walkers and courting couples. Next, he visited the several football and cricket pitches up there. Coppers often hung out on the goal lines to watch the games. The crown green bowling club's rustic timber pavilion was one of their most favoured spots. In there they could mash tea, play cribbage or dominoes, and in bad weather, dry their capes and tunics around a blazing stove.

He eventually found John Needham dozing peacefully, a newspaper over his face, in the police box at the top of Compton Street. Perched precariously on steep cobbles the cream and green painted kiosk was a favourite haunt of cat napping coppers.

'Oh blimey, it's you,' PC Needham groaned, struggling to wake up without falling off the standard police issue high-stool. 'Whaddayer want? Are you going to follow me everywhere?'

'You said you'd find out about the bank robbery,' Billy said with relentless determination.

'Oh –oh yeah. Well I did an' all.' He rubbed his eyes, folded his newspaper and straightened his tunic. 'There's nowt to tell.'

'What d'you mean?'

'Nobody was charged. There's no proof owt was stolen, and nobody admitted to losing owt.'

'I pretty much knew that,' grumbled Billy. 'I wanted you to tell me sommat new.'

'There's nowt to tell. All we know is that somebody got into the bank and found three safety deposit boxes damaged and blown open. None of the undamaged ones was touched. The attending officer even said that it didn't look like any robbery he'd seen before. The owners of the three opened boxes said they had no valuables in 'em, just stuff of no commercial value. Their names weren't recorded because no charges were brought. If the police had thought it necessary they could have applied for a warrant to get the names from the bank's files, but they didn't bother. They probably felt there was no point - and, don't forget, there was a war on.' PC Needham shrugged apologetically. 'I can't tell you owt else. Oh – except that we do know who the police sergeant in charge was…'

'Who?'

'An old friend of yours, a certain Sergeant Flood.'

'Sergeant?'

'Yeah, well he weren't born a chief superintendent, was he? He used to be just a sergeant back then.' He eyed Billy pityingly. 'Everybody was younger once, even Mister Flood.'

Billy looked at the floor, his shoulders slumping with disappointment.

'One more thing, I don't think it'll help you much, but we do know who one of the boxes belonged to.'

Billy straightened up, eagerly. 'Who?'

'The citizens of our fair city; it was registered to the town council, museums and libraries department.' He dug into his tunic pocket and pulled out his notebook. 'I got the name of the bloke in charge.'

'What did they keep in it?' Billy asked.

'Nowt apparently.' He leafed through his notebook. 'Aah, here it is. Mister Dillon.'

'Dillon? Where can I find him?'

'He's retired. He could have snuffed it by now.'

Billy sighed miserably, sagged back against the police box wall and slid down on to his haunches. 'Chuffin eck! I can't never get nowhere,' he groaned.

PC Needham laughed softly. He scribbled on the corner of his newspaper and carefully detached it from the page. 'Luckily he's not dead. He lives at this address.'

Billy perked up and grabbed the note. 'Linekar Road. Crikey, that's not far.'

'I don't know what you expect to learn. I've already told you, the box was empty.'

'Yeah, but you never know,' said Billy, trying to be positive.

He left PC Needham and cycled to Yvonne's house. She greeted him with an alarmed expression and pressed her fingers to her lips to silence him. Grabbing his hand, she led him on tiptoe into her mother's bedroom. There he saw Missis Sparkes feeding bits of bacon to a *Little Owl,* evidently nesting on top of her wardrobe.

Like her daughter, Missis Sparkes too had dark curly hair and large brown eyes, smouldering with Latin beauty. She made Billy think of flamenco dancers. He'd often wondered if she bit roses and stamped a lot. She was loud, eccentric, and oddly haughty. She was also generous, endlessly kind, a laugh a minute and a passionate animal lover. Possibly, only her husband, who tolerated her odd behaviour without a murmur, had a bigger heart.

After a few minutes of owl watching, Yvonne led Billy back to the kitchen. 'She found it on the path,' she explained as she filled two thick glass tumblers with Dandelion and Burdock. 'It looked dead, but now she's gorrit eating bacon. It likes Weetabix an 'all.'

Billy downed the Burdock in one. It was flat and warm. 'Did you get Missis Hepburn's address?'

'I said I would, dint I?'

'Where does she live?'

'Ranmoor. I bet it's a big posh house.'

'Humm, they're all posh up Ranmoor,' said Billy. 'Will thee mam gi' thee a lend of her bike?'

Yvonne shrugged. 'If we go now she'll never know. She'll be "owling" all day. My dad'll be lucky to get fed in the next two weeks, until the novelty wears off, or the cat gets it.'

'First we've got to see an old bloke in Linekar Road,' Billy told her. He led her outside into the Sparkes back garden, recounting what he had learned from PC Needham. Yvonne mounted her mother's bike and pushed off to follow him to Linekar Road.

Like most streets in Walkley, Linekar Road plunged into a river valley. Mister Dillon lived in a small, plain fronted terraced house at the end of a row of identical dwellings. Ornamental iron railings had once bristled proudly along the top of its low front garden wall. Alas, these had been chopped off and taken away *"to make Spitfires"* in the war effort, leaving behind a sad row of rusting stumps.

They found the old man at work in his back garden. Wrapped in concentration he was tapping earwigs into a jar from traps made of upturned plants pots stuffed with straw and hung on garden canes. 'Me and earwigs are just the same,' he said after Billy had introduced himself. 'We both love dahlias.'

He led the pair up his garden path to where a tin of tobacco and a box of matches awaited his attention on a bench seat. As the old chap filled and lit a pipe, Billy explained his mission.

'We never used it,' the old man said. 'The boss told me to get several boxes at different banks, but we never used any of 'em. It was a waste of money. Councils are like that. If I told you how much money they waste every day you'd never believe it.'

'Why did they want safety deposit boxes anyway?' Yvonne asked. 'I would have thought the Town Hall's got plenty of cellars and vaults for keeping stuff safe.'

'Oh some fool got into a bit of a panic,' he said, wafting gently at an inquisitive wasp. 'It was during the first war - 1916. The Gerries were bombing us from blimps.'

'Blimps?'

'Yes, those big balloons, you know – Zeppelins. They dropped bombs all over Sheffield. They killed quite a few people. The council panicked. Somebody said, what if they hit the art gallery or the museum? The council weren't bothered about people or hospitals. They just wanted to protect artworks and historical stuff. So, some bright spark came up with the idea of scattering the city's treasures all over the place in safety deposit boxes. They said that would make sure that if a bomb hit the museum we wouldn't lose everything all at once.' He drew deeply on his pipe and blew smoke at the persistent wasp, before pointing his chewed pipe stem at some invisible fact. 'That particular box was meant for the Ruskin papers. They used to be held at Ruskin's House years ago when it was a museum. There were some of his old notebooks and letters, and even some manuscripts of Keats or Byron. The ones I liked were some letters from Robert Southey to Ebenezer Elliot.'

'Who's Ebenezer Elliot?'

'Blimey! Don't they teach you owt at school?' Mister Dillon frowned. 'Ebenezer Elliot. Haven't you seen his statue in the park? He was a wonderful man, a poet. They called him the *Corn Law Rhymer*. His poems shamed Parliament into repealing the Corn Laws. Working folk were starving to death because of the Corn Laws. He helped to get rid of 'em.'

Billy scowled impatiently. 'So, if you never used the safety deposit boxes, what did you do with the city's treasures?'

The old man laughed soundlessly, his body shaking, his face growing red. Fearing he might choke, Yvonne ran to fetch a cup of water from his kitchen. He sipped it gratefully, spluttering between fits of laughter. After several moments of apparently not inhaling, he wiped a hand over his face and grinned brightly. 'I gave it to the greatest thief in all of English history,' he croaked.

'Tha did what?' hooted Billy.

'Robin Hood. You do know he was from Sheffield, don't

you?'

Billy and Yvonne gaped blankly.

'Aye, Loxley, just round the corner from Rivelin. I gave it all to him to sit on.' He laughed some more making Yvonne wonder if he would survive his upcoming anecdote.

'I had everything crated up and taken to the ganister mine in Little Matlock woods at Loxley. It's where Robin Hood and his merry men used to hang out.' The old man's eyes sparkled with pride. 'Well, the Sheriff of Nottingham never found him, nor his treasure, did he? So where better to hide our treasures? And what better thief to guard them than Sheffield's most famous son?' His silent laughter turned into a coughing fit. Yvonne ran to the kitchen again and refilled his cup with water.

Billy frowned and waited for the old man to drink and recover his composure. When he did, he asked, 'There's a poem about Spring Heeled Jack, did Ebenezer Elliot write that?'

The old man eyed him contemptuously. 'You silly boy,' he growled. Then standing abruptly, stomped away leaving the pair staring after him.

'I guess that's a no then,' said Billy.

Yvonne patted him on his forearm. 'You said it was going to be a waste of time,' she said. 'And it was. Do you realise what that means, Billy?'

He looked at her expectantly. 'What?'

'It means you got sommat right for a change.' She laughed and ran to get on her bike.

Billy shook his head dolefully and followed her. The old man was glaring rancorously from his kitchen window. Billy waved and pulled a face. 'Good luck to the earwigs.'

Out in the street the pair looked up the impossibly steep climb facing them, and started pushing their bikes on foot.

OoOoO

Chapter Seventeen

'We've still got Missis Hepburn,' Yvonne said, ever the optimist. 'Maybe she *will* talk to us. She might even give us a massive clue that makes everything fall into place.'

Billy didn't think so, but Yvonne's positivity was hard to condemn. He pushed his bike the last few gruelling yards up Linaker Road onto the level of Bole Hill Road, and looked back over the lush green of Rivelin Valley behind him. Yvonne was already pedalling away. He mounted up and followed her, assuming she would be heading for Ranmoor, Sheffield's wealthiest suburb, and home to the widow of the man whose death the newspapers had called the "Dance Floor Drowning".

Ranmoor lies to the south of Walkley on the far side of the same lumpy hill. Fringed by beautiful woodland, it looks westward to Ringinglow Moor and the Peak District. In its quiet avenues, mature trees overlook orderly stonewalls, built to defend the stately Victorian villas from the hoi polloi. Behind cast iron gates, evidently unsuitable for building Spitfires, gravelled drives sweep through large, leafy gardens. Ranmoor residences generally display fanciful names, rather than prosaic house numbers. Missis Hepburn lived in one grandly named *The Manse Grange*. Needless to say, it was not a Scottish vicar's house and had probably never contained more wheat or barley than could be found in a small brown Hovis.

Billy and Yvonne cycled up and down the avenue three times before eventually spotting the house name. It was carved into stone pillars supporting a pair of ornamental iron gates. One of them stood wide open, held there by a weft of ivy around its cast iron bunches of grapes and fleur-de-lis.

As Billy entered, he almost fell off his bike in shock at seeing Mister Flood emerge from the gates to the house next door. He had a white, excessively acrobatic poodle on a leash. The animal was out of control. It leapt and twirled in frenzied delight. Flood was kept so busy ensuring it didn't hang itself that he missed seeing Billy and Yvonne pedal out of sight up the Hepburn's drive.

The Manse Grange, a fine Victorian villa, occupied a low rise overlooking lawns that swept away into dense shrubbery. It had enormous bay windows and a front door, glazed with stained glass of churchlike proportions. Constructed of weathered grey sandstone, beneath a Welsh slate roof, it was typical of mansions built by wealthy steel-mill owners at the end of the nineteenth century. A large black dog, barking savagely, charged at them as they approached. It jumped at Billy, knocked him to the ground and licked his face ecstatically. Yvonne cowered behind her bike. Billy wrestled with the dog and struggled to regain his feet.

'My word, he certainly likes you,' observed an elegant, older lady, approaching sedately from the direction of the house. 'He usually bites visitor's heads off. Such a pity. I do hope he's not going soft.' She scrutinized the dog for a second or two. 'It's probably alright. He's an excellent judge of character. You must be acceptable.'

Billy managed to stand and take a firm hold on the dog's collar. He fussed it happily, rubbing its ears and scratching its back. The dog's enthusiasm calmed slightly and he released it to bound over to Yvonne who had secured a safer position behind a tea rose.

'He's very choosy about the company he keeps,' said the woman.

Billy smiled at her. He recognized her as the grand lady he had seen at Henry Darnley's funeral. It was not so much her face he remembered. Veiled and wearing a black straw hat her features had been almost invisible. It was her elegant, yet strangely unsteady walk, and the silver topped, ebony cane she so stylishly brandished.

The dog finished with Yvonne and stalked back to Billy, its head low, ears down, tail wagging so hard that it almost flipped itself off its feet. 'What's his name?' asked Billy

'Rayner.'

Billy frowned. 'Rainer?'

The woman rolled her eyes. 'Yes, Rayner. It's supposed to be funny - a legal profession joke,' she said. 'You see, my – er - late husband was a solicitor. He disliked Lord Chief Justice Rayner Goddard, his least favourite judge. My husband liked the idea of making him roll over and beg for titbits.' She shrugged, giving him a *what-can-I-say* look. 'Lawyers are not very funny, I'm afraid.'

'You – er – you are Missis Hepburn?' queried Billy, trying very hard to talk posh. 'Can we talk to you about your husband?'

'Well I'm – er - not sure, dear. What's it about?'

Billy introduced himself politely and then presented Yvonne, rather as if she were his dowager aunt. He began a long and unnecessarily convoluted explanation of their presence. Yvonne chipped in several times to straighten his meanderings.

'Well I'm not sure, but you'd better come inside for a moment. I think Rayner wants me to talk to you. You've made an ally there, Billy Perks.' She set off towards the front door. 'I must say, you're a rather mysterious young pair. I'm quite intrigued, though frankly, I don't think there's much that I can tell you.'

She led them through a panelled entrance hall, passed a huge grandfather clock, and into a vast, gloomy kitchen. A stern looking woman, whom Billy thought must be many years older than even Missis Hepburn, stood at a massive, scrubbed pine table. She was ironing a floral pinafore. Billy eyed her suspiciously. He remembered he had seen her with Missis Hepburn at the funeral. He felt instinctively that she would be trouble. She was short and wiry with sharp features. Her thin mouth looked as if it had not smiled in decades. On her head, a headscarf, badly arranged into a turban, threatened to fall off any second, but did not. Tangled silver hair protruded from it like barbed wire.

'I'm not stopping ironing to make tea for no girl guides,' she muttered, her pale blue eyes ranging disapprovingly over the pair.

'They're not girl guides, Bridget,' Missis Hepburn said flatly. 'This one's not even a girl. He's a boy called Billy. Rayner would like them to have ginger nuts and milk, if you please.'

They left Bridget simmering in the steam of her ironing, and went through to a bright, opulent room that overlooked the garden. A grand piano, its lid firmly closed, stood in the bay of the huge window. Billy's astonished gaze darted over gilt framed watercolours on the walls. Family photographs and ornaments of silver and crystal covered the room's many polished surfaces.

Rayner, his habits, preferences and idiosyncrasies, dominated the conversation as they consumed ginger nuts and milk. Missis Hepburn talked incessantly. Rayner, it transpired, had not been himself since "Jim's passing". He still waited forlornly at the foot of the stairs every evening, staring at the front door. His bowel movements too, they learned, had, to say the least, become unpredictable.

'Why do you think he was killed?' Billy asked without preamble.

Yvonne winced, her eyes rolling up in her head.

Following so closely on her observations about Rayner's troublesome motions, the question caught Missis Hepburn off guard. She looked flustered, and blinked away a tear. 'I'm sorry but I think you should go now. I feel a headache coming on. I need to lie down.'

Yvonne shot Billy a murderous glance. 'We're really sorry, Missis Hepburn,' she said, gently touching her arm. 'We didn't mean to upset you. You see, we want to know who killed Mister Hepburn. We think it was just awful and we're going to find the murderer.'

Rising from her chair, Missis Hepburn nodded, unable to speak. She dabbed her eyes and pulled back her shoulders, composing herself. 'Please go now, children. I'm sure you mean well, but I really must rest my eyes.'

Outside in the gentrified tranquillity of Ranmoor, Yvonne glared at Billy. 'Yer silly chuff!'

Billy pushed off on his bike. He didn't need to be told how badly he'd mishandled things, but guessed he was about to hear it anyway.

'Haven't you got no sense? Why couldn't you just let her chatter on for a bit? She was eating out of your hand. But no – you have to go wading in like a bull in a Chinese shop.'

'China shop,' corrected Billy.

'If you'd just let her get happier with us in her own good time, you could've asked her owt, and she would've told you. Now we'll never know. You've ruined it.'

'No I haven't,' said Billy. 'Tomorrow I'll go and ask her if I can take Rayner for a walk. I'll take him in Whitely Woods. I'll soon have her back on my side.'

He pedalled to the gate where he had seen Mister Flood and peered round the edge of its tall gatepost. A house, even bigger than The Manse Grange, stood at the top of a long drive through sweeping gardens. 'Wow, I didn't think coppers were rich,' he said.

'It might not be his,' said Yvonne. 'He might be on a case or visiting somebody.'

'Don't be soft, he had a dog. And don't tell me the police have started gerrin little white poodles for police dogs. And where worriz uniform? And another thing, if he was on a case his police car would be here, wouldn't it?'

Yvonne pouted and blinked snootily. 'I only flipping asked.'

*

It took Billy and Yvonne three outings with the dog, plus Kick clearing leaves and weed from Missis Hepburn's small fishpond, before her starchy coolness softened. Unfortunately, as Billy's relations with Missis Hepburn improved, he found himself increasingly at odds with Bridget. When he prepared to walk the dog, she would get its leash down from its hook and hand it over with all the charm of a Gorgon distributing serpents. He eventually discovered that Bridget enjoyed nothing more than stomping for miles across the moors with Rayner. She would tramp for miles in all weathers, returning, sweating like a horse, or frozen stiff, or dripping wet, but always with fire in her eyes and cheeks as red as apples. Billy, it seemed, was trespassing on one of her few pleasures.

In the garden, Missis Hepburn took the trio aside and walked them slowly to the shade of a pale red Acer. The sun beat down from a clear sky, as she explained the reason for Bridget's coolness. Then, she surprised them all by upbraiding Billy, whilst holding Yvonne entirely blameless. She made it plain that she understood perfectly why he was being so polite and attentive. 'You're just trying to get round me,' she said. 'I'm not a fool you know.' She gave him a challenging glare. 'The police will do what's best. You are children. These are matters for the police. It's not something children should be doing. What do your mothers say about you questioning people?'

Billy hung his head feeling caught-out and foolish. Kick surprised him by piping up. 'We know, but there's something dodgy going on. And anyway we like you, we want to help you. Somebody killed Mister Hepburn, but they're not bothering to do owt about it – the police. We don't think that's right. Billy and us only want to help. He's just not good at saying things without 'em sounding stupid.'

Billy gaped at Kick, whose face was a picture of innocence and cordiality. It put him in mind of the saints he'd seen drawn in the margins of old Bibles at school.

'If you don't want *us*, what about your neighbour?' asked Yvonne, nodding in the direction of Mister Flood's house next door, invisible behind a screen of sycamores. 'Would they help you?'

'Huh, chief superintendent or whatever he calls himself nowadays, no thank you. I would not ask them for anything.' She paused, looked at her feet and gathered her thoughts. 'They moved here in the winter of – er -nineteen forty-one. I took flowers round, and some eggs. We had hens then because of the war. Things were in short supply. I thought they'd appreciate it. Missis Flood didn't even invite me in, though she took my gifts, quick enough. I remember feeling quite hurt. I suppose I was being silly, but it didn't seem right. We've barely exchanged a word since.'

She looked at Billy from beneath her cream silk parasol and paused, weighing her options. Billy had been gently teasing Rayner with a well-chewed croquet ball. Even though his playing stopped and the mood changed, the dog was still gazing up adoringly, panting in the heat, his tongue hanging out of the side of his mouth. 'Let's go inside,' Missis Hepburn said decisively. 'It's too hot out here. I think we need some tea.'

Yvonne was glaring at Billy as if to say "Put a foot wrong, Billy Perks, and I'll kill you.".

Scowling murderously, Bridget brought tea into Missis Hepburn's sitting room and clanked it down onto an occasional table. Billy wondered briefly if she might have poisoned it. He watched nervously as the delicate china cups were filled.

Missis Hepburn took her tea with lemon and suggested Billy should try it. Ever the adventurer, he agreed. Missis Hepburn smiled and confessed it was the first time she had seen anyone take tea with lemon *and* milk too.

'Jim preferred coffee,' she said sadly. 'I had trouble getting it for him during the war. He hated the substitute stuff. And, of course, he would never buy anything on the black market. He called black marketeers "Hitler's cellar rats".

'You miss him a lot, don't you?' Yvonne said her voice softened by her growing fondness for her.

'I think of him all the time, dear. After a lifetime together there's nothing one can do that doesn't bring to mind some memory or echo of him.' She looked out of the window, a tear shining on her lashes.

'What do *you* think happened,' Billy asked her softly.

She sighed and looked into the teacup on her lap. 'I don't know, Billy. I've asked myself that question so many times.'

Silence fell on the room. Billy didn't know what to say next. He was terrified she would suddenly clam up and send them away if he said the wrong thing.

'It began when Arthur Shrewsbury died,' said Missis Hepburn, giving Billy a flat stare as though that would explain everything.

Beneath his outward calm, Billy was floundering. What would Sam Spade do, he wondered, raising a questioning eyebrow? It was the look he had seen in so many Humphrey Bogart films. If only he'd brought his trilby hat.

'Arthur was more than just a client,' she said, as if in response to the Sam Spade eyebrow. 'He was a close friend. Jim was shocked at what he'd found in his Will. He was his executor, you see. He had to read the will. He'd not seen it before. A firm in Lincoln had drawn it up, years earlier - some old family friend I think.'

Kick was not following. 'Exec – er …'

'Executor. He had to make sure the will was executed – er – carried out properly.'

Kick nodded and shuffled in his seat, content with the explanation.

'It took him completely by surprise,' Missis Hepburn went on. She glanced at a silver framed photograph on her mantle shelf. It showed a boating party; young women in large brimmed straw hats and summer dresses, the men in boaters and blazers. The trio followed her gaze. 'That's Arthur Shrewsbury, with the champagne bottle on his head. He was always a bit of a card. That was at their graduation. Jim's taking the photograph.'

Billy and Kick stepped up to the picture. A woman, her face partly hidden by the brim of her hat, held the bottle steady on Arthur Shrewsbury's head. Clearly they were having a very good time. Something about the young woman steadying the bottle caught Billy's attention, but he could not bring it to mind.

'What do you mean about the Will?' asked Yvonne. 'What was so surprising?'

'Well, for one thing it explained a mystery that had surrounded Arthur since the early years of the war.' She sighed and looked at the many photographs about the room. 'You see, around Christmas 1940, Arthur Shrewsbury came to see Jim. He was very agitated. They talked in Jim's study for over an hour. He had a question about safety deposit boxes. When he'd gone,

Jim told me all about it. He wasn't supposed to talk about clients, but if he worried about something, such as a client's family, or moral position, he would sometimes discuss it with me. We'd sit right here and talk.' She laughed softly. 'I know nothing about the law, but he used to say that I helped him more certainly than anything. He would suddenly relax and say everything was fine. Usually I had no idea what I'd said to put him at ease.'

'Well, that evening he told me he was worried about Arthur Shrewsbury. Apparently, there'd been a robbery at a bank in town. It was during the blitz. Arthur had a safety deposit box, you see. It was damaged by a bomb and some things were stolen. The problem for Jim was that Arthur wanted to keep it quiet. He was most insistent. It made Jim very uneasy. Arthur had asked him if he could legally refuse to answer police questions about the contents of his safety deposit box. As you can imagine, in wartime, that could make them rather suspicious. Nevertheless, Jim sorted it out for him somehow, but he didn't like doing so.'

Billy shuffled in his sumptuous chair. 'Is that all?'.

'He never told Jim what'd been stolen, if that's what you mean.'

Spotting a sudden cooling in Missis Hepburn's demeanour, Yvonne nudged the dog towards Billy, who absently responded by ruffling its ears. Missis Hepburn immediately relaxed and smiled, watching Rayner push his big head into Billy's playful fondling.

'Jim never knew what was stolen, until eighteen months ago when Arthur died. Jim had to read his Will. When he discovered the extent of the deception to which he had unwittingly been a party, he was very upset.'

Missis Hepburn rose from her chair and paced her sitting room. For a moment, she examined her reflection in a large, gilt framed mirror over the fireplace. It looked back at her sadly. She turned from it and faced the children, a tear glistening in her eye. 'There was a letter in the Will. Its contents worried Jim a great deal. He read it to me.'

Yvonne leaned forward in her chair. 'What did it say?'

'It was a confession. An admission by Arthur Shrewsbury that he'd stolen a document, called the *Pagez Cypher*, from the Bodleian library, whilst a student at Oxford. It said he'd bitterly regretted it and had even tried to return it without anyone knowing. He was about to make another attempt when it was stolen from his safety deposit box.'

'On the night of the Marples' bombing?' Kick queried.

Billy stared at Missis Hepburn. 'What sort of document was it?'

'Very old, and of course, priceless, as such things usually are.'

Yvonne patted the old lady's hand. 'What was it about?'

'At first, we didn't know, and we couldn't find out anything about it, except its name, the *Pagez Cypher*. We tried looking it up - went to the library – nothing. Jim didn't want to risk contacting the Bodleian, until he knew more about it.' She paused and shrugged apologetically before going on. 'There was Arthur Shrewsbury's widow and his two boys to consider, you see? They were innocent. A scandal of that sort can ruin a family's reputation. Finally, Jim decided to ring a friend of ours, a man called Henry Darnley...'

'The man whose funeral you went to,' interrupted Billy.

Missis Hepburn nodded sorrowfully and retook her seat. 'Henry was a professor of history. He was on the board at Sheffield Museum, and an expert on old documents. He rushed round here straight away, the very evening that Jim rang him. He sat in that chair.' She pointed at Billy, who looked at the seat beneath him as if he expected to see some vestige of the event.

'Jim asked me to join them. Henry was very agitated indeed. I'd never seen him so jumpy and cross. He wanted Jim to forget all about it. I must say, I was surprised by that. I rather expected someone with his special interest in old documents to have had a much more responsible attitude to such an artefact.' She paused and shook her head as if still puzzled by Darnley's behaviour. 'Anyway, Henry gave us a potted history of the letter. Its name came about because of a French man called Bastian Pagez. He was a servant and close friend of Mary Queen of Scots. In 1571, in front of the high altar in Sheffield Cathedral, Pagez secretly handed the queen a coded letter, the *Pagez Cypher*. It was from her supporters in France, and told of the gold they had raised to pay for an army against Queen Elizabeth. As soon as she'd read it, Queen Mary cut it in to two pieces and hid them in different places. She feared it might fall into her enemies' hands, but without both halves, it would be useless. Even if they could break the code they would never find the gold.'

Kick jumped to his feet. 'Gold! Crickey, It's a treasure map!' he cried his eyes almost popping out of his head.

Missis Hepburn shook her head.

Yvonne shuffled in her seat, gripped by excitement. Her dark curls fell across her brow. She flicked them back behind her ears and stared at Missis Hepburn. 'Forgive me, but, do you think this is why – er – Mister Hepburn was – er -...'

Missis Hepburn reached out and patted Yvonne's knee. 'I don't know, dear. All I can say is that, from the moment Jim read that dreadful Will, things moved from bad to worse. He became quiet and withdrawn. He couldn't sleep. He let things slip. We even began to lose clients.' She sighed and slowly wrung her hands. 'He looked so tired all the time. It preyed on his mind, you see. Then something happened between Henry Darnley and him. I don't know what. He wouldn't say. But I think they had a fearsome row. Jim didn't want anything to do with him. He even told me not to let him in the house. They'd been friends for years, but certainly not at the end.'

'How did they come to know each other?' Yvonne asked.

'Oh, the golf club, Rotary - you know how these things go. They weren't childhood friends or anything like that, but they both liked golf and angling. They often bumped into each other at their club and at the Turkish baths or the cricket.

Billy's ears pricked up. He wanted to ask about the Turkish baths but stopped himself just in time. 'Fishing? Did they ever fish at the Round Dam?' he asked, not really caring whether they did or not.

'I suppose so, dear. I sometimes went with him. We'd take a

picnic. We both liked Rivelin, but often we'd go to Dam Flask at Bradfield.' She went to her sideboard and selected a framed photograph from her collection. 'This's the pair of them at Dam Flask. It's before the war, of course. I'm behind the camera. It was a glorious day. Henry Darnley slept most of the time. Not surprising really, he ate almost a whole game pie. You wouldn't think it to look at him would you? He was as thin as a rake back then.'

Billy examined the photograph. Two youngish men in baggy shorts. One small and scrawny legged, with a large moustache. The other, more serious looking, is sitting on a small folding stool. He has a fishing rod out over a flawless reflection of soaring hills over the water. Billy pointed to the seated man. 'Is that Mister Hepburn?'

Missis Hepburn made a small, stifled sound and blinked her eyes rapidly. Yvonne jumped in quickly with a question to divert her. 'Was Mister Hepburn in the Marples Hotel when it was bombed?' she asked.

'No, dear.' She looked both surprised and bemused by the question, and dabbed her nose decorously with a lace handkerchief.

'Do you know anyone who was?' Billy asked.

'No. Not many survived that terrible night, you know.'

'I heard that Professor Darnley was there,' Billy said, watching her closely.

Her reaction gave nothing away. 'Oh no, I'm sure we would have heard about it if he had been. He and Jim were very close for years.'

'I suppose you know about the bank robbery, of course?' Billy said. 'We think the bank robbers killed a woman that night, to stop her telling the police. Mary Scott. She worked at the museum, just like the professor.'

Missis Hepburn turned her red-rimmed eyes from Billy to Yvonne and back again. 'Really? But that was ten years ago. I'm certain I never heard about a woman being murdered.'

'She was,' said Billy. 'They found her body in the old tunnels.'

'I don't recall hearing that,' she said. 'Jim never mentioned it.'

'He probably never knew. They didn't find her until about a week later,' said Yvonne. 'Her name was just added to the list of the Marples' dead. They never treated her death as murder. They didn't even investigate.'

'Missis Hepburn,' said Billy, taking the old lady's hand in his. 'We think whoever killed Mary Scott, may have killed your husband too.'

*

Billy would be late home. He fully expected a telling off. His chest tightened with apprehension. His mother would be behind the door, waiting. She would spring on him the instant his toe crossed the threshold. She might even be in the street, or round the next corner. It would not be the first time she had pounced as he had tried in vain to beat the clock.

A short cut through the back yard of the Heavygate Road chip shop through to Orchard Road would save half a minute, but its hidden brick rubble and snaring brambles could be rough on his bike. There was too the matter of negotiating a six foot high retaining wall, down into what he still thought of as the old Star woman's yard leading into the street.

He lay flat on the ground, lowered his bike down over the wall and then jumped down after it. Old man Sutcliffe suddenly popped up, as if out of the ground. He grabbed Billy's shirt, whipped him off his feet and shook him like a rag doll before dumping him down in a heap. Billy reared up defensively, wondering if Sutcliffe had left him with the same number of limbs, eyes, and ears as he had started out with. 'You chuffin idiot, you could have killed me.'

Sutcliffe grinned roguishly. It gave his broad, thuggish face the look of a Japanese kabuki mask. He was a tough old man, the father of eight huge, bellicose sons whose main aim in life was to fight anything that came their way. As paras and commandoes, the older brothers had distinguished themselves in the war. With Hitler now off the scene, the younger members of the brood had to content themselves with bashing Billy and his peers. Weirdly, the old man quite admired Billy, though that was rather a mixed blessing, like having a hungry wolf as a pet. He had formed the attachment during Billy's investigation of the Star Woman's murder.

'Does thi mam still want owd jackets?' Sutcliffe asked lifting Billy to his feet with one hand. 'I've gorra good 'en to sell her.'

'Aye, they're for me dad, for at work, but we don't pay for 'em. Folk gi 'em for nowt.'

Sutcliffe looked distraught. 'But this is a reight good 'en. Thi dad could wear it for Sunday best. It's Harris Tweed.'

Billy frowned. 'He dunt want 'em to wear. It's for keeping the heat off him when he's working in a furnace. He lines furnaces wi' bricks, while they're still hot. Anyway, weer did tha gerrit?'

'It's not nicked, honest, Billy. Straight up. I've just grown out of it, that's all. It's too tight under me arms, burrit'll fit thi dad.'

Billy remembered what PC Needham had said about the Man's Head murder victim not having a jacket. 'Euurgh!' he cried with disgust. 'I bet tha found it at Man's Head, dint tha? I bet thaz teken it off that corpse.'

Sutcliffe looked about shiftily. 'I never did. I found it up Attercliffe,' he said looking injured, but not so distraught that he forgot to pick an area og the city as far from Man's Head rock as possible. 'It were in t'middle of t'road, near t'Adelphi cinema. Tha dunt think I'd tek it off'n a dead corpse does tha?'

'I think tha'd take snot off a chicken's lip if tha thought tha could sell it. I don't think robbing a corpse would bother thee for a second.'

Sutcliffe gaped murderously. Billy wondered if he'd gone too far with this characterisation. Mercifully, the old man's mask slipped. He started laughing silently. 'Tha 'rt a reight cheeky little bugger thee, Billy Perks.' He dusted his palms together in a business-like fashion. 'Look, I'm making thee a reight good offer. I found it. It's not nicked, and all I want for it is ten bob.'

'Ten bob!' Billy pretended to faint with shock. 'We're not made o' money tha knows.'

Sutcliffe frowned. 'OK, how much then?'

'Give it here. I'll tek it to me mam and see what she sez. But I've gorra go now. I'm late. I'm gonna get killed when she sees me.'

'Tha'll get killed if tha tries to diddle me,' warned Sutcliffe. He handed over the tweed jacket. 'I'll be waiting for thee. Everywhere tha goes from now on, I'll be watching thee.'

*

Billy sneaked into the hen house, his favourite secret retreat. He had been making visits there since he was about three years old, but as he got older and bigger, he was finding it more of a struggle to climb in through the hatch and settle on an unoccupied nest box. The hens didn't seem to mind, and he enjoyed their company, particularly their soft crooning clucks as they dozed. He liked the half-light, and the warmth of the place. He even liked the smell, a pungent mixture of straw, bran, and chicken manure.

He leaned into a beam of sunlight spearing in through the hatch to examine the tweed jacket. There was a small stain on the left elbow. Peaty, crushed vegetation he thought, like a grass stain. The pockets were empty. No surprise there; Sutcliffe would have scoured them thoroughly. Taking hold of the jacket shoulders, he shook it into shape, wondering how big a chap Professor Darnley had been. Though it looked in excellent condition, he saw it would be far too small for his dad's muscular shoulders. As he folded it up again, he spotted a faint bluish mark running across the lapel to the shoulder. It was barely visible, even in the shaft of sunlight. He could not guess what it was; paint, chalk, or metal of some sort. It had no detectable texture or smell.

He climbed out of his secret retreat and headed up to his house. The coat would be no use to his dad, and without the contents of its pockets, it offered no clues about the killer either. It would not please Sutcliffe.

His mam hit him with a cucumber as he crept in through the door. It broke in half. One piece skittered under the settee. Ruff ignored it. Wirehaired terriers are not big on salad.

'It were old Sutcliffe, mam. It weren't my fault,' protested Billy rubbing his head. 'He held me up for ages. I wudda been 'ome on time, else.'

'Little fibber. Get to bed!'

'He gen me this jacket for me dad. He wants ten bob for it.'

His mother eyed him unmoved. 'You heard what I said. Get to bed. If you can't be here on time, why should I bother to cook for you? Your dad's never late and he has to come miles from work. So, my lad, no supper, no jacket, and no ten bob! I don't want to hear another peep from you until you're twenty-one.' She paused, her curiosity hijacked by the jacket. 'Is that Harris Tweed? It looks like it.'

'Mam, I'm hungry,' Billy whined. 'I'd 'ave been 'ome early but for Sutcliffe and this flippin jacket. I only did it for you.'

'Get to bed, but get that cucumber out from under the settee first. It's for Sunday tea.'

OoOoO

Chapter Eighteen

'Me mam waint pay thee for it. It's too small and anyway we usually gerrem for nowt from people.' Billy handed the sports coat to old Sutcliffe.

The old man grimaced. 'Burrits like a new un. Look, thiz norra mark on it,' he argued, trying to hide the blue stain on the shoulder with his forearm.

'It is marked, it's got paint on it. Me mam says tha must 'ave pinched it, cos if it were dry cleaned it'd be like a new un.'

Sutcliffe had pulled Billy into a narrow gennel running between the stone garden walls of two large villas, one of them the old St Mary's vicarage. Though only a few yards from Walkley's busy shopping street, overhanging trees, shrubs and creeping ivy, ensured its leafy seclusion. It was a steep cobbled path ignored by most save rogues and tomcats.

'Me mam says it's Harris Tweed, they cost at least forty quid. She says me dad would have to work ages for forty quid.'

'I'm not asking forty quid. I only want ten bob.'

'Look, Mister Sutcliffe, I think tha should take it to t'cops,' Billy said reasonably. 'It's evidence in a murder. Tha'll be in trouble if they find thaz gorrit. They'll think tha killed him.'

Sutcliffe's grizzled visage paled. 'I never…'

'I know that, burrit waint look good if they trace it to thee. It belonged to a murder victim. They're looking everywhere for it.'

'Thee tek it!' he said pushing it into Billy's hands as if it were red hot. 'I don't want nowt for it.' He stared about wildly. 'Tha can say tha found it. They'll believe thee. They never believe nowt I say.'

Billy was not surprised to hear that. The old man was behind every bit of skulduggery in the area, from black marketeering to burglary. Murder however, was out of his league. 'How can I take it?' Billy pushed the coat back into Sutcliffe's hands 'They'll want to know where I found it. They'll examine it wi' microscopes and Bunsen burners and stuff. It's called forensic science. They can find out everything about sommat these days. They'll soon know that it were thee who found it.'

Sutcliffe gazed miserably at the jacket then tossed it aside. 'Tha 'rt a lying little sod, Billy Perks.' He grabbed him by the shirtfront, almost lifting him off his feet. Billy smelled the old man's sour, beery breath. Spittle sprayed into his face as he raged at him. 'Thee take it! Tell 'em tha found it. Tell 'em owt tha wants, burrif tha tells 'em tha gorrit from me, I'll tear thee gizzards out and feed 'em to thee.' He shook him violently and threw him against the wall. Billy fell heavily on his knees and elbows. Sutcliffe bent over him, grabbed him by the hair and pulled his head back. 'Don't forget, Perks, if them coppers come after me o'er this, I'll get thee, and then I'll kill that bloody dog o' thine and all thee mother's hens.'

*

'There, that's fine now; Billy. No real harm done, old lad, just a grazed knee and a bruised elbow. It'll feel sore for a couple of days.' Doc Hadfield resealed a bottle of surgical spirit and popped it into a small kidney shaped medical dish. He moved to the sink in his tiny living room cum kitchen, washed his hands and then searched unsuccessfully for a hand towel. 'Tea's what you need,' he said cheerfully. 'The perfect medicine.' He gave up on the towel and shook his hands, flicking water everywhere before wiping them on his cricket flannels. 'So, aren't you going to tell me who did this to you?'

'No point. It won't change owt.' Billy slumped in the doctor's armchair, his head withdrawing into his tank-top like a wary tortoise.

The doctor filled the kettle and set it to boil on his electric stove. He rinsed two teacups, but not their saucers, and set them on the table with a messily opened packet of digestive biscuits. 'Did I mention that I saw your friendly copper just now, constable Needham. He told me he'd found Darnley's sports jacket. He was very pleased with himself.'

That was quick, thought Billy. Less than one hour had passed since his unpleasantness with old Sutcliffe. He had left the jacket in plain sight at the top end of the gennel, as near to the shops and the tram terminus as he dare.

'How does he know it's Darnley's? It could be any old coat,' said Billy attempting to distance himself from the object.'

'It's Harris Tweed, old bean. It had the poor fellow's name inside it; Savile Row, I expect. A decent tailor always puts ones name in ones jacket, see.' He whipped his suit jacket from the back of a chair, pulled open the inside pocket and showed Billy the label with his name inside. 'See. Huntsmans, always do it that way.'

Billy flicked a glance at it, and bit into a damp digestive. 'What's so special about Harris Tweed?'

'Rarity value, old bean. It has a very short season, the Harris. Every year the clans gather for one week either side of Burns' night, to trap as many Harrises as they can. They use haggis baited traps made from old Tam o Shanters. Some families have been using the same traps for hundreds of years. They pickle the Harris skins in single malt whisky, and sell them to the English to make sports coats.'

Billy shot him a sideways glance, and sniggered. 'You're a nutter!'

'Suit yourself, old bean. I try to please.'

Billy helped himself to a second digestive. 'I'm going to see that bloke at the swimming baths.'

'Which bloke?'

'Stan, the boiler man.'

'Stan, Stan the boiler man,' Hadfield cried brightly. 'It sounds like the start of a Limerick.' He began mumbling, unsuccessfully testing potential lines for a Limerick.

'No, shurrup,' laughed Billy. 'This's serious. I've gotta find out how the floater drowned.'

'Haargh, good question. Sarah thinks it's all a bit fishy. Her boss took her off the case and signed off the autopsy himself.' He clapped a hand over his mouth and blushed. 'Oh Crickey! I wasn't supposed to say anything. Sarah made me promise.'

Billy looked at him crossly. 'What's fishy?'

'I can't say. I promised Sarah. She'll be furious.' He inflated his cheeks and looked around glumly. 'Look, Billy, a chap's word is important, you know. I really didn't mean to tell you. She'll think I've let her down. I'll have to see her and explain.'

'Just tell her the truth. I'll come with thee if tha likes.'

Hadfield didn't hear him. 'I'm on night call tonight, but I'll visit her tomorrow. Maybe she'll believe me – face to face.'

'Take me with you. I'll make her believe you. I'm good at making people believe things. I can look all honest and pathetic and cringing, like this – look.' Billy worked his face, trying different expressions until he thought he'd mastered humility and dejection.

'Crickey, It's Uriah Heap!' cried the doctor. 'She may not believe it, but it'll certainly give her a fright.'

*

Cycling into the city from Walkley was a breeze. Billy loved it. It was easy to forget how high above the city centre Walkley was, until one mounted a bicycle. For Billy, the journey began with a break neck descent of Highton Street, down onto South Road, Walkley's main shopping street. Once there he had to keep his wits about him to avoid trapping the bike's wheels in the tramlines, otherwise acrobatically spectacular dismounts were inevitable. Like most tumbles, it was endlessly entertaining to watch, but never quite so enjoyable to perform.

Beyond Walkley were several switchback slopes of increasing gradient. The real fun started with the plunge over bone shaking cobbles down Barber Road. At the bottom, if ones teeth and wits were still intact, the road levelled off onto an arrow straight stretch, strung out like a tightrope. On one side lay a green park with a fabled deep lake, and on the other, a dramatic tumble of rough tussocks, down into the Don valley. After that came numerous university buildings, another park, and a couple of hospitals.

Billy inhaled the lemony, vinegarish smell of the Sheffield relish factory as he tore past it, and skirted the grim walls of the York and Lanc's barracks. Seconds later, he skidded to a halt outside the boiler room entrance to the Glossop Road swimming baths. The ride had been invigorating and spectacular. He felt great, and as long as he didn't dwell on the gruelling demands of the return journey, he could stay that way.

Stan Daniels was frying eggs and bacon on a shovel, balanced in the furnace door. He beamed broadly as he saw Billy. 'Ayup mi owd. Are tha alreight?'

Billy enviously eyed the sizzling shovelful. 'That looks good.'

'Aye it is, and it's not thine neither. Keep thee mucky paws off.'

Billy laughed and flopped onto one of three battered old dining chairs drawn up to the table in Stan's snug little tea break corner. A seriously thumbed travel magazine lay open on the table at a double fold about Route Sixty-Six in the USA. Billy pulled it towards him and idly flipped a page.

'That's my dream there,' Stan said, coming over and turning the page back to the double fold. 'One of these days I'm going to bike right across America.'

'Why not go on t'train? They've got buffet cars and tables and everything. I've seen 'em in t'films.'

'It's not about just going there,' Stan explained, casting a glance at his frying eggs. 'It's about motorcycling; the journey, the experience, the adventure. And I can nearly afford it too, wi a bit more overtime.'

'Are tha rich?' Billy queried.

'Nah, don't be daft. Would I be working here if I were?' He laughed and swatted Billy's tangle of red hair. 'I had this old auntie. She died and left me a house. It's only a little cottage, burrit's nice and it's gorra lovely big garden. Since my wife died, two years ago, I've been living there rent free and saving my money. Soon I'll have enough, then it's bye-bye Sheffield and hello Chicago. I'll burn up the Mother Road, *route Sixty-Six*, through Missouri, Kansas and Texas, and all the way out to

California and the Pacific Ocean.' He leafed through the magazine, a faraway look in his eyes.

'I wanted to ask thee about the dance floor drowning,' Billy said, brutally bursting Stan's dreamy bubble.

Stan frowned and sighed tolerantly. 'Huh, I thought as much.' He bustled to the fire door and flipped the sizzling bacon and eggs onto a plate. 'Tha can have all the answers tha wants, but not until I've had me snap. I've been here sin' five this morning tha knows. I'm knackered and I'm starving to death.'

'Shall I mash?'

'Aye, good idea, young un. Kettle needs filling.' He nodded at the tap in the corner. Billy filled the kettle his gaze wandering over a rack of steel shelves beside the sink. Bottles, flasks, packets of chemicals, Stan's crash helmet and goggles, and a weird collection of tools and equipment crowded the untidy shelves.

Stan sat down and began tucking into his breakfast, or supper, or whatever meal his stomach's disrupted chronology decreed it was. Billy poured the tea and handed him a mug. 'How did they drown Hepburn with the dance floor in position?'

'They dint.'

'What?'

'It's impossible. You couldn't have drowned anybody under that dance floor.'

'Why not?'

'For one very simple reason.'

'What reason?' Billy was agog.

'There were no watta in it. I'd emptied it to replace a broken filter cover.'

Billy gaped at him. 'But – but they said he was floating in the pool.'

'Aye, but he weren't drowned there.' Stan mopped his plate with a piece of bread. He stuffed his mouth and munched heartily. Billy waited, impatiently watching every chomp. Finally, Stan swallowed, and grinned. He clapped a hand on Billy's shoulder. 'Here, come wi' me. I'll show thee sommat.'

Taking his tea mug along, he led him to double doors at the far side of the boiler room and shouldered through them into a vast, windowless space. 'This's our storage area. We keep all sorts down here. There's a lot to running a swimming baths tha knows.'

He pointed to what looked like a giant pack of cards leaning against a wall. 'See them panels? That's the dance floor. Solid beach, polished like a baby's bum.' Billy was not sure that babies' bums were ever polished, but he got the message – smooth. 'That over there is our electric hoist. We use it for lifting 'em up to the main bath hall.'

Billy looked up at the ceiling, feeling slightly queasy at the thought of so many tons of water sloshing about above him. 'Blimey, I hope it dunt leak.'

'No, don't worry, it's just the Turkish baths above here. The swimming bath goes off in that direction, over solid ground.' He casually pointed away from the storeroom, then turned to point out a small door at the opposite end of the room. 'That leads to the cold plunge for the Turkish baths, and that staircase you came down when old Longden were chasing you.'

Billy gazed around at a jumble of wooden crates and cardboard boxes. There were drums of chemicals, and sacks of salts and powders with strange names. Apart from a weak glow leaking in through the boiler room doors, the only light in the place came down through an access hatch, a couple of meters square, where the electric hoist passed between floors. 'It's dark in here,' said Billy. 'How the eck do you manage to find owt?'

'We're used to it, and everything has its own place.' Stan slapped his big hand on one of the floor panels. 'Contractors erect the dance floor. It takes 'em a short day, or sometimes they do it on a night shift. I drain the pool for 'em. They erect the trestles and lay the floor on top.' He led Billy to where the electric hoist stood at rest. 'Everything has to go up in the right order,' he said with a regal wave over the ranks of floor panels. 'They're all numbered, see. They go up in sequence. It's my oppo, Mike, who usually looks after all this, but he's off sick. He's been off more than two weeks, now. Mind you, them balm-pots in t'office still expect me to do the same work. I've been doing overtime every day since he's been off. I've bin here sin' five this morning, tha knows.'

Billy peered at the hoist trying to imagine how it might work. It comprised a platform with gated sides and reminded him of the wooden crates in which film directors imprison gorillas in Tarzan movies.

'They were late gerrin here that morning,' said Stan. Billy guessed he meant the day of the murder. 'They were supposed to be here at five in the morning. I was desperate to get the pool filled early, because that old pump of mine takes hours. Swimming was due to start at seven that night - Monday - for two hours. That only gen us about twelve hours to do everything. First, they have to take the floor up and store it away down here. Nobody can do owt else while they're doing that. It takes 'em about half as long to take it down as it does to install it – about four hours. When they're done, me and Mike start reassembling the changing cubicles round the pool. They work like folding doors on hinges. We swing 'em flat against the wall when it's a dance, and open 'em out again afterwards. It's a lot of fiddling about. The 'oles never line up for the catches and slide bolts. I hate the bloody job, but at least we can start filling the pool while we do it. That takes ages. 'He held his palms out, as if shadow boxing. 'You see, I like to pump the water in through the filter and treatment vessel, instead of circulating it afterwards.'

Billy didn't have a clue what Stan was talking about, but thought it seemed irrelevant anyway. He was still trying to work out how the victim was put into the pool, and, if he wasn't drowned, how was he killed?

Stan was saying, 'You see, the chorine doesn't mix so well otherwise. You soon get people complaining about sore eyes and itching.' He stopped talking and flipped a switch to demonstrate the electric hoist. 'We'd never manage it without this. It's worth its weight in gold.' He lovingly patted the hoist's electric switch. 'Mind you, the panels have to be in the right sequence. If not, they wain't go down properly. It causes all sorts of buggerment. We had a bit of trouble the last time cos somebody had moved one of the trestles out of order. We never found out who it was; probably one of them daft buggers in t'office.'

Billy climbed half way up a trestle and leaned back over it to look up through the hole in the ceiling where the hoist travelled. High above was the bright glazed lantern roof of the main bathing hall. The cries and laughter of unseen swimmers bubbled down in its bluish glow.

'Anyway, I decided to start pumping without waiting for 'em to get here. I knew they'd be pissed off, but I'd waited long enough, and it served 'em reight for not being here on time.' He laughed shaking his head. 'You should have heard 'em. The air were blue. I think I learned about ten new swear words, and there was only a couple of feet of watta in the deep end when they got here. It were nowt to get fussed about. They just had to paddle about a bit. Of course, I stopped pumping as soon they arrived. And then the shout went up. They'd found the guy floating in the deep end. Somebody rang the coppers.'

Billy followed him back into the boiler room. Stan tapped a couple of gauges and balancing his tea mug, adjusted a wheel valve along the way.

'Well, I still don't see how did the killer got him in under that floor?' Billy said.

'Yeah, that's got me flummoxed an' all. You'd either have to be up there in the baths, and lift up one of the end floor panels so you could drop him in underneath it. But one man can't do that on his own. It's at least a two man job.'

'And what's the other way?'

'What?'

'You said "either", so what's the other one?'

'Er – no, I can't think of another – there int one.'

Billy scratched his chin. 'When they put the floor down, do they start at one end?'

'Yeah, the deep end. The trestle numbers run that way.'

'So you could have half the floor down, and the other half just trestles waiting to be covered over.'

Stan scratched his head. 'I suppose so but ...'

'So somebody could hide a body under the covered half and you'd never see it.'

'No, that'd never work. You couldn't carry a body in and shove it under the floor with all them blokes working there? They'd see thee.'

'Only if they were there,' said Billy. 'But what if they weren't?'

'What d'you mean?'

'What if they were down in the store loading the hoist or sommat? Or, what if it was their tea break, or better still, what if they were all having their snap?' Billy's face brightened. 'Where do they go for their dinner break?'

'If it's nice, some of 'em sit out in the sun. They come in here if it's raining. Sometimes they go round to the pub - the Raven, for a pint.'

'That means they leave the bath hall empty for at least half an hour at midday.'

Stan nodded slowly, his face creased in a fading frown. 'Aye, but you'd have to hide the body somewhere else until you could bring it out to shove it in there.'

Billy frowned and flashed a glare of annoyance at Stan for puncturing his theory. He ran the problem through his mind again, always coming back to the same dead end. The murder must have been committed somewhere very close by. The killer then had to keep the body out of sight until he could hide it in the pool without the dance floor fitters seeing him.

He remembered that the body had been naked except for a towelling bathrobe. That almost certainly placed the victim in the Turkish bath immediately before his death. Billy knew there was a connecting door between the main swimming bath and the Turkish bath. That could have been the killer's route in and out. But how? Once open for business the Turkish bath was always occupied.

'Can I have look round up there?' Billy asked, pointing to the door behind which he knew the service staircase led up to the

Turkish baths. He recalled his escape from Longden.

Stan frowned. 'Aye, but don't say I knew owt about it if tha gets caught.'

Billy left him and charged up the stairs to the door at the top. He eased it open and peered in. Steamy warm air hit him in the face. He wiped the ensuing fog from his spectacles and crept through onto the balcony that ran around the main hot room. He could see down into the curtained alcoves edging the room. A slumbering figure occupied almost every bed and chaise; none were moving, except to snore or yawn.

He descended the stairs, confident that all the bathers would be dozing peacefully. Sweat dripped off his nose as he stepped into the middle of the tiled room and stood on the star patterned mosaic floor and looked about. Nobody noticed him, not even when he extended his arms and twirled around in a balletic challenge to them all. Nobody moved in the soporific clouds of steam, save to snore and mutter unintelligibly.

As expected, he found the door to the main bath hall. He softly cracked it open and slipped through. The snorers in their sweaty, sweet dreams remained undisturbed. Once in the main bath hall he ducked into a vacant changing cubicle and hid there, watching the swimmers. Had the killer done the same? he wondered. He sat down on the cubicle's little bench seat, and gazed, unseeing, at the graffiti carved into its wooden walls.

That's how it was done, he told himself. The killer hid the corpse on a chaise in the Turkish bath. He bundled it up in towels. Nobody would see it was a corpse, even if they looked straight at it. Apart from the snoring, they all looked like corpses anyway. Then, when the contractors went for their midday meal, the killer crept back into the Turkish bath, made sure everybody was dozing peacefully, and dragged the corpse out and hid it under the half-finished dance floor. It remained there throughout the summer ball and overnight - in the dry, empty pool space.

On that morning when Stan was cross at the contractors for being late, he had started filling the pool. The corpse floated on the rising water. When the contractors finally arrived, there was a blinding row with Stan, who turned the water off. The contractors made a start on the floor. They take up the shallow end first so that everything will be in the right order for the next time. After taking up half of it, they find the body floating in about a foot of water. Somebody called the police.

Billy released a sigh of satisfaction. His theory worked perfectly, he thought. 'Simple,' he told himself, certain he had cracked it. He gazed at the cubicle's foldable walls and ran his mind through the whole process again. This time, however, his confidence suffered a slow puncture, and he felt himself slumping lower on the bench seat. The certainty that the corpse had been hidden in full view of the Turkish Bath's clients leaked away. Even worse, the inconvenient question of where the drowning had actually taken place, inflated massively. He puffed out his cheeks and headed back gloomily to the boiler room. He might be a little closer to an answer, he told himself, but he still had far to go.

0o0o0

Chapter Nineteen

In the greenhouse, his two friends listened with rapt attention as Billy reported his latest findings. Yvonne chalked up, rubbed out, rewrote and revised the MOM board eager to capture every nuance of both Billy's evidential and theoretical conclusions. Kick fulfilled the role of MOM board easel to perfection, except for leaning over and putting his head in the way whenever Yvonne tried to write on it.

'But even if he was drowned somewhere else, in the way you say, it still doesn't tell us who did it,' Kick said. He was thinking aloud, his face riven in concentration.

'What about that Longden bloke, the one you said walks like a sergeant major?' Yvonne asked. She was gazing at the whitewashed glass panes above her head, chalk poised, ready to write. 'If he's always in the Turkish bath, like you say, he might know sommat.'

'He might have done it,' Kick warned. 'Is he the same Longden that Professor Darnley was with in the Marples' cellar?'

'He could be,' said Billy, 'but whether he is or not, why would he kill Hepburn?' They're not connected to each other. Hepburn wasn't in the cellar that night.'

'Yeah remember, *means – opportunity – motive*,' said Kick, tapping the MOM board. 'What's his motive?'

'Well, they knew each other; they were both regulars at the Turkish bath. That means Longden had the opportunity to kill him and, with all that water, the means.'

'Opportunity is nothing if you don't have the motive. What's his motive? They're just two old toffs who like dozing in the steam baths. 'Billy argued. 'Without motive you've got nowt – zip - zongo – zoodle – err - zerrrr - nowt!'

'We need to find a connection between Professor Darnley and Longden,' said Yvonne. 'We know they were friends. How long for? Where did they meet? There has to be more to it than that. If we could find that out for a start, maybe we can begin to fill in the other gaps.' She drew a line under Longden's and Darnley's names. 'One of these fellers is the key.'

'Yeah, burrits three men not two; Hepburn, Darnley and Longden, said Kick. 'Only Longden is still alive. That makes him number one suspect as far as I'm concerned.'

Yvonne gaped at him for a second then sneered with disbelief. 'You think Longden killed them both? That's stupid, why would he?'

'Exactly!' cried Billy. 'And until we know if he had a motive we'll not be able to prove anything. But, remember this, Longden knew them both and he had the means and the opportunity to kill them. He also knew Mary Scott. He could have killed her too. He was there in that old tunnel on that terrible night ten years ago. Maybe he stole sommat that night; cash, gold, jewels, and Mary saw him, so he killed her to keep her quiet. Maybe this is all about Mary's murder and not the dance floor drowning. We need to find out the killer's motives. Once we know that, the rest is easy.'

Billy stood up and moved to the greenhouse door. Yvonne and Kick were staring at the MOM board as if willing it to give up its secrets. 'What time is it?' Billy asked. 'I need to tell the doc what I've found out.'

'Oh crickey!' cried Kick, leaping up suddenly. 'I bet it's late. I've not been home for me tea yet. Me mam'll kill me ageeyan. She killed me yesterday an' all.'

Billy shot him a worried glance. 'Me too.'

Yvonne, whose mother was never entirely sure what planet she occupied, let alone what the time might be, looked at the pair with mild amusement. 'He should be home by now. Surgery closes at seven.'

At the mention of the hour, Billy's shoulders slumped with disappointment. 'Chuffin eck! I've missed Dick Barton ageeyan.'

*

'Where the devil have you been until now?' Billy's mam was not pleased. He ducked as he sidled in through the door, just in case she was packing cucumber again. 'You know your tea's at six when your dad's on days. It's on the kitchen side - as cold as charity.'

'Ayup Billy. You missed Dick Barton,' his dad said with a wink. 'It worra brilliant one an' all. Snowy's really had it this time. He's tied up in a cellar that's filling up wi' acid. Thiz no way Jock can get out of the furnace before he burns to death, and Dick's unconscious in a Spitfire plummeting to earth.'

Billy sat at the table grinning. He knew his dad hadn't really heard the broadcast, because he told him the same thing every time he had missed one. Missis Perks set a plate of steaming hot tripe and onions in front of him. His favourite meal; pieces of tripe simmered for ages in milk and onions, seasoned with sage, parsley and pepper, and served with boiled potatoes that should just be about ready to fall.

'You don't deserve it piping hot,' she said. 'I really will let it go cold next time, so make sure you're in at six, or you'll get what for.' She brushed a hand over the back of his pullover as she passed by. 'What this mark?' She rubbed harder. Billy twisted round trying to see over his shoulder.

'Take it off. It looks like paint, or sommat.' She pulled his tank top off over his head and held it up to the window to inspect it in the evening sunlight. Billy juggled his glasses back onto his nose and peered where she was rubbing at the woolly. He saw a faint blue line about six inches long. It did look like blue paint, he thought, but powdery and dry, not fresh. It was like the mark he'd seen on the sports coat. On closer inspection, he saw it was flaky old paint, the same colour and texture as that on the battered surfaces of the dance floor trestles. He remembered leaning back over one of the trestles and guessed he had picked it up then.

*

At noon the following day Billy finally ran Doctor Hadfield to earth. He found him in his tiny living room cum kitchen, cooking eggy-bread. It smelled delicious.

'Can I have some?' he asked, peering into the doctor's frying pan.

'No.'

'Mardy arse!'

The doctor cast him a despairing glance. 'You're such a barbarian, Billy, even despite my best efforts to civilise you.' He flipped eggy-bread onto a plate and carried it to his table. A single rose, displayed in the sort of jar used for taking urine samples, shed its last few petals onto the table as the eggy-bread was set down beside it. 'Be quick, old lad. Tell all. I daren't be late back. I'm at the top of my dreaded leader's death list at the moment.'

'Hepburn wasn't drowned.'

'Yes he was.'

'No he wasn't. There were no watta in the pool.'

'Billy, old thing, his lungs were full of water. I've seen the pathologist's report. I can assure you, the poor man drowned – in water – chlorinated.'

Billy bit his lip and gazed at the sad little scatter of rose petals. 'Then the killer must have drowned him somewhere else and stuffed him into the pool later to make it look like he was drowned there.'

Hadfield chewed, eyeing him steadily. He swallowed and took a swig of tea. 'Hum, it's an interesting theory. It could be why that idiot Longden wants Sarah to let it seem like suicide. Drowning in a large public swimming pool instead of the cold plunge, used only by a small elite, would be far less troublesome for the police. It gives them more variables with which to confuse we lesser mortals.'

'What are you talking about?'

Hadfield was blushing bright pink. 'Nothing, forget it. Forget I said anything.'

'Huh, Longden again, isn't it?'

The doctor looked about him stricken, mouth full of eggy-bread.

'He gets everywhere. I think he's the same bloke who goes to the Turkish baths and was also in the cellar when Marples was bombed?'

Hadfield groaned, dropped his knife and fork with a clatter and struggled to swallow before answering. 'Oh flip! I wasn't supposed to say anything. I promised Sarah...' He blew a sigh and shook his head, furious with himself. 'Look, old bean, I'm sorry, but I can't say another word.'

'You have to!' Billy cried. 'The bloke who was with Darnley in the Marples bombing was called Longden. I have to be sure if it's the same bloke.'

'Darnley? D'you mean the Rivelin victim? Man's Head?'

'Yes.' Billy sat closer and stole a bit of eggy-bread. 'Him and someone called Longden were old pals. I know a bloke who was with 'em in that bombed cellar.'

Hadfield looked worried. 'Crickey! I'd better warn Sarah.'

'I'll come wi thee,' Billy said, a determined frown on his face. 'I want to see her me sen.'

Hadfield gaped, horrified by the idea. 'Good lord! That's absolutely out of the question, old bean. Why on earth would I introduce you to normal people, especially one's friends?'

'I've got to question her; it's vital. You won't tell me owt cos you've promised her not to, burrif I meet her me sen, she'll soon tell me everything. It's called charm. I'm brilliant at it.'

Hadfield almost choked on his lunch. He laughed aloud, trying not to spray Billy with eggy-bread. 'Billy, old bean, forgive me but - *charm* – are you quite sure about that?'

'Oh don't worrit thee sen, lasses like me when I turn it on.'

'I don't mean to doubt you for a second, dear boy. I'm sure you're the very epitome of gallantry and courtly love. However, nothing could induce me to take you anywhere near Sarah. It just wouldn't be cricket. She's very upset about the whole unpleasant business. She'll barely speak to me about it. She wants to forget it all, and I respect her wishes.' He chuckled at some afterthought and wiped his mouth on a crumpled napkin. 'No matter how undoubtedly charming you are, Billy, you are not meeting Sarah.'

Billy glared at him. It was happening again, he thought. As soon as a young woman appears on the scene, it renders Hadfield *useless – unhelpful - dopey*. It was just the same when they were investigating the Star Woman's murder. As soon as Yvonne's sister, Marlene, arrived on the scene, he started keeping secrets and holding out. Just like a lap dog, Billy reminded himself, He had caved in to Marlene's every wish. Now it was Sarah. He glared at Hadfield and tossed his head disdainfully. 'Never mind,' he said. 'I'll just have to question her without your help. It's a free country. You can't stop me seeing who I want to.'

Hadfield shrugged, more amused than threatened. The idea was ridiculous.

*

Grumbling under his breath, Billy left Hadfield to his eggy-bread. He knew where Sarah Becket worked, and immediately set off on his bike to find her. As he pedalled into town, he reviewed what little he knew about her and tried to work out how he should approach her.

At the hospital, he hid his bike in bushes and slipped into the main building, unopposed. At cluttered reception desk, a trio of harassed receptionists were dealing with injured and worried members of the public, as well as lots of paperwork, nurses and doctors. Billy marched swiftly by and looked round for direction signs to "Pathology". He tried various routes unsuccessfully, returning each time to the main entrance to start again.

It was midday. His stomach was rumbling and the memory of Hadfield's eggy-bread still preyed on his mind. The smell of hot food wafted down one of the corridors. He was about to explore it when a hand landed heavily on his shoulder. He spun round to find himself looking up at the biggest man he had ever seen. He was wearing a brown overall, and carried a bucket.

'Are you lost, boy?' The huge man had not moved his lips. The voice had boomed from behind him. It took a second or two for Billy to realise it was not ventriloquism. He leaned sideways and found himself looking up into Doctor Longden's outraged glare. A memory of the pompous pathologist with his willy hanging out through his Turkish bathrobe flashed into his mind, but Longden's cold unflinching gaze quickly banished it.

'No! No - er yes - yes I am,' Billy said, rapidly readjusting his response as a possible ruse took shape in his mind. 'I'm looking for – for – er - my cousin.'

'Your cousin?' Longden nodded slowly, eyeing him with undisguised disbelief. 'I know you don't I, boy?' he said. 'I've seen you somewhere. Where have I seen you?'

'I come here to see my cousin sometimes. Perhaps you saw me then?' Billy saw that Longden was not convinced.

'And your cousin is …?'

'Cousin Sarah,' Billy said, feeling as if the ground beneath him was turning into quick sand. 'Sarah Becket.'

Longden leaned forward, bringing his purple veined nose close to Billy's glasses. 'So, Doctor Becket's your cousin - eh?'

'Yes, she's a pathologist.'

'When was the last time you saw her?'

'Err – Sunday,' said Billy. 'She came for tea.'

'Was it very dark? I mean, presumably you could you see her quite clearly when you took tea with her?'

Billy sensed a trap, but couldn't quite nail it. 'Yes, of course I could see her.'

'Well then, why can't you see her now?' Longden asked triumphantly. 'She's right there under your nose.' He made a grab for Billy and pointed to a group of several young women standing at the hospital's reception desk.

Billy weaved out of his reach. Longden scooped only fresh air almost falling over. 'Ah yes, thank you,' Billy said cheekily. 'I never spotted her there.' The trouble was he still had no idea which young woman was Sarah Becket, and though he racked his brains, he could not think of a single distinguishing feature that might identify someone as being a pathologist.

'You're a fraud, boy,' Longden declared. 'Point her out to me if you're not. Which one is she?' Longden's fierce, accusing eyes burned into Billy's.

Billy knew it was a fair cop. Longden had lured and landed him like a tickled trout. Any second he expected to be booted outside. The brown coated giant was already gleefully warming up. Billy gazed around forlornly, blew a sigh and waited for whatever would happen next, but suddenly, he was inspired to seize upon his own salvation. 'Sarah!' he cried at the top of his voice.

One face, one beautiful face, instantly responded and turned towards him.

*

Sarah Becket was gorgeous. Billy gazed at her adoringly as she nibbled on the thinnest, daintiest, salad sandwich he believed he had ever seen. Her perfect pearly fingernails shimmered softly against the white fluffy bread. Her pillowy pink lips parted just enough to allow the bread to pass between her perfect teeth.

'How long was he dead before he was shoved under the dance floor?' Billy asked her, squinting in the bright sunlight.

After shedding the giant porter, and imploring her to save him from Longden, he had accompanied her to a city park close to the hospital. They were sat on a bench watching randy ducks clatter about on the river Sheaf. From the willow covered bank opposite, a precipitous woody hillside rose up to a cloudless sky. At their backs lay a broad grassy field dotted with people enjoying the sun. Distant tramcars raced noisily between the city and the terminus at Millhouses Park.

Sarah pouted slightly, and tilted her head, giving Billy a concerned look. 'Are you sure Doctor Hadfield wants you to ask me these questions? You seem rather young to be involved with such nasty things.'

Billy's heart almost flipped out of his ribcage and did a somersault. 'The doc's a man of his word,' he said, trying to appear calm as he swallowed his innards and coaxed them back into place. 'He won't tell me owt, unless you say he can.' He showed his palms in a gesture of hopelessness. 'I'm investigating a murder – two, no three actually, and all I get from him is that he promised you he wouldn't say owt about what you told him. That gives me only one alternative.'

'Alternative?'

'Yes. I have to charm it out of you.'

Sarah turned away, hiding her amusement. She pretended to watch an elderly couple playing cricket with several small children, as she recovered her composure. She was not entirely sure why she had saved Billy from Doctor Longden's wrath. She knew a little about him from Doctor Hadfield, and on seeing him in the flesh for the first time, had decided he looked pretty harmless. 'First, you tell me why you think I should tell you.'

Billy leaned closer, his demeanour conspiratorial. 'A long time ago, during the war, a woman was killed. A nice, ordinary woman who hadn't done no harm, nor nicked owt, nor hurt nobody. She was just looking forward to Christmas and to being with her family. But, she didn't live to Christmas. Somebody bashed her head in and buried her under some rocks. They found her body about a week later. For some reason the cops didn't investigate her death. They never even said it worra crime. If a fireman hadn't found her body she would have been left all alone in a stinking old tunnel where Spring Heeled Jack roams. Nobody would ever have known about her.' He looked at Sarah and held her gaze for a second. 'But now, me and my friends know about her. We've seen her grave. It says Mary Scott, born 8th December 1895 - died 12th December 1940. "*Brutally murdered in the Marple's Massacre.*".'

Sarah Becket looked away, dabbed her nose and resealed the small tin lunch box resting on her knee. 'You really care about this, don't you, Billy?'

'I never knew her. She was dead even before I was born. But two more people have died since – both violently, and I think they're all connected.'

'I'm sure there would have been an autopsy in a case like that. It's the law, there has to be for a death certificate to be issued, unless she was declared a victim of the bombing. But either way, the death has to be recorded. The process is perfectly transparent. I'll check the records for 1940.' She wrapped her fingers together nervously and looked down at them. 'As for the murders, Billy, if I were to tell you anything, I would be breaking the law …'

'What, because I'm only a kid?'

'No, it's not that. You're a very sensible and mature young man. I'm sure you could handle it. It's because these are matters of the law. What we pathologists do is try to uncover the facts to help the coroner determine the proper cause and nature of a person's death; such as was it an accident, or suicide, or what was it? I can't share that information with you or anybody else until the coroner has ruled on it. I was quite wrong to tell Reggie. And I would certainly be wrong to tell you.'

'Reggie?' Billy giggled at the unexpected discovery that his friend was called Reggie.

'Doctor Hadfield. I'm afraid he caught me on a bad day. I'd blubbed it all out to him before I had time to think.'

'But how am I going to find out then?'

'I can't help you, Billy; though I must say you're a very charming young man.' She eyed him coyly, a tear glistening on her eyelashes. She turned her head aside and dropped her gaze in a slightly coquettish manner. 'I guess it's common knowledge,' she said softly, 'that Mister Hepburn was knocked unconscious and drowned without struggling.'

Agog, Billy pricked up his ears and leaned closer to her.

'Lots of people know that,' she went on. 'It's not a secret so I can hardly deny it. And, as you probably know, we always check for bruising and signs of a struggle in such cases. We do other things too, Billy. For example, in the case of a drowning there will be water in the lungs. We analyse this to confirm, amongst other things, that it's the same as the water at the death site. If it isn't then we'd know that the victim was drowned elsewhere. Sometimes we can even determine where the water came from, and direct police attention to the actual death site. It's not uncommon for a victim to be drowned in their bathtub at home and have their body turn up in the sea or some lake or river.'

'Where was Mister Hepburn drowned?' Billy asked.

'Billy you know I can't tell you. I've said enough already'

'There weren't any water under the dance floor when he was shoved in there - not enough to drown him anyway. I think they probably drowned him in the little plunge pool in the Turkish baths. It was closed to the public, because they were repairing some tiles, but there was water in it. There are two doors to that room; one from the main hot room, and another for the maintenance staff. It leads to a big storage area and a flight of service stairs. From there you can get to the boiler room. There's also a service lift – sort of hoist - up to the big pool where they lay the dance floor.'

Sarah studied her polished fingernails as if utterly unconcerned. 'It's time I made my way back to work. The corpses will be wondering where I am.' She grinned at him and giggled, but his sullen expression saddened her, and she reached out and stroked his ginger hair. 'Oh Billy, I'm sorry I can't be more helpful. Unfortunately, they took me off the case before I finished the tests, officially anyway. And if someone had done an unofficial test and it proved that Mister Hepburn was drowned in that little pool, they wouldn't be able to use it in court.'

Billy felt a cold shiver run over his body. He watched Doctor Becket rise from the bench and carefully pack her lunch box into her shoulder bag.

'There, that was pleasant wasn't it? I often come here to eat my sandwiches.' She flicked her long blonde hair from her face. 'Well, as charming as you are, Billy, I managed not to tell anything you didn't already know. You and your friends are very clever. You'd already worked out that James Hepburn suffered an injury to the back his head, probably from falling, and drowned in the cold plunge pool in the Turkish baths. But if you ask me one more question, I'll have to report you to the police. You do understand, don't you? I hope we'll meet again. Please give Reggie my love.'

Billy watched her walk away across the grass, her hair swinging in the sunlight. She was lovely. Far too good for "flippin Reggie" he told himself.

OoOoO

Chapter Twenty

'We're stuck,' Yvonne said exasperated. 'We can't prove owt. We don't even have any suspects, except one and he's dead.'

'It's not my fault,' Billy said lamely. 'At least I've worked out how Darnley could've drowned Hepburn.'

'So what? Even if you're right, it still doesn't tie it all up properly.' Yvonne's large brown eyes challenged Billy's faltering, defensive stare and won. The three pals were sitting, swinging their feet, on a low wall beside the Ebenezer Chapel, a Victorian building of rather ostentatious design and proportions, considering the puritanical values of its congregation. Billy was chewing on a woody stalk of liquorice root. He'd been at it for a while and the resultant cud now resembled an orange paint brush.

'Well it's more than tha's come up with. All tha does is write daft notes in your book that never lead us anywhere. At least I could go to t'cops with my – er – my theory.'

'Go on then! Just go and see what happens,' she said. 'They'll laugh at you. You've got no proof. They'll just say there's no case because we've no witnesses and no evidence.'

'We have! What about the paint mark on the jacket?'

'Oh, big deal,' she sneered. 'You mean the mark that's the same as the one on your pullover? If you call that evidence, it could mean it was you who bumped him off.'

Kick laughed, almost falling backwards off the wall.

Billy dropped his gaze, feeling miserable and frustrated. Yvonne had torpedoed every notion and theory he had suggested. And annoyingly, she was right. He could not prove anything. All he had were ideas and fancies.

Yvonne gave him a sideways glance, feeling sorry for him. She gently patted his forearm. There was no satisfaction in knocking

down his ideas, but it was a good way of testing them.
'Remember the MOM board,' she said. 'You told us we must fill its columns with nowt but facts before we can find the truth.'
'That were my idea,' said Kick. 'He never thought of it. It were me.'

Yvonne did not react. She had spotted Doctor Hadfield and a large, snooty looking woman approaching from the high street. Hadfield was carrying a shopping bag and an onion-net bulging with groceries. 'Blimey! Is that his mother?' she asked from behind her hand.

Billy sniggered, accidently spurting yellow liquorice root juice down his chin. 'Nah, that's his boss. She's the one who took over after old Doctor Greenhough.'

'She looks a reight misery guts,' Kick observed gravely.

Seeing them, Doctor Clarissa Fulton-Howard crossed the road to them; her approach was measured, sedate and threatening. Billy dropped down from the wall and tried to palm his tasty cud of liquorice root as decorously as possible. Yvonne and Kick slithered down to stand either side of him. The trio waited with some trepidation for whatever was about to pass.

'How nice to see you, Billy,' Doctor Fulton-Howard said, through an invisible cloud smelling of lavender, surgical spirit, and mothballs. 'I'm so glad I've seen you. Are these your little friends?'

Kick groaned. As Bole Hill Juniors' ace centre forward, he was not fond of being referred to as somebody's *little friend*.

Billy laughed nervously and tried to distract her from Kick's rancorous glare with an animated introduction. 'Yeah, this's Kick – er - Michael Morley and ...'

'I'm Yvonne Sparkes. My dad knows you.'

'Really, good. Humm that's nice.' Clarissa cast around awkwardly, wondering briefly if Billy was quite right in the head. He seemed to be eating a handful of wood and turning himself yellow. 'I need a word, Billy,' she said edging him away from his friends. 'I wanted to ask you how your – er - enquiries are going? I understand you went to the morgue - why on earth would you do that?'

Billy was astonished to discover that she knew of his visit to Sarah Becket. He pulled himself up straight. 'The morgue – what makes you say that? I went to the hospital, that's all. I never went in the morgue. I was visiting somebody – a friend. I never went near the morgue. That'd be too spooky.'

The doctor flapped a hand before her face as if swatting flies. 'Oh never mind, I may have misunderstood. She studied him closely for a second as if counting his freckles. 'Were you there alone? I mean at the hospital.'

Across the street, Doctor Hadfield was juggling clumsily with croquet mallets and canvas chairs, as he tried to make room in the boot of Clarissa's shiny black Rover 75 for her grocery bags. He finished loading them, dusted his palms triumphantly, and crossed the road to join them. Clarissa shrugged with annoyance at his approach. 'Never mind. Perhaps we'll talk again,' she said. 'I would like to hear more about your - er - *detective* work.' She turned to face Hadfield, her expression cold and business-like. 'Is everything in?'

'Yes, I put the eggs on the back seat, as you said. The rest is in the boot.'

'You don't need a lift back, do you, Hadfield?' It was more of an instruction than a question. 'I'm in rather a hurry. I have a private patient in a few minutes …'

Hadfield blew out his cheeks. 'No, thank you. I have a call of my own to make. I would hate to take you out of your way.'

Clarissa plucked the ignition keys from Hadfield's fingers and marched to her car. Hadfield and the trio watched in silence as she started the engine and sped away, spinning the wheels on the tarmac. Kick grinned and pretended to waft exhaust smoke from his eyes. 'Chuffin eck! She could give Fangio a run for his money.'

Hadfield puffed out his cheeks. 'I don't know who she'll wear out first, me, or that poor Rover.' Turning to the children, he found them all staring at him expectantly. 'What's up?'

'You're stopping us getting anywhere,' Billy grumbled.

'That's what's up. We're pretty sure Darnley killed the bloke at the baths, but we can't prove it. The other thing is …'

'We don't have a clue who killed Darnley at Man's Head Rock,' Yvonne chipped in. 'We can't even say how he got there. And why wasn't he wearing his jacket?'

Hadfield appeared not to have heard her and sidled closer to Billy. 'Did I hear my dreaded leader mention that you were at the morgue?'

Billy blushed and stuffed his cud of liquorice root back into his mouth. He chewed steadily, avoiding Hadfield's gaze. 'I was just having a look round and I accidentally bumped into your new girlfriend.'

Yvonne pricked up her ears. 'New girlfriend! What new girlfriend?'

Hadfield's cheeks reddened. He turned, hiding his face. Quickly composing himself, he flashed Billy a rancorous look and turned to face Yvonne, smiling broadly. 'He's talking nonsense, Yvonne. Don't pay him any attention. Luckily for our enquiries, I have a friend in the pathology department. She's been helping us – secretly – so not a word to anyone. Her name is Doctor Sarah Becket. Billy is being rather childish about it, but one day, maybe, he'll grow up and be less of a ninny.'

'I shouldn't count on it,' Yvonne growled distrusting them equally.

'Did you really see Sarah?' Hadfield said drawing Billy aside.

'I told thee I would.'

Hadfield pinched his lips thoughtfully. 'Well, I don't expect you learned anything. Sarah is very careful. She has to be. Most of her work ends up in the coroner's court.'

'I learned plenty. I know that Hepburn died without a struggle. The water in his lungs came from the little cold pool in the Turkish bath.'

Hadfield stared astonished. 'Good Lord! She told you that?'

*

Later on, Kick and Billy lounged in hay in the loft above Mister Leaper's stables. Below them, Beattie stood quietly in her stall, eating her evening meal of oats, and occasionally stamping as if demanding a bit of personal attention from the lads.

'Fancy old Tweedy Knickers coming up to us like that?' Kick said.

'Clarissa Fulton–Howard, please' Billy corrected putting on a comically snooty voice.

'How did she know it was us?'

'I know her,' Billy said. 'She's seen me with "Reggie".'

'Reggie?'

Billy giggled. 'That's his name, old Hadfield. He's called Reggie.'

Kick looked at him crossly. 'What's to laugh about? My dad's called Reg.'

Billy shrugged, hiding his look of guilty amusement. 'I think I should go and see her,' he said. 'There's sommat going on there. Why is she suddenly so friendly? She's up to sommat. I'd like to know what.' He began to imagine what such a meeting might be like and soon wished he had not suggested it. 'Will tha come wi' me?'

Kick thought of Doctor Fulton-Howard's tweed bound frontage, stern face and icy glare and quickly decided that there were plenty more urgent calls on his time.

'I mean to say, all for one and one for all, like we agreed,' wheedled Billy.

Kick blew a sigh. 'Okay, burram not asking her owt. Tharz got to do all the talking.'

They slid down from the loft and squeezed passed Beattie, rubbing her neck and shoulder. The old mare whickered and leaned into their petting, thoroughly enjoying it.

They left the warm, horsey smell of Mister Leaper's yard and tramped thoughtfully up to the noise and bustle of South Road. Trams rattled by bringing home the last of the day shift. At his fruit and veg shop, the owner, Mister Lambton, was only just closing up, even though it was gone six-thirty, an hour past normal closing time. Lambton's fruit and veg, was often the last shop to close. He liked to clear his shelves daily, to make way for the fresh stock he would buy each dawn in the wholesale market. He tossed the lads an apple each and grinned at them – possibly – for Mister Lambton had a squint, and it was never easy to be sure who he was actually looking at. 'Billy! A word?' the fruiterer said, twitching his head conspiratorially.

Billy bit into the apple and followed him into the darkened shop. 'What's up?'

The greengrocer bent close to Billy's ear. 'I hope you're not gerrin thee sen mixed up wi' that owd rogue Sutcliffe,' he whispered. 'Thart not, are tha?'

'No, what do you mean?'

Mister Lambton looked about his empty shop as if to make sure they would not be overheard. 'One of my customers, I can't tell thee who, saw him steal a bloke's jacket from a car down Rivelin.'

Billy's spine tingled with excitement. He almost choked on his apple. 'Who were it? What sort of car?'

'I just told thee, I won't say who it were. I'm just giving thee a warning cos I heard he were trying to sell it to thee mam.' He eyed Billy suspiciously for a second. 'Everybody knows she takes old jackets for thee dad for work. I'm just warning thee, mek sure she dunt buy it. It's stolen goods. She could gerrin to trouble if t' coppers ever found out.'

Billy's shoulders slumped. 'Thanks,' he said miserably. 'She dint buy it. It were like a brand new 'en. He wanted ten bob for it. She dunt usually pay owt for 'em.'

'Good! I just wanted to warn thee, that's all.'

'Can't you even tell me what sort of car it was?'

Mister Lambton shook his head. 'No and tha can try as much as tha likes, but I waint tell thee his name neither, nor nowt else.'

'A man then? It were a man?' Billy's eyes bored into one of Mister Lambton's.'

'Who sez it were?'

'You did. Tha just said "his name" so it must be a man.' Billy gazed at him, willing him to weaken and divulge the name of the witness. 'A man who comes in here shopping,' he went on. 'It's mostly women who shop here. So, that means it's a man who shops for himself. An old man, whose wife's dead?'

Mister Lambton looked alarmed. He groaned and bustled Billy out of the shop. 'Go on, bugger off. I'm not telling thee. And think on, keep clear of Sutcliffe, he's trouble.'

Outside in the street, young men smelling of shaving soap and Brylcreem were dashing for the pubs; The Rose House, The Walkley Cottage and the Freedom. They had just enough time to down a quick pint before meeting their girlfriends in the Palladium queue. Realizing the lateness of the hour, Billy glanced at the time on St Mary's clock tower - ten to seven. Again, he was missing Dick Barton. He groaned and vowed that when he had solved this case he would never miss another episode, no matter what.

The doctor's surgery would close at seven. On the dot, Clarissa Fulton-Howard would close the blind, lock her consulting room window, and leave for home. Billy and Kick stood by her car parked in the surgery yard and waited quietly, their stomachs churning with apprehension.

Betraying no reaction on seeing them there, Doctor Fulton-Howard locked the surgery's front door and marched towards them across the gravel drive. 'What are you two doing here?'

'I thought you wanted to speak to me, Miss,' Billy said stiffly.

'Doctor. You say Doctor, not miss.' She fiddled in her large shoulder bag and fished out the ignition keys for her Rover. 'We said all we had to say earlier today.'

'I was wondering if you were friends with Professor Darnley, or his friend Mister Longden?'

'Doctor Longden,' she corrected. 'He's a physician ... Look, what's all this about?'

'A woman was killed during the war. She was their friend. She worked at the museum with Professor Darnley. Somebody smashed her head in and buried her under some rocks, to make it look like bomb rubble, same as the rest of them in the Marples Hotel. But it wasn't. It was cold blooded murder.'

'You bold boy! How dare you say ... What on earth does that

have to do with Doctor Longden?'

'There was no enquiry into her death. No Ortosky.'

'Ortosky?' she queried.

'Autopsy,' Kick put in, stony faced. 'They just added her to the list of them killed in the Marples' bombing.'

'Well if she was there, and her body was under rubble, what else could it be?'

'It wasn't rubble. It was building stone from when they built the main Post Office. It'd been piled on top of her to look like rubble.'

'Well I don't know,' she said crossly. 'Without the full facts it's impossible to say.' She opened the car door and slid inside, her face fixed like a stone carving.

'Every death should be accounted for, even in wartime,' said Billy repeating what he'd been told. 'This was murder, anybody could see that. So, how come there was no enquiry of any sort and no – er - autopsy?'

Doctor Fulton-Howard stared ahead as grim faced as a York Minster gargoyle. She fired up the shiny Rover saloon and lurched away spraying gravel about their shins.

OoOoO

Chapter Twenty-One

A couple of days later Billy arrived home to find his mam waiting for him. She looked pink faced and worried. 'What've you done?' she asked, meeting him at the door. Billy looked up from the bottom step, his mind rapidly sifting through all possible misdeeds, errors and omissions for which he might be culpable. As usual, there were far too many to concoct an effective defence, especially at such short notice.

'I've had the doctor here,' his mam said.

Billy took a step back and checked her over for any obvious signs of illness or injury; spots, pot leg, eye patch, crutches. 'What's up mam, aren't you well?'

'No, it's not me. It's you!'

'Thiz nowt wrong wi' me.'

'He was asking for you. He was very cross. What have you done?'

'He's me friend, mam. I expect he were just looking for me. I'll go round after me tea and see what's up wi' him.'

'He's not your friend, Billy. He's a doctor, a grownup. You're just a kid.'

'I've told you before, mam, he likes me, and he likes being a detective. We talk about all sorts. He knows all about the ancient Greeks and knights and cricket.'

Billy squeezed passed his mother into the living room. The smell of simmering cowheel and dumplings steamed his glasses up and set his mouth watering. He wiped the lenses with the thumb and finger of one hand whilst fending off his ecstatic dog with the other. It was time for Dick Barton. He pulled up his favourite stool, leaned close to the wireless set and tuned in the programme. His dad glanced up at him from his newspaper, gave him a secret wink, and tut-tutted theatrically. 'In trouble again –

eh? What've yer done this time?'

'I 'aven't done nowt. Doc Hadfield's a pal. I expect he wants to tell me sommat.'

*

Billy and Yvonne waited by Doc Hadfield's car after surgery the following day. They had found it parked in its usual spot in front of the coach house doors.

'Get in!' Hadfield snapped, as he bustled out of the surgery door, one arm in his raincoat sleeve, the other loaded with medical bag, university scarf and a bulging manila folder of patients' notes for the night round.

Mystified, Billy shrugged and squeezed into the little Austin Ruby's rear seat. Yvonne followed and sat in the front. Hadfield took his seat, banging and bumping about reproachfully as he stowed his scarf and bag and stuck the ignition key into the starter switch. 'What the devil have you done?'

Billy shot Yvonne a puzzled frown. She looked back at him equally bemused. 'Me mam said you came to the house yesterday. We've been looking for you since. What's up?'

'You've got to stop all this, the pair of you.' Hadfield turned awkwardly in the cramped driving seat and eyed them both sternly.

'Stop what?' Billy asked.

'You're upsetting people; Sarah – err - Doctor Beckett, and now my boss. I'm in enough trouble with her as it is. I don't need you adding to my problems. You're blundering around like a bull in a china …'

'Is this cos we spoke to old tweedy knickers?' Billy asked.

'She came to us first,' Yvonne said, springing to Billy's aid. 'You were there, Doctor. You saw her come and speak to us. She asked questions. Billy was just going on from there.'

'Yeah, on from there,' said Billy giving Yvonne an appreciative nod for the support.

'Well, she's been on my back all day. She said you and Kick were insolent monkeys.' He was glaring at Billy in the rear view mirror. The Austin's engine shuddered into life and Hadfield drove out of the coach house yard and headed up the leafy street of small Victorian villas. He was staring grimly ahead, his cheek muscles pulsing with tension.

'We asked her about Mary Scott's murder, that's all,' Billy explained. 'We wondered if she'd ever heard about it. I told her there was no - ort – ort – autopsy. I thought she might've known why. Did you know she's pals with the top man in the morgue?' He caught Hadfield's eye in the mirror. 'We were polite and careful. We weren't rude nor nowt. Then, all of a sudden, I don't know why, she got all stroppy and drove off.'

'You've got to stop this, Billy,' said Hadfield. 'First, you go bowling into Sarah's – er - Doctor Becket's luncheon break, then you upset my boss. It's got to stop.'

'Well, if we're nuisances, Doctor Hadfield, that's nothing compared to poor Mary Scott. She's dead,' said Yvonne passionately. 'Somebody killed her, and whoever did it has been free to enjoy over ten years of life since then; ten Christmases, ten summer holidays and ten birthdays stolen from poor Mary Scott. Whoever did it thinks they got away with it. Well I don't think they should. I think the least we can do is try to catch them, and it doesn't hurt anybody to answer a few questions, even snooty old lady doctors.'

Hadfield almost ran off the road, surprised at Yvonne's opinion. 'Crickey! That's quite a mouthful.' He shrugged feeling somewhat chastened. 'Huh, you're right, of course. Look, I'm sorry...'

'And I never upset Sarah Becket,' Billy said, piling in righteously. 'She were reight nice to me. I could've 'ad one of her sandwiches, burra dint. I were reight polite and just had a crisp.'

Hadfield pulled up outside his small octagonal house and switched off the engine. He sat in silence for a moment then grinned at his passengers. 'Jam and tea, anybody?'

A few minutes later, between sips of tea in the doctor's living room, Yvonne leafed through her ubiquitous notebook, attempting to summarise the progress of their investigations. A raspberry jam seed clung distractingly to her cheek as she spoke. Billy interrupted her indiscriminately, thereby ensuring their collective analysis was hopelessly random and confused.

'The paint mark on the jacket is crucial,' Hadfield said reviewing what he had heard. 'At the very least it connects the jacket to the dance floor timbers. It's a pity we can't prove that Darnley was actually wearing it at the time. Even so, it's pretty strong circumstantial evidence that he was either in that basement store, or under the dance floor. Both are locations in which he had no good reason, or authority to be.'

Yvonne wiped her face with her hand, but missed the raspberry jam seed. 'We need to make sure the coppers check that out, Billy,' she said, adding a line to her notes. 'They need to make all the same connections that we've done.'

'Yeah, I'll tell John Needham,' said Billy. 'He can pass it on to 'em.'

'Old Clarissa has been really strange these last couple of weeks,' Hadfield mused into his cup. 'I thought she might be out to get me, and now - well I know she is. She hates me you know. Can't think why.' He spread jam on another slice of bread and butter. 'She's as looney as a booby.' He laughed at some recollection. 'I remember she sprained an ankle at Oxford, and used to stamp around with a croquet mallet for a walking stick. Woe betide anyone who sniggered. She's still as crazy as ever, only nowadays she's only got me to pick on. She accuses me of everything that goes wrong. I think she even blames me for that scratch on her car. I'm waiting for her to pounce. It's like the sword of Damocles. Mind you, she might not. I think she knows very well who did it. She's been hitting the sauce, you know. Oh heck! I shouldn't have said that. For God's sake don't ever repeat that. Promise, promise me now, both of you.'

Yvonne and Billy mumbled their assurances and nodded bemused. 'What do you mean, "hitting the sauce" what sauce?' Billy asked.

'Nothing. Forget it. The old girl has a lot on her mind. She's under great stress.'

The three sat in silence for several moments, deep in thought. 'What will you tell Marlene?' Yvonne demanded suddenly, her tone dramatically restrained. Billy sat up, surprised, and saw that her dark brown eyes were boring into the doctor's.

Hadfield reddened slightly. 'I haven't seen your sister for several weeks, Yvonne,' he answered feebly. 'We – er – we had a drive out to Bakewell, as you probably know. It was nice. We picnicked by the river. In fact, we enjoyed it so much we promised ourselves a picnic at Chatsworth the following weekend. I don't know why, but it never happened. We just sort of - *stopped* - seeing each other.' He was quiet for a moment then shuffled in his chair before speaking again. 'To be frank, I rather thought that Marlene had dumped me. Though of course, you're absolutely right, I do owe her an explanation. However, I can assure you, Yvonne, Doctor Becket has nothing to do with it. We're just friends, nothing more.'

'Huh, not for long – Reggie,' Billy quipped, grimly sarcastic.

'Shut up!' Yvonne snapped at him, her angry reaction finally dislodging the raspberry jam seed from her cheek.

*

John Needham listened as Billy explained how he thought Professor Darnley could have drowned James Hepburn, and made sure the body remained hidden until he was far from the swimming baths and suitably armoured by a concrete alibi.

Billy had tracked the constable to the Rivelin Valley gardening association's clubhouse. It stood on a hillside at the edge of an expanse of allotment gardens, wedged between a school and a shirt factory. It was a dusty, wooden shed, about twenty feet wide and forty long. As dry as snuff, it smelled of blood-fish-and-bone fertiliser, tobacco and sisal. Around its walls were piled stocks of garden canes, bales of hessian, hanks of raffia, plant pots, balls of sisal, bags of lime, and a clutter of used gardening tools for sale. A couple of notice boards displayed posters announcing details of various gardening events and competitions. Want-ads, mostly scrawled on fag packets, convened in irregular groups on the wooden walls like moths at rest.

When Billy finished his presentation, John Needham agreed to pass his theory about the paint-stained jacket to a friend of his on the forensics' team. He led him to a corner of the shed where a wooden bench seat had just become vacant and sat down. He immediately turned his attention to Darnley's possible motive. 'They were well acquainted, you know' he said, thinking aloud. 'They went to the same clubs and social events …'

'And the Turkish baths,' Billy said sitting beside him.

'But not best mates. Close acquaintances, as you might say.'

Billy wondered whether to tell him about the unknown witness to Sutcliffe's theft of the coat from a car in Rivelin Valley, but decided not to, not yet anyway. First he would try to trace the man himself, and the car too. At worst, old Sutcliffe could answer both questions. If he couldn't trace him by other means he could always try to persuade the old devil Sutcliffe to talk. Huh, fat chance, he thought.

A group of allotment holders shuffled noisily into the shed, breaking the dusty silence. They all carried vegetables or blooms. Nodding amiably at John, they huddled round an old packing case, which served as a desk, kettle stand, and samples table, and laid out tomatoes, early chrysanthemums, and runner beans for inspection. John looked at his watch and jumped to his feet. 'Crickey, I've got to go,' he said. 'I'll get back to you about that paint mark, but I need to know where that jacket was *really* found. I know you showed it to your mother …' Billy blushed and started to protest, but John stopped him. 'Don't worry, I won't tell anybody, but I want to know how you got it. Whoever gave it to you could be in big trouble. I might be able to help them if they just tell me where they found it.'

'I can't say definitely, but I'm sure it was nicked when it came to me.'

'I expect it was that old rogue Sutcliffe. Don't worry, you don't have to tell me, but you'd better warn your mother anyway, just so she knows.' He edged towards the group of gardeners and pretended to pinch a tomato from their display. 'They look rubbish,' he teased. 'I can get better at Lambton's for tuppence a pound.

'Bugger off, them's prize winners,' cried one of the men in mock outrage.

John placed a hand on the man's shoulder. 'Here, do any of you lot know owt about a tweed sports jacket found on the vicarage wall. I've a good idea who nicked it but ...'

'Huh, no prizes for guessing who that might be,' one of the men said. His friends nodded and mumbled agreement. Billy heard the name Sutcliffe bandied.

John nodded, agreeing with them. 'Aye maybe, but nobody saw him do it. I can't nick the old rascal without proof. So keep your eyes and ears open, fellas. It could be important.'

Billy followed John Needham out into the fresh air. The allotments overlooked Rivelin Valley Road where a solitary car could be seen whining along beneath the lime trees. They parted at a low wall that encircled the shed. The constable went left towards the school and the police station at Hillsborough, Billy took the steep hill up to Walkley. He was due to meet his pals in the old greenhouse. By the time he got there, the sun was low in the late summer sky. Windows in the few houses scattered above Stannington Deer Park and Roscoe Wood reflected its brilliance like signal mirrors telegraphing across the tree filled valley.

Yvonne did not move as he entered. Notebook in hand, she was sifting through the various bits of evidence and conjecture they had collected. Kick had been in the city's main library poring over newspaper cuttings. He had been looking for reports of anything odd around the day of Professor Darnley's death. The only thing he had found, and copied out in his spidery hand writing, was a report that Doctor Longden had complained to the City Council about the lack of public access to *The Turret House,* an intact Tudor dwelling on the site of Sheffield's old Manor Castle ruins. In the article, Longden claimed that it was a public building of enormous historical interest and should be open to all.

'What's that got to do wi' owt,' Billy demanded sourly.

Yvonne sat up and faced him defiantly. 'Manor Castle was one of the places where they kept Mary Queen of Scots locked up. Kick did very well to spot it.'

Kick gaped bemused. 'Oh no, I dint do it for that,' he said as if defending himself against some terrible accusation, 'I just saw it was Longden's name so I copied it out.'

Yvonne sighed with despair and slumped back into her deckchair. She fanned her face with her notebook. 'You two don't know nowt. I'm gonna have to solve this case me sen.'

She folded Kick's hand written copy of the newspaper clipping and placed it in her notebook. 'Manor Lodge was quite new then,' she told them. 'It would have seemed like a modern, luxurious mansion, fit for a queen; and she was a queen. That's why they put her in there. I've seen inside it. My dad took me last summer. Somebody lives there, but you can go and look round. You have to knock on the door and ask the woman to let you in. She's called the custodian. She can't stop you going in, even though she lives in it.'

'Well why is Longden complaining then?' asked Billy.

Yvonne opened her notebook and consulted Kick's scrawled extracts. 'He wants it open all the time so you can visit when you like without some old woman following you around coughing if you touch owt, or if you stand on a window seat to feel at the curtains to see if they're really hand embroidered.'

Billy frowned. 'It says all that?'

Yvonne ignored him. 'Most of Manor Castle is in ruins, except that bit. It's called the Turret House. It's gorra flat lead roof. The custodian told us it was one of the queen's favourite places to sit and embroider in the summer time. Another woman called Bess of Hardwick, used to sit there with her. They were best friends. They sat together for hours embroidering.'

Kick suddenly remembered something from the article and interrupted eagerly. 'Yeah and the sewing they did is on show at Hardwick Hall and - er – somewhere else.'

'The Victoria and Albert Museum,' Yvonne said. 'That's in London, my dad says.'

Billy sneered. 'So what. It doesn't tell us owt. It's nowt special.'

Kick faced him angrily. 'Well it is special, big eeyad! If tha'd just listen and stop being a mardy arse, tha might learn sommat.' Billy shrugged and waited, disbelief sculpting his frown. Kick gathered himself and spoke calmly. 'The thing is, I went and saw that old cust – custodian woman. She were very upset by this story. She said Longden went there all the time. She told me she never stopped anybody going in, and that all he ever did was look at the lead roof.'

'Chuffin eck!' Billy leaped to his feet and began pacing up and down the greenhouse aisle, rocking dead plants and raising dust. 'There must be sommat hidden up there, but what? Longden must know what it is.'

'The golden treasure?' Kick cried his eyes sparkling.

'No, don't be daft,' said Yvonne. 'It has to be sommat small. I've been on that roof. There's nowhere to hide anything bulky like treasure. It's just an empty square with the flat lead roof that you can walk on. It's got battlements all around the edge to stop you falling off. There's a little tower in one corner with a narrow door in it. That's where you go in and out to the spiral staircase up to it.'

'I bet you could hide a letter up there,' said Billy, 'in a crack or between the old stones.'

'Or under the sheet-lead roof, more like,' said Yvonne.

Billy became increasingly animated. He paced about, breathless with excitement, as he tried to form his ideas into a credible theory. 'Remember what Missis Hepburn said? What if it's that letter – the Pagez Cypher?' Yvonne and Kick stared at him, transfixed, as they waited for him to go on. 'That could be what Longden's looking for.' His animated expression invited them to see his point. 'It could be the other half of the Pagez Cypher,' he went on. 'Remember, Missis Hepburn said, the queen cut it into two pieces so her enemies couldn't read it and find the gold. I bet that's it.'

Kick laughed dismissively, but could offer no alternative

suggestion. Yvonne was eyeing him thoughtfully, her expression showing her deep reservations.

Even more animated in the face of their doubting, Billy pressed on. 'I bet Doctor Longden discovered that Professor Darnley had the part of the letter that was stolen from – er – wotsit - Oxford library, and was looking for the other half.' He pointed at Kick. 'We've gotta go to Manor Castle and look at that lead roof. I think Longden has just handed us a massive clue.'

'You really think it's about that letter?' Yvonne's tone betrayed crumbling disbelief.

'Or if it's not that,' said Billy. 'Worrif she left a message telling somebody else where to find it?' He turned his back on the pair and again stalked the length of the greenhouse. Then, turning suddenly he said, 'I read that they were always moving her about so that she couldn't build up regular contacts to pass messages to.'

'So, now you're saying she hid the letter somewhere else and left instructions on the Turret House roof so her friends could find it.' Yvonne shrugged and sneered at the idea. 'This is crazy, Billy. You're just making it up. You're flippin dreaming,' Yvonne snapped. 'You can't just invent things, Billy. You said yourself we need evidence. Nothing you've said can be proved. It's not evidence.'

Billy sighed and flopped into his deckchair. He glared sulkily at Yvonne as she went on, 'I agree that we should go and have a look for ourselves, but we shouldn't expect too much.' She closed her notebook and eyed Billy scrunched up in his chair. Her expression softened. Maybe she was being a bit hard on him. 'All I mean is, let's not get carried away,' she said apologetically. 'We'll need an adult to go with us. That custodian woman doesn't let kids in on their own.'

'I'll get the doc to take us,' said Billy. 'He can drive us in his car.' As he spoke he pulled a bunch of newspaper clippings from under his tank top. 'I've got these. I saved 'em specially.'

Yvonne gave him a wry smile.

Billy pretended not to notice, and smoothed out the ragged

leaves of newspaper. He selected one containing a photograph. 'Do you know who that is?' Kick and Yvonne looked closely. It was a photograph of a silver haired man, wearing a dinner jacket. He was standing at a long table, laid out with white linen, silver candlesticks and Christmas holly. Seated around him were other equally distinguished looking men, evidently listening to him. 'That's Longden standing up. The bloke next to him is Professor Darnley. They were at a dinner at the Cutlers Hall last Christmas. Harry Clegg was there too. You can see him standing in the background. It says here that he wrote the story.'

'Crickey! You went right back to Christmas,' said Kick awed by Billy's diligence.

'Hum, amazing what you can find when you're tearing up lavvie paper,' Yvonne quipped harshly. Billy flinched and pretended not to have heard her.

'What was the dinner for?' Kick asked.

Billy scanned the cutting to remind himself of the details. 'It's for the reopening of part of the museum that was damaged in the blitz. The thing is, as well as Longden, Darnley, and Clegg, I can also see the back of Chief Superintendent Flood's scrawny bonce - look.' He stabbed his finger at one of the happy diners' heads. 'I bet James Hepburn was there too and maybe even that Arthur Shrewsbury bloke who died. What chance have *we* got? How can we hope to beat 'em? These toffs are all in each other's pockets. They cover up for each other all the time.'

'Maybe, but at the moment, they're killing each other too,' said Yvonne, adding chillingly. 'There's at least one corpse at that table. Who's next I wonder?'

*

'I'm sorry I was a little short with you, Billy.' Clarissa Fulton-Howard had pulled her car over beside Billy as he walked along South Road, a weighty shopping basket on his arm. The morning rush hour was over. Shopkeepers were busily building their pavement displays of everything from apples to tin bathtubs. He tried to move away feeling hemmed in by her sudden appearance and the shopkeepers' frenetic activity. The sleek Rover 75 revved gently and edged forward to keep up with him. 'I appreciate you coming to see me like you did. I had no right to be so offhand.' She eyed his basket of groceries. 'Can I give you a lift with those? Highton Street isn't? Get in, I'll drop you off.'

Billy felt hijacked. He meekly climbed in, his feet tangling with a pair of muddy walking shoes as he slid along the Rover's leather rear seat. The doctor laughed and shrugged. She hadn't expected him to sit in the back. 'Ooh, just like our new queen – hey?'

'Sorry, d'yer want me in the front?'

'No no, it's fine,' she said and steered out from the curb to head towards Highton Street. Billy liked the Rover, and didn't fear for a second that it might not manage the steep climb up to his house.

'Tell me, Billy; how do you know Doctor Longden?'

'I don't know him really. I just know who he is. I've seen him at Glossop Road baths.'

Clarissa Fulton-Howard sniffed with unrestrained disapproval. Billy watched her in the rear view mirror. She saw him watching and switched her expression to a sickly grin. 'Oh really. Do you like swimming?'

'Yes I do. Usually I go a lot during the school holidays. There was a murder there, you know. A man was drowned. I never heard if they had a proper post mortem. Do you know if they did, doctor?'

'Oh I'm sure they must have,' she said. 'The circumstances of a death – any death, must be properly established before a death certificate can be issued. The law is very clear. For example, what you told me about the woman in the old castle tunnels, that can't be right. I'm sure someone has misled you there. I'd like to hear more from you about that.'

'I don't know anymore. That's why I'm trying to find out.' He rolled back deep into his seat as the Rover turned and began the steep climb up Highton Street. 'It's halfway up on the left,' he said as a half empty bottle of scotch rolled out from under the front seat and bumped into his foot.

'You and your friend seemed very well informed. Your questions were most succinct.'

Billy wasn't sure what that meant, but thought it sounded like a compliment. He eyed the scotch and pushed it gently out of sight with his foot, wedging it in place with one of the muddy walking shoes. 'Well that's cos we thought you knew Doctor Longden, and as he works at the morgue, he should know something about it. I mean for example, was he working there back then, during the war?'

'Yes, but of course he wasn't the director then, just a humble pathologist.'

'So, who decides who they will – you know – autopsify?'

The doctor smiled but understood him perfectly. 'It depends,' she told him. 'Sometimes it's the police or the coroner's office. Most often it starts because a doctor, either in hospital or in general practice, refers it because they feel the circumstances warrant clarification.'

'You mean they suspect sommat dodgy?'

The Rover pulled into the curb and stopped. 'Will this do?'

'Thank you.'

'Billy, I want to help you. We should work together. I may be quite useful to you.'

From her window, Missis Perks watched her son's arrival in the shiny Rover. She recognized the driver and felt a flush of panic as she looked to reassure herself that her son was not injured or sick. Seeing that he was not, her relief, nevertheless, was short lived. A second flush of panic swept over her as she prayed he would not invite the doctor inside for a visit. There was no sugar left in the basin, and the tablecloth was not her best one.

'Billy you must stop bringing doctors home. They're not stray kittens,' she said as he shouldered in through the door with her groceries. 'What have you done this time?'

'Nowt. She just gen me a lift. I'm her friend now. She likes me.'

Missis Perks looked around her living room despairingly.

Billy wondered briefly whether she was looking for a cucumber. 'Honest mam. It's alright. She just wanted to ask me about the murders. I asked her sommat an' all. She's norras bad as she looks. Though she does use too many mothballs.

0o0o0

Chapter Twenty-Two

The newspaper article Kick had found and read out in the greenhouse, had greatly intrigued Yvonne. The memory of it still played in her mind. Why was Doctor Longden so concerned about public access to the old Manor Lodge? He was a pathologist not a historian. If anyone was going to write complaining letters to the council about such matters, she expected it would have been Professor Darnley. She wished that Billy's improbable theory could be right, if only because her desire to investigate the place was becoming irresistible. As the only one of the three to have already visited Manor Lodge, she felt duty bound to take charge of an expedition, and began by encouraged Billy to enlist Doc Hadfield as their "tame grown up" and chauffeur.

The following morning Doc Hadfield parked alongside Manor Lodge's crenulated ruins. With some relief, he released his unruly, squabbling passengers onto the pavement. Kick immediately scroamed up the wall and railings surrounding the castle site, for a better view.

'Get down!' snapped Yvonne. 'That's exactly the sort of thing that'll gerrus chucked out before we gerrin.'

'If we're norrin they can't chuck us out,' Kick replied defiantly, but slid off the wall nonetheless.

The sixth Earl of Shrewsbury built Manor Lodge, sometimes called Manor Castle, in 1516, as a luxurious hunting lodge. Mary Queen of Scots spent most of her fourteen years in Sheffield, imprisoned behind its walls. She is said to have found it most comfortable, which is probably why her ghost walks the old Turret House, the only remaining habitable part of the ruin.

'Right, now listen here.' Yvonne grabbed their attention and pointed to a sturdy, three-storey building topped with battlements, six ornate stone chimneys and a copper domed turret. It was a forbidding cube of weathered grey stone, that had stood sentinel before the crumbling grandeur of Manor Lodge for well over four hundred years. 'The woman who lives in there is called the custodian,' Yvonne explained. 'She's in charge of the place. She'll only let us in if we look sensible and polite. So, no messing about, or acting daft.'

The two boys sneered comically at each other. 'Oooo get her,' cried Kick. Doctor Hadfield raised an eyebrow. Such was the intensity of Yvonne's delivery that he was unable to stop himself from feeling included.

'She won't let you touch owt, or climb on owt,' Yvonne went on. 'So you have to behave yourselves.'

Hadfield nodded, already scared of the unseen custodian. Billy and Kick likewise, though they yawned and pretended to be bored.

They approached the Turret House in silence. Its iron bound door creaked open spookily before they could reach out to its bulky doorknocker. A bespectacled, middle-aged woman popped her head out from the dark interior and welcomed them with a warm smile. 'You're my first today. Welcome to Manor Lodge. This is the Turret House. Have you been here before?'

'My dad brought me,' said Yvonne, as the woman led her into the gloomy interior. Billy, Hadfield and Kick followed. 'We went up onto the roof.'

'And you can do so again today, my dear,' the woman said, closing the door behind them and beaming brightly. 'It's lovely on a sunny day like today. But imagine how much more wonderful it must have been when all around was beautiful deer park, right down as far as the river and the walls of Sheffield Castle.' She looked around dreamily, her hand encompassing the imagined scene with balletic grace. 'The earl and his friends would be hunting and feasting, even the fine ladies …' She paused and bent to take a closer look at Kick, who had stayed in the background, skulking behind Doctor Hadfield.

'Not you again!' she cried. 'I hope you don't think I've changed my mind. I told you the last time, I won't answer any more of your rude questions.'

Billy panicked and sacrificed Kick to keep the woman onside. 'Sorry about him, lady. He can't help it. He's got a mental disease. It makes him rude and bad mannered sometimes, but he doesn't mean it. He's harmless.' Surprisingly, Kick did not seem to mind being labelled as some sort of lunatic, and stiffened the idea by smiling soppily.

The woman backed off a pace. 'He was here the other day, asking silly questions. I wouldn't let him in.'

Billy distracted her with his newspaper cutting showing Darnley addressing the dinner-jacketed diners. 'We're doing a project for our school,' he announced. 'Did this man ever come here?' He pointed to Darnley.

'I don't think so, but he did,' the woman said sourly and pointed to Longden, shown seated beside the professor.

Billy looked at her in surprise. 'This one?' He jabbed a finger at Longden's image. 'Are you sure?'

'Excuse me, but I am not stupid, young man. I recognize him very well. He used to come here all the time, often several times a week.' She screwed her eyes up in concentration for a moment before going on, 'Doctor Longden, he's called. He's a very important man.'

Billy smiled apologetically. 'Er - yes, you're quite right. It's just that I thought you would know this man too.' He pointed to Darnley again, and held the clipping up for her to study at closer range.'

'He's very important too,' Yvonne put in shrewdly. 'He's a professor …'

At that, the custodian appeared much more interested. She gave up glaring at Kick and peered closely at the photograph. 'There was another man, once,' she said. 'I suppose it could be him. In fact I think he was the one who brought Doctor Longden the first time.' She took hold of the clipping and peered at it even closer. 'Is he from the museum?' She looked up for a second, seeming suddenly very pleased with herself. 'Yes I remember him. He's from the museum. Very important I believe. He came with the doctor that first time. Then they came together a few times after that, but then this one stopped coming and only the doctor came.'

'Why did they come so often?' Hadfield asked. 'Oh, forgive me, madam. I'm Doctor Hadfield. I'm responsible for these young – er - historians.'

The woman smiled coyly and shook Hadfield's extended hand. 'Oh, doctor, how nice to – err – yes –err –... I don't know really.' She leaned close to Hadfield and whispered, 'I suppose you have to look after him.' She flicked her eyes in Kick's direction, who was twitching his head and smiling gormlessly. Doctor Hadfield avoided the question by looking around the room as though fascinated.

'Doctor Longden often made rubbings from the lead sheet on the roof. I don't know why. We can go up and look at it if you like?' She waved them towards a narrow oak door, but stopped suddenly, struck by something she had seen through her window. 'Ooo–ooo-ooo dog! Look dog.' She squeezed by them and ran outside waving at a poor man walking his dog. 'No dogs! You there, no dogs. This is a historical monument, not a toilet for dogs. Get away, get away.' The alarmed dog walker ran for the gate, dragging his puzzled pooch behind him.

Kick looked at Billy and raised an eyebrow. 'She's a nutter,' he whispered out of the side of his mouth.

Doctor Hadfield gave the now flustered custodian a slightly embarrassed smile as she returned. 'Shall I go first?' she said in a singsong voice. 'It might be best if I did.' She opened the narrow oak door to reveal a spiral of steep stone steps immediately behind it. 'It's three floors up to the roof. It keeps me very fit.' Her laughter echoed in the dark stairwell.

Hadfield had a job keeping pace with her and the children. At the top, the woman pushed open another narrow door. Sunlight poured in. They trooped out into its brilliance, blinking and squinting, to find themselves on a flat, square roof, covered with lead sheet and surrounded by battlements. 'Here we are, the Turret House roof.'

Billy scroamed up the battlements to gaze out from the old walls, perhaps, he thought, as Mary Queen of Scots had done during her long imprisonment. In every direction, the steel city swarmed over its seven hills and five river valleys; certainly not the vista the Scottish queen would have enjoyed.

The custodian coughed and harrumphed loudly to net their attention. 'He used to kneel down here and stare at the lead floor. He brought a special kneeler with him; like from a church - a hassock. He had it in a Gladstone bag with all sorts of things; a magnifying glass, scrapers and pencils, notebooks and drawing paper. He would lay a sheet of paper over any special marks he found and rub the pencil over them to make a copy, you know like brass rubbings in a church.'

'What was he looking for?' asked Billy.

'I don't know. I'm not nosey with my visitors, young man. All I can say is he came two or three times some weeks. It went on for several weeks.'

'So he doesn't come anymore?' asked Yvonne.

The woman shook her head. 'Not for four or five weeks.'

'Huh, not since Darnley was killed,' Billy whispered to Doctor Hadfield.

After a quick tour of the rest of the Turret House, the custodian ushered them back to the entrance on the ground floor. Doctor Hadfield dropped some coins into a collection box and thanked the woman. Billy said, 'I wonder why he stopped coming?' He did not mention the professor's death.

'Humm yes, it's a puzzle,' said the woman. 'I remember, he was very excited the last time he came. I think he must have found whatever he was looking for. He put a ten shilling note in the box,' she nodded at them, as though such a thing could barely be believed, 'Humm, ten shillings. Then he rushed away, very excited.'

'Did he say what he'd found?' asked the doctor.

The woman shook her head looking very disappointed that he had not. 'I'm sorry,' she said apologetically.

The trio trooped out behind Hadfield. In silence, they climbed into the car. After a while Billy said, 'I feel worse now than before we came.'

'Well, don't,' said Hadfield cheerfully. 'I know we didn't learn very much, but it wasn't a complete waste of time.'

Billy blew a sigh filling out his cheeks. 'I was hoping for more.'

Kick glared at both of them. 'What are you talking about? We dint get nowt. It were a total waste o' time.'

'No it wasn't,' said Yvonne. 'For one thing, we can now safely assume that Longden knew about the letter, the Pagez Cypher, as well as Darnley did. Otherwise, why else would they have been scratching around the place where Queen Mary was imprisoned.'

'Yes,' agreed Hadfield thoughtfully. 'The letter could be the thing tying this place to our enquiries. I can't see any good reason for two professional men to be so obsessed about it otherwise, especially Longden.'

'I agree. I think they were looking for the other half of the letter,' said Billy. 'We know the queen cut it in two. How did she hide both halves? Where? She was watched all the time.'

Hadfield started the car and pulled away from the curb. 'Good question, Billy. It would not have been easy for her. History records that all her visitors, whether high born or lowly, had to endure body searches and very close scrutiny on their way in and out of her presence, to prevent her sending secret messages. The authorities obviously knew of the existence of the letter, because the Bodleian's half of it came from Wallsingham's papers after the Queen's execution. But where is the other piece?'

'Wallsingham?' queried Billy.

'He was Queen Elizabeth's spy master. He was ruthless and very good at his job. Old Queen Bess charged him with keeping the Scottish Queen locked up and quiet. He had to ensure her complete isolation from her friends, and any possible conspirators. Poor Mary endured regular searches of her apartments and belongings. The poor woman had no peace, or privacy, just a head full of useless secrets.'

'You realise what this means, don't you?' Billy said, thinking allowed. 'If Longden knew about the letter, which now seems certain, he could have stolen it from the bank. He was there that night ...'

'Opportunity,' said Kick, raising a finger.

'All he had to do was walk into the ruined bank and pinch it.'

'Means,' said Kick, flicking up a second finger.

'And he gambles on the horses, said Billy quietly. 'Stan Daniels says he's lost a fortune gambling.'

'Motive!' cried Kick, trying, but failing, to successfully raise a third finger in the count. 'He was skint. He needed the money. He was after the gold.'

Billy turned and looked back at the Turret House. His face was grave, his shoulders slumped in misery. 'If that's all true, it means it could be him who killed poor Mary Scott.' He looked at each of his friends in turn. 'That's why there was no ort – ort – autopsy. He covered it up. Once again, he had the means, the opportunity and the motive. Nobody else did. Not Darnley or Clegg - or ... anybody.'

When they reached South Road, Billy asked the doctor to drop him off outside Lambton's fruit and veg shop. He waved cheerio to his pals and for a second or two watched the little car drive away. Turning to Lambton's shop, Billy read the whitewash lettering on the window announcing irresistible offers on beetroot, onions and cabbages, and marched inside.

Mister Lambton groaned and looked up at the ceiling as he saw him. 'Oh no, what does tha want, Billy?'

'You've gorra tell me,' Billy said stomping up to the counter, 'otherwise it's called aiding and abetting, and withholding police evidence. You can go to jail for it.'

'Worriz!' cried the distraught fruiterer.

'I've been informed, by a police officer,' said Billy putting on his most authoritative voice, 'that you will be arrested if you do not tell me what you know about somebody nicking a coat out of a car down Rivelin.' Billy was now bluffing for all he was worth. He stood in front of the shopkeeper and shrugged despairingly, as if utterly helpless in the situation. 'Thiz nowt I can do to stop it, Mister Lambton. It's not my fault. They warned me that if I don't tell 'em who told me about it, I've had it. I'll go to jail - and so will you.'

Mister Lambton fixed one of his eyes on Billy's face, and quivered pleadingly. 'If I tell thee, does tha have to say it were me?'

Billy's spirits soared, but he struggled to cling on to his mask of dejection. 'If you tell me who it is, I promise, I'll keep you out of it, even if they torture me with red hot needles.'

Mister Lambton glanced shiftily around his shop as if it were not already obvious that he and Billy were alone. 'It was Ernest Tomlinson. You know him, the budgie breeder at the Cocked Hat cottages.'

Despite fireworks and streamers of delight going off inside his head, Billy kept a straight face as he expressed his deliberately muted gratitude. He marched out the shop and set off to find the witness. Half an hour later, he had the full story. Ernest Tomlinson had seen old Sutcliffe steal the jacket from an unlocked car parked outside the Rivelin Hotel at Man's Head. The car was a grey one, make unknown. Mister Tomlinson, a vinegarish, chain smoking skeleton of a man, had grunted sourly and said, 'It's the same make as belongs to that stuck up fancy piece at the post office.' Billy immediately ran round to the post office, but could find nobody there fitting the description of grey car owning stuck up fancy piece.

*

It was late afternoon when Billy and Kick cycled down to see Stan Daniels at the swimming baths. Billy had cajoled Kick into joining him for the journey by saying he needed his opinion on the boiler man. His real reason however, was to conduct an experiment to ascertain how clearly one could hear people talking in the cold plunge room, through the "chunter pipes" in the boiler room. Stan would certainly have helped him, but Billy was concerned that he might have taken over, or interfered in some way, whereas Kick would do as he was told.

Stan was delighted to see them. He made a big fuss of Kick, letting him wear his bright red crash helmet. Kick could not be parted from it, or the motor cycling goggles that came with it. He wore both even as they drank mugs of tea in Stan's cosy little tea break corner. After a while, Stan looked at the pair apologetically. 'I'm sorry lads, I don't want to rush thee, but I've gorra knock off soon. I've been here sin' five this morning, tha knows; twelve hours straight. Them in t'office said they were going to get me an assistant. Huh, weer is he? Scotch bloody mist! I have to do it all me sen.'

Billy smiled secretly. He'd heard it all before from Stan, a man who so obviously loved his job that he really didn't care how long he had to spend doing it. He drained his tea mug and told Stan about his proposed experiment. He explained that he wanted to go into the cold plunge room while Kick listened at the duct opening for the "chunter pipes" then he'd come back and ask Kick to repeat whatever test he had set for him.

'Well tha'll have to do it thee senz,' said Stan. 'I've gorra get ready to leave. I've no time for malarkying about.' He left the lads to it and bustled off to his jobs.

Billy's experiment confirmed that anything said in the cold plunge room could certainly be heard in the boiler room, provided the listener stood close to the pipe duct opening.

'Just like you said,' Billy told Stan. 'You can hear every word.'

Stan looked up briefly. He was packing the ex-army gas mask bag he used for his snap tin and milk. When he finished, he donned an old leather flak jacket and slung the bag over his shoulder. Kick reluctantly returned the crash helmet and goggles to him. Chattering all the time, Stan led them to the exit, pausing here and there to switch off a light or reset a valve. Billy wondered how, without Stan to coax and coddle the steam and water, the place would survive overnight without a flood or explosive disaster.

Outside, the street throbbed and clattered with rush hour traffic. Stan mounted his motor cycle, a scarlet Royal Enfield, and kicked it into life. The admiring, envious lads took a step back as he grinned at them, saluted, and roared away into the traffic.

OoOoO

Chapter Twenty-Three

Behind the relish factory, near the entrance to Walter's ramshackle gymnasium, Billy and Kick played heading tennis with Kick's ubiquitous tennis ball. They were waiting for Walter Mebbey to arrive. The evening sun was still above the rooftops though the relish workers (relishers I wonder) had knocked off leaving only lazy wafts of steam and the sweet, vinegary smell of Sheffield relish on the air. A couple of the gymnasium's patrons arrived, bandy legged, barrel chested blokes. They grinned and joined in the heading tennis. Weightlifters, Billy guessed. They had slicked back hair and towels round their necks. They might each be capable of lifting a Co-op dairy float with one hand – and the horse too, but mobility was not their forte. The youngsters were soon three games up.

Walter arrived a few minutes later. He looked shiny and pink and smelled of shaving soap. 'Ayup sithee!' he cried greeting the lads. 'It's the dare devil detective and his pal, England's next centre forward. What's up, lads? Tha must want sommat.'

He shoved a large, wear polished key into the door, jiggled, and teased the lock with it for several tense moments before throwing open the door with undisguised relief. The smells of stale sweat, rosin, liniment and dusty floorboards tumbled out to greet them. Walter inhaled it happily and proudly strode into his kingdom. Over the next half hour, an oddly shy dribble of men and boys arrived to join their fellows. They chatted quietly as they stripped down to gym shorts and vests, and began shadow boxing, chinning the bar, or skipping before the serious business of pressing weights began. Billy sat on a bench seat in a corner talking with Walter. He gently led the old man back along the years to the few hours he had spent in the tunnels under the bombed out shell of the Marples Hotel.

'Well there's Sally Snape,' Walter said, responding to a question from Billy about Mary Scott's friends. 'She was at school with Mary Scott, but I think they lost touch after Mary got married.'

'Married?' Billy hadn't thought of that. 'What about her husband then? Do you know where he lives?'

'He's been dead years. He died afore the war; pit accident - Treeton colliery. He were only about twenty-five.'

Billy sighed and leaned back against the wall. 'She dint have much of a life, did she?' he said sadly.

'No, but she weren't a misery or owt like that. She were a nice woman. She helped people, 'Walter told him. 'I dint know her that well, but I know she loved her job at the museum. She started as a cleaner, but they let her do more as she went on. She even used to set things out for displays. I think it was him who encouraged her – the professor.' He lowered his voice. 'To be honest, I think there might have been a bit of – er - hanky panky at some time. I don't know for sure, but tha knows - putting two and two together ...'

'Was Professor Darnley married?'

Walter straightened up suddenly. 'Here, now don't go building that up into sommat, Billy Perks. I dint say they were having a passionate affair or owt like that.' He puffed out his cheeks and shook his head, annoyed with himself. 'I shouldn't have said owt.'

'No, but was he married? That's all I'm asking thee.'

'Yes, but I've only just found that out, and I don't know where they lived; somewhere up Fulwood or Ranmoor I think.'

Ranmoor again thought Billy. There's a lot going on behind those high walls and big posh gardens. Walter scribbled an address on the edge of his newspaper and carefully tore it from the page. 'Here, this is Sally's Snape's address. As I say, I don't think she'll be able to tell you much. You'll just have to see for thi sen. I don't know the house number, but it's the one with lots of plants in old buckets and chimney pots. Her husband grows stuff everywhere; potatoes, sprouts, strawberries, he can grow owt – green thumbs tha sees.'

*

The school holiday was almost over. Billy was desperate to wrap the case up before he was sent back under the acid gaze of Sister Pauline and her gang of butterfly wimpled furies at St Joseph's school. Most of his teachers were nuns; Sisters of Charity, mainly from Ireland. They were notoriously strict, and devout believers in corporal punishment. Headmistress, Sister Pauline, could pick off a giggler at fifty paces with a blackboard rubber, and had eyes in the back of her head, even despite her huge, starched wimple. Billy shuddered as he pedalled passed his empty school. Only a few more days and a thrashing with the slipper or cane would become a constant threat, and in his case, a frequent reality.

He was heading for each of the three post offices in the area, Crookes, Rivelin, and Walkley. He needed to find out which one of them had a "fancy piece" with a grey car, so he could establish the make and model of the vehicle from which Sutcliffe had pinched the jacket. He finally found it at Rivelin post office. The postmistress, a delightful young woman with long earrings and wrists wrapped in jingling gold and silver, confirmed that her car was indeed the grey Morris Oxford, parked beside her shop.

If Longden owned a similar car, it would go a long way towards proving that he had taken Darnley to Man's Head that fateful day. To be sure, Billy decided he would also check with the landlord at the Rivelin Hotel, where Ernest Tomlinson said he had seen the car parked. If everything checked out as he expected, he would then tell PC Needham and the case could be quickly wrapped up.

He left the "fancy piece" at Rivelin post office. He could now confirm the make and model of the car. He had also learned what a delight a "fancy piece" could be. He cycled up to the football practice pitches on the Bole Hills. As expected Kick was there. Billy had to wait a few moments for him to complete a triumphal run, having just scored with an overhead bicycle-kick. It was an impressive feat, and would have been even more so, had there been any opposing players, in particular a goalkeeper. Kick ran around for a while, making hissing noises intended to sound like a crowd of forty thousand fans. It was some time before he stopped and recovered the ball from an imaginary net.

'We've got to go to t'hospital where Longden works,' Billy said.

Kick did not look keen. 'Why?'

'I want to find out what car he drives. If it's a grey Morris Oxford, we've gorrim,' Billy announced triumphantly.

'What do you mean?'

'It was that old misery Tomlinson, him who breeds budgies, who saw Sutcliffe pinching the professor's jacket from a grey Morris Oxford. He said it was parked outside the pub at Man's Head.'

'Did he get the registration number?'

Billy puffed out his cheeks, annoyed at his pal. It was certainly a flaw in the evidence, but not a serious one. 'That dunt matter. I'll show the pub landlord the newspaper photo. They must have gone in for a drink. They can't just park there without going in. A sharp-eyed landlord would see who was parking in the pub's spots, and if they weren't paying customers they'd get a mouthful of aggro.'

*

In the greenhouse that afternoon, there was lots of rubbing out, editing and updating of the MOM board. Actual hard evidence was still a bit thin, but at least, they could now explain the missing jacket. Its theft from an unknown car at Rivelin, near the murder site, pointed to Darnley having been in the car at some time. Was he alone? Was he the driver? If so, where was the car now, and how had it vanished from the scene? It seemed more likely that he had been a passenger, so who was the driver?

Billy chalked up an enigmatic note about chunter pipes. Yvonne gazed at it flat eyed and resisted the urge to seek clarification.

'Kick and me are gonna eyeball that car,' Billy said, acquiring an American accent. He adjusted an imaginary upturned raincoat

coat collar and expelled imaginary smoke from an imaginary cigarette. 'Did "the prof" get a lift to Man's Head? Who took him? Why did they go?' He turned to Yvonne, 'And remember, Toots, whoever took him was probably the goon that snuffed him.'

'Stop being daft; I know what to do.' She turned the MOM board around, grabbed the chalk and started writing. 'Kick can find out about the car,' she said, writing *Kick car*. 'You need to see Mary Scott's friend that Mister Mebbey told you about.' She wrote, *Billy Mary Scott friend*.

'Oh I wanna do that,' Kick said in a whining voice. 'Tha orlas giz me rubbish jobs.'

Billy took over. 'I don't care who does what,' he said crossly. 'We'll all be back to school next week and if we've not done it by then we waint have time. Chuffin murderer will gerraway wi' it! We have to get this all wrapped up and we've only gorra few days left.'

'OK, I'll do the car,' said Kick sulkily.

Billy underlined it and turned to Yvonne. 'Your job is to find out what Longden found at Manor Lodge that gorrim all excited and …'

'His Eureka,' said Yvonne.

Billy and Kick gaped at her for a second, stunned into silence.

She shrugged, grabbed the chalk from Billy and started to write *Eureka* on the MOM board, but abandoned the attempt, defeated by a swelling combination of disapprobation and spelling uncertainty.

Kick turned his surly frown on Billy. 'What tha going to do?'

'I'm going to find constable Needham,' Billy told him.

*

When Billy found him, an hour later, a harassed PC John Needham was booking the driver of a bread van for causing a traffic obstruction on South Road. The vehicle had two wheels on the pavement and two on the tram track. A delayed tram driver was stamping on his foot bell and yelling, unheard, through the tram's bowed glass windscreen. Irate pedestrians were squeezing passed the van, and complaining to John as though it was his fault. Several wanted to lynch the van driver from a gas lamp, like Mussolini.

Finally, the van pulled away and the red-faced tram driver drove after it, glaring at the constable and mouthing something unflattering. PC Needham blew a sigh and turned to face Billy with obvious relief. 'The daft bugger,' he growled. 'I'd have helped him carry the bread in and lerrim off if he hadn't started mouthing off at me.' He shook his head and glared after the departing bread van. 'He called me a "pointy head".'

Billy laughed explosively, struggling with his handkerchief to avoid splattering the affronted constable. He quickly controlled himself, on seeing that John was not amused.

'Whaddaya want, Billy?'

'Any news on the paint stain?'

'Yeah, it's just like you said. Forensics even matched it to the actual trestle. They won't confirm that the wearer of the jacket was probably hiding in the storage area, but they tipped me the wink. That's as good as a blind horse for me.'

Billy bit his cheek. Blind horse; what did that mean? He dismissed it. The paint stain was evidence of a sort, but it still left much unanswered. 'Is there any more? What about that – er – Detective Constable Wooffit? You said you'd talk to him. Has he come up with owt?'

'Look Billy, everybody's busy. There's a whole bunch of new collars every day. We can't drop everything to do errands for you.'

'But you said you'd ask him about the Turkish baths.' Billy gave him a hard look.

'I did ask him, he didn't have anything,' John said dropping his gaze guiltily. He thought for a moment and dredged up memories of his meeting with his friend D.C. Wooffit. 'All he said was some old boy had complained to Longden about him and Darnley making a noise – arguing or something. He said they went off into another room when he'd complained, so as not to disturb the others. It was nothing. Now scram. I've got to get on.'

Billy watched him walk away under the disapproving eyes of the shop owner. 'They should be out catching burglars, not harassing bread vans,' a woman passer-by said, to no-one in particular.

*

The following morning Billy followed the paperboy and the milkman into the simmering courts of Daniel Hill Street's back-to-back houses. Nineteenth century builders had crammed them into every available space with such ingenious frugality as to impress even honeybees. Though he found all doors tightly shut against the day, he felt drawn in to every household by an encompassing undertow of lives thrust unwillingly into interdependence.

Sally Snape lived with her bricklayer husband and their five children in three rooms beneath a similar family, with yet others adjoining at the back and at both sides. Being at ground level meant that her husband Tommy, could grow potatoes, lettuce, tomatoes and strawberries in old buckets, paint pots, biscuit tins, leaky saucepans and a couple of chimney pots. Rampant greenery thrived around their door and window and climbed to the bedroom where a window box trailed nasturtiums, marigolds and runner beans.

After a short delay and some twitching of the curtains, Sally Snape answered Billy's knock on the door. A thin, sallow skinned woman in her forties, she looked worn out. Her grey streaked brown hair was pinned under a hair net. Bare legged and wearing a faded floral apron over a mauve dress with baby milk stains on the shoulder, Sally was riding the tide of her life, weighed down by defeat and weary acceptance. She greeted Billy with hardly a glance, admitting him in as if she had no power to stop him.

'It looks nice outside,' said Billy discreetly acclimatizing to the foul smell of bed bugs, soiled children, one on a pot, and a pan of porridge simmering on the fire bars.

'That's Tommy. He can grow owt in a bit of horse muck. You

wouldn't believe what comes out of them old buckets.'

'I'm sorry to bother you when you're getting your breakfast, but it's just a quick question. I was wondering if you could tell me anything about Mary Scott.'

'She's dead, God rest her soul.' Sally crossed herself and kissed her thumbnail. 'She was killed in that terrible bombing on the Marples.'

'Yes I know,' said Billy. 'I was wondering about before that. She worked at the museum, didn't she?' He knew that she did, but wanted to get Sally talking.

Sally raised a teacup in front of Billy and tilted her head inviting him to have a cup of tea. Billy shook his head. 'She loved that job,' Sally said smiling dreamily. 'It took her out of this dump. She used to live round the corner in the top house. Her husband was down the pit. Then she started at the museum.' Sally clenched her hands beneath her chin in delight. 'Gerrin that job was a Godsend. And after a while she started getting on really well. She'd tell me all about it – right proud. They paid her more money and soon she even stopped the cleaning. She was setting things out - like displays and things. She moved house - up near Lydgate Lane in one of them nice bay windowed semis. They're lovely they are. They've got bathrooms and gardens.' She lifted the toddler off the pot, held its bottom under the cold tap and cleaned it with her fingers. The child howled deafeningly, without making the slightest impression on her. She served it up a dollop of porridge in a saucer, and sat it on the floor. It stopped screaming immediately and happily stuck its fingers into its breakfast and began feeding.

Sally lit a cigarette and rinsed her older children's porridge bowls under the tap, her eyes blinking rapidly in the tobacco smoke. 'Some of 'em round here sneered at her, but they always do if you get owt nice or show a bit of ambition.'

Billy wondered what Sally's ambitions might have been before her life was ground out. What spark had she possessed?

'They said it was that posh friend of hers, the professor, who moved her up the ladder and did her favours, just as long as he –

you know?' She looked sideways at Billy and reasoned that he probably did not know, and was too young to warrant an explanation. 'Anyway it wasn't that. I knew her better than anybody did. We'd been best friends for years. She was older than me, of course, but we were real friends – like sisters.'

'Had she gone to the Marples with the professor?' Billy asked, edging carefully towards the topic he really wanted to explore.

'No, not with him, not really. He was there of course, but it was a sort of a works outing before Christmas. A lot of 'em went from the museum and the university. She even said I could go with her, but I don't go in for that sort of thing.'

Billy supposed that Sally was lying. She would probably have loved to have gone, but didn't have the clothes for such a do, or would have felt awkward and out of place amongst such people.

'He never took her out in public, the professor. She wouldn't have stood for it, not Mary Daniels, as was. She was rather straight laced. She hated anything rude, or dishonest, or even just a bit cheeky. She would never have had an affair with a married man. I've seen her get all stiff and starchy over a seaside postcard. Chapel girl you see. She never missed a Sunday.' The porridge-eating infant was suddenly on the move. It crawled to Billy with alarming speed, tottered to its feet and smeared porridge on Billy's knees and socks.

It was time to leave.

*

Billy's mam had left him threppenz for a bag of chips for his lunch. It was a treat for being "a lovely helper". He had whitewashed inside the chicken shed and an alcove in the cellar, which had a stone table built into it. The family jokingly called it *the fridge*. It was used to keep butter, cheese and milk cool. Whitewashing was work he always enjoyed, for some perverse reason. He never flinched from tackling the cellar steps, the outside toilet or the washhouse, and particularly enjoyed doing the chicken shed.

He found Kick in the chip shop queue. 'I've saved thee pog,' he announced avoiding the petrifying glares of two queue jumped gorgons bristling in the wake of his generosity. 'Thaz got cobwebs all o're thee sen and white paint.'

'I've just done us chickens and t'cellar fridge.'

'I found Longden's car in the hospital car park. Grey Morris Oxford. I was just going to ask 'em at reception if it were his, but I saw him come out. He gorrin it and drove off.' Billy ordered his chips and put down his money, all in haypniz, on the counter. 'He's gorra big scratch on it same as old tweedy knickers.'

'She's on the sauce,' whispered Billy, still unsure of any significance for that.

'What?'

'Sauce. She's on the sauce.'

'We don't do sauce,' snapped the fish fryer. 'This's a bloody chip shop not the Savoy. Tha gets salt and vinegar nor nowt else.'

Billy winced and ordered his chips. 'Can I have some scraps on 'em an' all, please.' He loved scraps, those crozzled little crisps of batter that fizzled off the fish in the frying. Usually they were thrown away, unless begged by passing children.

'Threppenz. I ought to charge thee a penny extra for them scraps,' said the man sourly.

'Suit thee sen,' said Billy. 'I can gerram from Johnellis chip shop next time. My mam says his tail end's better than thine anyway.'

The fish fryer shot Billy a killer look and moved quickly on to his next customer, one of the Gorgons. She was still trying to turn Kick into stone, but a few others in the queue smirked and winked at Billy as he left the shop.

The lads ate their chips from the newspaper wrappings as they slowly walked up to the greenhouse. 'So if that was his car it proves he went to Man's Head rocks,' Billy said. 'But why did he have Darnley's coat in his car? Was Darnley with him? Had they gone there together? Had Longden killed him and left him there?'

'What I don't understand is,' said Kick, his exuberance almost expelling a half chewed chip, 'what did Longden see on the Turret House roof that made him so excited that he and the professor went dashing off to Man's Head rocks the first chance they got.'

Billy nodded thoughtfully. 'Yeah, we need to cop another look at that roof. Get thee bike. I'll go and borrow my granny's magnifying glass and we'll ride over there this afts.'

'What about t'warden though? She waint lerrus in if we've no grown up wi' us.'

Billy nodded. Kick was right. 'We'll need to create a diversion. Like they do in films.' He looked around frowning. 'I'll think of sommat on t'way there.'

*

A chattering gaggle of middle-aged ladies milled around the beaming custodian as they exited the Turret House door. She was smiling, nodding and tilting her head obsequiously as the women shook her hand and patted her shoulders. Billy dismounted and wheeled his bike in through the pedestrian gate. Kick followed and parked his bike next to Billy's. The party of well to do ladies had evidently enjoyed their guided tour, and were taking a long time about leaving. At last, amid much laughter and gentile squealing, they turned and started towards the gate. The custodian waved and almost curtsied before slipping back inside and closing the door.

The lads waited for the women to leave and then approached the door. Kick tentatively rattled its great iron knocker. The custodian appeared almost immediately, beaming expectantly. Her face fell when she saw the two boys. She had probably expected to see one of the ladies returning for a misplaced glove or umbrella. 'Oh, it's you two again.' She looked out and cast around, her disappointment growing by the second. 'Where's the doctor?'

'He's not here this time, but we'll only be a minute.' Billy hoped this would satisfy her.

'You won't because you're not coming in.' She started to close the door in their faces.

Billy launched into the diversionary tactic, he and Kick had worked out on the journey over. 'That bloke over there with the sheep dog said you'd lerrus in.' Billy nodded in the direction of the Manor Lodge's ghostly ruins.

'Dog! What dog?' The woman gaped in horror. 'Where is he?'

Kick pointed vaguely. 'There. He's just gone behind that wall.'

She pulled the heavy door shut, barged passed them and set off in the direction of the ruins. 'Show me. Come on quickly. Show me where.' Kick trotted beside her, pointing at the invisible canine intruder. Billy hung back a few moments then tried the Turret House door. He slipped inside and bolted the door behind him. In a minute, he was on the Turret House roof. He glanced over the battlements and saw Kick leading the excited custodian into Manor Lodge ruins in search of a non-existent sheepdog.

Billy turned back to the flat, lead covered roof and glanced around it. He remembered the custodian saying that when Longden had become all excited and run off, he had been kneeling in the far corner, peering at marks on the lead through a magnifying glass. His "Eureka", as Yvonne had called it.

Armed with paper and pencil and granny's magnifying glass, Billy knelt in the same spot and peered at the leaden floor. Pits and scratches from centuries of wear and tear covered it. Traces of ancient graffiti mixed with more recent references. *Up The Blades*, and *The Owls for ever* being a common theme. One told that Percy loves Doris, it was dated 1944. He slowly moved the glass from side to side across the marks, praying with every image that ballooned up in the lens that he would see the mysterious cause of Doctor Longden's excitement. There was nothing. He searched deeper into the corner, but still found nothing except badly drawn hearts with arrows through them and scratchy declarations of, Frank loves Theresa, or Bert = Gertie. He covered every square inch before moving on to examine the next bit.

The custodian began hammering on the door, shouting about calling the police. He heard Kick trying to convince her that he was not inside. He even tried alerting her to another invisible dog, but that merely enraged her more.

It was no good. The mission had failed. The outraged custodian was becoming hysterical. Billy knew that the game was up. He could do no more. He sighed miserably, his shoulders slumping, and let the glass and writing paper slip from his fingers. The shadow he cast in the afternoon sun seemed to mock him as he hunched over the lead sheeted roof. He got off his knees and walked to the battlements, looked down miserably at the ranting custodian and told her he was coming down.

Whatever Longden had found would remain a mystery. Perhaps it wasn't even important anyway, he told himself, and bent to retrieve his magnifying glass and pencil.

Doomster stares o'er water rounde
His needle plying skie
Wrought stones on shining iron ground
That a crownie head might plie.

Scratched into the lead, the words filled the lens exactly. They floated and loomed as he picked up the glass. He did not know what they meant, but the word *needle* attracted him. The Scottish Queen had spent her time sewing and embroidering up on The Turret House roof. She had sat many hours with her friend, the Earl of Shrewsbury's wife, Bess of Hardwick. Needles were part of her life. This obscure little poem could be important. Maybe Doctor Hadfield would know what it meant.

0o0o0

Chapter Twenty-Four

Polly Harrison opened her pub, The Rivelin Hotel at Man's Head, at eleven precisely every morning. Rain, snow, sun, or blow, she always crossed the narrow road to the pasture in front of her door and looked out fondly across the silent, wooded Rivelin valley. This particular morning she found herself sharing the view and the earthy scent of woodland, with a ginger headed, freckled faced kid. He was leaning back on a bicycle, his feet on top of the crumbling dry stonewall that enclosed the pasture.

'Hello. Who are you?' she asked cheerfully. 'I've seen you up here before.'

'Billy Perks, Missus.' He smiled at her and looked her over with innocent indiscretion. She was chubby, and middle-aged, with grey-blonde hair. Her face looked as though she was about to burst into laughter at any second. As she, in turn, studied him, she folded her fleshy pink arms beneath a large bosom cloaked in a floral wrap-over pinafore.

'Billy eh? My dad was a Billy; God rest him. So, what are you doing here then, Billy?'

'Nowt, just looking round a bit; I live near – above Walkley Bank Woods.' That was a true, though lame attempt at justifying his presence.

'I've seen you before haven't I?' She cocked her head as she studied him.

'I came when they found that dead bloke,' he told her. 'And I've been back since. I'm a detective. Not a real en. I'm norrin t'police force or nowt like that. But I like to investigate mysteries to find out who killed 'em.'

Her face lit with recognition. 'I remember,' she said, pointing at him as though inviting him to take a look at himself too. 'You're that lad who was in the paper, aren't you - threpenze or tuppence or sommat detective?'

Billy blushed and looked away shyly. 'It weren't just me. It were my friends an' all. We all did it.'

'I remember it because I knew that old lady,' Polly Harrison said, her expression softening. 'She used to sell the Star newspaper in town – near Coles' corner. She was a tough old lass. She stood out there in all weathers, as unshifting as a parson's gate. She had lungs like a bull; singing out the same old tune over and over. Mind you, you could never tell what she was saying. The only word I could ever make out was "Extraaaah".' She laughed, nodding as if to convince Billy. 'Oooh it were a sad business when she was killed.' She took a step back and held out both hands to Billy. 'So, that was you? You solved it. My word you must be a clever boy. Would you like a Tizer?'

Tizer was a favourite tipple of Billy's, a free one even more so. 'Oooh yes please.' He had pedalled from home, wondering all the way, how he would persuade the publican to open up and talk to him. As he followed her into the pub, for a free Tizer, he congratulated himself on his artful powers of persuasion and charm.

Polly Harrison led him into the saloon bar. It was a low ceilinged, dimly lit room, which smelled pleasantly of furniture polish and a million other things, mostly beer and cigarettes. As the only patron at that moment, he had the pick of the seating. He chose a high stool at the bar. 'What's it like having a famous murder right on your door step?' he asked.

Polly shuddered as she poured a disappointing measure of Tizer into a handled pint glass. 'Oooh I don't like it, love. The police are in here all the time, and the flipping newspapers. It was terrible at first. I had a queue right round the bar for days. There were folks coming from all over the world; Rotherham, Glossop, Barnsley. There's only me and my Harold to serve 'em all, apart from Bessie, who cleans, but she's as soft as a brush. Give her a shilling and she'll give you change for ten bob. Worse than that, they wanted food. Can you believe it? Food! I told 'em straight, "this is a pub not a flippin café".'

'Who do you think killed him?' asked Billy burping after a swig of fizzy Tizer. 'Oops! Sorry.'

Polly nodded, accepting his apology with the untroubled understanding of a seasoned professional. 'He was in here you know, the poor man. I remember it very well. It was a quiet afternoon. There was a man on his own - sat over there. I didn't know him.' She pointed to a seat by a window. 'He was a pint of Guinness. Then the two toffs came in. Campari and soda, one of 'em wanted. Can you believe it?' She shook her head despairingly. 'I told him straight, we don't do French nonsense in here. We're English in my pub. He had a cognac instead. The other one was a Famous Grouse. They'd parked their car across Ray's gate and I was a bit worried. Luckily, his sheep were up in Goody fields, behind the Man's Head, so I didn't say nowt. He can be a bit mouthy can Ray, if you block his gate, even when his damn field is empty.'

'Was it a grey car, a Morris?' asked Billy

'My word,' Polly gasped in awe, covering her mouth with her hand. 'You're doing it now, aren't you?' she said. 'You're being a detective. How did you know that?'

'I don't know it. I'm just asking.'

'Well it was. You're absolutely right; a grey Morris Oxford. I remember it because it's the same as my friend's at the post office. In fact I thought it was her coming, until I saw 'em get out - the two toffs.'

'Then what?'

'They sat in that corner, whispering a lot. I don't know what they were saying, but you could tell they were having a row about sommat. Then one of 'em, the cognac, not the Famous Grouse, stood up and stormed out in a huff. He stopped at this door for a second.' Polly pointed it out even though it was the only door in the bar. 'He was furious. I thought he'd explode. But he never said a word. He just walked out and drove off.' She looked at Billy and raised a quizzical eyebrow. 'They have funny rows, don't they, posh people? They never throw owt down, angry-like, or swear. And if they do swear it sounds so posh it dunt even sound like swearing.'

'What did he do then?'

'How do I know? I just told you, he drove off.'

'No the one who stayed,' said Billy. 'The Famous Grouse.'

'Oh him, yes, he asked me to get him a taxi. I started to phone for one but he stopped me because he realised he'd left his coat in the car with his wallet in it. Luckily they'd already paid me for the drinks.'

'Are you sure this was on the day of the murder?'

'Of course I am. It was the day my Harold went to the Walkley Cottage Inn about the fishing match with their dart's team.' Her head wobbled huffily on her shoulders.

Billy worried he may have compromised her goodwill, and dived in quickly with a question to divert her. 'Then what happened, Missis Harrison?'

'Polly, call me Polly, love.' She patted his forearm forgivingly. 'He left as well, but he brought the glasses back first. That was nice of him. Most of 'em just leave 'em,' she explained, her eyebrows shooting up her forehead. 'I followed him to the step and watched him go back up the path to the crag. I was surprised that he went up there. I expected him to go down to the main road to get a lift, or a bus, but he didn't.'

'Did you see him again?'

'No, that was the last I saw of him. The pint of Guinness left a bit later as well, but he didn't bring his glass back –typical. Mind you, he was on a motor bike, so what can you expect? Huh, bikers! They're all the same that lot – no manners.' She wiped a non-existent spot from the shiny bar. 'I was left here with an empty bar and no money coming in. They're hard work these places, Billy. You don't get rich having a pub. And now, what with people demanding food and frenchified drinks, it's no wonder is it? We were better off during the war. You knew where you were then. You couldn't get nowt for love nor money, and we got bombed every night, but we were happy.'

*

'What made you think it was old?' asked Doctor Hadfield. He,

Yvonne and Billy were leaning over his small dining table, their heads almost touching. Between them lay a crumpled sheet of paper from a school exercise book. Billy's efforts at copying the little poem were not too bad considering his necessary haste at the time.

'It looked faint and worn thin,' said Billy. 'The writing was sort of scrolly, you know, like a five pound note.'

The doctor reached into his jacket hanging on the back of a chair and pulled out his wallet from an inside pocket. He took out a big white fiver and smoothed it out on the table next to the poem. 'Like this?' He pointed to the copper plate lettering.

'Not as fancy as that. A bit plainer and not as neat.'

Doomster stares o'er water rounde
His needle plying skie
Wrought stones on shining iron ground
That a crownie head might plie.

Doctor Hadfield picked up the scrap of paper and walked around his tiny room scowling at it. 'Doomster. That could mean a seer, a sort of oracle, or prophet. Someone who sees all and knows the future. But, water round, I've no idea what that could be.'

'If we take it literally it would mean water that's round,' Yvonne piped.

Billy gave a derisory snort. 'Tha can't 'ave round water?' he hooted. 'That's barmy.'

'Put it inside something round,' Yvonne explained calmly. 'Then it can be round. Water in a jug is jug shaped.'

Billy frowned and curled his lip. 'Jug shaped? That's barmy.'

Hadfield held out the scrap of paper and stared hard at it 'No Billy,' he said. 'When you've nothing else to go on, you must accept what you have and start with that. So think, Billy, what could round water mean?'

Billy frowned thinking hard for a long time. 'D'yer mean like the Round Dam?' he asked tentatively.

Doc Hadfield looked up astonished. 'Crickey! The Round Dam. Yes that could be it. It's near where the body was found and…'

'It's right under the doomster's nose,' offered Yvonne.

'You mean Man's Head rock? That's not an oracle,' Billy sneered. 'You can't tell thee future there – not unless tha'rt falling off of it, head first.'

'It could be,' Yvonne argued. 'People have been coming to see it for centuries. I bet the cave men thought it was an oracle. I bet the Romans did and the Vikings an' all.'

Hadfield recovered his fiver from the table and stuffed it back into his wallet. 'It's the best we've got, old lad. It looks out over water. The water is in a round pond – so "water round". I think that's a reasonable start. That just leaves us with "Wrought stones on shining iron ground". That's a bit of a puzzler to me.'

Yvonne looked at him and held her hands up next to her shoulders. 'Not if you accept that round water means the Round Dam. It becomes pretty obvious then.' Hadfield raised his eyebrows and pouted, challenging her to back up her statement. 'The Round Dam,' she went on, 'was made for the Hind Wheel, an old cutlery mill back in Tudor times. Mister Greaves told us it was working in 1581, at least that's the first written record of it. It's the same time as when Queen Mary was imprisoned in the Turret House.'

'Who is Mister Greaves?'

'Her history teacher,' Billy said.

'Wrought stones, could mean the stones they carved into great big grinding wheels for grinding the knife blades, shears and scythes and stuff.' She looked at the pair expectantly. Their goofy, mystified expressions gaped back at her. 'The stones that *ground the shining iron*,' she paraphrased.

'Yeah I gerrit,' said Billy suddenly looking very pleased with himself. For once he felt ahead of the doctor. 'Er – er , but what about the needle plying sky?'

'That must be the needle, just up the road at Rivelin Rocks.'

'Rivelin Rocks?' Hadfield queried, the gaps in his knowledge of the local geography letting him down again.

'It's a big needle of rock about sixty-five feet high.' Billy explained. 'It's just up the road. Climbers love it. They're always falling off it.'

The three sat in thoughtful silence for several moments before the doctor spoke. 'This business about *ground the shining iron* and all that - it's a bit of long shot, but what if it means something like scissors or sewing needles being made in the old cutlery mill at Round Dam for Queen Mary? She was a crownie head. *"The crownie head - to ply"* That could mean for a queen to sew with.' The doctor shuffled and blushed with embarrassment at his own suggestion and flapped a hand dismissively.

Billy frowned and rolled his eyes. 'Yeah but look, we don't care about all this,' he said impatiently.

Doctor Hadfield eyed him questioningly. 'Why not? It's a terrific mystery. And there could even be treasure at the end of it.'

'We're not looking for treasure! What we want to know is why did Longden come here and why did the professor come with him? The treasure is not what we're after.'

Yvonne turned to the doctor. 'Yes, we just need to know if the poem Billy found was enough to bring the two of them here.'

Hadfield bowed his head and shook it slowly. 'You're absolutely right, of course,' he admitted, laughing quietly at the irony. They were trying to solve a murder, but at the first hint of gold, he had veered off course to search for it. 'It's the glister of gold. Fool's gold too, no doubt.' He looked at the pair and shrugged apologetically. 'Treasure - it hooked them both, Longden especially. We know he spent hours on his knees at the Turret House trying to find it. Obviously, he believed there was a message, or clue of some sort there. Perhaps it was the poem. I'm quite sure it describes the murder site.'

'Is it enough to bring them here?' Yvonne wondered, thinking aloud.

'I think so,' Billy said firmly. 'Stan Daniels told me Doctor Longden was a fool. He'd probably believe any old story that he thought might lead him to gold. Stan says he's lost loads of money gambling. We know that he went to the Turret House lots of times looking for clues. I think he's desperate for money and stupid enough to believe he could find buried treasure after four hundred and fifty years.'

Hadfield shook his head. 'No, he's an educated man, Billy. He'd never be that naive. There must more be to it than that.'

'He's broke and too snooty to admit it,' Billy argued forcefully. 'I think he drowned poor old Hepburn to keep him quiet about the Pagez letter, and he probably killed the professor too.'

'Now you're clutching at straws, Billy.'

'Who else then?' Billy demanded. 'We know he drove the professor to Rivelin. They were in the pub together. We know they had a row. Longden left in his car and the professor went back up to the crags. What was to stop Longden creeping back and murdering him? For all we know he might have killed before. He might have murdered Mary Scott.'

'And that's the worst part of all this,' Yvonne put in passionately. 'Poor Mary Scott was killed because she saw someone steal the stupid letter. Since then two more have died because of it. Its whiff of gold is still killing people.'

0o0o0

Chapter Twenty-Five

The narrow door to Walkley's police box swung gently on its hinges in a light summer breeze. Morning sunlight streamed into the cramped space finding the odd cobweb and highlighting dusty streaks on the built in desk top. PC Needham hunched over a police logbook, carefully entering his report. Billy was sitting on the threshold leaning against the door jam and reading the officer's newspaper.

'They make us print everything in this damn book now,' Constable Needham grumbled. 'It's Handley's fault. His bloody writing's so bad he can't even read it himself. So now the bloody sergeant treats us all like idiots.' He paused his writing and glanced down at Billy. 'Here, gerrof the floor and gimme back my paper, your messing it up.'

'How much does a sergeant get paid?' Billy asked folding and smoothing out the newspaper.

'Why? What peerless gobbet are you about to spring this time?'

'I was wondering how a police sergeant can afford a big posh house up Ranmoor. That's where Flood lives.'

'He gets paid loads. He's a chief superintendent.'

'Burree were only a sergeant when he bought that massive palace of his. How did he get the dosh for it back then?'

John Needham eyed him flatly. 'Massive palace, eh? Go on then, tell me, o wise and gingery freckled one.'

Billy thumped him playfully on the leg and stood up. 'I don't know, but just think about this; Flood was sent into the tunnels where the bank was broken open by the bomb. If he'd really searched the tunnels properly, like he was supposed to, he must have seen Mary Scott's body. He couldn't miss it! But we know he didn't say owt about it. It wasn't in his report and they dint find her until a fireman went in a week later. He also said he dint find Longden or the professor and the group that went the other way when Walter Mebbey escaped.'

'Yeah, that's right, so what?'

Billy looked perplexed. 'Well, he was sent in specially to find 'em. How come he didn't? How could he have missed 'em if he was really searching and not doing sommat else at the time?'

'What else?'

I don't know – robbing a bank, maybe?'

'Don't be daft.'

'He'd been told to search the tunnels, and yet he doesn't find Mary's body, and he doesn't find Longden and the others, and he doesn't even find how they got out. So if he wasn't searching the tunnels, what was he doing?'

'I don't know. Playing cards with Spring Heeled Jack?' John quipped offhandedly. 'I don't see the point you're making.'

'Three months later he buys a big posh house, but he's only a sergeant. Where did the dosh come from?'

'Are you saying it was him who robbed the bank?'

'You told me the cop's report said the bomb smashed open three safety deposit boxes. We know that Darnley stole the Pagez Cypher from one of 'em. All three box owners, including the one Darnley robbed, told the coppers nowt of value was stolen. Well, why did they bother having a box if they had nowt to put in it? That's daft, and it's also very hard to believe. So, what really was stolen? And who nicked it? Was it Flood or was it the others?'

John Needham pouted and raised an eyebrow. 'We don't know, and we can't make people report stuff stolen if they don't want to.'

'Yeah, but worrif Flood stole sommat that night? Worrif he found a stash of dosh in one of them boxes and realised it was illegal proceeds, or whatever you call it? He could fill his pockets and nobody would ever know. Then, to make sure the tunnels don't become a crime scene with lots of other coppers running about in them, he pretends not to see Mary's body and leaves her to rot in the dark.'

Needham looked at Billy and laughed softly, shaking his head. 'Illegal proceeds – eh? Have you swallowed a dictionary?'

'Int that what you call it when money is from a robbery or some swindle? I'm just saying, how could he suddenly afford to buy a big house just after he'd been in them tunnels?'

John chuckled softly. 'He could have used his wife's money. She's loaded. Her father died in 1940 and left her a mint.' He patted Billy on the shoulder. 'Never mind, Billy, it was a good idea. I had the same thoughts myself. That's why I asked my pal Terry Wooffit to check it out for me.' Billy's shoulders slumped. 'Keep plugging away, lad. We'll get there, eventually.'

'It doesn't change the fact that he lied about not finding Mary's body. Why did he do that? He must have seen her. The firemen did. And why was there no investigation or ort – ort – autopsy? And don't forget this …' he had Needham backing away against the police box wall, 'Longden was a pathologist. Doesn't that make you wonder about him and Flood. Worrif Flood made Longden cover her death up? Worrif he knew Longden had stolen sommat from the boxes and he blackmailed him into covering her death up and making it seem like she was just another victim of the bombing?'

'Blimey Billy, you've made me bust my pencil.'

'It's not funny,' Billy said squeezing back tears. He wiped them away quickly and coughed, trying to hide them.

John Needham swallowed the emotion rising in his throat. He understood the lad's passion and concern and was moved by it. 'Look Billy, I'll try to fix a meeting with that pal of mine, D.C. Wooffit. I know he's pretty fed up with it all. He's been getting the run around from Fletcher, his boss in CID. Flood and Fletcher are as tight as ticks. Terry wouldn't say so straight out, but I know he thinks something iffy is going on.'

Billy had composed himself. 'It's Mary I feel sorry about most,' he said. 'I never thought much of it until Wy said about her missing Christmases, and birthdays and stuff for ten years while her killer goes on enjoying life.'

'I know son,' John croaked. 'What was she – about forty-five? She had plenty of time left. Who knows what she might have done with it, and how it could have affected other people. I often think that about my little brother - Eddie. When he died, I lost more than a brother. I lost a whole lifetime of seeing everything he could have done with his life and mine too. Death is a thief, Billy, and murder is its vilest creature.'

*

It was half past three on Wednesday afternoon. The shops on South Road were enjoying a busy period. Tomorrow would be early closing day, and by this time in the week any meat and bone left from Sunday dinner had been stewed, pie crusted and "souped" to oblivion. Shoppers dashed from one side of the street to the other assembling fresh ingredients for their midweek evening meal; tea, as most folk called it, or supper if you were older, but never dinner, unless you held middle class pretensions. Butchers laid out liver, heart, cowheel, tripe and oxtail on their slabs. They would have to go in their back stores for chops or chump for the more well to do.

Sutcliffe grabbed Billy and yanked him roughly into a passage between two shops. 'Has tha said owt?' the old man snarled tightening his grip on Billy's wrists, making him wince with pain.

'No, I never.'

'They asked me about that bloody jacket. What did tha tell 'em?'

'I dint say nowt. They already knew thar'd gorrit and tried to sell it to me mam. But I never said nowt about it. Burrif tha dunt let go o' me wrists I'll tell 'em everything, and I'll get me dad on to thee.'

Sutcliffe relaxed his grip a little. 'Don't try threatening me, lad. I've flattened blokes twice as big as thee dad. I'm not scared o' nobody.' He looked hard into Billy's eyes and curled his lip to underline the point. 'I know thaz been talking to t'coppers. I've seen thee wi' that new bloke, Needham. What's tha been telling 'im?'

'Nowt. I'm norra snitch.'

'They said I'd nicked it from a car.' The old man's look of shocked indignation was hardly convincing.

'Well tha did,' said Billy, incredulous. 'Everybody knows it were thee. You're lucky they aren't saying that you killed him.'

'I never killed nobody.' Sutcliffe preened, his wild eyes flicking around.

'I know you didn't, but you were there, and you did steal the victim's jacket from a car parked near the murder site. Have you any idea how guilty that makes thee look? I'm amazed they haven't been grilling thee over hot coals ever since it happened.'

'Oy! Wharra tha doing to that lad?' Walter Mebbey's voice echoed angrily down the passage. 'Lerrim go or I'll spread thee nose across thee face.'

Sutcliffe released Billy and swung round to face Walter, who squared up to him boldly, his fists circling menacingly before him. Sutcliffe backed away a couple of steps and half-heartedly raised his own fists, clearly lacking Walter's determination and confidence. 'Thee keep thee nose out,' he told Walter. 'This is between me and him.'

'No it int,' Walter argued calmly. 'He's my mate, and if tha touches him, I'll peel thee apart like an orange.'

Sutcliffe needed no convincing. He turned and scurried down the passage into the back yard behind the shops. Billy was not sure how he would get out, but at least he was gone. 'Good 'en, Walter. Thanks.'

'Ah he's nowt. I could take 'im easy,' said Walter, looking relieved nevertheless. 'I've been looking for thee, Billy. I've got an address for another woman who were a friend of Mary Scott's. She's a cleaner at the museum like Mary used to be. I thought you might want to talk to her an' all.' He handed Billy a crumpled slip of paper. 'How's it going? Are you any nearer to solving it yet?'

Billy blew out his cheeks in a sigh. He leaned back against the passage wall. 'Well, we're sure Longden knew about that old letter that was pinched, but we can't say if he and Darnley both stole it.' They left the gloomy passage and walked out onto South Road in the bright, afternoon sunlight. Billy continued, 'Longden drove the professor to Man's Head after he found some sort of clue at the old Turret House at Manor Castle. We're not sure what the clue was, but we know for definite that him and Darnley went to Man's Head after he found it. They were seen in the pub there. We know they had a row and that Longden drove off and left the professor on his own. His jacket was nicked from the car there. Old Sutcliffe stole it. He thinks I told the coppers, burra dint.'

'Do you still think the professor drowned the solicitor, what's his name – Hepburn?'

'Definitely. He had a paint stain on his coat that came from the woodwork they use under the dance floor to hold it up. Both men were regulars at the Turkish bath. The cops have gorra witness who saw Darnley and Longden arguing in the hot room. One of the other bathers told them to keep the noise down, so they went into the cold room to avoid disturbing the others. That's where Hepburn was killed. I'm sure any honest pathologist could show that the water in his lungs came from the cold pool in that room. From what I can make out, it looks like he fell and bashed his head, and then was drowned while he was unconscious – he never struggled, you see.'

'Did anybody see it happen?'

'No, the cold room was closed to the public that day. They were fixing the tiles in there. But the great thing is, it's dead easy to get from there into the store room where they keep the dance floor panels. Darnley could easily have dragged him through and hidden him under the timbers. That's how he got the paint on his jacket.'

'But you said he was in the Turkish bath. He wouldn't have been wearing a jacket.'

'No, not when he hid the body the first time, but what about the following day when he crept back to hide it in the swimming pool under the dance floor?'

Old Walter straightened his shoulders and gave Billy a

sideways grin. 'Huh, you're clever little bugger, Billy Perks,' he said laughing softly. 'Tha makes it sound reight enough, but I'm no detective. It'd be easy for anybody to convince me that the moon's made o' rag cheese. What I want to know is who killed Mary, and why was it covered up?'

'Me too, Walter, but no matter what I do, it keeps coming back to the same dead end.'

'Hello, Billy. How are you?' It was Doctor Clarissa Fulton-Howard. Walter gaped at her, whipped off his trilby hat and stood almost to attention as he watched her. She had been striding along South Road, her crocodile skin medical bag in her hand, a dead fox around her shoulders. Billy wasn't sure how many other animals had died to dress her that day, but he didn't like it much. 'I've been hoping I might see you,' she announced, as if addressing the whole of South Road. 'I hope you've not been pestering them at the hospital again since we last spoke?'

'I haven't been to the hospital.'

'Good boy. Is this your grandfather?'

'No, It's Mister Mebbey. He's a weightlifter,' said Billy.

'Pleased to meet you,' Walter said bowing briskly, giving her a quick flash of his bald head.

Clarissa managed to look right through him and turned to Billy. 'How are your enquiries? Have you found the killer yet?'

Her snooty attitude towards Walter annoyed Billy and so he made sure his reply placed him at the centre of their conversation. 'No, but Mister Mebbey here, has been helping me,' he said pointing to Walter like a prize goose. 'He knew Professor Darnley.' Walter did not react. Instead, he continued to eye Clarissa curiously. Billy ploughed on, 'He was trapped in the tunnels with the Professor when the Marples was bombed.'

Clarissa looked shocked on hearing this. The colour drained from her face. She gaped at Walter and stepped back unsteadily, studying his face. Without a word, she turned abruptly and almost fled along the busy pavement, disappearing into the crowding shoppers.

Walter and Billy watched her go. Walter shrugged with comic

incredulity. 'What was all that about?' he said. 'Sommat flew up her pipes.'

The pair walked along through the distracted, intense shoppers. Walter veered purposefully towards a pork shop window. Billy carried on, unaware he had lost his companion. He chatted away happily to the amusement of passers-by until he realised he was alone. He turned to see Walter beckoning him back to his side. 'Ayup sithee, look at them.' He was pointing to a tray of chitterlings. 'Don't they look champion? Hang on here a minute, I'll just get me sen some.'

Chitterlings were not a favourite with Billy, though he did eat them, usually cold with salt, pepper and vinegar on them. But, if his mam was going to feed him uncooked meat with vinegar on it, he preferred tripe. It was obvious from Walter's beaming face that he did not.

Cheerfully tucking his parcel of chitterlings under his arm, Walter fell into step with Billy and they continued along South Road.

'I went to see the woman you told me about, Missis Snape,' Billy said. 'She told me Mary Scott was a bit straight laced, a chapel woman. She said she was too stiff and starchy for some people. Not much fun. Apparently, she didn't like pubs. She only went to the Marples' do because it was a special work's outing – for Christmas.'

'Poor lass. First time she goes to a pub, and it gets bombed.' Walter stopped at the tram stop and leaned on its iron pole. 'I hope you get sommat a bit more useful from this other woman.' He patted his pockets as if he'd lost something. 'I've gen you t'address didn't I?'

Billy waved the slip of paper at him. 'Yeah, I'll see her tomorrow. We're running out of time. I've got to wrap this case up before we start school again.'

A tramcar rattled into view. 'You sounded a bit American then,' Walter said, grinning.

Billy blushed and stepped back as the tram slid up to the stop. Walter boarded it with a friendly nod. 'Tell us how tha gets on.

So long, Billy.'

For a second or two he watched the tram pull away and head for the city, then crossed the road and made his way to the bottom of his own street. As he turned the corner, he saw Sergeant Lackey sitting in a police car a few yards up the street. The driver's door opened immediately. Lackey clambered out. 'Hey Perks! I've been waiting for you. Come here.'

'You'll have to speak to my parents. I've been told not to talk to you.'

'Oh really, well we'd better go and see your mother then. It's that house there int it, the one wi' the mucky curtains.' He pointed up the street to Billy's house.

'They're not mucky. There's nobody in. My mam works until four. She won't be home until half past.'

'Where's your father? Drunk in a boozer I suppose.'

'He's at work - and he dunt drink except at Christmas and cup final day.'

Lackey had slowly drawn closer, and was now towering over Billy, his manner sneering and threatening. 'Stay away from that hospital, Perks. People don't want smelly kids interrupting their work and getting in the way. Keep out of it. And don't let me hear that you've been pestering people at the Manor Lodge again either. We're on to you, Perks. Every step you take goes in my book. You know what Mister Flood told you. He said to keep your nose out of police business. If you don't, me and you will be ...' He stopped suddenly at the approach of a small man wearing housepainter's white overalls, spattered with the trophies of years of paint jobs.

'Are tha alreight Billy?' It was Mister Thackery, the Perk's next-door neighbour. 'What's up, officer? His dad's still at work.' Thackery approached rapidly on short bandy legs. His questioning frown making it clear that the sergeant would have to explain himself.

'Nothing for you to worry your sen about, sir,' Lackey said stepping back from Billy.

'Well, he can come wi' me now. I don't think you need to

shove him about any more.' He waved Billy to his side and stood pugnaciously between him and Lackey, his thin, sloping shoulders barring the sergeant from reaching the lad.

'And what might your name be, sir?' Sergeant Lackey asked coldly.

'Don't worry, Sergeant,' Mister Thackery replied calmly. 'I won't be complaining to Councillor Morrison and the Watch committee. I'm sure you meant well.'

Lackey looked about perplexed. He moved stiffly to the police car door, climbed in and drove off, careful to avoid looking at Mister Thackery and Billy watching him from the pavement.

'Tell thee mam when she gets home, Billy,' Mister Thackery said. 'She should be told about him.'

Billy thanked his neighbour, and chatting amiably walked with him to the footpath that served both their houses. 'As tha heard latest score?' Mister Thackery asked.

'At the Oval? No, I've been out all day,' Billy told him. 'Last I heard England had the Indians on the run.'

'Not arf. Bedser and Young Freddie Trueman are skittling 'em out,' Mister Thackery said. 'I reckon they'll be four or five wickets apiece when they draw stumps.'

OoOoO

Chapter Twenty-Six

Doctor Hadfield was washing his car with all the care and concern of a mother for her child. Billy sat watching him from a low wall. He was eating a handful of the first of the summer's blackberries, picked on a bit of waste ground, on the way over to the doctor's house. He had just asked Hadfield about Longden's movements on the day of Professor Darnley's murder.

'Sarah Becket said that she was with Longden in his office at the estimated time of Professor Darnley's death. She's sure he couldn't have killed him'

'But he was seen in the pub at Man's Head. He drove them there. Darnley's jacket was pinched from his car there.'

'I know, Billy, but don't forget, Longden left Darnley there – in the pub - and drove to the hospital. He was in his office by one-thirty. Sarah confirms it. What's more, she insists there was nothing about his demeanour, his clothing, his shoes – nothing at all to suggest he had been in a tussle with Darnley, or done any lifting or digging. If he had killed Darnley, at the very least, he'd have looked a bit dishevelled. She's adamant he couldn't have done it.'

Billy frowned, inflating his cheeks in a sigh. 'What time did he die?'

Hadfield scratched his head. 'It's very difficult to say, old lad. Obviously, we know he was alive at one o clock when he left the pub. According to the pub landlady, that was about ten minutes after Longden left. Unfortunately, whatever happened after that is a mystery.'

'But about the - er – autopsy?'

'Sarah didn't get a proper look at the corpse. Longden stopped her. Anyway, the body had been out there too long for a quickie analysis - three days, as we now know for sure. The pathology report notes skin marbling and the early intrusion of blowflies. Unfortunately, that does little but confirm what we already know from witness testimony - three days. The actual time he was killed can't be determined with much accuracy. Stomach contents, hypostasis, and hardening and such, are not all that helpful in this case.'

Billy gaped, bewildered. 'Hey, hold on – hypo wotsit – bla – bla-bla. Wharra yer talking about?'

'OK, in plain English, Sarah said he ate about six hours before death. If we assume his normal pattern of behaviour, he would have eaten breakfast at about eight. We know he didn't eat at the pub. According to Sarah, that would make time of death mid-afternoon, say about two or three o-clock. She can't say more, because Longden prevented any further examination and he took her notes from her.'

*

The weekend was the last before the start of the autumn term. Heavy rain kept Billy to the house. His dad was off sick again, but this time the doctor at the steelworks where he worked had referred him for a thorough examination at the Royal Infirmary.

On Sunday morning, Billy sat on his dad's bed reading the papers with him, mainly the Green 'un and sports' pages in the Empire. Apart from the start of the new football season, nothing much was happening. Sheffield Wednesday had drawn with Newcastle at Hillsborough, England beat the Indians in the Test match, the Korean war rumbled on, and Emil Zatopek still ruled the sports' world, weeks after his three gold medals at the Helsinki Olympics.

*

The following day, thoroughly fed up, Billy set out for school on the first day back. He sat miserably on the tram, reviewing his gloomy prospects; his dad was sick, it was raining, it was back to school, and the murderer was still free. His life was rubbish. He sighed and stared out at the rain. The tram was clattering past the university. He thought of his mam working there on the refectory hotplate. She had begged him to listen to the teachers this term, and not to mess about in class. He felt ashamed of himself, and sorry for her. He knew he was letting her down. He shrugged and resolved to try harder. He would try to make her proud of him. It might even help to take her mind off his dad. He knew she worried about him.

By the time he joined his classmates, he was feeling more positive and determined to work and study as hard as he could this term. He picked up his step and cheerfully shoved in to join his usual group in assembly. The teachers, moping about at the front, responded to his cheery nods with their usual hard stare.

Despite his good intentions, he spent that first day in a mist of bewilderment and enervation. His earlier enthusiasm and positivity wilted when he learned that an unfavourable report, passed down by his previous form teacher, had scuppered any chance that he might have had of a fresh start with his new one. Headmistress, Sister Pauline, thought by many to have trained under Goebbels, added to his woes. She singled him out for public castigation at morning assembly, citing various, long passed misdemeanours, and even mentioning something his dad had done as a boy thirty odd years before. Billy was not sure whether she was making the case that, - *evil was in the blood,* or that he should - *beware the power of her record keeping.* At day's end, he slouched out through the school gates feeling anything but charged and eager for the challenges and excitement of education.

Having spent his tram fare on bubble gum, he set off to walk home. As he trudged the incongruously named Daisy Walk and Meadow Street, between the husks of blitzed houses, a motorbike roared up alongside him. The rider raised his goggles. It was Stan Daniels. He looked chillingly stony faced, and pointed to a bombed out row of houses. 'I need a word, Billy,' he said sternly, 'in there.' He pushed his motorbike out of sight behind a bomb-damaged wall. Billy followed him, wondering what could be the matter. Stan parked the bike on its stand and stomped over the rubble into the ruins of one of the houses.

Billy looked around at the destruction. Half the roofs were missing. Patches of willow herb and dandelion thrust up hopefully from tangles of rubble. Shreds of wallpaper peeled from exposed plastered walls, and at shattered windows, rags of curtain material stirred in the air. Inside, he found bits of old furniture crushed beneath collapsed floors and walls.

'Nice place you've got here, Stan.'

Stan turned on him suddenly. 'Worra tha up to, Billy? I thought we were pals.' He was glaring with fierce accusation, his lips trembling with anger.

Shocked, Billy felt himself pale. He struggled for words. 'I – I don't know what you mean, Stan. What's happened?'

'Tha knows,' he snapped back at him. 'Thaz been pestering Sally Snape. Don't deny it. She's told me her sen.'

Billy shrugged turning his palms out. 'Sally Snape, yeah I went to see her, but I'm not pestering her. I just asked her a few questions about sommat.'

'Huh, a few questions about sommat,' Stan sneered, mimicking his tone.

Billy stiffened crossly. 'What the hell's wrong, Stan? Whaddayer being like this for?'

'I don't want Sally pestered. Leave her alone.' He paced about the rubble-strewn floor, kicking at odd bits of plaster and timber. 'I know thaz been trying to find out about that bloke who drowned. Well she's got nowt to do wi' it. Keep away from her. It were Darnley who did it. I thought you'd worked that out by now. Him and Hepburn had a row. He fell over and hit his head. Darnley drowned him. Tha knew that, surely.'

Billy did know it, but it was useful to hear Stan say so too. 'I – I didn't ask her about that. I asked her ...'

'I know what tha asked her,' Stan yelled with undiminished fury. 'And I don't want her asked owt again. I've told thee now, Billy. Stay away from her. I won't tell thee again.' He stomped out of the shattered room and headed for his motor cycle.

Billy rushed out after him. 'Stan, who killed Mary? Is that

what this's about? Tell me who did it. Wait, Stan. Stan - don't go.'

Stan Daniels straddled his motorbike and kicked it into life. 'You don't know what you're messing with, Billy. That bastard Flood's behind all this. He's gonna pay too. I'll make sure of that. He covered it up. It was murder, Billy. I've worked it all out now. I know exactly what happened, and he's gonna pay. I'll make sure of that. He's got to pay as well.'

The motorcycle engine roared, spinning the back wheel and throwing up a barrage of dust and brick rubble. It swerved away into the Meadow Street traffic. A passing lorry skidded to avoid it, its brakes screeching. Billy ran out onto the pavement and saw the bike snaking away at speed. In seconds, it was gone.

'He's got to pay – "*as well*"?' Billy said to himself, repeating what Stan had said. 'What's he mean, "*as well*"? As well as who?' He rapidly reviewed everything Stan had said from the start of their brief and unpleasant meeting, and then went over their previous meetings. He was certain he had never mentioned the Marples' bombing, or Mary Scott to Stan. They had only ever talked about the drowning. Stan had been very helpful. He knew a lot about it, but they had never discussed the other murders. And, why was he so interested in Sally Snape? Sally didn't know anything. She hadn't said anything. What was bothering him about her?

He started walking home, Stan's troubling outburst playing over in his mind. He reviewed everything, analysing every phrase and nuance. It was then that a thought hit him like an explosion in his mind. *Daniels!* That was it. He stopped dead in his tracks, remembering suddenly that Sally had called Mary Scott, "Mary Daniels". She had immediately corrected herself and Billy had all but forgotten it.

The strident blare of a truck's horn blasted into his thoughts, shocking him back to reality. He looked around bewildered and found himself in the middle of the road. A truck was bearing down on him. He jumped out of its way and shrugged apologetically to the driver who glared back at him, mouthing angrily through his windscreen.

Daniels had been Mary's maiden name, he told himself. Stan and Mary could be related, perhaps even brother and sister. He felt so foolish. It had never occurred to him, and Stan had not mentioned it. This was why Stan was so angry. His bitter references to Flood were now completely understandable. He recalled how Stan hated Flood. That had been obvious from that first day when he had hidden in the boiler room. "That slimy toad Flood" Stan had said. Now he understood why. Obviously, Stan blamed Flood for covering up Mary's death, but was there more? Did he think Flood had killed her? After all, the same idea had crossed his mind.

A cold shiver ran down his spine. He felt sick. For a second he thought he might swoon, right there in the street. Stan had said that Flood had to pay, *"as well"*. As well as who? Who else did he mean? Who else had to pay, or had they paid already? Was it Darnley? Did he mean him?

'Oh my God!' cried Billy staring at a brick wall plastered with old posters. A woman with a toddler in a pushchair accelerated passed him as she heard him speak. No doubt she wondered what was so terrible about the circus poster he seemed to be gaping at.

'The pint of Guinness in the corner!' Billy cried, recalling how Polly Harrison had scorned the man for not bringing back his glass. 'She had said he was on a motorbike.'

The mother prepared to take a defensive swing at Billy as he leapt over her toddler in its pram and sprinted for home. It was a steep, gruelling run of about a mile and took in Blake Street, a killingly steep hill. Even so, it passed in a blur. Luckily, his mam was not back from work yet, saving him the need for explanations. Without pausing, he grabbed his bike and pedalled off to find Doctor Hadfield.

He felt sick with worry about Stan. It was obvious he was going after Flood. He feared that in his present state of mind, deluded by grief and vengeful fury, Stan could easily do something he would regret forever. He pedalled harder, skidding round corners and dodging between the rush hour trams. He would soon be there. Hadfield would know what to do. He could help him to find Stan and calm him down. An image of Stan crashing into Flood's office and killing him at his desk, flashed through Billy's head as he pedalled in to the Doctor's quiet, leafy street of Victorian villas. They had to stop him. Hadfield could drive him to Police Headquarters. He could stop Stan bursting in there and doing anything stupid. It wasn't Flood he wanted to protect. He couldn't care less about him. It was Stan. He had to stop him from becoming a murderer and facing hanging, especially for killing a scumbag like Flood.

Hadfield was not at home.

Billy pedalled down to the main surgery, half a mile away, hoping he might be there. Seeing that his Austin Seven was not parked in its usual spot, he did not bother to go in. Instead he pedalled round to the ironmongers on South Road, hoping to find PC Needham. Mister Nicholls, the owner, grabbed him before he could reach the storage shed. 'Let go of me. I've got to find John,' he panted. 'It's an emergency.'

Mister Nicholls eyed him suspiciously, but was quickly convinced by his demeanour. He released him. 'He's not in there. I haven't seen him today.'

Billy looked about, feelings of panic rising in his chest. 'Can I use your phone? I have to ring the cops. It's an emergency.'

'I don't have a phone,' said Mister Nicholls, as if admitting the errors of a misspent life. 'They've got one at the post office. Here, lad, come wi' me. I'll tell 'em you need it.'

The postmistress listened to the ironmonger's tale, occasionally peering at Billy with obvious distaste. 'I'm just closing up,' she said. 'It's gone half past five.'

Billy stared at her unmoved. Finally, she sighed and began looking up the number for Police Headquarters. Billy thanked her profusely for her kind help, not suspecting for a second that she was simply making sure he did not ring some auntie in Australia. She dialled and handed him the phone. Eventually he was put through to Flood's snooty assistant. She told him the chief superintendent had gone home for the day. The postmistress and the ironmonger hissed in chorus that he should ask her to take a message. He did, but the woman refused. She also declined to give him Flood's home telephone number.

Billy looked at the two worried adults. The postmistress, now fully engaged, whipped through the telephone directory shaking her head with worry. 'I can't see his number in here. He must be ex-directory.'

'Don't worry,' he told them. 'I know where he lives.' He ran out of the post office, mounted his bike and pedalled off, first to Yvonne's house. She joined him without question. Her mother stroked her owl, mumbling something about how nice it was for two children to be so thoughtful. The pair pedalled off to pick up Kick Morley on the way to what Billy called "Flood's massive-mansion-palace"

The three of them tackled the gruelling climb up to Ranmoor, as Billy breathlessly updated them. It was about six-thirty when they arrived at the walls of Flood's leafy garden. The evening summer sun gilded the gently swaying heads of the trees. There was no sign of Stan Daniels or his motorbike. Apart from a large black car, parked a few houses away, the street was empty. They did not go straight up to the house. Billy suggested they should try to find Stan first, and convince him not to do anything stupid. If they did find him and could turn him around, the whole thing might be forgotten, though in his heart Billy doubted it. They split up and searched the street, peering in shrubberies and behind garden walls hoping to find Stan's motorbike.

After a while, they had to give up. They hid their bikes in bushes. Billy suggested they should watch the house and try to catch Stan as he arrived. Keeping well out of sight of the windows in Flood's house, the trio crept up the drive. At the large sweeping lawn, they crouched in a thick shrubbery. They could get no closer without the risk of being spotted crossing the lawn. 'You two stay here,' said Billy. 'I'll go and see if Stan's here already. He might be round the back. If I don't find him …' He stopped and hung his head. 'Well, I don't know what we'll do then. I expect we'll have no choice. We'll have to go and ring the doorbell.' He turned and eyed the house, readying himself for the dash across the open lawn.

His heart felt as if it would leap out of his mouth as he dashed across the open ground, but he was determined to help his friend. He knew that grief and anger had shaken Stan's powers of reason, knocking him seriously off balance, so that all he wanted was vengeance. But that would bring about his own destruction. Somehow, Billy had to stop him.

He commando rolled into the shadow of the house and pressed back against its wall, panting for breath. He got a rapturous thumbs-up from Kick, who disappeared quickly, presumably dragged back unceremoniously into cover by Yvonne.

Sideling along against the wall, his shoulder blades in contact with it, he came to a door and window. He guessed it was probably the back kitchen. A couple of buckets and a yard broom stood beside the door. He reached for the door handle, listening all the while for any sound. It was unlocked. He opened it silently, and slipped inside. It was a kitchen, large, empty and dimly lit. Crouching by a scrubbed pine table, he froze, listening for any sounds. He heard adult male voices, distant and muffled. He couldn't tell what was being said, but sometimes they were soft and low and then would swell up louder and more passionate, as if in argument. He listened at each of the two internal doors before gingerly trying the second one. It opened into a large dining room, furnished with antique furniture. The room was unoccupied, the curtains drawn. At its far end, light showed around the edge of a door into an adjoining room. He crept across to it and peered through the crack.

'Aren't you joining us?' It was Sergeant Lackey. He had whipped the door open just as Billy leaned to put his ear to it. 'You'll hear much better inside.' Billy stumbled into a brightly lit sitting room. A crystal chandelier and bright matching wall lights sparkled around the room. Heavy curtains covered two large windows, though outside the evening sun still shone.

Flood was pointing a pistol at Stan Daniels, who took

advantage of the distraction and dived to grab it. Flood was too fast. He spun around and clubbed Stan to the ground with it. He dropped like a sack. Billy ran to him and tried to help him to his feet. Blood oozed from a wound on Stan's head. He moaned softly and covered it with his hand. After a few moments he was able to stand, leaning heavily on Billy as he struggled to his feet.

Flood was grinning, almost giddy with delight. 'This is excellent,' he said. 'Thank you, for coming, Billy. It's good to see you again. Now we can tidy everything up at once.' He turned and pointed to Stan. 'I suppose you've worked out that he killed that fool Darnley? He eavesdrops at pipes all day, don't you Daniels?'

Billy gaped at Stan, and immediately remembered the menthol sweet wrappers on the floor near the chunter pipes. Had Stan been listening near those pipes? Had he heard them arguing? Perhaps he'd heard even the killing.

'He learns all sorts of secrets that way. That's how he learned Darnley had hidden his sister's body. I suppose he heard Hepburn accuse him and threaten to tell the police. That's when it all started. He flipped. He began making a nuisance of himself, stirring up trouble for everybody. But he's a fool. He's stupid. He killed Darnley instead of waiting to let things take their course. We would have nailed Darnley eventually for Hepburn's murder.'

'You lying toad. I never …'

'No matter now. I'll see you're blamed anyway. The evidence is a bit thin, but my good friend Doctor Longden will make sure it sticks, and the drowning too.'

'He didn't drown Hepburn,' Billy cried.

'Yes, I know, but it'll look a lot tidier that way. Longden can fix it. He'll wrap it all up in a nice neat bundle and everybody will be happy we got the right man.'

Lackey was at the window peering out into the garden through a chink in the curtains. He turned to Flood. 'Sir, quick, look here.' His voice sounded tense and panicky. Billy's heart sank. If Lackey had spotted Kick and Yvonne, they'd be dragged in too. Flood backed towards the window keeping the pistol aimed at Stan. He snatched a quick look where Lackey was pointing. 'There's nothing there, you idiot,' he snapped.

'For God's sake, Flood,' Stan cried. 'He's just a kid. You can't mean to kill …'

Billy retched and vomited on the carpet. His face was ashen. He swayed and reached for the support of a table. Until Stan spoke up, he hadn't thought of being killed. Now he realised that if Flood was happy to incriminate others in his presence, such as Longden, he clearly had no intention of ever releasing him, or Stan. Obviously, he intended to kill them both, and if he spotted his pals outside, he would have to kill them too. He was insane.

'You can't kill us both,' Stan said. 'Even you're not that mad. How would you explain two violent deaths; a child and an adult?'

Flood paced the living room. 'No problem. I've got the perfect solution in mind. You're going to vanish, no bodies, no blood, no evidence.' He turned to Lackey. 'Have we got handcuffs for both of 'em?'

'There are some in the car. I parked it up the street a bit, like you said.'

'Good, get 'em.'

'What are you going to do, chief?' Lackey was pale and sweating fearfully. Things were moving too fast for him. He was struggling to keep abreast of his deepening personal involvement and adjust to it. How far had he gone? Could he still get out?

'Get moving! Fetch the bloody car.' Flood's violent glare sent Lackey scurrying to obey. He paused briefly at the door, his face white with fear.

Flood reached out a hand in a conciliatory gesture. 'Don't worry, sergeant. I'll explain it all when you get back, but I promise you, when we're done, there won't be the slightest whiff of evidence to point to either of us.' He patted his sergeant on the arm and gently pushed him into action. 'Now, go and fetch the car, and remember, be casual and calm, no rush.'

Stan keeled over in a faint. Billy tried to help him. 'He needs some water.'

'Don't worry about him, Billy. If he dies, it'll save me having to kill him.'

A few minutes later, Lackey returned. Flood eyed him curiously. 'You alright?'

'Yeah, I took a closer look in the shrubbery. I was sure I'd seen something, but it's all clear.' He handcuffed Billy and Stan and started as if to leave.

Flood moved to the curtains and glanced outside. 'Hang on. We're not going anywhere yet. It's too light. We need it dark. There are eyes everywhere in this bloody street.'

'Huh, that'll be another hour or so,' grumbled Sergeant Lackey.

'I don't care, we can wait. It goes dark by about eight-thirty - nine. That'll be just right.'

*

Time passed slowly. Billy was bursting for a pee. 'I need to go.'

'Go? Go where?' Flood asked.

'The lav. I'm bursting.'

'Do it in your pants,' said Flood, and looked out again through a chink in the curtains. 'It's almost dark enough, I think,' he told Lackey. He pointed to Stan, who was still lying on the floor. He had barely moved in the last hour. 'Get him up and let's get going.'

Lackey took hold of Stan's leather flak jacket and started to drag him towards the door. Stan suddenly leapt up and kicked the sergeant sending him sprawling. Flood grabbed Stan's arms which were handcuffed behind his back and spun him round. He crashed him into the wall like a rag doll. Family photographs and ornaments scattered, a glass fronted cabinet toppled and shattered. Stan sagged to his knees. Flood leapt on him and pushed him facedown into the shards of glass on the carpet. Lackey struggled groggily to his feet. He swung a couple of kicks at Stan before Flood stopped him. 'There'll be plenty of time for that later. Right now, I need him walking, not crippled.'

They half-carried and dragged Stan out to the car and bundled him onto the floor in the back. Billy followed dumbly. He didn't try to run. He wanted to help Stan. Lackey picked him off his feet and dumped him on the back seat. He slid in beside him, slapping him a few times to make him move to the far side of the car. Flood got in the driving seat. He passed the pistol to Lackey, who waved it about threateningly.

Flood adjusted the rear view mirror and started the car. He steered it round slowly on the gravel in front of his house and drove sedately down the drive. Billy couldn't see, but at the gate, he felt them turn left, towards the city centre. He'd thought they would probably go right out onto the wild moors, a good place for murdering and burying bodies.

In the thick shrubbery, Yvonne and Kick had formed a plan. They waited for the car to leave. Yvonne followed it on her bike, keeping well out of sight. Kick pedalled off in the opposite direction. His job was to find John Needham and Doctor Hadfield. Yvonne had told him she would get a message to him through Walter Mebbey on the telephone at the relish factory. She felt sure the old guy would help them, and think of some way of passing on her messages. She also hoped he would know what to do if Hadfield was flummoxed.

Unaware that Yvonne was following, Billy tried to sneak a look out of the car window whenever Lackey was distracted. He had no idea what Flood had in mind, and heading into the city had completely foxed him. Traffic was quiet. Rush hour was long past. Most people would have eaten by now and be sitting in front of their fires, listening to the wireless. He thought about his mother. She'd be worried sick about him, and fearing the worst. She'd be right too, *the worst* is exactly what was happening. He imagined her running round to Yvonne's and other neighbours' houses to ask them if they had seen him. Yvonne's mother would flap and start weeping and make things worse.

Flood swung the car into Fitzalan Square, passed the ruins of the Marples Hotel. He turned down the hill next to the main Post Office and swung left into the street where the Queens Head pub stood. Billy stretched up trying to see what was going on. Lackey punched him back down again and shoved him to the floor. The car swung left again into a dark, quiet street. Billy had seen enough to remember it. It was opposite the Queens Head. Ruby had pointed it out when she'd told them about the old castle tunnels. He knew it headed into a single flyover arch beneath Commercial Street and the tramlines. Where it went after that, he had no idea.

The car stopped sharply under the flyover. Flood climbed out looking about warily. The poorly lit street was deserted. 'Quick get 'em out before somebody comes,' he snapped at Lackey.'

Lackey relished the task. He dragged Stan out onto the road bumping him cruelly on the pavement edge. Billy followed and bent to help Stan, but couldn't with his wrists locked behind him. Flood was facing a narrow doorway built into the stone arch. A rusty iron barred gate sealed it off. Billy could see nothing beyond the vertical bars but pitch-blackness. Flood was fiddling with a bunch of keys, trying to fit one into a large padlock. Cursing, wrenching and twisting, he eventually managed to release the lock. He shouldered the bars, pushing hard to swing the gate. It squealed as though it had not been moved in years. Grabbing Billy by the shoulder he shoved him ahead through the gate. Stone steps led down into blackness.

Yvonne had seen enough. She thought of asking Ruby for use of the telephone, but decided against it, remembering her curmudgeonly husband. She pedalled to the telephone box near the main post office, looked up the relish factory number in the directory and dialled it. She was weeping but trying hard not to admit it to herself. A night watchman at the relish factory agreed immediately to fetch Walter to the telephone. The sound of Walter's voice on the line was such a relief that she couldn't speak for several seconds. Once she started, she couldn't stop. When Walter had the gist of the story, he put a hand over the telephone mouthpiece. 'Here Barry,' he whispered, passing the receiver to the young man beside him. 'Try to calm her down a bit. I've got to get going.'

*

In the tunnel, Flood was pushing Billy ahead of him, deeper into a damp, silent blackness. He swung a torch beam along narrow tunnels and alcoves. 'These are the old castle tunnels,' he said, his voice strangely gleeful. 'I first came here during the war, but I expect you know all about that by now, don't you? I've been here quite a few times since. Go left.' He pushed Billy leftwards where more steps led down towards the sound of running water. 'Down here is where you'll spend - eternity. I hope you like it. You can make friends with Spring Heeled Jack. This is his world. Did you know that?'

The tunnel opened out into a vaulted area about twelve feet square. Another tunnel and a narrow staircase fed into it. In one corner was a black hole about two feet square. Billy could hear running water in it. He peered closer, but could see nothing. On the opposite side, a wider tunnel sloped down into the room. It seemed to curve in from above.

'I'd like you to climb down there please, Stan.' Flood pointed his torch at the hole in the stone flagged floor. 'It's a bit of a squeeze, but you'll manage it. Billy will follow you. You'll be company for each other. In a couple of weeks we'll discover your bodies. No bullets or stab wounds.' He laughed and glanced at Lackey, then back at Stan. 'Huh, it's the perfect murder. Nobody lays a finger on you.'

He cocked the pistol. 'Take off his handcuffs, Sergeant. And – er – make sure they've got no pencils or scrapers – nothing that could be embarrassing. Put 'em in head first. That'll make sure they don't climb out. There's a slab over in that corner that you can pop over the top of 'em.'

Sergeant Lackey froze suddenly. 'Shush, I hear something.'

Flood gaped around, his brain sifting every sound. Billy and Stan listened too. There was something. Lackey was right, thought Billy. What was it? It sounded like rustling, like stiff cloth or dry leaves in the wind ...

Flood lost patience. 'Oh get him in there quick. We can check it out later.' Lackey started with Stan's handcuffs. At that very moment, a face appeared in the black mouth of the opposite tunnel; a wicked, cruel face with a wide, vicious mouth and staring eyes. It floated on a strange, indefinable mist. Flood gaped, 'Spring Heeled - ,' he murmured in disbelief.

Stan broke free of Lackey and kicked Flood's legs from under him. The pistol fell to the ground and rattled across the flagstones. Stan gathered it up in a second. Sergeant Lackey shrank back and clutched his head as it was pointed at him. He stumbled, his feet finding only air as he plummeted down the shaft into the water below. Flood capitulated immediately. He stood up, his hands raised.

The apparition stepped forward, its fiendish face vanishing as it walked. It shed its weird mist, which, on closer inspection, turned out to be a plasterer's dustsheet spattered with gobs of dried plaster and paint.

'Walter!' Billy cried. 'That was brilliant.'

Walter struggled to remove a pencil he had stuck across his gape. It came away, ridding his face of the wide, leering grin it had given him. That simple device and a torch placed strategically under his chin, had given him the horrific, ghostly façade of Spring Heeled Jack. A plasterer's dust sheet had done the rest. Three hugely muscled men, wearing gym shorts and vests filed in behind Walter. One of them wrestled a small key from Flood and released Billy from his handcuffs, instantly transferring them to Flood.

Beams of light were flashing down the tunnels in both directions. Detective Wooffitt and a uniformed police officer appeared from one tunnel. Yvonne, Kick and Constable Needham emerged from the other. Hadfield followed them in. In seconds, the dark, silent tunnels had become a bright, thronged area, with people milling about, happily congratulating each other. D.C. Wooffitt got two of the weightlifters to haul Sergeant Lackey out of the shaft. A young police constable, who was very excited to be involved, gleefully handcuffed him.

PC Needham and Detective Wooffitt spun a coin to see who would have the honour of formally arresting the Chief Superintendent. John Needham checked the coin and craftily declared himself the loser, thereby avoiding possibly hours of paperwork.

More police officers arrived and began escorting everyone out into the pleasant night air. Billy found the street full of police cars, two ambulances and a fire tender. A few spectators had gathered. He recognized Ruby from the Queen's Head pub, and another familiar face, Harry Clegg. 'Billy, don't talk to anybody but me,' he hissed from the gathering crowd. 'I want the exclusive on this.'

Billy glared back at him, annoyed that Clegg seemed to think this was all some sort of game. He nodded crossly and brushed him aside. He was more interested in finding out what was happening about Clarissa.

Hadfield was talking to Yvonne near his car. She was peering about, grim faced, looking for Billy and Kick. She cheered up as she spotted them, and steered Hadfield towards them.

'Look, old lad,' Hadfield said pulling Billy gently aside. 'I need to find Sarah. Her boss, Longden, is in this up to his rotten neck. I'm worried about what he might do.'

'Do? What do you mean?' asked Billy.

'Well, he and Flood have been in cahoots, we all know that now. The police want him for fixing evidence. He might try to intimidate Sarah or something. He's a desperate man, Billy. He could do anything. He's gambled away all his family's money. He's finished, in more ways than one. Sarah needs to know. I don't want her getting caught up in …'

'Is that where you're going?' Billy asked, glancing across to Hadfield's car.'

'I have to see her, Billy. To make sure she's safe. I've explained to PC Needham, and asked him to take you all home. He will do, but you have to talk to the police first. They're taking on-the-spot-statements. They'll see us all again tomorrow. They're letting me go because of Sarah.'

Billy shrugged, letting Hadfield dash off to his car. He looked around for the constable and found him with D.C. Wooffitt and a knot of police officers, listening to a senior officer who announced himself as Superintendent Roberts. He was taking charge. Meanwhile, other police and forensics officers were moving in and out of the gated tunnel. Flood was sitting handcuffed in the back of a police car. Medics were loading Sergeant Lackey into an ambulance, still handcuffed, but now cursing Flood and breaking every confidence they had ever shared.

Billy spotted Walter Mebbey in the growing crowd of rubber-neckers. He and his weightlifter pals, one of whom had driven him to the tunnels in a Bedford truck, were chatting quietly with Ruby and some of her customers from the Queen's Head. Walter happily nursed a frothing pint of stout. Billy threaded his way through the throng and sidled up to him. 'Can you get me out of here?'

'Yeah, what's up?'

'I have to see Clarissa,' he said from the side of his mouth. 'She's involved. In fact after what's happened here, I'm sure it was her who killed Mary.'

Walter gasped. 'Old tweedy knickers? Why would she?'

'Can you give us a lift? We can try the surgery first, burrits late, she'll probably have gone home. She lives at Litton Mill, near Millersdale.'

Walter turned to his driver pal. 'What do you say, Barry? It's Walkley, the surgery just off South Road?' He decided not to mention remote Litton Mill out in the Peak District.

Barry's face lit up. He was enjoying his adventure, and eager to be of use again. 'Yeah, come on then. Let's get cracking. You navigate, Billy.'

'Just a second,' said Billy. 'Weerz mi pals? I need to tell 'em.' He ran to find Yvonne and Kick and explain what he planned. Both wanted to come too, and stealthily backed away from the circle of police activity and sneaked into the back of Barry the plasterer's truck.

*

At the surgery they found Dr Fulton-Howard's car crazily parked with two wheels in a flowerbed and two in front of the coach house doors. Billy checked its coachwork. The keys were in the ignition. He looked under the seats and checked the boot.

They found the surgery's Victorian double doors firmly locked. Barry lifted Billy up to the fanlight above them, as though he weighed no more than a loaf of bread. 'I can see her,' Billy whispered. 'Her office door's wide open. She's just sat there - wobbling a bit.' Barry lowered him to the doorstep. 'We've gorra get in there,' said Billy. 'She might take pills or sommat daft.'

Walter asked, 'Has tha got thee universal door key, Barry?'

Barry exposed a mightily muscled arm. 'Does tha mean this one?'

'That's it,' said Walter.

The weightlifting plasterer took hold of the handles of the narrow double doors. He leaned back slightly, and then shouldered them in with ease. Grinning, he bowed and ushered Billy inside.

Walter stood back. 'You don't need me for this, Billy. Me and Barry'll wait out here, in case the coppers come.'

Clarissa raised her head and sneered as Billy, followed by Yvonne and Kick, entered her consulting room. She lounged inelegantly at her desk, a glass and a bottle of whisky in front of her. She refilled the glass, clearly not for the first time that evening. Yvonne and Kick hung back nervously as Billy approached her.

'I suppose you're feeling pretty pleased with yourselves,' she said her speech slurred, her gestures clumsy. 'I thought it wouldn't be long before some idiot came through that door. I expected that fool Hadfield, but it's you. Huh, *The Three Stooges*.' She laughed, almost choking as she took a swig of scotch.

'I'm sorry about Doctor Longden,' said Billy, assuming she knew the police were looking for him, and why.

'Why? He's a fool. A weak fool. Clearly, he never cared about me. He was a liar. I was in love with him, but he lied all the time. Treated me worse than ... All he thought about was money –

gambling. That's all I ever was to him. A money supply.' She topped up her glass again and drained it noisily. 'He'll never know what I gave up for him. What I did for him.'

'You mean killing Mary Scott, to stop her blabbing.' Billy watched her closely.

'Don't be silly,' Clarissa sneered. 'I didn't kill her.'

'Somebody did. You were there. It must have been you,' insisted Billy. 'You buried her in that tunnel and left her to rot. When they found her body, a week later, you and Longden fixed the death certificate to make it look like just another bomb casualty.'

Clarissa blinked a tear from her eye. It spilled down her stony face like an ice crystal. 'It wasn't murder, you silly child,' she said. 'It was an accident. She ran off into the dark and fell. I never touched her. I didn't want her to die.'

A disturbance at the back of the room made Billy turn round to look. Mister Roberts, the police superintendent, had arrived. He paused in the doorway and glanced around, quickly assessing the situation. John Needham followed him in, frantically miming that Billy should shut up, underlining his concern by drawing a finger across his throat and nodding crazily.

The superintendent took a step forward, 'That's enough, young man,' he said sternly. 'Doctor Fulton-Howard is not a murder suspect. We have the killers safely locked up.'

Billy stretched up and looked the officer in the eye. 'Well you've missed one – er - Sir. She's a murderer, and I can prove it.'

The officer smiled and lowered his gaze, before quietly addressing Billy full faced. 'Billy, isn't it?' he enquired pleasantly. 'Billy Perks. I've heard a lot about you. I know you've been very helpful to us in the past, and frankly, I don't think we've always treated you with the respect you deserve. You're a bright lad. Your parents should be proud, but you've got it wrong this time, I'm afraid.'

'I haven't, sir,' said Billy, squaring his shoulders. 'She's a killer, and if you let her go, you'll be making a big mistake.'

Silence fell on the group, as the man and the boy faced each other. A tear slid down Yvonne's cheek. Kick clenched his fists, ready to tackle anybody who went near Billy. Doctor Hadfield arrived with Sarah Becket and Harry Clegg. They pressed through the gathering crush of police officers and curious members of the public. Hadfield nodded and gave Billy an encouraging smile.

'But, Billy, we've got them all,' Roberts said softly. 'We know the whole story.' He glanced around bringing Yvonne and Kick into the discussion. 'Professor Darnley drowned poor Mister Hepburn, because he'd found out about the theft from one of the safety deposit boxes. I'm certain we can show that Stan Daniels killed the professor, and I'm satisfied that Doctor Longden and the professor probably killed Mary Scott.' He patted Billy on the shoulder, and smiled at him. 'It's all over, son; just the loose ends to tie up. You've done a very good job.' He turned to face his officers crowding in the doorway. 'Now come on everybody, clear the room. Constable, get everybody out, and see that these children are safely taken home. Their parents must be worried sick.'

'No, wait! She is a killer,' Billy cried. 'I can prove it!'

Clarissa stood up sharply, reeling unsteadily. She backed into shelves behind her, scattering pill bottles, medical equipment and books. 'I didn't kill her,' she cried. 'I was angry with her, but I didn't kill her.' She turned to the superintendent, and pointed to Billy. 'He's right about Darnley. He was a cheat and a thief. Mary Scott saw him steal from the safety deposit boxes. She was going to tell the police. I couldn't allow that. They would have arrested Amos too – Doctor Longden. I tried to persuade her to keep quiet. I said we could make them give it back later, but no, she wouldn't budge.' She wiped her face and tried to straighten herself up. 'I didn't kill her. She ran away into the darkness. I didn't have a torch, just a cigarette lighter, but I chased after her. I found her eventually. She'd fallen, tripped over some rubble. I tried to stop the bleeding. It was her head. The cranial fossa. The meningeal artery was severed. I couldn't see in the dark. I couldn't stop it. I didn't kill her. I didn't. It was all Darnley's fault. He's poisonous. He killed everything. He killed my life … my heart.'

Mister Roberts laid a hand gently on Billy's shoulder. 'You see, Billy. I believe her. She's not a killer.'

Clarissa was glaring drunkenly at Billy. 'Don't you see, you silly child?' she yelled, slurring her words.

'You may not have killed Mary Scott, but you're still a killer,' Billy said flatly. 'You killed Darnley.'

Clarissa bristled combatively. 'Don't be so stupid. How could I have done?'

'You were following Longden in your car. You saw him drive Darnley to the Rivelin Hotel, but instead of parking there, like they did, you parked up on the lane by Goody Fields, where they couldn't see you.'

'Don't be ridiculous …Stop this foolish child now.'

John Needham reached for Billy's shoulder, to take him away as Mister Roberts had instructed, but the superintendent raised a staying hand, his curiosity evidently aroused. He stood back watching the exchange between Billy and the doctor.

Billy looked around, suddenly feeling sick. He realised he was in the spotlight. The seriousness of the situation weighed on him as he tried to speak. His voice would not work, his knees felt weak and panic was welling up in his stomach. Luckily, Humphrey Bogart was not put off by the tension crackling in the room. Inside Billy's head, he took over, though his accent sounded a bit more Sheffield than Chicago. 'You scratched your car up there, your Rover 75. The paint mark's still on the wall.'

Mister Roberts immediately sent a junior to alert the forensics team. Billy – or -Humphrey, went on relentlessly. 'You crossed the sheep field. I guess you wanted to look down on Longden's car from the crag. You'd be able to see 'em leave without them spotting you. My guess is you were gonna follow 'em again.'

'Why would I?' she snapped.

'To have a go at 'em about fixing – ort – ort – autopsies.'

'This is ridiculous.' She turned angrily on Superintendent

Roberts. 'You're supposed to be in charge, here. How much longer are you going to permit this farce to continue?'

'You put on your walking shoes,' Billy went on, 'because the field was muddy and slippery. They're still in your car. The mud on 'em will prove you were there.'

'I – I –I often walk there. It's – it's one of my favourite spots. Of course there's mud on my shoes. It's always muddy in those fields.'

Billy was relentless. 'You watched old Longden leave and drive away, but professor Darnley stayed in the pub for about another ten minutes. But you waited. When he came out you watched him walk up to the Man's head Rock.'

'What nonsense! How much longer are you going to allow this foolish child to…'

'There he was,' said Billy dramatically, adjusting an imaginary trilby hat.

Roberts lifted an eyebrow, noticing that Billy seemed to have acquired a slight American accent.

'It was Darnley, the guy who'd messed up your life,' he said eyeing her steadily. 'He'd spoiled everything for you. He'd spoiled Longden, hadn't he? He'd turned him into a crook and a cheat. You might have married him, but for Darnley. And, he might never have fallen into Flood's clutches, with all his dirty tricks and swindles.' Billy glanced at the faces gathered at his shoulders. 'There he was, all alone. You saw your chance. You climbed down the rocky path at the side of the crag, crept up behind him and belted him.'

'What nonsense. What am I supposed to have hit him with?'

Roberts turned to Billy, enquiry written all over his face. 'Well?'

Kick stepped up, taking defensive stance beside his pal. He hadn't a clue what the answer to the question was and feared that Billy might be running out of steam. 'Go on, Billy, tell 'em.'

Billy looked at the faces in the room. He saw Doc Hadfield smiling, willing him on. No one moved. No one spoke. He turned back to Clarissa. 'A croquet mallet,' he said. 'From the back of your car. I guess you took it with you, because it was slippery in that muddy field. You were using it upside down as a walking stick.' He turned to Roberts. 'It's still there, in the car boot. My guess is you'll find Darnley's blood on it.'

Clarissa lunged at him but missed. 'You vile little boy,' she shouted, spittle glossing her sneering lips.

Yvonne quickly stepped in close at Billy's side and squeezed his forearm encouragingly. He looked back into her large brown eyes and smiled gratefully. 'Yeah, and "Here's looking at you, kid."'

THE END

Epilogue

They charged Doctor Clarissa Fulton-Howard with Darnley's murder, concealing a crime and perverting the course of justice. The list of charges against Chief Superintendent Flood filled several pages, and included, conspiracy to murder, attempted murder, abduction of a minor, blackmail, concealing a crime, and innumerable counts of perverting the course of justice.

A coroner's enquiry concluded that James Hepburn, had been murdered, by drowning, by a person, or persons unknown. Popular opinion agreed with Billy's analysis that Professor Darnley had done it, which is how Harry Clegg reported it. The court did not attempt to explain the post mortem damage, or injuries, to Darnley's corpse. The police sought Stan Daniels to help them with their enquiries, but quickly lost interest when he could not be found.

Sally Snape received the keys to Stan's cottage. A handwritten note in the blank rent book for it, suggested that if she should feel like paying a rent, she should instead donate to Walter's Gym at the relish factory. Sally and her Tommy soon began growing ever more children and a lush variety of vegetables in their large garden.

Polly Harrison continued her determined resistance to the public's rising demands for pub food and "frenchified" drinks. She also told Harry Clegg, "Not everyone who fails to return their empty glasses, is a killer.".'

For a week or so Billy and Kick pondered over the Pagez Cypher with its hints at buried treasure. Their outrageous ramblings kept Yvonne amused for hours until their interest faded and the football season got fully into its stride.

A week after Christmas, Billy received a postcard, from Man's Head Rock in Montana, USA. It said simply, "Scotch mist - Will o' the Whizz." It was signed, Roy Lenfield. Kick wanted to know who Roy Lenfield was. Yvonne reminded him, disdainfully, that Stan Daniels's motorbike had been a Royal Enfield. Kick shrugged bemused, until the penny dropped.

Glossary of Sheffield – eeze

Alreight:	(pron. as in eight) All right
An'all:	Also, as well, and all
Andrew:	"*The Andrew*" sailor's slang for Royal Navy.
Aypenny duck:	Savoury meat ball or faggot.
Ayup mi owd:	Hello my old friend
Back-naks:	Back gardens
Beeyart:	Without, not having, minus.
Bob:	Shilling (twentieth of an old pound sterling)
Bobbies:	Police officers
Chabby:	Toddler (also pron. chavvy)
Clemmed:	Feeling cold
Crozzled:	Crisped, scorched, (from slag in steel making)
Dee-ad:	Dead
Dee-in:	Dying
Dint:	Did not
Donkey-stoned:	White chalk drawn edge to steps, as used in the wartime blackout
Dunt:	Does not
Gen:	Given
Googly:	A sneaky, crafty and often highly effective style of bowling in cricket.
Laikin:	Playing
Mardy:	Grouch, sulking, whining
Little Mester:	Self-employed cutler or metal smith.
Mester:	Master, or man in authority.
Moant:	Must not
Mun:	Must
Nay:	No
Neet:	Night
Netty:	Outside toilet.
Nithered:	Feeling cold
Nowt:	Nothing
Nowty:	Poor quality, small, shabby
Owt:	Anything

One-n-tuppence:	A shilling and two pennies (old money)
Pog:	Personal space, place in queue, usual seat.
Racked:	Plodding of packhorses. Rivelin Street follows The line of the 4000 year-old Racker Way, a packhorse track.
Rantied:	Rocked, wobbled, unsteady
Ranty:	Children's see-saw
Reight:	Right, intensely, very
Reight badly:	Very sick
Scroamin:	Climbing, scrambling
Scutch:	Smack, slap
Sen	Self
Shurrup:	Be quiet
Sin':	Since
Sithee:	See you, pay attention, observe.
Skoyl:	School
Snek:	Latch
Sprottling:	Reclining
Tanner:	Silver six pence coin.
Th'art:	You are
The Blades:	Name of the best or second best football team in Sheffield. *(This will be energetically disputed.)*
The Owls:	Name of the best or second best football team In Sheffield. *(This will be energetically disputed.)*
Thee sen:	Alone, your self
Threpenz:	Three pence
Tup:	A ram
Tuppenz:	Two pence

Tommy Ward's elephant was put to work during WW1 because of the shortage of horses.

T'owd:	The old
Tranklements:	Bits and pieces, odds and ends, thingamabobs.
Watta:	(pron. As in hatter) Water
Waynt:	Will not

Wellows: Wellingtons, (Never Wellies back in the fifties)
Weshin: Laundry
Wunt: Would not

A Sheffield-eeze Ditty   (Speech exercise)

Oh weer reight dahn in coyl oyl,
Weer muck splarts on t'winders.
We've used all us coyl up,
An' weer reight dahn to cinders.
When bum-bailiff cooms eel never fint us,
Cos weer reight dahn in coyl oyl,
Weer muck splarts on t'winders.

(bum-bailiff, so called because they always came round the back.)

Translation

Oh, we are right down in the basement,
Where the dirt accumulates on the casement.
We have used all our anthracite,
And are right down to the residue.
When the landlord's representative calls,
He will not discover us,
Because we are right down in the basement,
Where the dirt accumulates on the casement.   Anon.

Spring Heeled Jack o' Sheffield

Prowls Spring Heeled Jack on nights of black,
The steel city's leaping ghoul.
In filth he scroams Satan's foul domes,
Hunting the unwary fool.

One face time weather'd, spring heels unleather'd,
He watches with baleful gaze.
In dark his other, self-same not brother,
Drags liars to his maze.

Jack leaps o'er spires, sucks life from liars,
Garners proud talking fools.
From dungeons deep on them he'll leap,
Those keenest of Satan's tools.

From lost stone ways, or oak beamed his gaze,
Sees all and waits to leap.
Proud liars beware the night's dark air,
Spring Heeled Jack will never sleep.

Acknowledgements
Many thanks to all those who helped me, especially my wife Jeannie, who patiently tracked down my many typos, despairing when I changed anything without telling her, for all the new ones she knew I'd have introduced.
Thanks also for:
JR Wrigley's book, A Walkley Camera, Pickard Publishing, Sheffield.
Walkley Through the Ages by Albert Staley, DS Publishing.
Around Sheffield Then and Now, by Geoffrey Howse, Sutton Publishing.
Water Power on the Sheffield Rivers, Sheffield Trades Historical Society, University of Sheffield, and Sheffield City Museums.
Reminiscing Rivelin by Roy Davey, DS Publishing.
Sheffield archive www.picturesheffield.com

About the Author
Brian Sellars was born in Sheffield in 1941 where he attended St Joseph's primary and St Vincent's secondary schools. Aged fifteen he started work in the steelworks as an apprentice electrician, but switched to become a sales rep, and later sales manager. He travelled extensively, mainly in the Far East, USA and Australasia, selling engineering services and capital equipment to oil companies and governments engaged in large civil engineering projects.

Brian has been married over fifty years. He and his wife live in a village near Bath, England. Now retired, he spends his time writing, doing woodwork, exploring old British towns and villages, and doing what his wife calls, "Looking at bumps in fields."

READ A SAMPLE OF THE WHISPERING BELL.

This historical fiction, for ADULT readers, is set in the Peak District around 650 A.D. It's an adventure story about an Anglo Saxon warrior's wife. When her husband is lost in battle, she is cheated out of her home, inheritance and even her children. This is the story of her fight to win them back.

Chapter One

Mercian England circa 620 AD
After the great sickness famine gripped the land, garnishing it for riot and murder. Abandoned farms fell into ruin. Weeds shrouded rotting ploughs in neglected fields and yards. Bands of vengeful wealhs picked over their lost lands, preying on the few English incomers who had managed to save a little food. In smouldering settlements corpses lay unburied, their flesh a

gruesome harvest for the dying. Beyond limp stockades and deserted city walls secretive groups of fearful refugees scoured the great shire-wood for berries and roots.

Twice Ettith had defied famine and plague. Despite the aches of her old bones she had outlived her entire family, strapping sons and daughters with their rowdy broods. She was a loner deeply suspicious of others. That was how she had survived so long and though weak from hunger and as frail as a rush-light flame her old eyes still burned defiantly in their waxy sockets.

She came upon a hamlet deep in the forest on a soft summer's morning piped with glistening dew and birdsong. As usual she hid and settled to study the place assessing its situation. Did the inhabitants have food? Might they be dangerous or hospitable? If she saw they too were starving she'd pass them by. It would not be wise to linger.

All was silent: no dogs, no smoke, no hens scratching in the road, no children playing near the pond, no men in the fields, or women hunched over the washing stones beside the well. Like so many farms and settlements she had seen it stood abandoned, stripped and ravaged by plague and famine. Already the greening haze of disuse covered its single street as the forest reclaimed the rutted earth.

"A mouse would be lucky to fill its belly in this place," she said, as if to craning onlookers.

She was about to leave when she spotted a cat cleaning itself beside the door of one of the small, windowless houses. It stopped its grooming and eyed her as she stepped from cover. "Cat is meat," she whispered, stalking it like a wolf on a lamb. "Cat is meat, good meat." Such a cat could feed her for a week or more. "Here kitty kitty."

A sound burst upon her, scaring away the cat. Her old joints froze as stiff as sticks. She tilted her head and flicked her gaze around trying to pinpoint the source of the sound. It was several moments before she recognized the sounds of the snapping crash and rip of someone forcing their way through the forest, with no care for who might hear them. She freed her joints and hobbled back to her hiding place. Moments later a man burst from the tangled undergrowth at the far side of the village. He was short and muscular with greying hair and a thick, wild beard. He wore leather armour and had a sword slung across his back. A stocky saddle pony bearing his shield, spears and a large pack trailed behind him. On the end of a long leash attached to the horse an amiable milk cow followed.

Though weary and bedraggled by his journey, the stranger's fearless bearing showed the arrogance of the warrior kind. He barged into the village, sweeping aside the vegetation, clearly expecting a deferential welcome. Though far from arrogant, the milk cow followed, equally self-assured.

Ettith had not seen a cow for months, let alone a fine, meaty horse. She imagined eating the succulent red meat they could provide. Her mouth watered, though she knew it was a foolish daydream. Without the magic of salt or a smoke house, fresh juicy meat would soon rot into a stinking flyblown mess. She had seen plenty of those.

The warrior was striding through the village searching the houses. After poking his head into several of the meaner dwellings he entered the largest where he remained for some time.

She cursed him for the loss of the fat cat. Her old body creaked as she crouched in hiding. Her stomach rumbled with hunger. Again she thought of roasted cow meat, its juices dripping over a fire. She must have food. Clasping her hands together she prayed for the man to go away and leave her to her scavenging. When at last he emerged from the house, he carried a bundle wrapped in cloth. She thought it looked big enough to be a whole ham or a side of bacon. The certainty that it was food burned into her brain, and again she cursed the warrior. If only she had arrived sooner, that ham, or whatever it was, would be hers now. But what could it be; smoked pig meat, a salted side of mutton? What was this arrogant thief stealing from her?

The man lowered the bundle to the ground and hurried back into the house. He re-emerged carrying a spade. Ettith watched him choose a spot of earth near a small shrine to Eostre, the spring goddess. He poked the spade at the ground a few times and then dug it in deep, piling his weight behind it.

"Food, he's burying the food," she told herself, before doubts dismissed the notion. No, not food, she thought, but what? She stared at the bundle, trying to make sense of the swaddled shape. Is it a little child? She shuddered as the idea that it could be grew in her mind. It could be a bairn – perhaps his own. She smoothed her palms over her cheeks and stood up, watching him work. Sadness chilled her like shadows. She pitied him. Despite her years of trouble and loss, the sight of this lone warrior digging a grave for his small child struck her deeply. She stepped out of hiding and hobbled towards him, determined to offer whatever comfort she could.

Startled, the man spun round to face her, wide eyed. "Oh gods, mother!" he said. "You scared the marrow out o' me. I didn't think there was anybody here."

She was about to reply when, from the corner of her eye, she caught a slight movement in the swaddled bundle. "It's alive!"

"Aye, just about. It's the mother who's dead. The bairn seems right enough," he said, sweat dripping off his nose and vanishing into the wilderness of his whiskers. He studied Ettith for a moment then asked, "You're not their kin are you? I don't remember seeing you before."

"No."

"Aagh — pity. She died just now while I was in there. You'd have thought she was waiting for me. She just handed me the bairn and died - never made a sound."

Ettith eyed him closely. "So, you're not kin either?"

"No, but I knew 'em. Not her so much as her man. He was a comrade, a blood sworn friend," he said. "It's the least I can do for him. He was killed."

He began digging again, but with a fierce energy. Ettith watched him, wondering where such strength came from. After a while he stopped and mopped his brow. "I know these parts well, but don't recall seeing you, old mother."

"No, I'm just passing," Ettith said, adding hopefully. "Have you any food?"

He waved a hand in the direction of his pony. "Aye, there's a pack on the horse. I brought it for the woman. Her man was killed alongside me in the shield wall. I promised him. She'll not need it now. I brought her that damned cow too. It's slower than winter honey. Can you take it off me? I've urgent duties. I can't be slowed by a stubborn cow."

Ettith could hardly believe her luck. The pack was full of such food as she had only dreamed of in months; bread, salt pig, cheese, a sack of dried white beans, some coarse flour, a block of salt, honey and a skin of ale. She sat beneath the horse's belly, stuffing her mouth as fast as she could; afraid she may be dreaming and might wake up before she'd had her fill.

When the grave was finished, the man carried out the body of the child's mother and gently lowered it into the ground. Ettith stood beside him looking down at the scrawny corpse wound in a sheet.

"She were a real beauty in her day," he said, his voice thickened by emotion. "You'd not think so now, would you?"

"Huh, so was I, once upon a time," said Ettith.

The man inspected her, unconvinced. "Aye well, that's the way of things I suppose." He shovelled earth over the corpse leaving the face until last.

Ettith left him to his task and wandered towards the dead woman's house, pausing for a closer look at the child sleeping in its bundle of cloths. It was a little girl about three years old. A pretty child, even though her tear-stained face was thin and drawn. Her tiny hands were slender and delicate. A leather thong, shiny with wear curled around one hand and threaded through a hole in a purple gemstone, about as big as a pigeon's egg. Ettith handled it, admiring its colour and river-polished smoothness.

"Is she all right?" the man called from the grave side.

His voice startled her, scattering her thoughts. "Oh, aye she's fine. She just needs a few good meals." She tucked the child in its soiled rags and left her sleeping to go and peer into the open door of the house. Of course, she did not dare enter. It was a house of death. Spirits would still be lurking inside hoping to catch another unwary soul.

The warrior finished his sad work and tossed the spade aside. Wiping his hands on his front, he approached Ettith, stopping on the way to pick up the sleeping child. Ettith watched with trepidation as he tried to gather up the infant. His clumsy struggle to balance the child safely woke her up. She began to howl with such a voice that its echo bounced around the village like the wail of some other-worldly creature. With a pained look the man came close to Ettith. "Do you want to come with me, or stay here? I'll leave you the cow if you're staying. Only, I must travel quickly. I don't want it slowing me down again. Treat her kindly and she'll milk well. Milk's better than meat in these times, old mother."

Ettith thanked him, praising him ecstatically as he mounted his pony. He barely heard her as he struggled to calm the screaming child in his arms. At the forest edge, Ettith stopped and watched him disappear into the enveloping green. A wave of apprehension swept her. Perhaps she should go with him? What was she to do? The solitude and secrecy of her life had become open and complicated. She now had a cow and a great pack of food to protect. Instead of being free to wander she would have to stay put, at least until the food ran out, or the cow died or wandered off. As she reviewed her new situation, she looked around the empty village. Its oppressive silence bore down, intensified by the distant, fading sounds of the warrior's departure.

She was alone now, but for her cow munching contentedly at the living turf roof of one of the houses. The silence heightened her sense of dread. She thought of yoking the cow beneath the pack of food and chasing after the warrior, and was on the point of doing so when a new sound chipped at the emptiness. It was a feeble cry, like a kitten's mewing. With relief, she remembered the cat and looked about for it. Now it could be company, not food.

Again, she heard the sound, but this time it did not seem quite so feline - more like a gurgling cough. It came from the dead woman's house.

"Spirits!" She backed away in terror. "Oh Holy Mother Frigg spare me," she cried, falling to her knees.

The sound grew louder, becoming unmistakably an infant's cry. Something deep inside her awakened, transforming her fears for herself into concern for the mysterious, unseen child. She edged towards the house, trembling at the realisation that she must go inside that place of death. She chipped a handful of salt from her newly acquired supply, and summoning courage, hobbled to the house. As she stepped over the threshold she scattered the sacred charm before her. Her courage stiffened as the charm did its work. Inside the large single room she met not even one lurking spirit.

It was a well-to-do house with many of the trappings of prosperity. There was a sturdy oak table with a bench and stools drawn up to it. A large bed had embroidered curtains. Against the walls were two elm-plank coffers, a shrine to the goddess Frigg, and a standing loom. Beside the loom a finely carved, ash-wood mydercan caught her eye. Beneath its polished lid she found sewing yarns, needles and pins. This she realised explained how two hangings of extraordinary quality, such as only a wealthy thegn might own, dressed one of the room's lime-washed walls. Taken with the loom and the mydercan, Ettith could see that this was the house of a successful seamstress, a woman whose work adorned the houses of the rich.

The child's crying stopped, jerking her from her thoughts. She looked about with a start. In a corner she saw a wooden crib. The babe inside it was a girl of about a year and a half. She was painfully thin, her little bones pushed against her skin. Ettith's old heart went out to her. "Oh my little love, how could he have missed seeing you?" she said. "Trust a man to do only half a thing."

She reached to pick up the child, but stopped herself on

noticing that she still clutched the leather thong and its bluish purple gemstone in her hand. Panic gripped her. She had not meant to keep it. It belonged to the little girl. She must give it back. Rushing from the house, as fast as her old legs would carry her, she went after the warrior, calling out for him.

It was too late. He had gone.

....

Chapter Two

Mercian England 633 AD

The longhouse shuddered, its timbers groaning as a tree, torn from the earth for a battering ram, smashed again into the wattle wall. Scabs of plaster broke away, revealing the coarse weave of hazel lath on oak studding beneath. Smoke rippled down through the thatched roof, smothering beam and rafter. Wynflaed watched it ooze menacingly above her. It swelled and barged, gathering bulk, before flopping down the wall and splashing towards her across the earthen floor.

"They've torched the roof!" she cried, bridled fear cracking her voice. She pressed a kerchief to her nose and tightened her grip on Buhe's hand.

Buhe's father beckoned. Like a rock in a sea storm, he stood amidst the chaos of his burning hall calmly directing his terrified household. "Come by me, you two," he said. "They'll soon be through the wall and the thatch'll go up like a marsh devil when the air gets to it."

Though he tried to appear calm, Wynflaed sensed his apprehension. She allowed herself and Buhe to be ushered away from the fiercest burning, pretending not to see the old thegn's fearful, secret glances at his smouldering roof.

"Pull that table against the wall - get under it," he said, inserting his fist into the iron boss of his lime-wood shield.

Spears punctured the wall. Cold air rushed in, feeding the hot, glutinous smoke. The under-thatch was aglow, as red as sunset. It burst into flame, sucking the breath from Wynflaed's lungs. Noise crashed in through the broken wall, dragging men with swinging swords and axes behind it. In their refuge beneath the table Wynflaed and Buhe clung grimly to each other. Between them and certain death stood Buhe's father, the old warrior, magnificent in his battle harness — though it no longer fitted. He stood his ground, exchanging blows with the raiders, mocking them as smoke and the unexpected ferocity of the heat shrivelled their thirst for blood, driving them back through the shattered wall in scrambling disarray.

The old man pressed them, prodding and slashing as they fell back. "Cowards!" he yelled. "You came to kill Uhtred. Well, I'm here. Come and fight me, you scum."

As the last frenzied raiders retreated ignominiously, Buhe scrambled from beneath the table and ran to her father. She was sobbing, but more from love and pride in him than from any sense of fear for herself. She threw her arms around him and stretched up to kiss his bearded cheek. "Father, we must get out" she said, tugging on his shield arm. "I'd rather be fleshered by an axe than fried like pig meat."

Startled, the old thegn gazed into her soot-stained face, as if trying to remember who she was. He looked around his hall at the faces of his frightened servants and then back at Buhe. In her blue eyes, so painfully scoured by smoke and tears, he saw her fear. He gathered her gently behind his shield and kissed her forehead.

"Think of Wynflaed and Luffa and the others," Buhe said. "They might not kill the servants. We have to get them out to give them a chance."

"You're right, little mother," he said. "It's better we die out there where the gods can see us." He took a short dagger from his belt and pressed its handle into her palm looking at her with tear-glossed eyes. "You'd better take this," he said. "You mightn't think yourself quite a woman yet, my sweet Buhe, but those men out there ..."

Buhe looked at the knife, then at her father. Despite her youth, she needed no further explanation. "What about Flaedy?" she asked, glancing towards her friend.

"I'm all right," Wynflaed cried, scrambling out from beneath the table. She brandished a small boning knife and forced a pugnacious smile. "They'll get some of this if they touch me."

Uhtred chuckled and held out his sword arm to encircle her as she joined them. "That's it then," he said, hugging the two. "We're ready. Let 'em do their worst."

Turning to his household, he summoned them to follow him. Flames now barred escape by the door, so he led them to the broken wall, his shield held aloft to fend off flaming gobs of thatch and pitch dripping from the burning roof. Buhe followed then Wynflaed and the other servants, jostled into line by old Luffa the senior house woman. Gasping for air in the smoke and heat, they clung to each other like a string of blind beggars at a harvest fair.

Outside in the chill night a ring of cruel, eager faces, lit as bright as lamp-drawn moths, confronted them. Uhtred rushed at the nearest man and felled him with a single blow. Astonishment still showed on the dead raider's face as Uhtred advanced over the corpse.

Coughing and choking, Wynflaed struggled out blindly. She stumbled over smouldering debris, gasping as fresh air drenched her face, stripping stinging threads of smoke and heat from her eyes and lungs. Her ankle turned on something round and hard as her bare feet probed for safe footing. It was the head of a corpse, almost severed from the neck. Trying to focus, she peered with tear veiled eyes and recognized a friend. Her legs faltered. She swayed on the brink of collapse. Instinctively she reached for Buhe's arm. "Look what they did, Buhe," she sobbed. "They killed Quiet Eadie."

Buhe caught her hand. She was sobbing, her sooty face riven with tear-washed lines. She clung to Wynflaed's hand as the pair gazed about the longhouse garth, seeing for the first time the bloodied corpses of Uhtred's ingas, his slaves, servants and tenants; friends and neighbours she had been raised with. At the far side of the enclosure, huddled in the smith's compound, the few who had so far survived, mostly women and children, cried out to their master as they saw him.

The raiders had begun wrenching open the doors of Uhtred's great barn. Others were driving his oxen, horses and mules from their stalls and harnessing them to carts, yokes and pack-harness to haul away their plunder.

Wynflaed watched them, the true worth of all that the barn contained impressing itself upon her. Years of work and planning had yielded a good harvest. The villagers had thanked the gods and feasted around a bonfire. They had sacrificed a sheep to Nerthus the Earth Mother, and placed flowers and fruit on the little shrines to Frigg in the fields and lanes, to thank her for the magic of fertile seed. In Thunner's glade virgins had danced naked around his oak, praising him for restraining his anger and granting them soft rains and fine weather. Now it was all to be lost in a single night. There would be nothing left - and nothing to replace it.

Desperately wondering what she could do Wynflaed gazed around her. She saw two raiders squaring up to the old thegn. Others milled around him like snarling dogs, eager to jump in should their comrades fail to cut him down. The hopelessness of their situation struck home even deeper, bathing her in cold sweat. Something snapped like a bowstring inside her brain. She found herself running, blind to danger. She leapt between the posturing men and threw her arms around Uhtred's neck, placing her slim body between him and his attackers.

"No - no stop! Please don't hurt him," she cried. She had not an idea in her head, except that she must stop them killing Uhtred. She would not allow it. She would not let them slaughter this kind old man, her father in all but blood. Twelve years earlier Uhtred had saved her, a helpless orphan no more than three-years-of-age. Now she would save him. It was not bravery. What she did was pure impulse, the blind reaction of one much loved and loving.

Despite being a widower, the old thegn had brought her up like his own. Whatever his daughter Buhe had, so had she. The girls had studied, eaten, slept and played together. Each had borrowed clothes and toys from the other. Never was there a hand-me-over, or make-do-and-mend that they did not both endure. Uhtred had never done a thing to make Wynflaed feel unwanted. She would not see him killed.

The lightning slash of a knife flashed from the hand of one of the raiders. Uhtred spun away, following his out-thrown shield as though borne up by a powerful gust of wind. Blood spurted from his neck, salting Wynflaed's lips. She turned on the attacker. "Stop! Stop!" she screamed, flinging herself to her knees and wrapping her arms around the startled raider's legs. The man gaped down at her, an odd look of embarrassment and confusion smoothing the murderous creases from his brow. His comrades too seemed baffled. For a moment they lowered their axes, glancing nervously at each other and laughing in bewilderment.

An officer approached and stood between his men and the wounded thegn. His eyes flicked from one to the other. In all the chaos and sickening confusion, a strange calm enveloped them. It was as though Wynflaed, by some magic in her actions, had drawn an enchanted circle around them driving out chaos and violence.

The silence spread to the horde, honouring the officer's raised hand and his steady gaze along their churning ranks. In the enjoining quiet, Uhtred's groans and curses seemed harsh above the crackle and hiss of burning and the choral murmur of quieting voices. Buhe fussed beside her father, overlooked by old Luffa, fat and wheezing tearfully. Wynflaed watched the officer, her heart pounding, stomach sick with anxiety.

He was tall and broad at the shoulder. His chest was heaving from exertion beneath silver studded armour of dark red leather. Blood bespattered his scarred, muscular forearms. He wore brecs of dark green wool and boots of soft leather, bound to the calf. Wynflaed returned his gaze, annoyed to see that he seemed to find the situation amusing. "I'm commander here," he said, his sword seeking out a silver trimmed scabbard at his belt.

"I trust you find nothing to be proud of in that."

Her boldness surprised him, though he tried not to show it. "Is he your granfer?" he asked, nodding in Uhtred's direction.

She took a step towards him. "No, your honour," she said, and pushing her red hair from her eyes went on. "He is my lord Uhtred Bergredsunnu, master here. I am his bonded seamstress."

The commander looked thoughtful for a moment, his gaze switching from her, to Buhe and her father, then to his men pressing about him. "I know the rebel's name," he said dismissively. "I meant to know who you are."

"Wynflaed," she said, adding as an afterthought, "Alfwalddohtor." She cursed herself inwardly for trembling as the full realisation of what she had done began draining her strength. "May I know your name?" she asked, summoning boldness from somewhere.

The officer smiled and cast a jocular look at his men.

Despite everything Wynflaed could not help noticing his smile. The faint hope that he might not be the cruel killer he had seemed flashed through her mind.

"You're a strange one," he said, with a chuckle. "You say you are bondswif here, a seamstress, yet you demand my name and look me in the eye like any freeman of rank ..."

"I am of family," she said. "I told you ..."

"Yes — yes. Alfwalddohtor," he said, mocking her, and grinning at his men. "I'm sure we all heard you. Yet here you are in this nest of traitors."

With anger surpassing her fear, she watched him remove his battle helmet and push a hand through his mop of light brown hair. His face was pleasant, if rather roughly hewn, when not squashed between the silver cheek plates of his helmet. He was younger than she had expected, perhaps not more than twenty, yet he bore the scars of many battles. One, a faint blue line running from his right eye to his ear, intrigued her. It tugged at his eyelid, lending his eye a mischievous glint. His nose, which had clearly been broken more than once, showed him capable of much more than simple mischief. Still, she told herself, as her hope rekindled, it was not the face of a brutal man.

"Well, daughter of Alfwald," he said smiling, his clear blue eyes mocking her, "as you demand it, I shall tell you." He saluted her with an extravagance intended to amuse his men. "I am Wulfric Aelricsunnu of the Cenwulfingas. I come to this rebel's house for supplies. I serve Lord Cenwulf. He marches to join King Penda. I don't suppose your rebel master cares that our lord Penda and the Wealh king, Cadwallon Gwynedd, march to face the Northumbrians. He's obviously content to hide here in this house of women while loyal men fight and die."

Resisting the urge to rise to his mocking, Wynflaed pulled back her shoulders and looked him in the eye. "Your men have already stolen all they can carry," she said. "Killing us will neither swell their packs, nor help them carry what they have." She eyed him haughtily as she went on. "Or do you simply want an old man's blood on your swords for sport?"

Wulfric bristled, but made no reply. He crammed his helmet on, tied its straps beneath his chin and turned to his men. "Put the rebel and his whelp in the smith's yard with the others. Let's get out of this traitor's midden."

An officer at his shoulder relayed the order. Buhe and her injured father were led away. Luffa and the other servants followed. Wynflaed alone remained, held there by Wulfric's gaze. His anger was clear, yet he seemed torn by indecision. She glared at him, wondering what sort of man he could be. How could he do what he did? She felt confused and angry. Part of her wished she was a man, wished she could strike him for his violence. He should suffer for what he'd done. Yet he raised feelings inside her such as she had never experienced.

Wulfric turned and strode away towards the main body of his men. Wynflaed remained, a small, solitary figure in the bright, hot space before the burning hall. She watched him go, wanting to hate him but unable to take her eyes off him. Just before he vanished into his crowding warriors he turned and looked back at her. She knew there was something about that glance that she would never forget, but harder to accept was that she feared she would never want to.

All around her raiders rushed about loading carts and mules, gathering up all the copper and bronze, and stripping precious iron from plough and hearth. She scanned their faces expecting to see evil, but saw only ordinary men, working and sweating like field hands, their swords and axes encumbrances now, slung across their shoulders.

Wynflaed wandered about the burning village as if searching its ruins for the hatred and anger she expected. What she saw was certainly distressing, but she was denied the hatred she wanted to feel.

Later, as the fires died and the noise and chaos subsided, a grimy faced youth approached leading a skittish white mule. Skinny and dressed in torn tunic and cow-skin brecs he kept his eyes lowered in the manner of a slave. His unkempt hair blew across his face. As he neared her, he stopped and waited, as if for permission to speak.

Wynflaed was puzzled. "Do you want me?"

The young muler nodded and looked up through his tangled hair. Now he saw clearly the young woman he had seen only from a distance, boldly standing up to his master. She was every bit as beautiful as he had thought. She had long, coppery hair that fell about her face and neck in the deep, glossy remnant of linen-bound braids. Her large, green eyes were bright and haughty. They shone at him like lamps from beneath thick, coppery eyebrows and dark lashes. Even through the soot and grime of her ordeal he could see her skin was clear and smooth. She wore a shift of wool held at the waist with a belt of plaited, holly-green leather. Her small, maiden's breasts pushed gently at the faded green. A plain circlet of gold at her wrist reflected the light of the fires around them. Otherwise, her soot-marked arms were bare to the shoulder. She was about his age, he guessed, certainly no more than sixteen, though her manner lent her maturity beyond her years. No wonder his master wanted her.

"What is it?" Wynflaed resented his searching gaze.

"My master commands me to say ..." He stopped and gulped for breath. "And I'm to say exactly these words, my lady ..."

"You needn't address me so," she interrupted. "I'm a bond-servant like you."

"Lord Wulfric was precise, my lady," the youth insisted. "I am to say that you are free to travel where you wish. But my master wants you to know that *his* wish is that you will travel with him. Me and my mule are to ..."

"Travel with him?" she cried. "Huh! In what capacity I wonder?"

The muler dropped his gaze and took a step back. "I — err — I'm to say that you'll be well cared for ..."

"Huh! I don't doubt it," she said. "I expect your master is well used to caring for such — travellers." Her clenched fists beat slowly on her thighs as she tried to contain her mounting fury. "Tell your master — tell him, that if he were the last man on middle earth, I would rather prick out my eyes than ..."

***

When Wynflaed reached the blacksmith's yard, Buhe greeted her with tearful relief. "Oh thank Thunner you're safe," she cried. "We thought — well — we didn't know what to think. You are all right aren't you? I mean they didn't ..." Buhe's facial acrobatics told a fearful story.

"I'm fine," Wynflaed said. "How's father?"

"Oh, they say he'll be all right." She threaded her arm in Wynflaed's. "That commander sent us his healer. He's in there now." She nodded towards the smith's cottage. "Where were you? Gods, Flaedy!" she said. "You saved our lives. We'd all be dead but for you. You were so brave. I don't know how you could do it — just stand up to him like that."

"Neither do I, but maybe I didn't save us at all - just postponed our deaths. We'll likely starve over winter," she said, her eyes sweeping the destruction around them. "They're taking everything, even the bell from its pole."

"But we're alive," said Buhe. "And you did it. At least we've a chance. And if father's not too badly hurt, he'll soon think of something."

Setting Wynflaed walking, Buhe snuggled close and squeezed her arm. She was half a year younger than Wynflaed, and although they shared the same clothes, somehow on Buhe they seemed always to be in delightful disarray. Wynflaed was groomed and shining by comparison, and where she was calm and deliberate, Buhe was giddy and excitable. Buhe giggled a lot, often for no apparent reason, though she had the most infectious laughter. When Wynflaed laughed however, men noticed her, much less her laughing. The two were best friends, seldom seen apart. Accomplished in many skills from farming to music, they both worked hard. Buhe was a fine needlewoman, though she could not match the artistry of Wynflaed's work. She lacked patience, Wynflaed often told her. She could seldom sit for more than half an hour at anything. If her work went badly she would fling it down and become unbearably bossy. Throughout these outbursts, Wynflaed would remain serene, something Buhe found exasperating.

"Of course, father's been expecting this for a long time," Buhe said, her eyebrows shooting up in a gesture of bored inevitability. He always said they'd come for him one day." Then, frowning, she whispered, "Let's face it, he's said some pretty harsh things about King Penda."

"Is that the healer?" Wynflaed interrupted, on seeing a dark, solemn faced man emerge from the smith's hut.

Buhe nodded, eyeing the figure in flowing black cloak and large floppy hat. "I heard them call him Crowman," she whispered, with an elaborate shudder. "Gods! He looks like old Grim his-self, doesn't he?"

"I've got to speak to him," said Wynflaed, rushing off, leaving Buhe bemused.

The healer saw her running towards him and paused. He was tall and thin. His black clothes flapped about him like great black wings. His long, sad face wore a distant, weary look. At first Wynflaed thought his expression reflected Uhtred's condition and she wondered if his injuries were worse than Buhe had told her.

"What is it? Is he dying?" she asked.

The Crowman studied her for a moment. "We are all dying child, but your master no sooner than most of us."

"So he's all right" she asked, flustered by his answer.

The Crowman nodded.

"Oh, thank the gods," she said, and then checking herself smiled gratefully.

He nodded and started to move off, but she grasped his arm. "Don't worry," he said, patting her hand. "He'll recover. In a week or so he'll be fine." He peered into her face, wondering at her reluctance to release him. "Is there something else, daughter?"

She nodded with a grateful urgency. "I — I wanted to ask ..."

Crowman frowned impatiently. "Well Child?"

"I want to know about — your master."

"My master?" he queried. "I serve only Wyrd. Only by the whim of Wyrd may we serve even the gods. We are the dolls of Wyrd to be danced and toyed with."

"No, I mean Lord Wulfric," she said.

Crowman shrugged. "You know his name. What more would you know that cannot be seen in his eyes?"

"I wondered - what sort of man he is."

Crowman prized her fingers from his arm and squared up to her. She fell back a step, bracing herself. He was gazing deep into her eyes. She felt as if her soul was being laid bare before him. "In time, child, you will know everything," he told her. "You have a long journey ahead; far beyond a place of streams and lime trees. I see your chains broken by sunlight where there is no sky."

"Journey? What journey? What chains? I'm not going anywhere."

He turned away and set off towards the woods beyond Uhtred's smouldering fields. "Your journey starts soon, daughter of Alfwald," he called back.

"No. No, you're wrong. I'm not going anywhere. This is my home. I'm staying here. I'll never leave."

Buhe joined her, slipping an arm about her. "What's wrong? You crying. Is it father? What did he say?"

"No, it's not that," Wynflaed sobbed. "He's wrong, Buhe. I'm not going on a journey. I'm staying here. I don't want to leave."

"Of course you're staying. We all are," Buhe said. "What are you getting so upset about?"

"He said that I'm going on a journey, and something about sunlight where there is no sky breaking my chains. What chains? I have no chains. I'm free and I love Uhtredstun and you and your father."

"Sunlight without sky?" queried Buhe. "That's silly!"

……..

Website:- **www.briansellars.com**
Email:- **bsellars6@gmail.com**
Follow me on Twitter @briansellars

Made in the USA
Charleston, SC
17 September 2014